HAWK ISLAND

by George A. Platz

Blue Lake Press

BLUE LAKE PRESS
A Western Division Subsidiary of the
Chicago, Whitewater & Mad River Company
P O Box 797, Blue Lake, CA 95525

ISBN: 978-0615520827

HAWK ISLAND

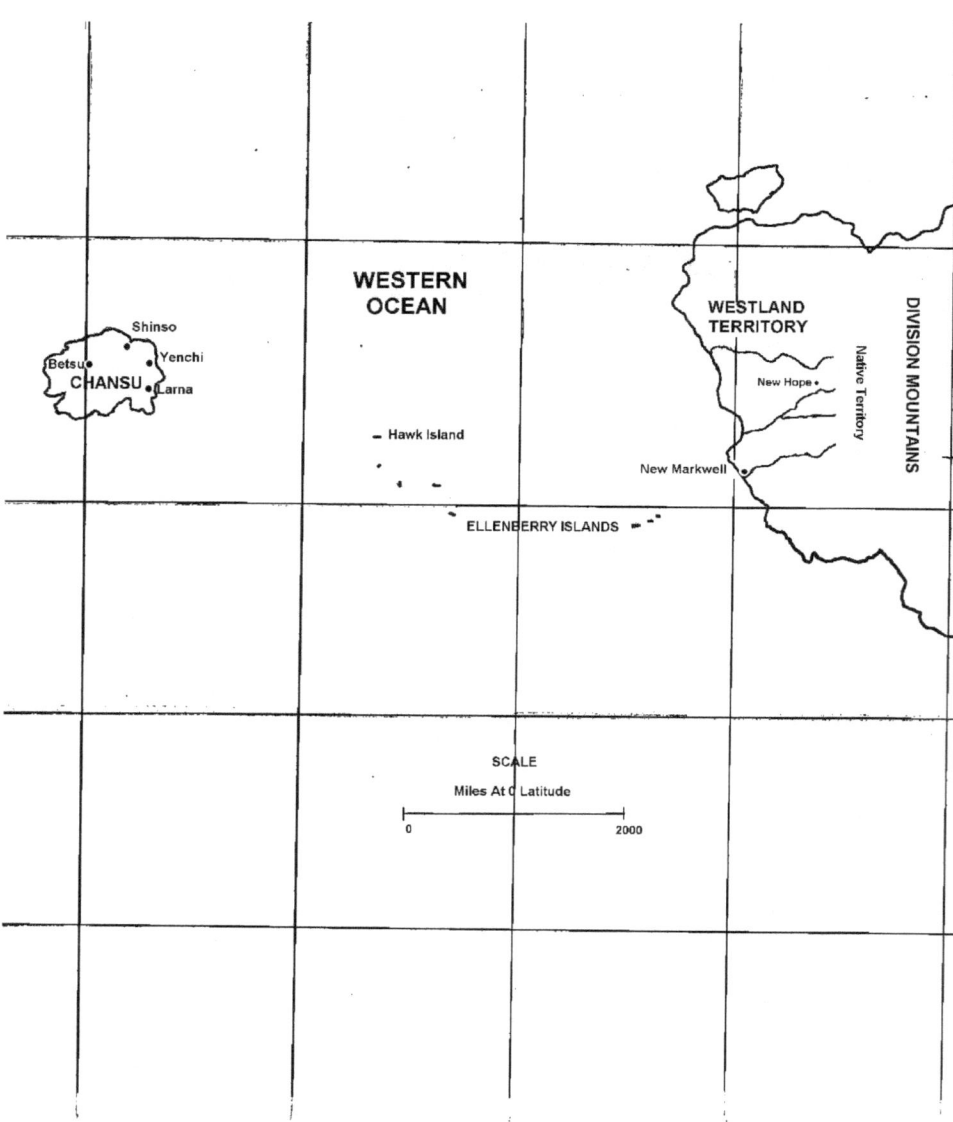

WESTERN
OCEAN

Shinso

Betsu • • Yenchi
CHANSU •Larna

— Hawk Island

ELLENBERRY ISLANDS

WESTLAND
TERRITORY

New Hope •

New Markwell •

DIVISION MOUNTAINS

Native Territory

SCALE

Miles At 0 Latitude

0   2000

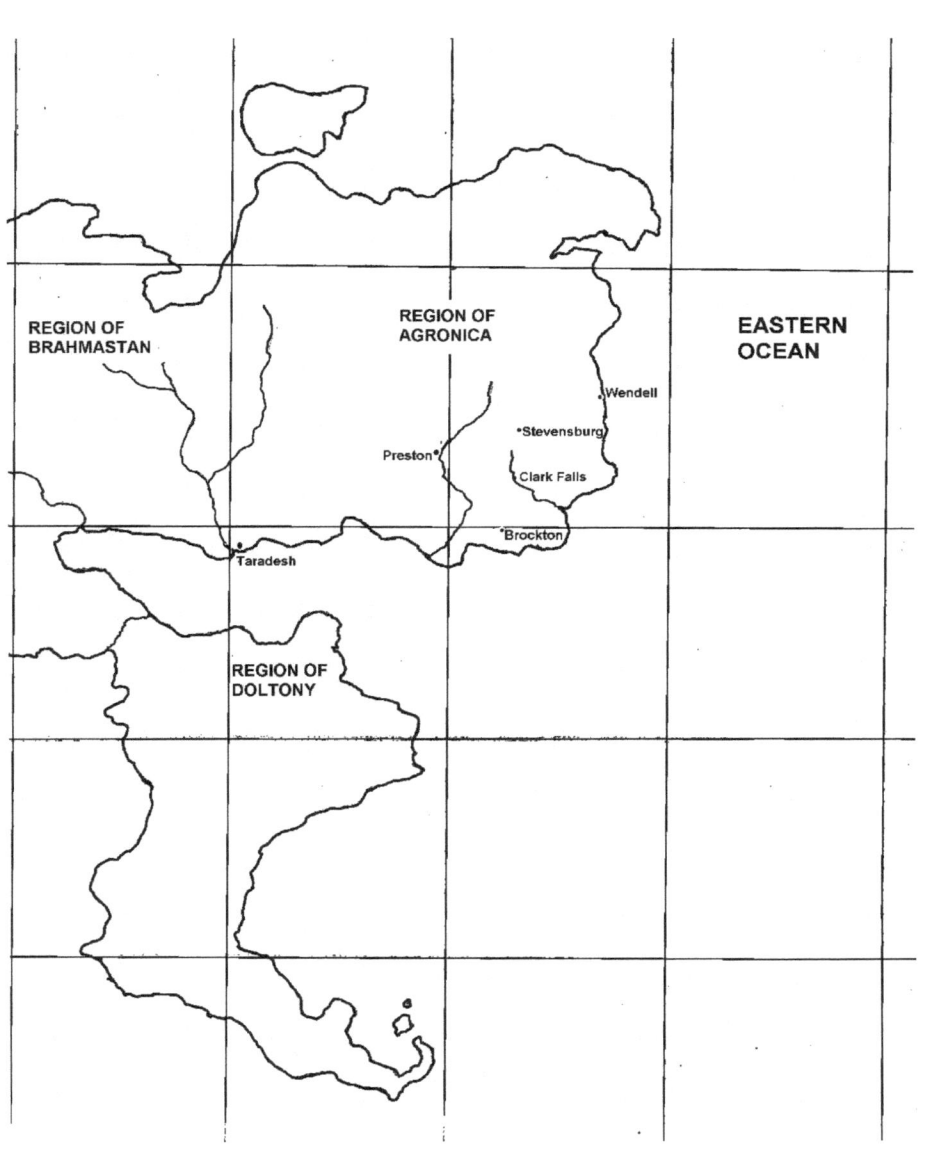

REGION OF
BRAHMASTAN

REGION OF
AGRONICA

EASTERN
OCEAN

Wendell

Stevensburg

Preston

Clark Falls

Brockton

Taradesh

REGION OF
DOLTONY

PART ONE

1898-1910

1.

One slow step at a time, the boy climbed the wide wooden stairs. As he went, he ran his finger along the cracked plaster wall, adding a minute amount to the accumulated stains left by years of dirty-fingered children. He had a long, thin somber face to go with a rather ordinary six-year-old frame, and he wore the brown cotton shirt and shorts that were the autumn uniform of the Pinedale School.

When he reached the top he stopped and looked down the musty-smelling, high-ceilinged corridor. The nearest door was open. A sign on it read "Counseling Office," but the boy did not bother to try to decipher it. After a long wait, he gave his little shoulders a shrug and marched past the door and into the room behind it.

A woman in a high collared white blouse sitting at a desk inside the room looked up as the boy entered. "Are you here for a counseling session?" she asked crisply.

The boy looked at her and nodded.

"Have you ever been here before?"

The boy shook his head.

The woman smiled a little. "Well, it's not as bad as they

say. What's your name?"

"Eric Faolin."

The woman picked Up a stack of cards and thumbed through them. She pulled one out. "Dormitory B?" she asked.

Eric nodded again.

"You've been with us a long time," the woman remarked, looking at the card. Eric made no response. "Well, you're to see Mr. Williams. He's talking to someone else now, so you'll have to wait." She pointed to a row of heavy wooden chairs across from her desk, and Eric sat down in one. He waited, as he did so often at Pinedale.

Eric watched the woman working. He sensed a kindness beneath her businesslike manner and wondered if she had children of her own at home. He thought about what it would be like to have a real mother. Pinedale was the only family and the only home Eric could remember. He had been an infant when he and his parents had boarded the government emigration boat in Agronica and made the voyage through the new canal to the Westland frontier in 1898. His mother and father had died soon afterward, in the flu epidemic of 1899, and the United World Government Welfare Ministry had immediately brought Eric to this facility it operated near New Markwell, Westland's only city.

Footsteps passed in the corridor outside and Eric heard someone go down the stairs. A few minutes later a tall, gray-haired man with a threadbare jacket walked into the room and up to the woman at the desk. When he turned Erie recognized him as someone he had seen from time to time around the grounds. The man approached Eric and extended his hand.

"How do you do, Eric," the man said. "I'm Mr. Williams. I guess we have something to talk about." Eric shook the outstretched hand. Then they walked down the corridor to Williams' office, Eric hanging his head.

"Well, Eric," Williams said when they were in his small cubicle, barely big enough for his desk and two chairs, "you've not been following the rules, I understand."

Eric continued to avoid the man's eyes.

"According to this report, you did two things last week that aren't allowed." He shook his head. "We don't often find our first offenders doing two things wrong. But perhaps there's some reason. We'll get to this in a minute. First, though, I must tell you what you're charged with and give you a chance to defend yourself."

Williams looked down at the small boy sitting in the chair beside his desk. Eric's feet could not reach the floor. They stuck straight out from the chair, one rubbing against the desk.

"According to the report, last week you pushed one of the boys in the First Level class and made him give you his dessert. And the next day you called one of the girls in your class a bad name. Now, do you have any answer to these charges?"

Eric shook his head, looking at his knees.

"You are guilty, then?"

Eric nodded. Williams reached over and raised the boy's face. There were tears in the corners of his eyes. "Now, now," said Williams, "there's no need to cry. What we must do is find out why you did these things so we can be sure they don't happen again. I'll be seeing you every day for the next two weeks. I'm sure we can work it out in that time."

Williams pulled a sheet of paper in front of him. "First of all," he said, "I'd like to make a note of some facts about you." He copied some data from the card the woman in the other office had given him. This took several minutes. Then he looked up at Eric. "Tell me, Eric," he said, "have you been going to all your Behavior lectures?"

Eric nodded. "I think so," he said.

Williams made another note, then pushed the paper aside. He leaned back in his chair and folded his hands across his chest. "All right," he said, "since this is your first offense and you've never been to a counselor before, I'll take this session to tell you about a few things."

Williams stared at the ceiling, his eyes half-closed. He put his hands behind his head. "The first thing I want to say is that, no matter what you may hear from the other children, we don't treat you any different here than you would be treated if you didn't live at Pinedale. We have the same rules, and the same kind of counseling for people who break the rules, as they have everywhere else.

"The second thing I want to say is, we aren't going to take away your freedom. As you ought to know by now, freedom is one of the basic principles of the United World Government. People should be able to do as they wish, and that includes children. Why do you think we let you choose your own meals and your own bedtime? Well, we're not going to change that.

"But the UWG is founded on other principles, too. Such as equality, and individual rights, and productivity. You've learned all that. That's why we have the behavior training. So that you will learn to control your own behavior and exercise your freedom the right way. And it works pretty well, too. But once in a while someone goes astray, like you did last week, Eric. And that's why we have counselors. To make sure you see why what you did was wrong and to help you keep it from happening again.

"Now, here's one more thing. What we're doing here, Eric, is to prepare you for a happy, productive life when you grow up. And we think the best way to do that is to make your life here as much like grown-up life as we can. You've got your job, and you earn pretty much the same as everyone else. You can change the job if you want to and if you qualify for another one. You've got freedom. You won't have behavior lectures when you grow up, but you'll have counselors to help you when you do something wrong.

"Now," said Williams, shifting forward in his chair and looking at Eric, "do you have any questions about what I've said?"

"No, sir," said Eric, who really hadn't paid much attention. He had been watching a fly crawl up the wall behind the counselor.

"All right, Eric," Williams said, patting the boy's head. "You're a good listener, and I can see we're going to get along just fine." He looked at his watch. "There's still a lot of time left, but I think we've covered enough for today. We've got two more weeks to work this out. You run along, and I'll see you tomorrow at the same time."

Eric got out of his chair and said good-bye. He backed out of the office and walked slowly and respectfully down the corridor to the stairs. He peeked in the door of the Counseling Office to see the woman but she wasn't at her desk. He looked around and saw no one else. With a little jump he grabbed the railing and, holding it tightly, flew down the stairs two and three steps at a time. He didn't stop at the bottom but raced out of the old brick building as fast as he could and dashed across the open lawn to join his friends in the playground next to the dining hall.

2

Prior to 1898 no UWG ship had called at a Chansu port in the UWG's entire hundred-year history. Nor would one have been welcome, for after the expulsion in 1608 of the last foreigners to set foot on their island, the traders of the old Doltony Empire, the Chansu had resolutely sealed themselves off from the continental civilizations on the other side of the globe and cold-bloodedly executed the few outsiders who thereafter attempted to make contact with them.

It came, therefore, as a great surprise to the leaders of the UWG when, in the autumn of 1897, they received an invitation from the ruler of Chansu's Northern Kingdom to pay him a visit. They would, of course, never have considered imposing themselves on the Chansu without such a request; after all, barbarians are entitled to their human rights too, including their right to be left alone. But here, completely unsolicited, was an invitation to spread the UWG's gospel of freedom and equality to the last remaining untouched segment of mankind. What an exciting prospect!

Thus it was that on May 15, 1898 (the same date, coincidentally, that the infant Eric Faolin and his parents boarded the lumbering old side-wheeler at Prestmouth, Region of Agronica, for their emigration to Westland), the UWG ship Liberty, after a long voyage across the Western Ocean, steamed into Shinso, capital of Chansu's Northern Kingdom. The most comprehensive eyewitness account of the events of that historic day is that of young David Halburton, then an assistant interpreter for the expedition:

I arose before dawn this morning and

went directly up to the deck. It was cold and the
sea was rough and throwing heavy spray across our
bow. I almost went back below but decided to wait
for a little while. In a few minutes it was light
enough to see some distance, and soon I was able to
make out the mountains of Chansu rising out of the
sea ahead of us. The sight made me forget the cold
and the wet, and I stood stunned by it for a long
time. It is very difficult to describe the feelings
that sight awakened in me. I had not expected
anything so forbidding. It was difficult to believe
that any safe harbor lay within that immense
fortress of rock. I could understand easily how the
Chansu had managed to keep the world out for three
centuries.

As I stood there I couldn't help
thinking about the horrible fate of the last
recorded voyage to Chansu, well over a century ago.
I reminded myself that our expedition came at the
invitation of the Chansu, but I worried about what
inconsequential act might possibly offend the
island's rulers, whose customs were so unknown to
us. Possibly I would have stood there all morning
had my thoughts not been interrupted by the ship's
bell announcing the morning's crew meeting. The
common room was almost full when I arrived, and the
excitement was clearly noticeable. Mohendi, from
the Information Ministry, gave a somewhat longer
invocation than usual, emphasizing the importance
of demonstrating Equality to our hosts. We served
ourselves breakfast and then split up into the
usual groups. Ralph Wintergreen, the Prime Council
delegate, and Rita Marzone, from the Congress,
joined our group.

With Loren Carpenter, the Senior
Interpreter, leading the discussion we again

reviewed the initial statement Wintergreen would make to King Torgoona. First, he would describe the peaceful nature of UWG society and would offer the people of Chansu the benefits of our experience. Then he would offer gifts to demonstrate our technological achievement as well as our good will. And he would ask permission to establish a mission in Chansu to teach the UWG way.

Before we had a chance to finish our review, a woman from the Pilot's cabin rushed into the common room to announce that three small boats had been spotted dead ahead, less than two miles away, moving directly toward us. We all hurriedly got into our heavy wool overcoats and went out on the forward deck. It was still cold, and the biting wind, coupled with nervousness, made my teeth chatter. We clung to the wet rail, peering into the distance. Sooner than we expected the boats were abreast of us. I was surprised at how small they were and admired anyone who would put to sea in one. They swung around in a half circle so as to come up alongside. At the same time the Liberty reduced speed and came to a virtual stop.

On the deck of the nearest vessel I saw a muscular man with reddish brown skin motioning excitedly at us. He seemed to be shouting, but I couldn't hear his words. He was clad only in light trousers and a sleeveless shirt, despite the cold wind and spray blowing over him.

Finally one of the deck hands realized what the man was calling about and tossed a rope to him. In a few minutes the Chansu sailor had drawn his vessel up next to the Liberty and climbed up the rope to the Liberty's deck. He pulled a ladder up with him and tied it to the deck railing, then

returned to his own little ship. He disappeared
below deck then reappeared a moment later
accompanied by two other red-skinned Chansu, both
of whom were dressed in brightly-colored jackets
and baggy trousers. The sailor bowed low before the
others, who brushed past him and strode over to the
ladder. They climbed up it quickly and stood
together on the deck of the Liberty, apparently
waiting for someone to approach them. In their
bright yellow, red and brown costumes they looked
to me like circus clowns. After some hesitation,
Wintergreen and Marzone walked over to the two
Chansu, followed by Carpenter. Michael Lawrence,
the other assistant interpreter, and I moved close
enough to be within earshot but stood several paces
behind the others. Wintergreen extended his hand to
the Chansu but they acted as if they didn't see it.

    "Welcome to the Liberty," Wintergreen
finally said. "We have come at the invitation of
your King Torgoona." Carpenter attempted to
translate the statement into Chansu. The two Chansu
looked at each other blankly. One of them spoke in
response to Carpenter. I listened closely but
recognized nothing. The sounds were entirely
different from what I expected.

    Lawrence and I exchanged worried
glances. Had we somehow deceived ourselves about
our ability to translate the Chansu language? King
Torgoona's invitation was written in exactly the
same language that the Doltony traders had recorded
three centuries ago, and we had therefore assumed
that, with our mastery of the old Doltony
glossaries and grammars, communication would be no
problem.

    "That's not the language we learned,"
Lawrence whispered to me.

"But why would they have written the invitation in a language they don't speak?" I asked.

"I can't understand them," Carpenter was explaining to Wintergreen and Marzone. The Chansu began to look impatient. Carpenter again tried to tell them of King Torgoona's invitation, but the Chansu simply stared back at him. Wintergreen, I noticed, was glancing nervously at the other Chansu fishing boats, which had all now drawn alongside the Liberty. Was he thinking, I wondered, about how quickly the men on those boats could board us?

Then, in exasperation, Carpenter reached into his inside coat pocket and pulled out a copy of the invitation and held it in front of the two Chansu. They looked at it, nodded, and chattered at Carpenter. I still couldn't understand, and I'm sure he couldn't either. Finally, in a stroke of inspiration, Carpenter pointed to the words on the invitation and pronounced them carefully, according to the old Doltony pronunciation chart. Immediately the two Chansu began to grin. They looked at each other and the grins turned to laughter. One of them gently took the document from Carpenter's hands. He pointed to the words and pronounced them himself. The sounds were entirely different from the ones Carpenter had spoken.

With this the mounting tension dissipated. We soon realized that, while the written language of the Chansu had changed hardly at all in the last three hundred years, the pronunciation--at least that used by government officials--had changed drastically. Communication with the two Chansu now came easily, first by

writing and then, as we learned the new
pronunciation, by halting speech.

These two Chansu, we were told, were
members of the Chansu Warrior class and had been
sent by the King. The one who spoke most appeared
to be in his late twenties or early thirties. He
was short and thin, with a long, straight scar that
looked like it might have been made by a blade
running down the right side of his face. He said
his name was Yim Jinsa, and that he was the First
Assistant to the Chief Minister. The other, whose
name was Kyn Litna and who was some sort of
cultural adviser to the Chief Minister, was a
bigger man, and the creases in the dark reddish-
brown skin of his face indicated that he was much
older than his companion. Both men had the wide-set
eyes and coal-black hair that, along with their
skin color, distinguished the Chansu from other
peoples.

"We have been sent," Jinsa stated, "to
express King Torgoona's great appreciation for the
acceptance of his invitation by the people from
across the ocean. The King acknowledges his duty
and obligation to make his visitors' stay as
pleasant as possible.

"We have met your great ship here in
the coastal waters," Jinsa continued, "because you
would not be able to sail up the fjord that leads
to the harbor of Shinso without assistance. We have
brought with us two pilots who know the channel
very well. We apologize for asking you to take two
members of the Worker class aboard your ship, but
in our land all tasks of seamanship are performed
by that class. We realize that this is not the case
for a seafaring nation such as yours."

This last statement puzzled me until I

realized that the Chansu knew nothing of the changes in the political situation of the world in the last 300 years. When the Chansu last had contact with people from outside their island, the Doltony Empire was at the height of its power, controlling most of the Northern and Southern Continents, and possessing a strong, elite navy. The Chansu had no way of knowing that the Doltony power had been crushed in the great revolutions of the late 1700s that gave rise to the United World Government.

"We are most grateful for the King's invitation," said Wintergreen, "and we would like to meet with him as soon as possible. There are many things we have to discuss with him. Your pilots are welcome aboard the <u>Liberty</u>."

"Very well," Jinsa said. "The King has planned a great feast to honor you this evening. But he also wishes us to present to you now a small initial gift, a token of his obligation."

Jinsa nodded to his companion, who stepped forward, producing from beneath his robe a small glass vial filled with a white powder. "This," he said, holding up the vial, "is a rare spice of great power. A few grains on the tongue-- no more, I caution you--will heighten the senses and produce a great joy. The King hopes that you may enjoy this in your moments away from obligation."

Wintergreen did not reach to take the vial from Litna's outstretched hand. He turned to Carpenter after translation was completed and asked softly, "Is it some kind of a drug?"

Carpenter shrugged. "I believe so," he said. Wintergreen turned to Marzone. "This might be a trick," he said. Marzone made no reply.

Wintergreen faced the two Chansu again. "The King's offer is very kind," he said, "but in our land we don't use stimulating drugs. We cannot accept the King's offer."

The Chansu looked at each other solemnly when Wintergreen's statement had been translated. They spoke rapidly, in low tones that we couldn't hear well enough to translate. Then, seeming to have reached some sort of decision, they wrote down a question and handed it to Carpenter, rather than continuing the fumbling oral communication. "Do you have laws against the use of such drugs?" Carpenter translated.

Wintergreen looked silently at the faces of the Chansu for a moment. "No," he finally said, "it is not forbidden by our laws, but by our choice."

When this was translated for the Chansu, they became very angry. Jinsa stepped up to Wintergreen and spoke loudly and heatedly, his face almost touching Wintergreen's. Before waiting for a translation, he turned around abruptly and, with his companion, started for the ladder back to their boat.

"Wait," Carpenter called, rushing after them, without translating their last remarks or stopping to consult with Wintergreen or Marzone. They stopped. "Please wait for just a moment," he asked. Then he returned to Wintergreen. "We have insulted them," he said. "They are very sensitive about social obligations. We can accept their gift without using it."

Wintergreen spoke briefly with Marzone, then apologized to the Chansu and claimed that he misunderstood them. He accepted King Torgoona's gift. The Chansu smiled and appeared to be satisfied. They brought the two pilots aboard the _Liberty_ and then departed, promising to see us again later that day at King Torgoona's palace.

The _Liberty_ sailed on toward Shinso. It was clear why we needed the Chansu pilots. They guided the ship right up to the towering coastline. Several times I was certain we would smash into that wall of rock. Then, suddenly, an opening appeared and we steamed up a narrow fjord that was as beautiful as the coastline was terrifying. We saw no people, although occasionally we glimpsed a small wooden building or a roadway up on the cliff.

Finally, as we reached Shinso, the steep cliffs receded and made room for a valley that sloped gently to the water. The city itself was situated in this valley, while numerous stone towers stood behind and above it in the surrounding hills. Shinso did not appear to be as large as the largest UWG cities, but it must have held close to 250,000 inhabitants.

The _Liberty_ dropped anchor in the middle of the fjord outside Shinso. It dwarfed the few other boats we saw in the harbor, most of which appeared to be fishing vessels. We waited there for over two hours. For all we could tell, it was as if we had arrived unnoticed. We ate a hurried lunch in the common room, then went back to the deck to watch. Finally, in the early afternoon we spotted a rowboat coming slowly out to meet us. It held six shirtless rowers, sweat glistening on their red backs, another shirtless man in the bow, and Jinsa and Litna, the two emissaries who had visited us earlier. The rowboat drew alongside, and Jinsa and Litna came aboard.

"It is good to see you again," Jinsa said. "This is Shinso." He waved his arm in the direction of the city. "King Torgoona wishes to meet with you as soon as it is convenient. He waits for you in the Old Citadel, which has been specially prepared for your visit." He pointed out a large gray stone fortress with a high tower, located on top of a hill that overlooked the city from the south. From our vantage point, the fortress reminded me of the crumbling pre-Doltony castles one still finds in the border area between Agronica and Brahmastan. Like those castles, the Old Citadel had probably been--and for all we knew, still was--a major defense point against attackers by land from the other side.

"We are most anxious to meet with your King," Wintergreen said. "But we would like a little time to prepare ourselves."

Jinsa looked surprised. "Please excuse us. We thought we had given you enough time."

"Oh, but we didn't understand . . ." Wintergreen began. Before he could finish, Marzone interrupted. "What we mean to say is, we have many gifts for the King, and we would like to get them ashore so we can take them with us to the Old Citadel." Carpenter translated this, and the two Chansu nodded understandingly.

"We will send another boat for you that is large enough to carry your gifts. The King will expect no more than ten in your party, please."

After a short discussion with Wintergreen, Marzone and Carpenter that I did not hear, Jinsa and Litna left, taking the two Chansu pilots with them. As far as I know, they did not ask whether we had used the drug they had given us. I guessed that they would not.

Not long afterward another rowboat came out to the Liberty, much larger than the first, carrying six men in addition to the rowers. One of the six wore a yellow and brown outfit similar to those worn by Jinsa and Litna, while the others wore plain gray trousers and light gray shirts.

The brightly-dressed man came aboard first and told us that he was the Dock Supervisor in charge of the group of Workers who would unload our cargo that we wished to take with us to the King. It would not be necessary for us to speak to the Workers, he said. It was his honor to relay our instructions to them.

The five Workers followed the Dock Supervisor aboard and bowed numerous times before him. He passed our instructions on to them with harsh commands. I couldn't help but be shocked, as I had been over the treatment of the Chansu pilots by Jinsa. The Supervisor displayed an attitude of superiority over these Workers far in excess of anything necessary to the proper performance of their jobs. The Liberty crew members, I noticed, also watched the Chansu Workers in amazement. Clearly we had much to teach the Chansu about equality.

It took about an hour to load our gifts into the boat that had been sent for us and to get ourselves ready to go. The entire complement aboard the Liberty met briefly in the common room and, as I expected, chose Wintergreen, Marzone, and Mohendi, representing the Prime Council, the Congress, and the Information Ministry, respectively, to attend the initial meeting with King Torgoona. They got into the boat and Carpenter and I joined them. Lawrence stayed on the ship to handle any communications with the Chansu that were necessary while we were gone. The Dock Supervisor and his Workers followed and sat in the back of the boat, and the rowers cast off. I tried to start a conversation with one of the rowers as we headed for shore, but he was either deaf or pretending not to hear me.

In only a few minutes we arrived at the dock and climbed, somewhat unsteadily, up the wooden ladder. It felt odd to have solid ground beneath our feet again. I looked back at the Liberty and suddenly missed its security. But there wasn't much time to think about such things. Yim Jinsa and Kyn Litna were waiting for us, and they ushered us immediately into a large maroon and white horse drawn wagon. Though obviously constructed with great care, the wagon, with its hard wooden seats, did not compare at all favorably in comfort or design with the carriages used in Preston or the other large cities of the UWG. The horses pulling it were much smaller than the standard Agronican carriage horse. It took six of them to draw us up the winding road toward the Old Citadel.

The first part of our journey carried us along the water, between the docks and rows of large open stalls. We saw a few fishing boats in the docks, and in the stalls men were loading and unloading wagons . They stopped to watch us pass, but not for long. I doubted very much if they knew who we were, although the mere presence of our ship in the fjord should have aroused more curiosity than it appeared to. Soon the road curved away from the fjord and passed through an area of large, plain wooden shingle buildings. As we began to rise up above the city, we went briefly past some densely packed, unpainted wooden houses that seemed to stretch on for a considerable distance. But then

we abruptly turned left into a wide, tree-lined
boulevard that largely obscured our view of the
city.

The areas of Shinso we had passed
differed greatly from any city I had ever seen
before. There were none of the swarms of carriages
and wagons that fill the streets of UWG port cities
such as Sedgwick or Taradesh. The few wagons we did
encounter pulled off to the side of the road as we
passed. And the people we saw, all men dressed in
plain grays and browns, were like so many
automatons mechanically going about their jobs. I
wondered to myself if perhaps the drug we had been
given was a part of their daily life until I
recalled that Litna had described it as very rare.

The boulevard led us, through numerous
switchbacks, up the steep hill toward the Old
Citadel. As we neared the fortress our two hosts
became slightly less formal and more friendly.
Litna gave us a brief description of the Old
Citadel. It had been built, he said, nearly a
thousand years before by the first king of the
northern area of Chansu. King Torgoona was his
direct descendant. The Old Citadel was now used, he
added, chiefly for ceremonial occasions like this
one.

At last we reached the Citadel. It had
no wall around it, but its sheer sides, windowless
for at least forty feet, presented a formidable
obstacle to any would-be attacker. We entered,
wagon, horses and all, through a huge door set in
the thick stone and found ourselves in an enormous,
poorly lighted room that looked and smelled like a
stable. Some Workers came forward to take the
horses and we all went on foot through another
smaller door opposite the one through which we had

entered.

We walked down several echoing corridors and up I would guess six long flights of stairs until we were ushered through a polished wooden door into a room with ornate carpets covering the floor and walls consisting of brightly painted panels. There were open windows on two sides overlooking the fjord and the city. The colorful decor contrasted sharply with the grim stone walls outside. Litna and Jinsa asked us to wait and they went through another door at the other end of the room. We did so, with growing impatience, for at least ten minutes. Then our two friends bustled back into the room, followed by a group of six men. Their gaudy, loose-fitting clothes, like those of Jinsa and Litna, were very different from the dark wool suits, with vests, high collars and neckties, that we all wore.

As the group of Chansu reached us, one of their number stepped forward apart from the others. He was, I would guess, about 50 years old, thinner and taller than the others, with a finely-chiseled face and wise eyes.

Jinsa spoke from off to the side. "We announce the presence of King Torgoona, chief Warrior of the Northern Kingdom."

The other Chansu bowed slightly. None of us did, and I felt uncomfortable about it.

Wintergreen stepped forward, Marzone close beside him, and spoke. "I am Ralph Wintergreen, authorized to represent the Prime Council of the United World Government." He put his hand on Marzone's shoulder. "This is Rita Marzone, representing the Congress of the United World Government. We thank you for your invitation and come in peace." Then, to my surprise, he and

Marzone both bowed ever so slightly toward
Torgoona.

Torgoona then spoke for about a minute,
saying something of which I could understand only
snatches. When he finished, Jinsa handed to each of
us a piece of thick paper with words handwritten on
it in Chansu. It was the text of Torgoona's
statement, and it read as follows:

"We welcome you to the Northern Kingdom
of Chansu. The Warriors of our lands have been
separated for too long. We would be shamed if we
were to continue the isolation of the past. We
extend our hospitality and offer to you every
pleasure your duty allows you to enjoy. It is our
wish only to learn from you the ways that have made
your nation so powerful."

Next Wintergreen handed to Jinsa a text
of his speech which we had translated into Chansu.
Wintergreen asked Jinsa to read it to Torgoona and
the others, since our pronunciation was so poor.
The speech took almost ten minutes.

The Chansu all wore smiles when the
speech started. As it went on, their expressions
changed. Jinsa stopped several times during the
reading, as though he thought there was some
mistake in what he had said.

When the speech ended the Chansu all
bowed politely. Torgoona again thanked us for
coming. "We have much to discuss," he added. "But
first, we must have refreshment." He nodded and one
of the others went to the door from which they had
entered. He returned, followed by three young
girls, dressed demurely in white, pushing a large
cart. They were the first Chansu women we had
seen. Their cart held trays, some with glasses of a
brownish liquid, some with small pieces of fried

fish.

        Torgoona directed one of the girls to pass a food tray among us. Wintergreen and Marzone each took a piece of fish. As the girl turned from them to Carpenter and me the tray bumped on Wintergreen's shoulder and several pieces of food fell to the floor. One of the Chansu men stepped forward hurriedly. He snatched the tray from the girl's grasp and struck her across the face with the back of his hand. He spoke quickly to her, but I believe I caught the meaning of his words. "Do not shame us with your clumsiness," he said. "Return to the kitchen and send another." The girl turned slowly and did as she was told, her eyes downcast. Another girl came out a moment later and resumed the serving.

        Oddly, neither the man who spoke nor any of the other Chansu apologized to us for the incident or mentioned it in any way. They averted their eyes for a moment, then went on as if it had never happened. I wanted very much to say something in defense of the girl, for I--and I imagine the rest of our party--was outraged at the way she had been treated. But the behavior of the Chansu never allowed us the opportunity.

        Next Torgoona directed one of the girls to pass a tray of drinks among us. "This is one of our finest wines," he said. "I hope that it pleases you."

        Wintergreen looked around at the rest of us, then turned back to Torgoona and held up his hand. "I'm afraid we can't accept your wine," he said. "We do not drink wine."

        Torgoona looked hurt. The other Chansu watched him closely, obviously waiting for a reaction.

"This wine is offered as a token of our good will," Torgoona said carefully. "Is it against your laws to accept it?"

Wintergreen cast a questioning look at Carpenter. Apparently they had anticipated this problem. "Our duty forbids it," Wintergreen said.

Torgoona appeared to relax a bit. "We understand," he replied. "We too are bound by our obligations, though they be different from yours. Our wine will be here for you if your duty permits later." He called the serving girl back and told her to bring us some water. Then he asked us all to go through another door which led to a larger room, where a series of small tables with chairs behind them were arranged in a circle. Torgoona and his advisers sat at the tabes on one side of the circle, and we sat at the tables opposite.

"Now," said Torgoona, "there is much you said that interests us. I will begin by asking about your rulers and your nation. Our records show that when people from the east were last here, their nation was known as the Doltony Empire. Yet you did not mention that name in your speech. Why is this?"

Rita Marzone answered. "The Doltony Empire was overthrown more than a hundred years ago. The United World Government has replaced it."

"Your new ruler must be a very powerful king, then. What is his name?" asked Torgoona.

"We no longer have a ruler," Marzone said. "We are governed by a Congress, elected by the people, and by a Prime Council, elected by our Congress. I am here on behalf of our Congress, and Mr. Wintergreen was sent by the members of the Prime Council."

"I do not understand how you can have two bodies ruling over the same nation," said Torgoona.

"They have different responsibilities," put in Mohendi, from the Information Ministry. "The Congress makes the general laws, and the Prime Council sees that they are implemented."

Torgoona looked at Mohendi and shook his head, as if to clear it.

Mohendi smiled. "It is not a matter that is easily explained to one who is not familiar with it. But we have brought many books about our land and its government for you. We will be happy to translate some of them into Chansu if you wish."

"We wish to learn your language. Then we can translate for ourselves," Torgoona replied. "I would like very much to know," he went on, "how you were able to overthrow so great a nation as the Doltony Empire. Their weapons were very powerful."

"We had no advantage in weapons," Wintergreen said. "We had a strong will and a just cause."

Torgoona looked disappointed. "Yet your great nation must now have powerful weapons," he ventured.

Wintergreen smiled. "We no longer need weapons. All our people live in peace, because we are a nation of equals."

"We would like to make all of Chansu one nation, but there are evil men in the southern lands who oppose this dream," said Torgoona. "It is our hope that you can help us to overcome them."

Marzone shook her head. "I'm afraid that is something we cannot do," she said. "We have happily given up forever our military services. We come here only to exchange information. But it is our hope that once the people of Chansu have seen the wisdom of our way, they will all, north and south, east and west, wish to unite with us as full and equal partners."

Torgoona looked thoughtful. "Tell me," he said after a moment, "do these books of yours discuss military matters?"

"Certainly many of our older books do," said Mohendi. "But we didn't bring any of those with us. We would like you to understand the peace and harmony we have achieved, not the warlike ways of our past."

Jinsa spoke up. "Of course, but we would like to know everything about your nation. We can't appreciate your accomplishments without knowing what you have overcome."

Torgoona smiled at these words. "Yes, that is right," he said. "We hope that this is but the first of many exchanges between our nations. We would like to know everything about your country and its history, and we would like you to learn about Chansu. Full understanding leads to a better relationship, don't you think? But if there is some reason you do not wish to give us information about yourselves, please tell us."

Mohendi shook his head slowly. "No. No reason," he said. "The UWG puts a high value on the freedom of information. We don't believe in censorship. We look forward to the exchange you propose, and we will open our entire libraries to you."

"Very good. Very good," replied Torgoona, obviously pleased. "Now I would like to discuss something else you mentioned. You spoke of equality as an important part of your government. The meaning of this is not clear to us. Do you mean that everyone in the Warrior class receives the same income?"

"We mean," said Marzone, "that everyone receives roughly the same income. There have to be some differences, of course, to provide incentive. But the differences are very small."

"This is an amazing concept," said Torgoona. "It would be much too degrading to impose on our Warriors. Tell me," he went on, "do your Landlord and Worker classes have the same system?"

"We have no Landlord classes or Worker classes," said Marzone proudly. "We have eliminated the classes."

Torgoona's mouth dropped open. He looked at the other Chansu, who appeared equally surprised. Then he asked that the statement be repeated and re-translated.

"That is a most drastic policy," he said, after the second translation apparently confirmed his earlier understanding. "Please excuse us if we seem shocked. Who does the work in your land?"

"We all share in the work, of course," said Marzone. "We have developed machines and industrial techniques that make the work easier."

"And increase the production," added Mohendi.

"Machines?" said Torgoona. "What sort of machines?"

"All kinds of machines. Machines to make clothes. Machines to harvest crops. Vehicles," said Mohendi. "We have brought some machines for you as gifts."

"I would like to see them," said Torgoona. "But we could hardly use anything that is going to require elimination of the Worker class.

Tell me," he continued, "did your revolution simply
. . . exterminate the Workers?"

"Oh my no," said Wintergreen with a
little laugh when the question was translated.
"Obviously you have misunderstood. No one has been
exterminated. The only people killed in our
revolution were the Doltony rulers and their
armies. We have eliminated classes, not people. We
are truly a classless society."

Torgoona now appeared even more shocked
than before. "What is your family?" he demanded of
Wintergreen.

"I beg your pardon," said Wintergreen.

"What is your family?" Torgoona
demanded. "Your father. Was your father Warrior
class?"

"We have no classes," said Wintergreen
earnestly. "My father was a blacksmith. My mother
made shoes. I am very proud of them."

"What of the others?" said Torgoona,
waving his arm at the rest of us.

Wintergreen told as much about our
families as he knew. When he had finished Torgoona
stood up and, without another word, strode out of
the room. The other Chansu followed, leaving us
alone.

"What did I say?" asked Wintergreen. I
shook my head. I was thinking in that moment of
what had happened to the last expeditions to
Chansu, before the UWG.

"Does anyone remember how we got to
this room?" asked Marzone.

"I think I could find the way out," I
volunteered.

"Maybe we should leave," said Marzone.

"I don't see any point," said

Wintergreen. "They can easily stop us if we go out the way we came in." He went over to one of the windows and peered out. "This is no good. There's a straight drop of at least fifty feet."

I was beginning to feel very frightened when the door opened and Jinsa, alone, returned to the room. "King Torgoona does not desire to meet with you any longer," he announced. "You falsely implied that you were of an equal class and rank. Now we find this is not so. You are of inferior status. Henceforth you will communicate through me and my assistants."

"We had no intention of offending the king," Wintergreen said.

"The king is not offended," replied Jinsa. "He bears you no ill will. It is simply that it would be improper for him to continue to meet with you as equals. Perhaps he will arrange an audience for you at some other time, with the appropriate formalities."

"What about the gifts we brought for the king?" asked Wintergreen.

"And the king's suggestion that we exchange information," Mohendi added.

"There is no change. We gratefully accept your gifts. I will discuss with you on behalf of the king and his Chief Minister the exchange of books and other such matters."

"Very well," said Wintergreen. There was a long pause. "Do we just . . . er . . . go forward with our talks here?"

"I am afraid not," said Jinsa. "It would be inappropriate for us to continue to meet in the Old Citadel. We will resume our talks at the New Palace. There are halls there for meetings with the lower classes. But because of the lateness of the day, we will wait until tomorrow to discuss matters further. We have made arrangements for you to stay at the New Palace."

"Stay there?" asked Marzone. "What about the ship?"

"You may stay on your ship if you wish. We are unaccustomed to having persons of your rank staying in the palace rooms, so there is no obligation broken if you refuse our offer."

Wintergreen looked around at the rest of us. "I think we would be pleased to stay at the palace. Is there room for the others from the ship?"

"There are rooms for only ten."

This presented a problem. We could, of course, accept lodging at the palace if it was functionally necessary for the performance of our jobs, but it would be unjust and unfair to the others for us to stay at the palace only to escape the cramped quarters of the Liberty. I was glad I was not asked to make the decision.

"Well, then," said Wintergreen, "I believe it would be proper for this group here to accept your offer, but when our talks are over we must return to the ship."

"As you wish," said Jinsa. "I will take you there now and you may refresh yourselves. We will serve you food, but I am afraid that the banquet we had planned would not be appropriate now. Also, if the men would like, we offer you some lovely girls from the temple--very well-trained-- for your entertainment." He looked at Rita Marzone. "I am afraid we have no men to offer you. It is not our custom to have women in such a position as yours."

Marzone blushed. Wintergreen looked around uneasily. He cleared his throat. "Thank you very much," he said, "but our duty forbids such pleasures."

"Very well," Jinsa replied brusquely. "Please follow me." He led us down to the room where we had first entered the Citadel. We climbed aboard the wagon, which still held our gifts, and it took us back toward Shinso on the same road we had travelled before. When we reached the place where we had previously entered the boulevard, however, we did not turn but continued on for perhaps another mile. The road led us straight through a gate in a high stone wall and into a large courtyard, at the other side of which stood a number of brick or stone buildings of various shapes and sizes. The wagon took us around to the right and up a narrow passageway between the wall and a long, low building. We soon emerged into another courtyard, lying on the other side of the cluster of buildings. Beyond this were the wall and another gate. The wagon stopped here and Jinsa directed us out of it and into the building we had just passed.

"This building is where the rulers of the mountain kingdoms stay when they visit us," said Jinsa. "I am sure you will be comfortable here."

The interior of the building was finished with the same polished wood and bright panels we had seen at the Old Citadel. Our quarters consisted of a meeting room, a dining room, a kitchen (though very unlike any UWG kitchen), and a number of bedrooms. All the rooms were smaller in scale than those in UWG buildings, but they were vastly more comfortable than the Liberty. The furniture was made almost entirely of wood of various types--even the beds, which were small platforms about six inches high, covered with thin quilts.

Shortly after we arrived at the New Palace, Wintergreen and Carpenter went briefly to the ship to inform the others of our situation. When they returned, a group of young Chansu girls brought many courses of hot food to us in our dining room. The food, consisting primarily of various sorts of fish and vegetables, much of which was unrecognizable and all of which was highly spiced, tasted very good after six weeks of the monotonous fare served aboard the Liberty. The serving girls watched us closely, with poorly concealed curiosity, but they did not speak or even acknowledge the few questions we asked them. They left immediately after we had eaten, and we saw no more Chansu that day. We talked late into the evening, speculating about what tomorrow would hold, then finally retired to our uncomfortable beds.

3

Halburton stayed on in Chansu and assumed an administrative role. The following report authored by him recounts developments in Chansu through the end of 1900:

```
        Report to the Information Ministry
              Re:  Initial Report
        From:  David Halburton
        Date:  January 15, 1901


        Your letter appointing me as Secretary
to the Chansu Mission and requesting me to begin a
series of reports on Chansu and on the effects of our
presence here was delivered last week when the
steamship Freedom arrived in Shinso. In this report I
shall attempt to answer your initial inquiries, with
the understanding that additional data will follow in
subsequent reports, which I shall make monthly.


    1. Chronology of Developments in Establishing UWG
                Mission in Shinso


        May 15, 1898—Liberty arrives in Shinso
for initial contact with Chansu.
        July 2, 1898—Liberty sails back to UWG,
leaving Mohendi here to continue discussions
regarding permanent contacts.
        September 12, 1898--Liberty and three
other ships return to Shinso, with engineers and
cargo of books and machinery.
        October 1, 1898--King Torgoona signs
agreement permitting UWG to build permanent compound
just outside Shinso.
        January 1, 1899--We sign technical
assistance agreement with King Torgoona (actual
assistance had commenced the previous October).
        March 1, 1899--John Bridges arrives and
```

begins duties as Director of the Chansu Mission. Mohendi returns to the UWG. Regular monthly shipping schedule is inaugurated between UWG and Chansu.

June 15, 1899--First building in UWG Mission compound is completed, and we move our offices in.

August 1, 1899--Residence building at the compound is completed, and all UWG citizens in Chansu are required to move into the compound.

January 20, 1900--We establish informal information exchange program with the Scribe of the Temple at the New Palace (thus far this is the only outlet we are permitted for our information regarding UWG philosophy and government).

July 1, 1900--Limited trade agreement between Chansu and UWG is signed by King Torgoona.

2. Highlights of Technical Assistance Programs To Date

April 15, 1899--First small electric generating station completed in Shinso.

July 10, 1899--First production from Nongoto steel mill.

June 20, 1900--First leg of Shinso-Nongota railway is completed.

January 1, 1901--As of the date of this report, at least fifty factories are completed or under construction in the Shinso-Nongoto corridor using machinery or technology imported from the UWG.

3. Chronology of Chansu Political Developments Since 1898

(The following dates are only approximate;

most of this information was obtained from the priests of the New Palace Temple and, because of the restrictions on travel by UWG citizens, has not been confirmed.)

February, 1899--Skirmishes are fought in the mountain passes on the border between the Northern and Southern Kingdoms of Chansu.

August, 1899--King Torgoona declares war on the Southern Kingdom.

October, 1899--Northern Kingdom destroys Southern Kingdom border forts, using newly developed cannon. Northern Warrior troops begin invasion of Southern Kingdom.

April, 1900--Northern Kingdom uses newly-developed metal-clad warships to penetrate Southern Kingdom harbors and bombard principal coastal cities.

June, 1900--Northern Kingdom wins decisive battle at Minko-Lan in western sector of Southern Kingdom, using newly-developed semi-automatic rifles, and begins encirclement movement eastward along coast of Southern Kingdom.

August, 1900--Southern Kingdom surrenders.

November, 1900--Small semi-independent mountain states between Northern and Southern Kingdoms in east central Chansu conclude treaties pledging allegiance to King Torgoona.

December 15, 1900--King Torgoona proclaims himself Emperor of all Chansu and announces betrothal of his son, Laka, to Princess Shala Noshusha, eldest daughter of the deceased king of the Southern Kingdom.

4

When Eric Faolin, at the age of eight, began his Fourth Level classes at Pinedale in the fall of 1906, he had a new instructor named Perkins who had just emigrated to New Markwell. On the second day of the term Perkins showed the class a box of small foil-wrapped candies of the kind that the school administration normally distributed to the chldren only on Equality Day.

"I can see by your faces that you know what these are," Perkins said to the class, holding the box out in front of them. "You probably wonder why I've brought them here today, since it's just an ordinary Tuesday." He watched the children for a moment. "Well, the school had these left over from last term and didn't know what to do with them. So they told me I could pass them out to my class."

Twenty-four faces suddenly brightened.

"But," Perkins said, "I couldn't decide how to divide them among you, so I thought I'd let you do that. I'm going to put this box on the table in the front of the room and walk back to my desk. Then you children can help yourselves. You can take as many as you like, so you'd better get up here before they're all gone."

Perkins put the box of candies down and went to his desk. The second he sat down the children scrambled to the front of the room. Eric managed to get to the table in time to snatch one of the candies, but not without suffering a banged shin and a bruised elbow. The students in the back of the room failed to get anything, and one began to sputter, struggling to hold back the tears, "That's not fair. I didn't get *any*."

"You're not very happy, are you?" Perkins asked the

blubbering child.

　　　The boy shook his head vigorously.

　　　"Well," Perkins said, "how would you feel if that happened every time you wanted something?" He paused for emphasis. "You know, life was like that once--before the UWG."

　　　At first Eric didn't grasp Perkins' point. But as the instructor continued to talk, the meaning of the incident with the box of candies emerged. For the first time, Eric understood that the way of life he had been taught from birth wasn't inevitable. And, with Perkins' guidance, he realized his great fortune to be born in this time, in this place. The session left young Eric a dedicated believer in the UWG.

　　　After that day, Eric developed a very strong affection for his teacher. He talked with Perkins almost every day after classes, begging Perkins to tell him more about how it was before the UWG and how the new government solved all the old problems of slavery, poverty, and unhappiness. Eric liked particularly to hear over and over again the stories of the revolutionary heroes--the selfless men of all classes who gave up everything they had to overthrow the Doltony Empire and found a new world on the great principles of equality and freedom. Many late afternoons Eric would walk with Perkins after classes along the wooden sidewalks that led to the small apartment building where Perkins lived, just outside the walls of Pinedale,

　　　On one of the first occasions Eric accompanied Perkins, he asked the teacher if he could come inside Perkins' home to finish their discussion. Perkins explained, politely but firmly, that as much as he might want to invite Eric in, it would amount to a showing of favoritism for him to do so. Perkins told Eric, though, that he planned to invite each of his students for dinner once during the year. If Eric would be patient, his turn would come.

　　　Eric looked forward to that dinner. Once the invitations began, he tried to keep track of which of his classmates had received them. He resented the fact that others, who cared so little about the great things Perkins had to tell them, had the same amount of time at Perkins' home as he would. Finally, shortly after the mid-year holidays, Eric received his invitation--a note placed on his desk in Perkins' class. Eric remembered to get the permission of his dormitory counselor to go, and he saved a clean uniform for the occasion. When the evening arrived, Eric carefully changed clothes, brushed back his hair, and walked briskly to Perkins' apartment.

He knocked at the door, then waited for a minute. No one came. Could this be the wrong night? He knocked again. After a moment he heard stirring inside, and the door opened slowly. A woman's face peered out--a young, slightly plump face with an amused smile. She was wearing a long green robe, and her feet were bare.

"Yes?" she said.

"I'm sorry," said Eric, blushing. "I thought this was Mr. Perkins' apartment."

"Oh, it is," said the woman. "I'm Mrs. Perkins." She looked at Eric thoughtfully. "I suppose you're our dinner guest?"

"Yes, I am," said Eric. He was greatly surprised. He hadn't realized that Perkins was married.

"Well," said Mrs. Perkins, you're about fifteen minutes early. But you might as well come on in and wait." She held the door open for Eric.

"Thank you," Eric said as he walked in. As he passed close to the woman, he sensed a warmth and softness that made him feel uncomfortable. Why did she have to be here anyway? The apartment was small and seemed crowded to Eric. It was also rather dark.

"You wait here," Mrs. Perkins said when they reached the living room. "We'll be in in a few minutes." She went into another room and closed the door behind her.

Eric stood there for a moment, then took off his jacket. He sat on the edge of a worn sofa with the jacket on his lap and looked around him. One end of the room contained bookshelves filled with thick books. Eric wondered if Perkins had read them all. At the other end of the room the late afternoon sunlight tried to squeeze in around the drawn shades. Across from Eric was a fireplace, where a few small lumps of coal glowed softly. In the middle of the room stood a table, empty except for two half-filled glasses sitting on one side.

Eric sat quietly for a few minutes. He shivered and wondered if it would be all right for him to put his jacket back on, or to stir up the fire. That would be indulging himself, he finally concluded, thnking about what old Mr. Garrett, his Third Level Fitness instructor, would say. Then he heard muffled voices from the room where Mrs. Perkins had gone. The voices were followed by giggling, then silence.

After another ten fidgety minutes, the door to the other room opened, and Perkins and his wife came out. Perkins wore a tight, starched collar, a thin red tie, arid one of his frayed black classroom suits. Mrs. Perkins now had on a long white skirt, with a high-collared blouse and a red jacket.

"Well, Eric," said Perkins, "how are you this evening?"

"Just fine, sir," said Eric, standing up.

"You met Mrs. Perkins sit the door, but let me introduce you properly." Perkins stood stiffly in mock formality. His manner was far more jovial than Eric had ever seen it. "Florence," Perkins said to his wife, "I'd like you to meet one of my favorite pupils, Master Eric Faolin. He's the lad who's got more questions about his lessons than I do." Perkins started to laugh at this, then stopped himself. "And Eric, this is my lovely wife Florence." Eric bowed slightly. Mrs. Perkins grinned and curtseyed.

Perkins' eyes, slightly puffy and squinting, surveyed the room. They came to rest on the two glasses on the table.

"Our drinks, Florence, our drinks," he said. He looked at Eric. "You haven't been tippling at these, have you now, Eric?"

"Oh no, sir," Eric answered, He paused. "What is it, Mr. Perkins? It looks very good."

Perkins smiled and glanced at his wife. "It *is* very good, Eric," he said, holding the glass up in front of him. "Good old Westland grain wine." He raised the glass and then quickly downed its contents.

"Oh, Peter," Mrs. Perkins said, a note of concern in her

voice. She turned to Eric. "He's just kidding you, Eric. Why don't you come out in the kitchen with me and we'll see what's for dinner."

"I am not kidding. And I want to talk to Eric," said Perkins. He stepped unsteadily across to the sofa and dropped onto it. His wife watched, an expression of alarm now on her face.

Perkins looked at his wife. "Come here, Florence," he said, beckoning with his hand. "It's not the end of the world." She walked slowly over to where he sat. Suddenly he reached up and took her arm, pulling her gently but firmly down onto his lap. They embraced and kissed, once quickly, then again passionately.

Eric sat watching, shocked. He had never seen anything like this before. Without thinking, he withdrew to the other side of the room.

Slowly Perkins and his wife separated. He helped her to her feet, then patted her on the bottom. "Now you get out and get that dinner ready while I talk to Eric." Mrs. Perkins turned and, without expression, walked out of the room through a swinging door that Eric assumed led to the kitchen.

Perkins stared at Eric, a slight smile on his face. "Well, tell me, Eric," he said, "what do they teach you at Pinedale about grain wine?"

"Not very much, sir," said Eric, disturbed and unsure of himself. "Is that an alcohol drink ?"

"You bet it is."

"They say alcohol drinks are . . ." he searched his mind for the word, " . . . counter-productive, I think. People who drink them don't do their work properly."

"You learn your lessons well, Eric," Perkins said bitterly. "But let me tell you, it's all a big joke." He patted the sofa next to him. "Come over here and sit down." Perkins' speech was slightly slurred. Eric followed the command reluctantly. He didn't like his teacher's behavior.

"You want to know why it's a joke? I'll tell you. Actually, it's not a joke. It's a damn lie. The government hires us to tell you how great it is. How *free* we are. Equal and *free*. Free to live our lives the way we want. But then we fill you full of crap about not drinking wine and not making love and not doing about a thousand other things that are fun to do. And everybody believes it." He paused. "What difference does it make," he said, gesturing broadly, "if there aren't any laws against doing things? We don't need laws because we're all afraid to do them anyway. We're no more free than a Doltony slave." He stared at Eric for a long time. Eric was beginning to feel very uncomfortable and maybe a little sick to his stomach. "Well, what do you think about all that, Eric? You agree with me?" Perkins slapped Eric on the leg.

Eric jumped. His leg stung. "I . . . I guess so, Mr. Perkins."

Perkins continued to gaze at Eric. Then he turned away and flopped back into the cushions of the sofa. "Oh, hell, what's the use," he muttered. He folded his arms in front of him and closed his eyes.

All Eric could think of now was how much he wanted to get out of this place. For weeks he had dreamed of this chance to talk with his new friend. Now he felt relief when the conversation stopped.

They sat in silence until Mrs. Perkins returned to the room a few minutes later. She stood with her hands on her hips, looking at her husband. His eyes were closed and he was breathing heavily.

"Peter," she said. He didn't answer. She glanced over at Eric. "Peter," she repeated, louder.

"Yes, yes, I hear you," Perkins mumbled. He straightened up and rubbed his eyes.

Mrs. Perkins looked at Eric again, then back at her husband. "Peter, honey," she said. "I can't make dinner. The . . . food is spoiled."

Perkins looked at his wife questioningly. "Why did it take you this long to find that out?" he asked.

She didn't answer but turned to Eric. "I'm sorry, Eric," she said, "but you can come back and have dinner with us some other time."

Eric looked at her, then at Perkins. Slowly he stood up. "Maybe I'd better be going, then," he said. "I'm feeling kind of sick anyway." He put on his jacket while Mrs. Perkins watched. "Thank you very much for inviting me."

Mrs. Perkins walked with Eric to the door of the apartment. Her husband remained on the sofa. When they reached the door, Mrs. Perkins lowered herself to one knee and looked Eric in the eye. "Eric," she said, "Mr. Perkins has said some things he shouldn't have. Please don't pay any attention to them. He's not feeling very well, either. And I would appreciate it if you don't repeat them."

"Sure, Mrs. Perkins," Eric answered. "I won't say anything."

Eric said good-bye and left. He walked slowly back toward his dormitory, feeling alone, unhappy, and cheated. It had become colder with the setting of the sun, but Eric scarcely noticed it. He didn't go inside his building right away but walked back and forth across the grounds until he was sure he had his tears under control. Finally he joined his dormitory mates just in time for the evening behavior lecture, after which he went quietly to bed.

5

Robert Strongarm sat, sweltering, in the crowded railroad coach, waiting for the train to move out of the station. Exasperated, he half stood and, with considerable effort, managed to force the window open a few inches. It was futile. The exertion made Strongarm sweat even more, and only the faintest draft of air circulated through the open window, along with the irritating sounds of clanging bells and puffing steam engines.

Strongarm looked around him. He was the only Nauryan in the coach this morning. He couldn't help but feel that his gray skin stood out among the brown faces like a black thread on a white cloth. As always, of course, none of the others in the coach gave any sign that they noticed his distinctiveness.

Strongarm became aware of the middle-aged woman in the yellow skirt and jacket sitting across from him, glaring at the open window. As soon as the train began to move, Strongarm realized, she would ask him to close it, and with good reason. The smoke and soot that would pour into the coach would blacken her clothing in an hour. He closed the window resignedly and sat down, nodding to acknowledge the woman's smile of thanks. Perhaps, Strongarm thought, once the train began to move the fans would work. He glanced at the still blades hanging from the ceiling of the coach.

A wave of impatience swept over Strongarm. He clenched his teeth and tightened his grip on the wooden armrest that separated him from his neighboring passenger, an old man with white hair and a stubble of white whiskers on his light brown face. Strongarm reached into his vest pocket and pulled out his silver-cased watch. Nine-thirty. The train was already half an hour late. At this rate, he might not get home to Clark Falls before dark. His stomach churned. He didn't want this extra time to doubt the wisdom of this trip. If the train would only get on its way, he would be committed and could put these nagging second thoughts out of his mind.

Strongarm held the watch to his ear. It was ticking strongly. He allowed himself a long, admiring look at it before returning it to its pocket. He still felt a fleeting pride in owning such a fine instrument. His parents had given it to him just six months earlier, on his graduation from Southern Agronica General College. They must have saved for some time to buy it, he guessed, for he had seen others like it selling for almost two weeks' pay.

Strongarm thought of his mother and father. What were they going to say when he walked in the door of their apartment this evening? Like most Nauryans, Strongarm felt a strong attachment to his parents. Probably a holdover from the extended family relationship around which the "unadapted" Nauryans--many of whom still lived in their various tribal groups on the slopes of the Division Mountains-- organized their lives. Not that Strongarm's family was fresh out of the foothills, though, like so many Nauryans were these days. Both his parents were descendants of Doltony slaves. Strongarm' s ancestors had been full-fledged citizens of the UWG since its beginning and had been "civilized" for centuries before that. Strongarm guiltily admitted to himself a certain pride in his heritage.

A jolt shook the coach. It began to move, ever so slowly, out of the station. Strongarm felt a momentary anxiety about pulling away, but it quickly subsided and he settled back for his trip, more relaxed now than at any time in the last two days.

Train No. 402 left Brockton, a city of 300,000 in the marshy flatlands of Southern Agronica, every morning. Sixteen hours later, according to the schedule, it was to arrive in Stevensburg, about 800 miles to the north. A little more than halfway there, it stopped at Clark Falls, a much smaller town, known principally for its textile mills. Strongarm had lived most of his 20 years in Clark Falls, and his parents still did. He had, in fact, spent a good part of the last six months there. It was only ten days since he had come down to Brockton for the start of the July Term at the University. But now, on this hot day in late July, 1910, he was going home again.

The train picked up speed once it emerged from the station and switched onto its northbound track. Strongarm stared absently at the rows of apartment buildings, the steamy green parks, and the furniture factories that passed by his window. He had seen them all before, for he had taken this trip many times during his three years at the General College. He didn't look forward to nine more hours of watching the familiar landscape slide by. He shifted in his seat. Somehow the movement of the train made him feel cooler, even though the ceiling fans were still motionless.

Strongarm settled back and stared up at the fans. How

different he felt now than he had just ten days ago when he rode this train into Brockton. Then he was full of curiousity, nervousness, and exhilaration as he approached the beginning of his legal studies. Yet he did also feel then a thin undercurrent of concern over the difficulty that now filled his mind. The treatment he received at the law school had not come as a surprise; perhaps, indeed, he had been looking for it.

Strongarm remembered vividly his very first class, where he sat, toward the back of the room, at the end of one of the long wooden benches. The lecturer didn't reach Strongarm until late in the hour. He had been discussing the UWG laws on the acquisition and ownership of property. "Mr. Strongarm," he said, looking down at his seating list, "may I ask you a few questions based upon what we have just discussed?"

Strongarm stood up, very tense. "Yes, sir."

"We've learned," said the lecturer, "that our property equalization policy operates primarily through the income tax. Now, what do you see as the major legal difficulties with that policy?"

Strongarm's mind was a blank. "Er . . . the tax rate?" he ventured.

"Well . . . yes," said the lecturer reluctantly. "That is a factor. If the rate is not correct, the tax may not have the desired effect. But that's what I would call an administrative problem, not a legal one. Don't you see any definitional problems here?"

Strongarm swallowed. His mouth was suddenly very dry. "I'm afraid I don't follow you," he said finally.

"Let's look at it this way," said the lecturer. "What about a gift? Should that be considered income? or money inherited? How about that?"

Strongarm stood tongue-tied, unable to think, perspiring heavily. "Well," he finally said, "a gift isn't exactly the same as income you earn at your job."

The lecturer looked Strongarm over. "Does that help us solve the problem?" he said gently. Then he riffled through some papers on the desk in front of him.

"All right," the lecturer continued before Strongarm answered the last question. "You probably don't have any reason yet to know how gifts and inheritances are taxed. What I'm getting at is that there is a legal problem in the definition of "income." And we solve the problem by looking at the policy of the tax. If we just wanted to raise revenue, we might decide that gifts should be excluded. But if the major purpose is equalization of wealth, as it is, then gifts and inheritances should obviously be included. By so doing, we make sure everyone has roughly the same wealth." He paused. "It's really the same thing, only in reverse, as our educational equalization policy. I'm sure you know about that." He smiled benevolently at Strongarm.

The remark hit Strongarm like a physical blow. He remembered now that he had stood there, shocked, for a few seconds or minutes, but he didn't remember anything distinctly about the rest of the class. The next thing he recalled clearly was sitting in his dormitory room, feeling ashamed and embarrassed.

Strongarm had not taken advantage of the Nauryan educational equalization policy before. There were no test requirements for the General College or the lower schools. It was only the graduate and professional schools--and, of course, the professional occupations-- that had to weight Nauryan scores so as to admit Nauryans in proportion to their distribution in the population. It was a policy that dated from the beginning of the UWG, but it bothered Strongarm nonetheless to be its beneficiaary. He had hoped it was a matter he could keep locked tightly inside him, but now it was exposed for all to see.

Strongarm had returned to his classes the next day, wary of another such incident. None occurred, but Strongarm perceived a distinct patronizing attitude toward him by both his instructors and his fellow students. The following day the condescension increased. And then came last night.

Last night, as he sat alone in his law school dormitory room, Strongarm had picked up one of his law books to prepare for the next day's class. After five minutes of looking at it he found himself unable to concentrate. Try as he might, he couldn't read a sentence.

Frightened, he began to worry about being unable to keep up with the lecturer the next day. Then, slowly, the depression began to envelop his mind. Before he knew it, he found himself sweating, confused, and consumed by morbid thoughts. There was barely enough rationality left for him to realize he had to get away, at least for a few days. And so he had packed his bag and walked the three miles to the train station, each step away from the school clearing a little bit more of the mist from his mind. He had sat on a bench at the station the rest of the night, waiting for the morning train to Clark Falls. Now he was on his way.

Tired from a sleepless night, Strongarm leaned his head in the space between the hard wooden window frame and his seat back and closed his eyes. He dozed almost immediately, but woke with every lurch of the coach. Finally, after the train hit a new section of track just past Vernon, Strongarm fell into a deeper and mercifully dreamless sleep.

In the middle of the afternoon Strongarm woke as the train stopped at Bigelow. The woman in yellow and the old man who shared his seat were gone, replaced by a young man in a dark suit with a large briefcase. Strongarm felt very hungry, but he had spent almost all of what was left of his student's monthly allocation on his train ticket. He could get something when he reached home. If the train was not further delayed, he would be in Clark Falls in three hours.

When the train was underway again Strongarm tried to go back to sleep but couldn't. He spent the three hours painfully watching the minutes creep by, staring out the window, finding excuses to pace up and down the aisle. At long last, shortly after 7:00 p.m., the train pulled into the Clark Falls station.

Strongarm was tempted to call his parents from the station, but there was only one telephone in their building, and he didn't want to speak to neighbors. He caught a trolley outside the train station that carried him slowly up the hill from the river beside which the railroad line ran and then across town to his home. It was still light out when he got off. Somehow Strongarm wished he had waited until dark, so that fewer questioning eyes would regard his return.

He walked up the familiar stairs of Building No. 3 to the third floor, turned right and stood in front of his parents' apartment. He still had his key, but he decided to knock. His mother opened the door.

"My goodness, what are you doing here, Robbie?" she exclaimed. "Father," she called into the other room, "come here."

Strongarm heard a chair scraping in the other room, then his father's footsteps. His parents must have been eating dinner, he thought. Mrs. Strongarm stood examining him as his father came and stood beside her. They looked older than they had ten days ago. Both were thin, and the bones and sinews of their faces stood out in their tight gray skin. His father's leanness and bald head contrasted with his son's already stout frame and thick hair.

"It's nice to see you, son," said Strongarm 's father. "But what are you doing here? Why didn't you tell us you were coming? Is something wrong?"

"There is something that's bothering me, Father," said Strongarm, "and I need to talk to you and Mother about it. But I haven't eaten since last night. Could I have some food first?"

"Oh, yes," said Mrs. Strongarm. "Father and I were just having dinner. There's plenty of stew left. We thought your grandmother was going to join us, but she went out." She took her son's arm. "Come on in. No reason to he standing here in the doorway."

The three of them went inside and sat at the table in the small dining alcove. Mrs. Strongarm stepped to the kitchen to get a plate.

Strongarm's father sat, looking at his son from across the table. "Are you in some kind of trouble, Rob? Do they know you're gone?"

"Later, Father," Strongarm said. "But it's nothing like that. I haven't done anything."

Mrs. Strongarm returned and ladled out the rest of the stew from an iron pot. Strongarm ate rapidly while his parents sat watching, too concerned to continue their own meals.

When he finished, Strongarm leaned back in his chair. He felt more at ease now. He hated to start the discussion, though, but he knew he couldn't put his parents off any longer.

"Mother, Father," he said, "they know I'm in law school on the equalization factor."

Mrs. Strongarm wrinkled her brow. "Who knows?" she asked.

"Everyone. The teachers. The other students. One lecturer mentioned it in class."

"So?" asked Strongarm's father.

"Father, it's demeaning. I feel like a second class person."

"But everyone knows about the equalization," said Mrs. Strongarm. "It's done a lot of good for the Nauryans."

"Not everyone knows which people are getting equalization points." Strongarm began to feel angry.

There was a pause. Strongarm's parents sought each other's eyes, carefully avoiding their son's.

"Is this the whole thing, Rob?" Mr. Strongarm finally said.

"Of course it's the whole thing. Isn't it enough? I've been so depressed I felt like . . . ." Strongarm didn't finish the sentence.

"Rob, you've got to stop being so sensitive," said Mr. Strongarm. "Look, people know we're Nauryans. We can't hide that. And they go out of their way to treat us well. There aren't enough Nauryans in certain jobs, so they make sure there are. You should he grateful, Rob, not upset. I'm a lot more concerned about what people think about your missing classes today than about what they think of your equalization points. Now I'm not going to tell you what to do, Rob. I believe a twenty year old man should decide things for himself. But it sure seems to me you ought to get yourself a good night's sleep and hop on that train back to Brockton tomorrow."

Strongarm barely held back an outburst against his father. "You just don't understand," he said finally. "You just don't understand." Tears came to his eyes. He looked up at his mother. "What do you think?" he asked.

She glanced at her husband, then cleared her throat. She reached out a hand and put it over that of her son. "Robbie, I'm afraid I agree with your father. We are treated the equal of anyone else. When the government gives us something we haven't earned, we should accept it humbly and be grateful we have it, not try to hide it. Sometimes I think it makes them feel good to know about it--to know they've helped us out." She patted Strongarm's hand gently.

Strongarm rose from his chair. "Mother," he said, "the problem is that you and Father both believe Nauryans really aren't as good as others. Well, I don't accept that. But if it's true, then I don't want to be reminded of it all the time." He stood and looked at his parents for a long while, his hands gripping the back of his chair. Then he straightened up and started for the door. "I've got to go out," he said. "It's too hot in here."

"Where are you going?" Strongarm' s mother asked.

"I don't know. Just to get some air. Maybe I'll go see Smallbear." He didn't wait to see what his parents would say but walked quickly out of the apartment, down the stairs and into the courtyard.

It was funny, Strongarm thought to himself, how John Smallbear's name had popped out of his mouth. He hadn't really talked with Smallbear since before college. Yet now that he thought of the man he felt better. He pictured Smallbear--small, thick, stooped, like his namesake. A man to be admired. Born in the Westland foothills of native parents, John Smallbear had come to civilization at the age of three when his tribe, starved in the famine of 1845, voted to join the UWG. In the dispersal of the tribe arranged by UWG officials Smallbear's parents had chosen to come to Clark Falls. Smallbear, as he grew, had done well, and had even studied at Agronica National University at Preston. He taught for several years at one of the Central Agronica colleges, but some trouble, so it was rumored, forced him to resign. He returned to Clark Falls, where he had now taught two generations, including Strongarm, in the secondary school.

It was nearly dark as Strongarm walked down the brick sidewalk toward town, hoping that Smallbear still lived in the old apartment building overlooking the city center. The walk seemed shorter than Strongarm remembered it. In fifteen minutes he was reading the list of occupants of Building No. 12 on Carriage Street. Smallbear was still there. After a moment of indecision, Strongarm went back to Smallbear's room and knocked.

Smallbear opened the door. He looked exactly as he did when Strnngarm last saw him, loose-fitting clothes, perpetually scowling mouth, small wire-rimmed glasses, and an abrupt, affirmative manner.

"Rob Strongarm," Smallbear said, in his thin voice, with still a trace of the Nauryan accent. "Haven't seen you for a while. What do you want?"

"You remember me?"

"Sure. I remember all my Nauryans. I remember your mother and father, too. How are they?"

"Fine . . . fine." Strongarm stood there, not knowing exactly what to say next.

"Well, what do you want, Strongarm?"

"Could I . . .er . . . could I talk to you for a little while?" Strongarm asked, embarrassed.

"It must be important, or you wouldn't be all the way up here from the law school. Come on in."

They walked into Smallbear 's sparsely furnished living room. It looked scarcely lived in. They sat down.

"You know about my law school, too?"

"I keep track. You didn't come all the way up here just to see me, did you?"

"I came up to see my parents," Strongarm said slowly. He felt he had to measure his words carefully in speaking to Smallbear. "They couldn't help me. That's when you came to my mind. Though now that I'm here I think maybe I knew all along that you were the person I wanted to talk to."

"Troubles at the law school?"

"Yes."

Smallbear scracthed his cheek. "You there on

equalization points?"

"Yes. Did you know?"

"Wasn't sure. You were borderline. Wouldn't have been surprised if you'd made it without equalization. Not surprised you didn't either. Not many Nauryans do."

"You did, people say."

"Yes, I did. So did a few others from Clark Falls, but the last was quite a few years ago."

"You may not be able to appreciate my problem, then."

"Try me." Smallbear, despite his years, sat cross-legged on a bench next to the radiator. He leaned back against the wall.

Strongarm edged forward in his cane-seated wooden chair and described the events of the last week. "I couldn't stand to stay there any longer," he said after he finished. "Yet when I got home tonight and talked to my parents, they acted as if I'm ungrateful. They think I should hurry back and apologize for missing classes. They say no one thinks less of me because I'm there on equalization points." He waited for a reaction from Smallbear.

"You are not the first Nauryan to talk to me about this problem, Strongarm. Nor are you the first to experience this terrible depression." Smallbear took off his glasses, cleaned and replaced them. "I dislike interfering in things like this, Strongarm, but your parents are wrong. What they say would be right if they were in your position, but they're not. They are trained dogs, like most 'civilized' Nauryans. You are a cat. You don't follow others. You think about yourself too much-- too much for your own happiness, I should say. I'm not judging you."

Strongarm felt relieved, but his situation was still unresolved. "What can I do?" he asked.

"In my opinion, the first thing is to get out of law school or it will ruin you, if it doesn't kill you. Do a job you can do as well as a non-Nauryan. Get married and have children. Try not to think too much about what is happening to you and to other Nauryans."

Strongarm thought over Smallbear's advice. "Is that the only solution?" he finally asked.

"The only one you can live with."

"But . . . how do you know?"

Smallbear's eyes narrowed. "Because I'm an old man. I've seen a lot of things and talked to a lot of people. Especially Nauryans. If you question my advice, why did you come here?"

"I'm sorry. I don't doubt your advice. I just wanted to know how you come to it."

"Well, I've told you. Sixty-eight years of experience."

Strongarm grew uncomfortable. He sensed that Smallbear was tiring of the conversation, yet he didn't want to leave. "Do other Nauryans getting equalization feel the same way I do?" he asked. "I mean, is there something wrong with me?"

"Some do. Some don't. Don't ask me who's right and who's wrong. I don't make judgments."

"How would you feel, Smallbear?"

Smallbear opened his mouth, then closed it. He looked steadily at Strongarm, then cast his eyes downward. "I would find it absolutely intolerable--a degrading and inhumane custom," he said, very softly.

"You would?" Strongarm smiled. "Then you agree with me! You don't know how much better that makes me feel."

"Why should it? My opinion doesn't solve your problem."

"Can't the system be changed? Have you ever thought of that?"

Smallbear got up from his bench and walked across the room. For a moment Strongarm thought he noticed an almost fatherly expression on Smallbear's face. But it didn't last. It wasn't Smallbear's way.

"I thought about it a great deal, Strongarm, long ago, when the memories of the foothills were fresher and the equalization policy was a lot newer. I even tried to convince others that something should be done. But it's not just the equalization policy, Strongarm, it's the whole framework of this society. This may sound like heresy to you, but maybe a little inequality wouldn't be such a bad thing." Smallbear stopped. He waved his hand past his face as if swatting away an insect, then turned and went back to his bench. "You've got me talking too much," he continued, his back still to Strongarm. "I don't want to think about this. They beat me down once and that was enough." He turned. "They'll beat you down, too. And they're probably right. You can't mistreat the dogs in order to save a few cats." He wiped his forehead and sat down again. "Take my advice, Strongarm. Get out of that law school and do something you're qualified for. Forget all this nonsense." He leaned back and closed his eyes. "You can go now. Please shut the door tight when you leave."

Reluctantly Strongarm got up and went to the door. Sadness welled in him, for himself and for this little misplaced man. "Thank you very much, Smallbear," he said. "This talk has meant a great deal to me." Smallbear grunted, and Strongarm left the apartment, making sure to close the door securely behind him.

George A. Platz

PART TWO

1916-1928

1

Report to the Information Ministry
Re: Southern Lands of the Chansu
From: David Halburton
Date: May 1, 1916

The Ministry has requested an
evaluation of the situation currently prevailing
in the lands of the former Southern Kingdom. As
the Ministry knows, travel in this area, as in
most areas of Chansu away from Shinso, is still
limited to personnel providing engineering and
other technical assistance. The information in
this report has been compiled from the

observations of such personnel and from
communications made to us by our informants at the
palace temple. The report is believed to be
accurate, but is subject to the limitations of its
sources.

1.   Social Situation

Despite their historically different
government, the people of the Southern lands seem
always to have maintained the same rigid class
structure, and the same panoply of deities, as in
the Northern lands. For this reason, the Torgoona
Conquest of 1900 appears to have had little
effect on the basic social structure, except in
the instances discussed below in connection with
the economic situation. In general, the classes--
particularly the Worker and Priest classes--
perform the same functions and maintain the same
rituals as in the North.

2. Political Situation

As the Ministry is aware, the former
chief of the Southern Kingdom, King Lan Noshusha,
killed himself after his defeat by Torgoona. After
the Conquest Torgoona removed all members of the
Southern Kingdom Warrior class from their
administrative and military posts. He re-staffed
the posts with Warriors from the North and
permanently forbade any Southern Warrior born
before the Conquest ever to return to such jobs.
The families he considered most dangerous he
removed to isolated Northern provinces. The rest

he placed under severe restrictions as to their communications with each other, but he did grant them modest stipends (financed of course by taxes on Southern Kingdom lands). And, as a conciliatory measure, presumably to give the Southern Warriors hope for the future, he arranged for the marriage of his only son and heir, Laka, to the princess Shala Noshusha, daughter of his late foe.

In 1905 several of the Southern Warrior families attempted an insurrection. The details of the attempt are not well known, but apparently it was put down rather easily and rather brutally. At present the Northerners continue to hold all the ruling posts in the South. This situation may, however, change in the not too distant future, for it will not be many years until Southern Warriors born after the Conquest will be old enough, and eligible, to take over such jobs. It should, incidentally, also be noted that Torgoona will soon be 70. Laka, his heir, is still married to a Southern wife.

3. Economic Situation

The Southern Warriors naturally faced a major dislocation of their lives after Torgoona's ban. Many have turned to a life of culture, but a large number have done something Torgoona may never have contemplated--they have taken up occupations of the other classes. The ranks of the temples have increased enormously in the South. But perhaps of most interest and concern has been the affiliation of the Southern Warriors, including close relatives of Princess

Shala, with members of the Landlord class.

There has always been a rather close relationship between the Landlord class of Chansu and the Warrior class, since traditionally the Warrior families do not own villages or other tracts of productive land outright. Rather, they own rights to the income of land that is nominally "owned" by the Landlords. Often in the past young Warriors have been sent to work with the Landlord whose land produces the Warrior's income.

When the Warriors of the South lost their jobs after the Conquest, they were welcomed and given permanent places to live by the Landlords. At first, we are told, the Warriors did little more than enhance the prestige of their hosts. Soon, however, in order to support the additional people and pay the ever higher taxes, they found it necessary to contribute their efforts to the administration of the large agricultural estates. Agricultural output in the South has increased greatly as a result, and the benefits of the increase have accrued largely to the displaced Warriors. At present there are many places in the South where the Warrior families and the Landlord families pursue virtually indistinguishable careers. The Warriors continue, however, to maintain their social status.

The story of the Southern Warrior is the story of the South. They both find themselves locked into the economy of the land which has prevailed in Chansu for centuries. This is in contrast to the North, where, undoubtedly because of our influence, the government and the wealthy Warriors are demanding the goods and services of an industrial economy. Warriors, Landlords, and Workers in the North have begun directing their capital and labor into manufacturing. Taxes on the produce of the land throughout Chansu are being increased to pay for industrial goods, while taxes on manufacturing output are being kept low to stimulate expansion. This situation is having an unfavorable economic effect on all classes in the South, where there is yet virtually no industry.

2

In 1923, as now, the rolling hills of central and northern Westland, when viewed from a distance, appeared soft and smooth and inviting, particularly in May after the spring rains had turned the land a cool green. On closer inspection, however, the softness and smoothness disappeared. Most of those hills were densely covered with low, wiry bushes whose roots reached deep into the earth for the moisture that in the summer would be so scarce. So tough was this growth that in some areas a man considered a five mile journey through it a two-day trek.

But the soil of Westland was fertile, and if a man could clear the land and dig wells to irrigate it, his labors were rewarded. He still had to endure the blazing summer, of course, and one way of doing this, if his land was near enough, was to journey eastward into the foothills of the Division Mountains, whose towering peaks sealed Westland off from the civilization of Brahmastan two hundred miles further east. Better yet, a man could establish his farm in that narrow gradient between the fertile bushland and the grassy foothills, if he could find a suitable place that did not lie within the territory which the UWG had preserved for the native Nauryan tribes and their grazing flocks.

Eric Faolin was looking for just such a site when, on the morning of June 28, 1923, tired and discouraged, he came upon that huge rocky outcropping that would later become known throughout the native territory as the Hill of the Protector. On that morning, however, the huge wall of granite threatened to end Faolin's quest. For a month and a half he had been moving northward, on foot, along the native territory boundary, searching in vain for homesteads for the band of pioneers who waited in New Markwell for his return. They had come to New Markwell during the early spring and hired Faolin as their scout soon afterward. In the beginning of May Faolin had reached the southern foothills aboard a grain barge being towed back up the Strange River that flowed from the Division Mountains down to the sea at New Markwell. He had then set out on his journey, staying next to the native territory boundary stakes as he moved northward. There were many good sections of grassland in the first three hundred miles along the boundary, but all had been settled. Then, early in June, Faolin had crossed a number of small rivers and suddenly found himself in true wilderness. Here the bush grew right up to the boundary markers, forcing Faolin to make part of his journey within native territory. There was little danger, for the UWG's benevolent policies had left the natives friendly and without guns, but Faolin knew that he was trespassing nonetheless. Occasionally he would be able to cross back into the Westland territory, but nowhere west of the boundary was there sufficient open land to remotely satisfy his clients. They were young, strong people, who would not shirk at hard labor, but even they would starve before they could get this land cleared.

After almost two hundred miles of fruitless tramping through the wilderness, Faolin's spirits were low. As he stood looking at the enormous obstacle before him, he debated whether to turn back. The hill of rock clearly extended for several miles both to the east, into native territory, and to the west, into free land. Scaling the sheer cliff appeared to be impossible, and Faolin estimated that circumnavigating it through the dense growth on the western side might take him three or four days. He could get around it on the east, but he would have to go much deeper into native territory than he had gone before. If Faolin went back now, he might be able to get in some exploring along the coast or the rivers before winter set in.

Faolin made his decision. They had asked him to find land along the foothills, and he would either find it or know it wasn't there. How could he turn back when, for all he knew, huge meadows lay right on the other side of the outcropping? He shifted the pack on his back, turned to the east, and stepped resolutely forward.

Four hours later, Faolin wondered if he had chosen the right path. He had left the thick undergrowth soon after entering native territory, but the narrow stretch of grassland had given way to a seemingly endless, dense stand of pines, in the midst of which Faolin now found himself. He sat on a log to rest from the uphill climb, then, removing his pack, lay down on the soft cushion of pine needles on the forest floor. As he rested there, staring at the sky, he heard a noise, a snapping of a branch in the forest not too far away. He sat up quickly. Fellow scouts in New Markwell had told him there were bears and wild pigs in the Northern forests, but he had never heard of any this far south. He listened, then heard the sound again behind him, and he spun around. He could see nothing. Frightened now, he removed his rifle from his pack and loaded it. Then he moved slowly toward the nearest large tree. In the next moment he suddenly found himself lying face down on the ground, his head buzzing and a burning pain spreading through his right leg. He gasped for air and struggled to regain his feet. His hand touched the wooden shaft protruding from just above his right knee as he felt himself being enveloped by a paralyzing blackness.

The next thing Faolin saw was a bearded man in a wrinkled white coat standing a few feet away, looking in the other direction. Confused, Faolin looked around. He was lying on a cot inside a building constructed of gray, unpainted logs. Light came from a window and from a lantern hanging from the logs overhead.

The bearded man turned toward Faolin and smiled. "Well, it's about time you woke up. How do you feel?" He was tall, thin, and light brown-skinned and obviously not a Nauryan native.

"Where am I?" asked Faolin.

"Safe now," answered the man. "And your leg is going to be all right. But you're lucky you weren't killed. What were you doing out there in native territory?"

Faolin didn't answer.

"Look," the man went on, "I'm not going to report you. But I hope you know how foolish you were. You created a lot of unhappiness here, too. Those poor boys who shot you feel just terrible, and chances are they'll be punished for it. They thought you were a bear."

"Who are you?" asked Faolin.

"Newberry. Bill Newberry. I'm the Medical-Indoctrinational man here. Been working with this tribe for twelve years now. You're lucky I happened to be in this village yesterday or you would have lost that leg for sure. Those boys knew how to stop the bleeding all right, but they couldn't do much else."

"Yesterday? I was shot yesterday?"

"Yep. Yesterday afternoon. Almost twenty-four hours ago."

"How far are we from where I was shot?"

"About five miles. Those boys carried you all the way here."

Both men were silent for a moment. "How do you feel, anyway?" Newberry asked. "You don't look too hot."

"My head hurts and my leg hurts. But I feel like I'll live." Faolin smiled slightly. "I sure could use a little food, though. There ought to be something in my pack."

"The boys had to leave your pack when they brought you in, but they went back for it this morning. In the meantime, I'll get you some food from the natives. This is the Komisaw tribe, in case you didn't know. You probably won't like what they have to offer, but it's better than nothing."

"How long will I have to stay here?"

"I want you in bed for a few more days. It's going to be a lot longer than that, though, before you can start tramping through the woods by yourself again. Which reminds me, you didn't tell me what you were doing out here."

"I'm a scout for a party in New Markwell. I was looking for homesteads."

"In native territory?"

"I was trying to get around that big rock so I could go further north."

"Hmm. Well, you took an awful chance going that far into native territory without getting clearance. Not all the tribes are as friendly as this one."

Faolin started to rise up, then sank wearily back onto the cot.

"You'd better rest a bit before we talk more," said Newberry. "I'll see about that food. Incidentally, I assume your name is the same as on your papers: Eric Faolin?"

Faolin nodded. Newberry grunted and left. Faolin closed his eyes and soon dozed. He woke again when Newberry returned with a large boiled root of some kind for him to eat. As Newberry had predicted, it did not appeal to Faolin's "civilized" palate, but he was hungry and ate it all.

"You can't be in too bad shape if you can put all that away," said Newberry when Faolin finished. "Now wipe your mouth and sit up. The boys who shot you are outside. They've come to return your pack and to apologize. If you ask me, you're the one who owes the apology, so you watch yourself."

"Wait a minute. What do I say? Do they speak our language?"

"What do you think I've been teaching them for the past twelve years? As far as what you say, just remember that they saved your life."

Newberry left the building for a moment. The two "boys" who returned with him were shorter and thicker than Faolin, but appeared to be almost his age. Both avoided Faolin's eyes as they approached and were obviously uncomfortable.

"Eric Faolin," Newberry said, "This is Forest Path and this is Swift Stream. They have something to say to you."

The young men glanced at Newberry, then at each other. They knelt at Faolin's cot. The one called Forest Path, who appeared slightly older than the other and whose gray skin was rough and pockmarked, spoke, fluently but with a distinct accent, in the language of the UWG. "We carelessly endangered your life. We've brought shame on us and on our houses. We beg your forgiveness."

"Please stand up," said Faolin from his cot. "I'll forgive you if you'll forgive me for trespassing on your land."

"The Council of Elders wish for you to choose our punishment," said Forest Path.

"I can't punish you," said Faolin.

Newberry cleared his throat. "I hadn't realized the matter had gone that far. If you don't choose a punishment for them, the Council of Elders will."

Faolin thought quickly. From Newberry's tone, it sounded as though punishment by the elders might be harsh. "All right, I will. But I must talk with Dr. Newberry first."

"That's a good idea," said Newberry. "I'd like to discuss it with the Council."

Faolin smiled at the two natives. "Don't worry. I'll take care of you the right way."

Forest Path and Swift Stream acted surprised. They rose and backed away from the cot. They looked as if they wanted to say something more but before they had a chance Newberry ushered them out of the building. When he returned he looked at Faolin approvingly.

"Did I do all right?" Faolin asked.

"You did fine. We'll work out something relatively easy for them. Poor devils. Tell me, why did you make that last statement?"

"Which statement?"

"The one about taking care of them the Right Way."

Faolin scratched his head. "I really don't know. I didn't want them to be afraid, I guess. Why?"

"Oh, it's just a native expression--from their religion. Maybe you picked it up from reading about the natives."

"Could be." Faolin paused. "Speaking of that, Doctor, those men weren't at all what I expected. I always thought Nauryan natives were bold and proud. Those fellows seemed rather pathetic."

"Yes, I know what you mean. The natives you read about in the UWG are usually the ones from the ruling houses. These boys aren't. Forest Path is from the Blackbird clan, and Swift Stream is from the Muskrat clan, two of the lowest-ranking houses in the tribe. Their clans don't own any sheep. They raise crops, and that's generally considered the least significant occupation in the tribe. Their low status explains their manner. It also explains, I'm afraid, why they're being punished for putting an arrow in your leg."

Memories of history lessons long forgotten returned to Faolin. "That's horrible. What a terrible existence. Why don't they join the UWG?"

Newberry shrugged his shoulders. "I don't know. They have loyalty to their tribe. They feel they must do what their ancestors did. I've certainly explained the benefits of UWG citizenship. That's one of the reasons I'm here." He started to move across the room, then turned back to Faolin. "We can't force the tribe to accept equality, you know. That's why the UWG still preserves the territory for those who want to stay."

"Well, it makes me angry. I'm going to find a way to help them." Faolin noticed that his hands were beginning to shake. He leaned back in the cot.

"This has been a lot for you to handle in your condition," Newberry said with a note of concern. "Get some rest and we'll talk about those boys later."

Faolin nodded and closed has eyes. He was too tired to pursue the subject further now, but he definitely was not going to forget about it.

3

Faolin's first five days in the native village passed uneventfully. Forest Path and Swift Stream didn't return to the hospital, and Faolin didn't venture outside it. It wasn't until the fifth day that Faolin's leg had mended enough for him to move about inside the building.

In the early afternoon of the sixth day Faolin lay on his back on his cot in the deserted hospital building and stared at the ceiling. He craved activity, and the enforced rest did not suit his temperament. Furthermore, it was threatening to end his scouting job.

The door opened and Newberry came in, carrying two crooked wooden sticks. He grinned broadly. "Well, Faolin, come on, let's go for a walk."

"Don't kid me. It's not funny," Faolin said sourly.

"Hey, the patient's disposition is terrible. Come on, I'm not kidding. Look at these." Newberry held up the sticks.

Faolin's eyes brightened. "Crutches?"

"You bet. Made them myself. I think you can handle them now. Come on. We've got someplace to go."

"Best news I've heard in two months." Faolin got up from the cot, hopped over and took the makeshift crutches from Newberry. He put them under his arms, stepped gingerly forward, and almost fell.

"Careful, you've got to get the knack of it."

Faolin tried again and took several steps toward the door. He remained steady. He smiled.

"Very good," said Newberry, "now we'll go. You can

practice on the way there."

"Where are we going?"

"The house of the Blackbird clan. It's time for you to pronounce sentence. Just remember what I told you."

They went out the door into the bright early afternoon sunshine. It hurt Faolin's eyes, and he had to stop until he got accustomed to it. Then he looked around. At first it appeared that the log hospital building was totally surrounded by a helter skelter assemblage of hide-covered dwellings. Then he saw that there were several pathways leading away from the hospital and through the closely-packed houses. Newberry started down one of the paths and Faolin hobbled along after him.

"Hard to believe that this whole village is portable, isn't it?"

"What do you mean?" said Faolin, breathing hard.

"Every one of these houses can be taken down and moved in less than a day. The hides are attached to collapsible wooden frames. Very ingenious. The only permanent buildings in the village are the hospital and the meeting hall. It's on the other side of the hospital."

"Why are they made that way?"

"Every summer a large number of the sheep are taken up the mountain to graze. When they go, a whole clan goes to take care of them. The clans alternate the job, so they all have to be able to move."

"What about the clans with no sheep?"

"Well, they don't go up the mountain, but they've got the same kind of houses. I guess maybe they hope some day they'll have sheep."

They went on silently for a while. It seemed to Faolin that the houses were getting smaller, with more and more patches. After about five minutes they stopped to rest in a little clearing.

"This is where a group of houses goes," Newberry said, indicating the area in which they stood. "They'll be back in the fall."

Faolin suddenly remembered something. "Doctor, I had an idea earlier today that I wanted to ask you about. Do Forest Path and

Swift Stream know this area very well?"

"They know where the crops grow. They don't know where all the meadows are for the sheep."

"Well, I was wondering if there's any possibility that one or both of them might be able to help me find the homesteads I'm looking for. They might know of some place that's relatively clear on the other side of the border."

"No, they don't," said Newberry curtly. "Besides, they don't have time to help you. They're too busy. Come on, let's go. We're going to be late." He moved on ahead of Faolin down the path. Faolin followed, disappointed and somewhat surprised at the sharp answer to his question.

Eventually they arrived at the houses of the Blackbird clan. Faolin noted that the houses were far from the center of the village; he thought he could see open country just beyond them. The houses themselves were considerably smaller and of much poorer quality than the houses Faolin had seen near the hospital building. They were torn and stained and covered with patches and looked every bit like the discards of the wealthy families, which Newberry said they were. The crop-raising clans who owned no animals could afford only the skins the other families no longer wanted.

Newberry took Faolin to the largest house of the group. It stood in the center of a cluster of smaller dwellings, away from the path. On it, unlike the others, designs were painted in oranges, blues and blacks. Over the large flap of sheepskin which served as an entrance Faolin recognized the symbol of the clan's totem--a docile-looking, plain figure very different from the striking eagles, serpents, and other creatures he had seen emblazoned on buildings of other clans. Newberry held back the flap and Faolin ducked down and limped inside the structure. It was dim, with only a little light seeping through open flaps at the tops of the two ends of the building. A strong smell of sweaty bodies and musty earth met Faolin's nostrils. As his eyes adjusted to the semi-darkness he saw that a large number of people had already gathered inside. They sat silently on the ground, eyes fixed on a slightly raised platform at the other end of the building. There, seated on small stools beneath another painted blackbird, were Forest Path, Swift Stream, and another person Faolin had not seen before.

"Looks like the show has started without us," Faolin whispered to Newberry. He was answered with a stern look. He hobbled behind Newberry to the raised platform. When they got there, Newberry, with his arm on Faolin's shoulder, guided him before the stranger.

"Eric Faolin, this is Running Fox, from the high house of the Coil Snake. Running Fox has been sent by the Council of Elders to oversee the punishment you will decide." Running Fox stood stiff and straight and barely acknowledged Faolin's presence with a slight nod. He was wearing a leather shirt and trousers stained with a red and yellow geometric pattern. Even Faolin could tell that his garments were much finer than the woven fiber clothes of the others in the room.

At Newberry's urging, Faolin sat down next to him on the platform. As soon as he did, Running Fox turned and spoke in the native language to the assembly. Then he nodded at the two Nauryan boys. Forest Path rose first.

"We have carelessly injured the man from the UWG. We are ready to accept our punishment," he said and sat down. Swift Stream rose and repeated the words. All eyes shifted to Faolin. With a gentle push from Newberry Faolin rose and stepped gingerly to the center of the platform. He cleared his throat and looked out over the gathered members of the Blackbird and Muskrat clans. Those he could see well appeared sad and tired. They obviously were not enjoying the ceremony. Faolin glanced at Running Fox. He sat smugly, arms crossed, watching with aloof detachment. Forest Path and Swift Stream, next to him, wore no expression at all. They were prepared to accept their fate without complaint.

Faolin looked again at the audience. "It is a privilege to appear before you," he said carefully. "I am honored to be invited into the Council House of the Blackbird clan." He glanced again at Running Fox, but there was no reaction. "I am glad the Council of Elders has delegated to me the task of naming the punishment for Forest Path and

Swift Stream, because only I am in a position to know the degree of their fault. And I know that their fault was very little. The careless person was myself, not them." Out of the corner of his eye Faolin noticed Newberry beginning to squirm. Newberry knew that Faolin was departing from their rehearsed message. "And so," he continued, "it is my decision that Forest Path and Swift Stream suffer no punishment at all." There was a sudden stirring among the assembled natives. Running Fox no longer appeared so smug. He rose from his stool, a startled expression on his face, and stepped toward Faolin.

"I further say," continued Faolin, "that because the fault is mine, I am the one who should be punished. I have carelessly caused your clansmen to be wrongly accused, and I am ready to accept my punishment. From you, not from your Council of Elders."

The stirring changed to a murmur, then to a rumble. Shouts of "no" and "no punishment for anyone" stood out. Running Fox, standing at Faolin's side, could detect the spirit of the assembly. With a final angry glance at Faolin he quickly walked off the platform and out of the building.

Newberry was at Faolin's side. "A very foolish thing, young man. Very foolish," he said into Faolin's ear. "We must get out of here and back to the hospital where it is safer." But Forest Path and Swift Stream were also at Faolin's side, and before Newberry could shepherd him out of the building, they picked him up and, with the help of several of their clansmen, were carrying him around the meeting hall on their shoulders. The people cleared a path, clapping and shouting, as they made two full circuits of the hall. Faolin's leg was bent at an awkward angle and began to hurt but he couldn't complain.

Finally Forest Path and Swift Stream took Faolin out of the building and put him on the ground. They asked him to follow them, and he limped along after them, still surrounded by many of the natives. They made their way around and between several of the closely-packed buildings until they arrived at a long, low house with a torn door, hanging partway open. Once inside, Faolin was guided through another door into a small room where colorful blankets lay across the hide flooring and low wooden benches stood around all the walls. On the benches sat clay bowls filled with items that were unrecognizable to Faolin.

"Where are we?" asked Faolin. "Where's Doctor Newberry?" The crowd had been left outside the house. Now only Forest Path, Swift Stream, and a group of five or six adults surrounded Faolin.

Without a word the Nauryans fell to their knees and bowed their heads. Faolin expected them to say something but they remained silent. "Please," he finally said, "I don't understand this." Still silence. "What do you want of me? Please rise." With these last words the others stood and smiled at Faolin.

"What's this all about? I demand that you tell me."

Forest Path took a step forward. "It is our way of showing our thanks. You have greatly honored our house."

"I just hope I haven't got you in more trouble. Doctor Newberry seemed very worried."

"We aren't concerned. There's no need for you to be."

Faolin looked around him. "What is this place? And who are these people?"

"This is the house of my family," Forest Path said. He stepped aside. "These people are my mother and father, my mother's mother and father, and my mother's sister and her husband." The relatives bowed to Faolin as they were introduced.

"You have greatly honored our house and our clan and the clan of our friend Swift Stream," said Forest Path's grandmother, a wrinkled, thin old woman whose voice carried a note of authority.

Faolin didn't understand all the attention and talk about honoring the house. "I only told your people the truth," he said tentatively. "That's the way of my land. Where I come from telling the truth is no great feat."

Forest path smiled again. "The truth is often difficult here when the ruling clans are present. They don't always want to hear it."

"I must say," said Faolin, "that I was shocked to learn

from Doctor Newberry the way the Blackbird and Muskrat clans are treated by the Council Of Elders. It's not the right way. In my land all people are treated exactly as equals. That's the way it should be here."

The Nauryans looked at each other, then turned back to Faolin. They didn't say anything.

"What is this room?" asked Faolin after a moment.

"This is our shrine, where we give thanks to the spirits for our good fortune," said the grandmother.

"We thought you would wish to see it," added Forest Path.

"What's in all these bowls?" asked Faolin, stepping toward one of the low benches along the wall for a better look. Forest Path reached out to restrain Faolin, but the grandmother touched his arm to hold him back.

"These are the sacred relics of the Blackbird Clan," said the grandmother. "No one from outside the Blackbird clan has ever seen them before, not even Swift Stream."

Faolin was about to reach down to touch one of the bowls, but he quickly drew his hand back. As he did, he noticed a movement at the door just behind the Nauryans. "I won't be the one to violate the secret of your relics." He pointed to the door. "I thought I saw someone move just outside there."

Forest Path looked toward the door. "That was probably my sister, Dawn Breeze. As the heir of this house, she is the keeper of the relics."

"Shouldn't she be here, too?" asked Faolin.

Swift Stream spoke up for the first time. "She is still just a child. You would have no interest in seeing her."

"In my land children are encouraged to share in the events of adults, so they'll be prepared for adult life."

"We apologize for excluding her," said the grandmother. She clapped her hands and called, and in a moment the girl appeared in the doorway. Faolin could see that she was about eleven or twelve and quite thin. As she approached Faolin noted that the girl had striking features, large brown eyes, and a clear complexion very different from the wrinkled or scarred faces of the others.

"Dawn Breeze," said the grandmother, "this man is Eric Faolin, who has defied the elders and refused to punish your brother and Swift Stream. He has come through the wilderness and brings us new ideas. He is a friend of Doctor Newberry. He has asked that you be present here."

The girl knelt before Faolin as the others had done. Faolin looked at Forest Path and Swift Stream. Swift Stream appeared uneasy. "Please rise," Faolin finally said, "it's my honor to meet you." The girl did so but didn't look at Faolin.

Faolin's leg, which had been aching dully, was beginning to hurt more now after all the standing. He also was beginning to feel very tired. He noticed that the Nauryans were still standing around him, as if waiting for something. "Where's Doctor Newberry?" Faolin asked. "My leg is beginning to bother me, and I think maybe I should be getting back to the hospital."

"Doctor Newberry is waiting for you outside," said Forest Path. "He's not permitted to enter our shrine." Forest Path made no move to allow Faolin to leave.

Faolin was surprised. It made no sense that he should be allowed to enter the shrine and not Newberry, who had been living in this village and helping these people for twelve years. He now wanted very much to see Newberry and talk with him. "Could I see Doctor Newberry now?" he asked.

Forest Path looked to his grandmother. She cleared her throat. "May we have some assurance that you will return here to help us?" she asked.

Faolin looked at the Nauryans. "If you'd like, certainly I'll return. When I'm stronger and can stay for a longer time."

The grandmother smiled broadly, as if Faolin had bestowed a great honor upon her. The other Nauryans stepped aside and cleared a path to the door. Faolin made his way out of the room. He saw Newberry standing next to the outside door of the building and went to him, the Nauryans following. Newberry seemed relieved at seeing Faolin.

"I've been to the Blackbird clan shrine," Faolin said.

"I know. They told me," said Newberry. He looked around at the Nauryans, whose faces were still beaming. "Apparently you satisfied your hosts, but we don't have time to talk about that now. We've got to get back to the hospital."

"All right. I feel pretty tired." Faolin turned to the Nauryans. "Thank you for admitting me to your shrine."

"It is we who thank you for the honor you have given us," said Forest Path. He extended his hand and Faolin shook it.

"I'll return as I promised. But please visit me when you can."

"We will," said Forest Path. Swift Stream nodded but his eyes regarded Faolin warily.

With that Faolin and Newberry left the house and began making their slow way out of the cluster of Blackbird buildings and back to the path that led to the hospital. Newberry walked slightly ahead, setting a pace that Faolin found difficult to keep.

"Please, can't we go a little slower, Doctor Newberry," Faolin said.

"I want to get you back to the hospital. You did a very stupid thing this afternoon. For all I know the Council has people out looking for both of us. We're going to the hospital and we're going to stay there until we find out what the repercussions are. It's the safest place."

"It may have been stupid, but it was right," replied Faolin, puffing. "It would have been wrong to punish those boys, even the way you suggested."

"This is not the UWG. This is native territory. They live by different rules."

"Then they ought to change their rules. You don't seem to have had much influence on them in your twelve years here."

Newberry stopped for a second and glared at Faolin.

Then he spun around and moved on, even faster than before.

Faolin tried to hurry after him. "Wait, Doctor," he said, "I'm sorry. I didn't mean that. I was just reacting to what you said. It's stupid for me to pretend I know more about these people than you."

Newberry slowed. "Perhaps I shouldn't have spoken so harshly. But you don't understand. My task is to convince these people to join the UWG. Not some of them, but all of them. I have to work through the leaders. If I alienate them, there's no hope of succeeding."

"I hope I haven't interfered with your work."

"I hope so, too. Time will tell. But I know your intentions were the best."

They walked on for a bit in silence. "What was the shrine like?" Newberry finally asked.

"Oh, not much. A small room. Benches all around the sides with bowls on them. Containers for relics, they said. They didn't want me to look inside." Faolin thought for a moment. "They told me you had never been admitted to the shrine. Why is that?"

"Usually no one but clan members are admitted. It's a very strict rule."

"Then why did they admit me?"

"I don't know. It must have had to do with what you did for those boys. Their religion is something I don't know much about. They don't like to talk about it with outsiders."

"They sure didn't say anything to me about it in there. What kind of a religion is it?"

"Fairly primitive. Worship of spirits. Not personal gods so much as forces of nature. But as I understand it the whole thing is intertwined with legends--myths--about sacred animals and men who reveal the way to live in harmony with the spirits. The scholars say that there's a strong resemblance to the old religions of Brahmastan, but I wouldn't know about that."

In a few more minutes they reached the hospital building and went inside. Faolin lay down immediately on the cot. "I've had it," he said.

"It was pretty rough for your first day out. Medically, I never would have advised it."

"It's good to be back. This is getting to seem like home to me."

"I'm glad you like it. You're going to be spending a lot of time here."

"What do you mean by that," Faolin asked, sitting up.

"I mean, I'm confining you to this building until your leg is well enough for you to leave the village."

"Why?" The prospect of spending another week or more in this room depressed Faolin almost more than he could bear.

"Because the Council of Elders will insist on it. They'll insist that you stay away from the natives. Let's hope that will be enough for them."

"How long until I can leave."

"At least a week. Maybe two."

Faolin lay back on the cot to contemplate his sad fortune. His hopes of finding the homesteads were looking very dim indeed.

4

In the days that followed Newberry strictly enforced his ban on Faolin's movements. Occasionally Faolin was permitted to step outside the door of the hospital for a little air, but the rest of the time he was confined inside the dark building. No new patients were brought to the building. Newberry said nothing about this, but Faolin wondered if his presence was forcing the doctor to treat the natives elsewhere.

After a week Newberry relented to the extent of allowing Forest Path and Swift Stream to visit Faolin late in the evenings, after dark, when they could slip in unobserved. Faolin learned that the two had pleaded with Newberry for the opportunity at great length before he finally gave in. Soon a pattern was established, and the two Nauryans would arrive every other night and the three of them would talk into the early morning. Faolin learned a great deal from them about life in the native village, and they became good friends. Faolin looked forward to their meetings and hated to see them end.

As the days went by, Faolin felt that his leg was improving rapidly. By the end of the second week after his injury, he had stopped using the crutches. At the end of the third week he was running and jumping inside the hospital building. But, to Faolin's surprise and frustration, Newberry continued to find the leg unsound. His estimate of the recovery period seemed to grow longer, rather than shorter.

On the day that marked a full month's stay in the Nauryan village, Faolin persuaded Newberry to examine the leg again. The doctor prodded and poked and asked Faolin to bend it and extend it.

"Still not up to normal," Newberry said. "It's not coming along very well at all. Have you been doing your exercises?"

"Every one. I don't understand, Doctor. It feels great. I've been staying on my feet for hours and it doesn't give me a bit of trouble."

"Well, it's not sound enough to take any kind of extended vigorous activity. You be careful."

"How long until I can get back into the bushland?"

"Not for at least another month."

"That's what you said last week," said Faolin accusingly. "If I have to wait another month, I'll just barely have time to get back to New Markwell before winter."

"I'm sorry. There's nothing I can do about it."

"You don't understand. I've got a contract to deliver a scouting report. If I don't get the scouting done, I don't get paid anything. Besides that, there's eighty people just biding their time until I find something for them."

"You told me before that you didn't think you were going

to find anything suitable out here anyway."

"I may not, but I can't tell them there isn't anything without looking."

"Well," Newberry said slowly, "you're not ready to do any looking right now." He stood up and went to the other side of the room, where he began arranging some instruments on a shelf. Faolin remained sitting on the high wooden table, his legs dangling over the side. He watched Newberry's back for a long while, thinking.

"Tell me, Doctor Newberry," he said finally, have you ever heard of a place the tribe calls the 'western meadow'?"

Newberry stopped his work for a moment, then continued with it. "No, I haven't," he answered. "Where did you hear of it?"

"Swift Stream mentioned it the other evening when we were talking."

"What did he say about it?" Newberry asked cautiously.

"Not much. He didn't know where it was. It was just an expression he had heard from one of the shepherd clans."

"I suppose it refers to the lowland meadow around the village where they graze the sheep in the winter. They go eastward up the mountain in the summer."

Faolin rubbed his chin, eyes still watching Newberry's reaction to his question. "I guess so," he said, lowering himself down from the table. He bent over to put his boots back on. "By the way, Doctor," he added, "when I do start back I'm going to have to get some directions to where I was shot. I don't remember the trip here, you know. Which way is it?"

Newberry turned and looked at Faolin. "Almost due west," he said. "There are some steep downhill slopes. You won't be in any condition to make those for some time."

"I know. I know," Faolin said. "You don't have to keep reminding me."

That night Faolin lay awake in his cot, waiting, until several hours after Newberry retired to his room in the back of the building. When he felt reasonably sure Newberry was asleep, he slipped out of bed and across the dark room to the opposite wall, where his pack was hanging from a hook. He felt through it for his flashlight, and with the aid of its illumination returned to his bed with the pack. He went through the pack carefully, checking each piece of equipment. He kept out the flashlight, a small alarm clock, and several other items. Then he placed the pack under his bed and set the alarm. He crawled into bed fully clothed but after a moment got up again and went to the table on which Newberry kept some of his instruments. After a frustrating search, he found a scrap of paper and a pen. With the light from his flashlight he scrawled a message, folded the paper once and left it in the middle of the table. Then he went back to bed.

The fitful sleep that followed was not at all restful, but it did pass the time until Faolin believed it was safe to proceed with his plans. When the clock showed 3:00 a.m., Faolin flipped off the alarm and slid out of bed. He felt wide awake as he pulled on his boots and lifted his pack to his back. He checked to make sure he had left the message on the table and then went quickly to the door and silently slipped out of the hospital building.

The night felt surprisingly cool. Insects chirped. Faolin smelled the smoke from a fire somewhere, but he moved down the path he had walked with Newberry several weeks earlier without seeing or hearing anyone. The quarter moon overhead provided barely enough light for him to thread his way along. His heart beat rapidly and his palms sweat as he proceeded along the seemingly endless path, but finally he came to the place where he recognized the houses of the Blackbird Clan. Just as he had thought, there was open land beyond. He walked on into it and then began to circle through it to the west side of the village. He had correctly predicted that, with the sheep now up the mountain, there would be no one around outside the village. When the stars told him he was due west of the village, he struck off on a heading directly away from it, striding as rapidly as he could through ankle-deep pasture grass and past stands of fir trees.

By the time the sun was up Faolin had almost reached the boundary of the native lands. The grass was thinning out, and Faolin noticed clumps of the bush that covered the ground on the other side of the border. The land had sloped downward a little coming westward from the village, but, as Faolin had suspected, not nearly as much as Newberry had said it did. Faolin's leg felt fine.

Faolin crossed over a low rise and then suddenly saw before him the huge rocky ridge that jutted out into UWG territory. Surveying the country, Faolin estimated that he was a mile or so north of the place where the arrow had entered his leg. To the south he could see the beginning of the pine forest through which he had walked that day. He sat down and ate some of the rations from his pack and drank from his canteen. It was a bright, warm, cloudless day with a light breeze that felt especially invigorating after weeks of living indoors. Reluctantly, Faolin stowed away his supplies and stood up. He looked again briefly toward the south, then raised his pack up high on his back and set out toward the north, into the unexplored land.

As soon as he rounded the end of the ridge, Faolin went westward again until he reached the boundary markers. Now he was back in the UWG bush country, which stretched off as far as he could see to the west and north. Determined, Faolin resumed his northward journey, his compass guiding him along the boundary line. At noon he was still at it, making his way slowly through the rugged growth which seemed to go on forever.

Then, in mid-afternoon, Faolin noticed that the thick brush seemed to be thinning out. Excited, he pressed forward, half-running. Abruptly, the brush ended and there before Faolin lay the vast expanse of grassland he sought, extending far into UWG territory.

Faolin wandered with delight through the open land until night came. He ran through the thick grass. He knelt, took handfuls of soil, and let it run through his fingers, smelling its richness. He began to pace off the open area but did not come to the end when daylight failed. He took out his pack, made a camp, ate silently, and lay down to sleep. His right leg ached, but only from tiredness.

The next morning Faolin was up before dawn. He spent the day further exploring this new-found tract of land. With every discovery his elation increased. The open area extended at least six miles to the north. At that point Faolin found a sizeable lake, apparently spring-fed, ideally situated to provide irrigation if the land required it. He didn't have time to explore north of the lake. For all he knew, the open area might continue beyond it. To the west Faolin was unable to measure the breadth of the clearing. He walked five miles into UWG territory and still there were large stretches of open grassland only occasionally interspersed with patches of brush or trees. Faolin was confident that the land could meet the needs of the group that had sent him, and more. He speculated with increasing excitement about the riches they would share, with the blessings of the UWG's exploration incentive tax laws.

As Faolin lay, exhausted, in his blanket that night, he faced the hard decision he had to make. Should he now return straight to New Markwell, or should he first go back to the Nauryan village? Faolin was certain that the shepherd families knew about this land and used it for winter grazing. Newberry probably knew about it as well, and neither he nor the Council of Elders would want Faolin to return to New Markwell and bring back men and women to farm it. They might even try to restrain him. The safe thing to do would be to go straight back home. He had all his equipment, and he was sure his leg was sound enough to make it.

Yet Faolin was reluctant to follow that course. For one thing, he felt that he owed Newberry an explanation of what he was going to do. But there was another reason. Faolin lay back and reflected on the future of the area. There was as much land here to cultivate as any man could want. The harvest would be limited only by the supply of men and women to gather it. The Nauryans' help would be invaluable. Perhaps the shepherds would consider it beneath them, but what of the other families, the clans of the Blackbird and the Muskrat? Here was their opportunity to break their bondage without having to adopt a whole new civilization.

His decision was made. He was not here to take from the

Nauryans, but to give to them. He should not steal away like a thief; he should openly proclaim the great future that he would bring to those of the Komisaw tribe who wanted it.

The next day Faolin returned directly to the village. He waited a safe distance outside it until well into the night, and then he went as silently as possible along the path he had taken previously among the Nauryan houses. When he finally entered the hostpital building it was well after midnight. To Faolin's surprise, Newberry was still awake, sitting alone at his work table. He looked up as Faolin entered the room.

"Well, you came back," Newberry said. "I wasn't sure you would."

"You've been waiting for me?"

"I figured you'd be back tonight or not at all."

"I did think of going straight to New Markwell," Faolin said. "I couldn't, though." He looked around the room. "Does anyone else know I was gone?"

"No one asked where you were, so I didn't tell anyone. It wasn't difficult to keep it quiet. No one except Forest Path and Swift Stream ever see you anyway."

"You could have reported to the Council of Elders. Why didn't you?"

"I don't know."

Faolin walked over and sat down on the edge of the cot. Newberry watched him.

"I found it," Faolin said.

"I figured you would."

"My leg stood up fine."

"Yes."

"I think you were wrong in trying to keep me away from it. It's exactly the kind of area I was looking for."

Newberry stood up. "The western meadow is very

important to these people. They'll be resentful if you take it away. The natives will be alienated from the UWG for a long time."

"It's got to happen someday. It's not their territory."

"But not so suddenly. If civilization approaches slowly, the Nauryans will get accustomed to the idea."

Faolin stood up also and faced Newberry. "If they can get accustomed later, they can get accustomed now."

Faolin turned and walked away from Newberry, over to the door. He looked out into the darkness. "What we will bring to this land will be as good for them as for us. We'll ask the natives to join us, those who want to. Surely the Blackbird clan and the Muskrat clan and some of the other low-ranking clans will be much better off. We'll make them full and equal partners. We'll help each other. Isn't that the UWG way?"

"They don't want to change. They like things the way they are. They're a cohesive unit. You can't just tempt a few of them away with your promises. We must acclimate the whole village to the ways of the UWG."

"All we'll offer them is more food, more leisure, more freedom, a greater opportunity to be productive. There can't be anything wrong with that. And we'll welcome them all, from the lowest to the highest, if they'll come." Faolin turned back to Newberry. "You can't talk me out of this, Doctor. I'm going to do it, because I know it's the right thing, for the Nauryans as well as for my people. I wish you would help me convince them it's the right way. I'd like to speak to the Council."

"If you do, you'll never get out of the village, I guarantee you that."

Faolin rubbed his chin and thought about Newberry's words. "How many of the clans raise crops?"

"I don't know. Perhaps half. Some of the clans that own animals also have to do a little farming."

"Then I'll tell those people about what we can accomplish."

Newberry shook his head. "You don't understand. Just because they raise crops doesn't mean they like it."

"I'll tell them that their occupation is a noble one."

"Even if you could convince them, the Council of Elders won't let you speak to them." Newberry moved over to Faolin and placed his hand on the younger man's shoulder. "I wish I could talk you out of your plans. I love these people, and I don't want to see bad feelings develop between them and the territorials." He looked into Faolin's eyes. "But I like you and admire you, too. I don't want anything to happen to you. If I can't convince you to abandon your plans, then for your own sake get on with it. Get out of here tonight or you may never leave."

Faolin thought silently for a while. "I'll go tonight," he said finally. "But before I go I'd like to speak to Forest Path and Swift Stream one more time. Can you bring them here?"

"Yes, I think so," said Newberry slowly. "They'll be asleep, but I can tell them I need them to help me." He pulled on a heavy wool sweater and went out of the hospital building into the night.

Fifteen minutes later Newberry returned with Faolin's two friends.

"Hello, Eric," said Forest Path. "Doctor Newberry asked us to come right away. Is something wrong?"

"No, nothing is wrong. But I wanted to see you both one more time. I'm leaving the village tonight."

"But what about your leg?" asked Forest Path.

"It's well now," said Faolin. "I think the doctor has been a little too cautious in treating it."

Forest Path and Swift Stream looked at Newberry apprehensively.

Faolin smiled. "The doctor has done his best to keep me here, but I finally realized what was going on. My leg is well, and I'm going back home because I've found the western meadow. Next spring I'll be back with families to farm it."

"Eric has discovered that the western meadow lies

outside of native territory," added Newberry. "Under the laws of the UWG he and his people are entitled to claim it and have it for their own to farm. I've tried to talk him out of it, but I can't."

"Eric, you can't do this," Swift Stream said. "The Council of Elders will not permit it. The shepherd clans use that land in the winter."

"My friends," said Faolin, "I admire your sense of loyalty to your people. But before you decide what that loyalty requires, I wish you would let me explain." He pointed to some chairs in the corner of the room. "Let's sit down and talk.''

When they were seated, Faolin began. "We're going to farm the western meadow because it's the right thing to do. For my people and for your people. The people of the UWG need to open up this land to provide enough food. But your people can share as equals. Think of it. With that land under cultivation there'll be no more worry about enough food. Your people will have more than they can ever use. And with less work.

"But the important thing is what this will do for your families and the other clans who aren't wealthy. This is your opportunity to acqure what you've always wanted. We'll sell the surplus grain to the UWG for money. For Nauryans who aren't UWG citizens there will be no taxes. You'll have more than enough to buy livestock from the UWG. You can be shepherds if you want to, although after you have had a taste of life on the farms, you may not want to leave.

"Look," Faolin continued earnestly, "your clans raise crops now. How will it be worse to work on the new farms, where your production will increase by ten or twenty times?"

"You paint a good picture, Eric," said Forest Path, "but you forget that you must take away the winter grazing land to do this."

"Surely you who own no animals can't complain too much about that," answered Faolin. "But the loss won't be important. We can't raise crops in the winter. The sheep can still graze on the stubble. If that isn't enough, we can arrange to supply feed for the sheep from the grain we harvest." He paused and looked at his Nauryan friends. "I give you my word," he said, "that if your people cooperate with our plans, no sheep will ever die from winter starvation."

"What you say may appeal to us and our clans," said Swift Stream, "but you will never persuade the Council."

"I don't need to persuade the Council if I can persuade you and others in the tribe like you. The Council will be reluctant to oppose a plan if half the tribe supports it."

"But how are you going to speak to so many people?" Swift Stream asked.

"I'm not," said Faolin. "You are. I want you and Forest Path to think about what I've said. On my life it's the truth. If you agree that the cultivation of the western meadow will benefit your people, I ask you to spread the message among them. Remember always, that you have my word that this project will go forward with the full and equal participation of all Nauryans who wish to share in it. That is the UWG way."

"Eric," interjected Newberry. "You are asking these boys to take a terrible risk. That's unfair."

"We're willing to take the risk, if it's the right way," said Forest Path. "We know how to do it."

"I want you to know that I'm very much against your participation. It will be very disruptive to your tribe," said Newberry.

"This is a difficult decision," said Forest Path. "This plan of Eric could mean much to the poor clans of our tribe. Yet we don't want to abandon our tribal ways."

Faolin got up and went over to Forest Path. "The decision is yours. You've heard me. You'll hear more from Doctor Newberry. It is the way of the UWG to allow all to speak their mind, so that decisions may be made fairly." He put one hand on Forest Path's shoulder, the other on Swift Stream's. "Whatever your decision, I'm proud to have you as friends. Now you can go back to your beds. I'll be leaving in a few minutes. I'll be back as soon as the snows are gone next spring."

Forest Path and Swift Stream said good-bye and left. Faolin and Newberry faced each other.

"I hope with all my heart that you're doing the right thing," said Newberry.

"It is the right thing," Faolin replied.

"Well, good luck. To you and your friends."

"Doctor, what about you?" Faolin asked. "If they do go along with my plan, will it endanger you?"

Newberry grinned. "The elders know me well enough to realize I had nothing to do with this. Besides, they need me."

"I'm glad to hear that. Your safety was the one thing that's troubled me most."

It was now nearing 2:00 a.m. Faolin thought of taking a short nap before starting his trek back to civilization, but decided instead to wait until he was safely into UWG territory. He bade farewell to Newberry, slipped out of the village again unobserved, and headed for home.

5

```
Report to the Information Ministry
Re:  Accession of the New Emperor
From:  David Halburton
Date:          January 1, 1924
```

Laka Torgoona was today officially proclaimed the new King of Northern and Southern Chansu and Emperor of All Chansu at a ceremony in the Temple at the New Palace. Apparently the three month delay since the death of Laka's father was attributable only to the fact that the

old Emperor had adopted our calendar, and it is
the custom of the Chansu to officially begin a
reign at the start of a new year.

No information has been received that
changes our prior evaluation of Laka's political
views. He appears to be dedicated to the policies
of his father. We see no reason at this point to
make any changes in our programs regarding
Chansu. There is a slight hope that in time the
new Emperor will relax the restrictions on our
direct communications with the people of Chansu,
but this will not take place in the near future.

Laka's eldest son, Changa, 15, now
becomes the likely heir to the Empire, although,
under Chansu custom, the second son, Han, 12,
could also inherit the throne if specifically
designated by his father instead of Changa.
Their mother, of course, is Shala Noshusha,
daughter of the last independent King of the
Southern Kingdom, who was deposed by Laka's
father. She continues to maintain contact with
her kin in the South and no doubt is familiar
with the problems there, but we have no reason to
believe that she will be able to alter existing
policies of the Empire toward that region.

6

The mid-winter festival was over. The guests had left
early in the morning. The new Emperor dined alone with his family for

the first time in weeks. To Han, the dining hall seemed strangely cold, empty and silent after the celebration, the first since his father had ascended the throne of the Empire and the most lavish he had ever seen.

The coldness and silence of the hall were matched by the mood of Han's mother. He watched her thin fingers spoon small quantities of spices onto her plate. She had scarcely spoken since they sat down to eat. Han could see that even his father was beginning to notice her distance. The Emperor did not always readily discern the moods and feelings of those around him, as Han knew only too well.

"You don't seem to be your normal cheerful self, my dear," Han's father said at last.

Han's mother glared at her husband. Han noticed that his brother Changa had stopped eating. Changa didn't like confrontations between their parents. Han secretly enjoyed them, for he knew who always prevailed.

A servant came to take away some bowls. With a slight flick of her hand Han's mother sent her back out of the room.

"You know very well why I'm upset," she said after the servant had gone.

"The festival is over. When the festival is over, the guests leave," the Emperor said matter-of-factly.

"But my family isn't permitted here at other times under your father's abominable laws. You could at least let them stay long enough for a proper visit."

"Your people have always left immediately after the festival was over. I can't understand why you are making such a thing of it now." Han was hanging on every word. Changa had slouched down in his chair, staring at his food.

"I wasn't the Empress before. You weren't the Emperor. It isn't an insult to send your friends away when you have no choice. It is when you do."

"My father's customs have sound reasons. I intend to continue them. Chansu has prospered greatly under his leadership, and I intend to rule exactly as he did."

"Those policies you praise so much are dangerous. The land tax is far too high. If you keep it there, you will discourage production and cut your own income."

The Emperor laughed. "I can see now that we didn't send those relatives of yours away too soon. They've been filling your head with nonsense."

"The taxes are driving the Workers off the land. You know this is true."

Han's father became serious. "Of course, but that's for the good. We need the Workers to operate the factories. Chansu is changing. You are a mere woman. You know nothing of these matters, and I don't wish to discuss them with you any further."

"Not all people of Chansu care for this change," Han's mother said sullenly.

The Emperor stood up, his face red. "That's enough," he said. "Please leave this table. You'll dine in your apartments, and you'll stay there until I'm ready to receive you. And when you next write your kinsmen in the south, please tell them that their efforts to influence the Empire's policies through you will only result in their disadvantage." He glanced around the table and, as if for the first time, noticed Han and Changa. "And please take your children. They're confined with you."

Han's mother and brother arose immediately and, heads bowed, began to shuffle away from the table. Han arose also, but more slowly. Frustration and conflict welled within him. How he wanted to say: "Father, you're right. I agree. You've properly rebuked her. Let me stay. I'm with you, not with her." But how could he show his devotion to his father without disobeying his father's command? He knew, too, from much experience, that he couldn't get out the words without being interrupted and chided. The Emperor had no time to listen to a twelve-year-old boy. Reluctantly, Han followed his mother and Changa out of the hall.

7

Faolin's footsteps crunched on the frosty ground as he walked across the meadow, puzzled by yet another mystery. To confirm his observations, he knelt down and poked at the stiff clumps of grass, frozen under last night's clear sky. The clumps were long and bent flat to the ground. He was right. No sheep had grazed here for a year.

Two men ran up behind Faolin, puffing and panting. One, whose name was Hiram Jones, was a tall gangly man of about Faolin's age. He had hired on as the assistant guide during the winter in New Markwell. The other, Parker Watson, was a stout, balding man in his mid-forties. He was the organizer of the expedition and had already been elected as president of the soon-to-be-formed settlement.

"My boy, it's everything you said it was. Everything," said Watson, clapping Faolin on the back. "You've done a terrific job. It's better than any of us ever hoped."

Faolin looked past Watson at the band of settlers slowly making their way out of the bush and into the clearing. Eighty of them: twenty-five married couples, some of them with children, and fifteen single men, adventurers like Faolin, who would work for several years, taking advantage of the tax incentives for frontier development, and then move on, leaving the families behind to carry on. Faolin prided himself on bringing all of them, their animals and equipment, safely through the wilderness to their goal.

"How long do you think until we're ready to start plowing?" Watson asked, rubbing his hands together for warmth.

"We've been getting temperatures above freezing during the day," Faolin said. He looked up at the late March sun, above the distant mountains. "With that sun, it shouldn't be too long. A few weeks, maybe. What do you think, Hiram?"

Jones scratched his head. "It's hard to say. This far north over on the coast the ground is usually thawed by now. But we're higher and drier here."

"Well, we'd better get started right away building some shelter. There won't be much time for that once the plowing starts," Watson said.

"You go ahead," Faolin replied. "I want to check the area out a bit." Watson left and headed back toward the others.

Faolin shielded his eyes with his hand and looked along the horizon to the east. The settlers had entered the meadowland at its southwest corner, after taking two days moving through the bush country on the UWG side of the rocky outcropping that marked Faolin's first contact with the natives the previous summer. Faolin had been reluctant to take his party along the easier path around the rock on the native side, especially after what he had just seen when he attempted to go to the native village to announce his return from New Markwell.

"You looking for something?" Jones asked.

"I'm trying to see the other side of the boundary. I think we're too far away."

"What do you expect to find there?"

"I don't know. Something that will explain why half the houses are gone from the village, I guess."

"You should have just asked the natives."

Faolin turned to Jones. "The houses that were gone were the ones where the poor families live--the people I invited to join us. I'm not about to show the rest we're here until I find out what happened to our friends."

"I guess you're right."

"There's something else strange. Look at that grass." Faolin kicked at a clump in front of him. "No sheep have grazed here since last spring. Yet this is what the natives use for their winter pasture."

Jones shrugged. "Maybe they've all moved away because they knew we were coming."

"Maybe." Faolin squinted toward the east again. "Come on, Hiram, let's go over to the boundary and see if we can find out."

It took them an hour and a half to reach the boundary stakes. They stopped when they got there.

"Do we go on?" Jones asked.

"I don't know," Faolin said, his eyes on the slightly rising ground to the east. He pointed. "Doesn't the cover look different in there, about fifty yards?"

Jones looked too. "There appear to be some trampled spots." He shifted his gaze. "Well, look. Up there. That's got to be a flock of sheep. And what's that square thing?"

Faolin smiled. "That's it. The sheep and a hide hut for the shepherd. Hiram, I'm going up there. You wait here for me, just in case." Jones nodded.

It took Faolin another fifteen minutes to reach the hut. It wasn't as large as a native house, and it was made of hides that were brown and cracked. As Faolin approached it, He heard the murmur of voices and a burst of laughter from inside. "Hello there," he called.

The noise from inside the hut stopped. A moment later a head peeked cautiously out. It belonged to an old, thin man with sun-blackened skin and missing teeth. He stared at Faolin for a few seconds, then came all the way out and stood up. He was very short.

"My name is Faolin. My friends and I have come to settle the UWG land on the other side of the boundary." Faolin waved his arm toward the west. The old man followed the movement without expression. Then he looked back at Faolin curiously.

Faolin noticed another pair of eyes watching him from just inside the hut. Then another man came out and stood next to the old one. The second man was much younger, perhaps in his early thirties, but not much bigger.

"My father does not speak your language," said the younger man. "He understands only a little."

"You speak it very well," Faolin said. "Did you learn it from Doctor Newberry?"

"Yes, and from his other students. Do you know Newberry?"

"I met him last summer."

"You are then the man from the UWG who came here last summer."

"I am."

The young man turned to the old one and spoke in the native tongue. The old man looked at Faolin, then spat on the ground and returned inside the hut.

"My father doesn't like you. You've taken our winter grazing land away and caused trouble among our clans."

"You could have used the land this winter."

"There is no point. We must learn to do without it, and we will. We're here to keep the sheep on our side of the border. We've lost some this winter, but not too many. We'll survive." He shook his head. "You don't know this land. You'll suffer much."

"We'll meet the challenge," Faolin said. "Do you know where my friends Forest Path and Swift Stream and their clans have gone?"

"I know those names. They are the ones who brought the message of your coming. At first the Council wanted to punish them, but their people voted against it. So they were banished, and their clans, too. Some other clans went with them. They are no longer members of the Komisaw tribe."

"Where are they? Are they alive?"

"I don't know where they are. I assume they're alive. They were allowed to take all their food stores with them. We hadn't expected to be without grain this winter, but we'll manage." The young man shrugged and smiled smugly at Faolin.

"How can I find out where they went?"

"You can ask at the village, if people will speak to you. I last heard they were going to the big rock to await your coming. But you would have seen them when you came."

"Not if they are on the east or north sides." Faolin faced toward the south, estimating the time it would take to return to the area of the rocky ridge. He really must help with the settlement today. Perhaps tomorrow he would seek his friends. He turned back to the young man, who was still staring at him.

"You may resent us now," said Faolin, "but five years from now you'll be very glad we came. We'll bring you greater prosperity than you ever dreamed of."

The man stood stiff and straight. "We're happy with our life. We pity those poor souls who have chosen to join you. But in five years you will be gone. Then we can return to our old ways." He started to go back inside his hut. "We haven't touched your land. We expect you not to touch ours. It's our right under the treaties. Please leave."

Faolin watched the young man disappear into the hut, then ambled back down the slope to join Jones on the other side of the border.

8

The next day Faolin set out, alone, to locate his friends. He found them just where the young native had suggested, camped in a clearing near where the pine forest gave way to the grassland, to the east of the rocky hill. As soon as Faolin entered the edge of the camp a shout went up from the first natives who saw him. Within minutes a hundred yelling people had surrounded him. At the edge of the throng Faolin spotted Forest Path and Swift Stream. They edged their way toward him.

"How are you, my friends?" Faolin shouted over the

noise.

"We're happy, now that you're here," Forest Path shouted back. "We had faith in you."

"The people want to see you. Will you walk through the camp with us?" asked Swift Stream.

"Anything you say," Faolin answered, grinning.

Forest Path and Swift Stream led Faolin through the camp, the crowd following behind. Amid the shouts Faolin heard songs and chants. He noticed the natives' ragged and dirty clothes, their thin bodies, their dilapidated houses. These people had suffered from their banishment. Yet what they lacked in material wealth they made up in spirit. Their adulation surprised Faolin.

The two young men led Faolin to a smallish building in the center of the camp. On the hide flap that served as a door were drawn the symbols of a number of clans--Faolin guessed they were all the clans that had come here. Inside it was apparent that this structure was not a home. It held only a low wooden platform and a number of wooden benches. As Faolin's eyes grew accustomed to the dim light inside, he noticed that five or six older men were gathered there.

"These are the chosen leaders of our camp. We have elected them," Forest Path said proudly. "It's appropriate that you speak with them first." He bowed low before the men, and Faolin did likewise.

A short, stocky man in his sixties spoke first. "You chose your messengers well, my friend Faolin. These young men have spoken with such strength and conviction that they have caused us to cast away all we had to spare their lives and join your venture. Not," he looked around him with a smile, "that we had that much to lose."

Another of the men stood up and bowed slightly toward Faolin. "My name is Sturdy Oak," he said, "and as the elected chief of this camp I would like to welcome you to it." He introduced the others. When he came to the short, stocky man, whose name was Thundercloud, he said, "Thundercloud simplifies things too much. But he correctly gives credit to your two friends. We only hope that they have spoken rightly about your purpose."

Faolin cleared his throat. "The success of my friends amazes me. I'm sorry that my actions have caused you to lose so much, but I assure you that a glorious future lies ahead for every man, woman and child in this camp. We need your help and accept you as equal partners in our enterprise."

The other men showed relief from a tension Faolin had not perceived until it was gone. "But where is your party?" asked Thundercloud hesitantly.

"They are already on the land. We came up through the UWG territory. There are eighty of us. We're building shelter now."

"We have much to talk about. Much to plan, then," said Sturdy Oak.

"We do indeed, and I would like to begin. You must realize, though, that our group has a governing board, too. I'm merely their adviser. I can't make decisions myself."

"But they will follow your advice, surely," said Sturdy Oak.

"I hope so. They have so far."

"Good. Then let us begin. Won't you join us here?" Sturdy Oak made room for Faolin to sit next to him on the bench. As he did, Faolin could not help but notice the unpleasant odor of the man's body--he remembered the smell from the Blackbird Clan meeting on his previous journey.

"First of all, we are ready to move onto the land and share our lodgings with you," Sturdy Oak said eagerly.

A slight frown passed across Faolin 's face. "We must consider that carefully," he said slowly. "If you move onto UWG land, you may be subject to tax as UWG citizens. If you continue to live here, but merely work on our land, you won't be."

Thundercloud appeared disappointed. Sturdy Oak said, "Well, we will do as you think best. Perhaps we should make this camp more permanent."

"We would like your help in putting up our buildings,

though."

Sturdy Oak looked questioningly at another man. "Yes, if you wish," he said.

"When do you plan to begin your planting?" the other man asked.

"Oh, as soon as the ground thaws, of course. We'll plow the ground and then plant. Before the beginning of May, surely."

"But what of the rains?" asked Thundercloud. "The rains aren't over then."

"Rain? Surely that won't stop us. Rain is necessary." Could it be, thought Faolin to himself, that these men did not know even the importance of moisture for their crops?

The others looked at each other and shook their heads. "What crop will you plant? The barlum, such as we have raised?" asked one of them.

"Yes, barlum. But not like what you've raised. This is a new strain, developed only recently by our scientists. It grows longer-- well into October--and yields three times as much as the old strains."

"Into October?" asked Thundercloud.

"Yes. This strain won't be harmed by an early frost," Faolin said smugly. Then he became worried. "You don't have hard frost here before October, do you?"

"Oh no," Thundercloud said slowly. "It is warm until October. But we have always harvested our grain in early September. It is a very strong tradition."

"Well, traditions are going to be broken. We're going to show you what modern, scientific farming can do."

"Please tell us what you wish us to do," said Sturdy Oak.

"That will depend upon how the work goes. But I have some ideas. I think I'm right that you don't use animals in your farming?" Several of the others nodded. "So the plowing with the horses will be done by us. If there aren't enough horses, you can help with the plowing by hand, of course. Then you can help with the sowing--that might be a good job for the women and children. You can cultivate the crops--keep out the weeds. Irrigation ditches must be dug, that you can certainly help us with. And, of course, the harvesting. That must he done by hand, at least at first. Someday, of course, we hope to bring in some harvesting machines, but that's too difficult and too expensive now." He stopped for a moment. "Does that give you enough of an idea?"

"I think so," Sturdy Oak said. "Tell me," he went on very seriously, "how we will share in these rewards with you."

Faolin smiled. "In the UWG, that would have been the first question asked. You and your people will share directly in the harvest. As to the surplus beyond what we need--and I assure you there will be much of that--we'll take it to the river and send it to New Markwell to be sold, and you'll receive a share of what we sell it for. We'll have to cut a road through the bush to do that, though, so we may not be able to ship until next year. Now, in figuring everyone's share, we must of course take into consideration that we are subject to some tax and you are not. Also, we'll be supplying the animals, and the seed, and some equipment, as well as our labor. But your labor will be rewarded, and amply."

"At harvest time," said Sturdy Oak.

"Yes, at harvest time."

"We will have our own plots, too?" Thundercloud asked tentatively.

Faolin considered. "I don't think so," he said. "This will be a common enterprise, in the true spirit of the UWG. We'll all share in the bounty of all our crops. If your people have time to do more work, it should be for the joint good of all, don't you think? There's more than enough land there for us all."

"Yes, of course," Thundercloud said meekly.

Sturdy Oak looked around at the other men. They looked back at him, silent and expressionless. Then he stood up. "Our friend Faolin," he said, "we have waited long for you, and now you are here. We place ourselves in your hands. Will you please tell

Thundercloud what you wish us to do when your own Council has decided? Your friends can find him for you. Until then, we have much to do here." He nodded, and Faolin realized, after a moment, that this was the signal for him to leave. He thanked the other men and said good-bye to them, then joined Forest Path and Swift Stream and left the building. The crowd had disappeared, and the few people they saw now left them alone.

"Your people won't regret the choice they've made," Faolin said, feeling a need to justify the present bleak circumstances of the natives.

"It will be difficult until the harvest," Forest Path said.

"Yes, it'll be hard work for us all," Faolin said. "Now I'd like to hear everything that has happened since I left. You two must have gone through a lot."

Forest Path exchanged glances with Swift Stream. "We would like to talk about that very much, but first there is something you should know that Sturdy Oak did not say."

"What's that?"

"When we came here, we brought our grain stores, but we had already traded a large part of our grain to the shepherd clans. We don't have much left, and the clans in the village won't give us any more of their food."

"How much do you have?"

"Enough for a month, perhaps, in ordinary times. We can possibly stretch it to two."

"What about hunting and fishing?"

"There is very little game near here. Our men must travel far to find it, and even then it is scarce. If they travel, they can't work in the fields."

"Surely under these circumstances your brothers in the village will help."

Forest Path and Swift Stream shook their heads. "Only if we all go back to the old ways and refuse to help you. But we don't want that."

"Well," Faolin said reluctantly, "we brought food for ourselves to last until the first harvest. We might be able to share some, but not much. How many are there in your camp?"

"About three hundred, including the children."

Faolin did some quick mental calculations. The natives, of course, being accustomed to privation, could get along on less food than the territorials. "Perhaps we could give you each a quarter of a pound of grain a day after your supply runs out." That would, Faolin estimated, leave only a little over half a pound a day for the territorials. He wondered if the settlement board would approve.

Forest Path and Swift Stream smiled. "That would be very helpful. We'll tell Sturdy Oak."

"You should wait until our board considers it. I'll let you know their decision."

"Yes, of course. Now we can talk about what has happened since you left us."

They sat down in the dirt outside the houses of the Muskrat clan and talked into the afternoon.

9

After a fruitless search throughout their apartments, Han finally found Changa sitting in the library. Han paused at the door, then walked quietly into the room and sat on the thick carpet across the low table from Changa. Changa was buried in one of the large old hand-copied volumes that in recent years had gathered dust behind the shelves of the newer, printed books.

Han waited for a few minutes, watching his brother. Changa didn't even look up. "What are you doing here so early in the morning?" Han finally asked. "Especially in the middle of the summer festival."

Changa marked his place with his finger, then looked up. "This is the only time I can find to do this," he said impatiently. Then he returned to his book.

"Are you going to the games this afternoon?"

"I suppose so," Changa muttered with his face still in the book.

Han let his eyes wander around the room. The new shelves that had been added to accommodate the recent books almost entirely obscured the delicate designs on the centuries-old wall panels which had been moved to the New Palace from the old Citadel. Even Han could remember when the room held only half as many books. He had heard his mother complain about covering up the ancient art, but Han himself liked the room better this way. New books were far more interesting than dull old paintings and drawings.

Han decided to pursue his objective. "Does that book have anything to do with the meeting you went to yesterday?" he asked.

"What meeting?" Changa looked up again.

"The meeting you went to with mother and her relatives."

"What do you know of any such meeting?"

"I saw you go in the room with them yesterday afternoon."

"Oh, that. It was only a social visit. We haven't seen mother's relatives since last winter."

"Then why wasn't I invited?"

Changa went back to his book. "I suppose because you're still too young."

"Do you know what I think?" Han asked. "I think it was more than a social visit. I think you talked about other things. And I think you went to the meeting because you are the heir to the throne, and I am not."

Changa slowly closed the book and put it aside. "That is

partly true."

"Father doesn't like those meetings. Remember what he said after the festival last winter? He doesn't want us to listen to these wrong ideas of mother's relatives. I'm going to tell him you were there."

"Please don't do that, Han. It will make him angry at me for no reason. Look, if I tell you what we talked about, will you keep it quiet?"

"Oh, all right," Han said with a reluctance he didn't really feel. He knew that the Emperor probably wouldn't listen to him anyway.

Changa pushed his closed book around on the table for a moment before speaking. "It's really not all that important. It's something mother and her relatives have been talking about for years. They're very concerned, for one thing, about the land taxes. Those taxes have hurt mother's relatives and other people in the south a lot."

"But father says that the tax is necessary for progress. Surely he's right."

"Well, that depends upon what you think about progress. Mother's relatives say that everything we're doing is a mistake--the factories, the railroads, the power plants, all of it. They say that the ways of the past were successful, so why change them? That's why they suggested I look at this book; it was written about the administration of the Northern Kingdom three hundred years ago. This," he tapped the book, "is the way they think Chansu should be run, not the way father and grandfather have done it. Mother's relatives think it was wrong to let the UWG people come. They think that adopting the UWG's methods is going to destroy our society and bring Chansu under the control of the UWG."

"What do they think we should do?"

"Expel the foreigners and return to our old ways. Get rid of the contamination the foreigners have brought."

"Do you agree with them?"

"Some of the things they say make sense."

"Well, I don't agree. I think that father and grandfather have done the right thing. They've made Chansu stronger and more important."

"But not if they bring us under the control of the UWG. Then Chansu is nothing."

"That won't happen. The UWG may have more people and more machines, but they ignore the gods and the natural order of things. They don't have our will and our spirit. We can always resist them."

"I know," said Changa, "that that's what father says and that's what our tutors say. But the UWG is very powerful."

"The tutors say the UWG's power comes from machines that were created by the Warrior classes of the UWG many years ago. But the UWG is now controlled by weak, classless people. Chansu is strong. Someday Chansu will defeat the UWG and restore the natural order of the classes."

Changa smiled. "I hope you're right. But you're speaking the dreams of a child. We do have the will and the spirit. But fighting the UWG would be very costly even if we won. And what if we should lose? Chansu would be destroyed. It's the safer course to go our own way, to forget about the UWG."

"Father wouldn't like to hear you saying such things."

"I'm only repeating the ideas of mother's cousins. But you won't tell father that I listened. You gave your word."

"I won't tell him. I told you I wouldn't."

And Han did not repeat what Changa told him. But he filed the conversation away carefully in his memory, for use at a more appropriate time.

10

The first year almost destroyed Faolin's settlement, which the inhabitants had ironically named New Hope. They had roofs on only a few of their new buildings when the spring rains came. It rained hard every day until the first of June, preventing all plowing and planting. After that, as the natives could have told the territorials if they had been consulted, which they were not, it didn't rain at all. The irrigation ditches they worked around the clock to build in July and August saved only half the crops. And more than half the remainder was lost to the blight that infested them in late September and early October, just before the harvest.

Despite the setbacks, all the settlers decided to stay on through the winter. Faolin understood how they felt. They had accepted the challenge of the land, and they would fight it to the end. The secure world of the UWG cities would no longer satisfy them.

The settlers managed to survive the first winter without anyone starving. Unfortunately the same could not be said for their native Nauryan partners, notwithstanding the food rations the territorials reluctantly supplied. But the next year was better. The settlers threw out the rest of their scientifically-developed late-maturing seed and planted the traditional varieties. With irrigation, they had a decent harvest, though not enough to sell at New Markwell. The following year saw a slightly better yield and great promise for the future, for Faolin and Jones discovered a means of preventing the late September blight.

Early in the spring of 1927, filled with great hopes, Faolin paid what had now become a ceremonial call at the camp of the native exiles, which had been moved closer to the fields. There were speeches in the native language, which Faolin had not bothered to learn, and dancing and singing. Faolin noted that not only was the spring ceremony becoming more elaborate, but he was becoming a more central figure in it. Toward the end of the ceremony Faolin gave a little talk about how he was proud to be a partner with the natives in their great enterprise, and how this year ought, for the first time, to produce the considerable rewards he had been promising.

At the end of the ceremony Forest Path invited Faolin to the house of the Blackbird clan. With his work and his involvement in New Hope, Faolin had been seeing much less of his Nauryan friends than during the first year of the settlement. This was, in fact, his first visit in six months. The main structure was still stained and patched, but somehow it seemed less drab than the last time Faolin had seen it. Faolin paid his respects to Forest Path's parents, grandparents, aunts and uncles, but he could not keep his eyes off the thin, dark-haired girl who stayed in the corners, away from the rest of the family.

When Faolin had finally spoken with all the elders of the family and it was about time for him to leave, he drew Forest Path aside. "Who is the dark-haired girl?" Faolin asked. "I didn't have a chance to speak with her. I don't believe I've seen her with your family before."

Forest Path laughed. "You must mean Dawn Breeze. She has certainly grown, hasn't she?"

Faolin was surprised. He looked around for the girl but didn't see her. "I can't believe it. Are you sure? She looked much older."

"Dawn Breeze was the only girl here. She's not so young any more. She will be sixteen years next winter. And then she will wed our friend Swift Stream." He smiled. "We are very pleased about the betrothal. All the arrangements were made this past winter."

Faolin returned the smile and put his hand on Forest Path's shoulder. "I'm very pleased for both your sister and Swift Stream. They are a fine match. It will be good for both your clans. I'd like to congratulate them personally, but I'm afraid I must be going back before the dark. Please give them my best wishes and tell them I'll make it a point to see them later in the season."

"I will. The family will be glad you are pleased."

Faolin moved to leave. He turned back to Forest Path. "And when will you wed? After all, Swift Stream is younger than you."

Forest Path smiled again. "I might ask the same question of you. After all, you are older than I."

They exchanged farewells and Faolin, bearing the gifts he had received at the ceremony--a colorful blanket, some pottery-- mounted the horse he had requisitioned for the day and headed back for the cluster of houses in New Hope.

As Faolin rode, Forest Path's last remark stayed in his thoughts. When would he marry? Faolin had never had any close relationships with women. For most of his short adult life he had felt little need for the companionship of women--or of men, either, for that matter. He liked the solitary life of an explorer and a tamer of the wilderness. But now that he, too, had in effect settled down here, at least for a time, he saw how the lives of many of his fellow territorials were made fuller by sharing them with a spouse. Nor could he deny the sexual appetites he felt from time to time, especially during the long, cold idle hours of the winter. Some of the other single men among the territorials had gone this last winter to New Markwell or one of the newer towns springing up along the Westland coast, where there were places catering to such desires. But Faolin could not help but think less of these men for doing so. Like most other citizens of the UWG, he had been strongly indoctrinated with the idea that sex outside marriage, though not illegal, was wrong. So his cravings went unfulfilled, and he turned to whatever work could be done to assist him in repressing them.

As he thought further, Faolin realized why Forest Path's remark had had such an impact on him. He would soon be confronted with a crucial decision. Was he to remain here, in New Hope, devoting his days to this enterprise he had helped to found, or would he soon move on, perhaps to found other settlements? He could not leave this land and these people without breaking very strong ties; yet at the same time he doubted that he could be satisfied with the uneventful life New Hope would offer once the struggle against the wilderness was won. The question of marriage was bound up in this larger question. For if he was to stay, he didn't want to do so alone.

The question, then, was what his future was to be. Until he decided that, he couldn't think about a wife. Comforted somewhat by that analysis, he put aside the problem for the remainder of his trip home.

11

The spring rains came. Faolin spent the time working inside and drawing up plans for the planting. This year, with good reason to believe they could control the late September blight, they would plant fully half the land with the late-maturing grains.

When the rains stopped, Faolin went out into the fields to supervise the plowing and sowing and to inspect the damage the rains had done to the irrigation system. On his first day in the southwest quadrant he saw a group of Nauryans working on the plowing under the supervision of one of the territorials. He was suddenly surprised as he recognized the thin, dark-haired girl in the group. It was Dawn Breeze. He watched her lithe figure straining against the weight of the plow she was trying to guide. Then, against some invisible resistance he could not define, he edged his horse closer. Now he could see the girl's body pressing against the loose folds of her plain gray clothing, the sweat glistening on her smooth child's face. This was no work for someone so young and so small. Something about the sight disturbed Faolin, made him feel vaguely but acutely irritable. He wheeled his horse around and rode swiftly away. At the next meeting of the New Hope village board Faolin proposed and the board passed a rule limiting the kinds of work the Nauryan women could do in the fields.

The planting went well, the irrigation ditches were put in order, and in late August the early-maturing grain was harvested. The August harvest alone was enough to see both Nauryans and territorials through the next winter. Faolin began to calculate what they could sell the rest of the crop for if they stopped the blight. The figure surprised him. It greatly exceeded the tax credit the territorials would receive for developing the land. Indeed, if the remainder were shared with the Nauryans, they, with no taxes at all, would get more than the territorials. Faolin began to plan how that problem could be avoided, possibly by investment in more animals and farm machinery.

When the early harvest was finished, preparations were made to flood the remaining fields. It was by such a technique that Faolin expected to prevent the blight, which thrived on the extreme dryness of the early fall in these regions. Forest Path was supervising this work in the southern fields. One morning in early September when Faolin was working nearby, a native runner brought an urgent invitation from his friend. He rode over and he and Forest Path sat down in the shade of the small hut the Nauryans had erected in which to keep their shovels and other tools.

"You seem to be right on schedule," Faolin said.

"Yes, we are. The digging is hard work, but we're used to hard work." Forest Path paused and looked away toward the horizon. "Eric, I have some news that's of much greater concern than our work here. I would have come to see you last night, but I knew you would be in our area this morning."

"What is it?"

"For several weeks we have been concerned about things happening in our old village. We noticed that the people there have already brought their flocks down from the high meadows. They usually don't do that until much later. And we have also noticed that no one has been leaving the village."

"What could it be? Some sort of disease?"

"That's what we thought at first. But we didn't know. We have almost as little contact with our brothers there as you do. But yesterday we found out. Early yesterday morning several of our people saw the men of the village leaving, marching northward. They were carrying their bows and hatchets. It can only mean that they're going to a battle."

"A battle? I don't understand. With whom?"

"It must be with one of the tribes from the north. They live in a hard climate, and when they can't sustain themselves, they raid tribes like ours."

"I didn't know that. I thought warfare between the native tribes was abolished."

Forest Path shook his head. "It is as it has always been. Many of the people in my camp are worried now. If the others fail to stop the raiders, the raiders may move against us next."

Faolin stood up. He could ignore battles between the Nauryan shepherds high up on the mountain. But if the raiders threatened Forest Path and his people, they also threatened the entire New Hope community. Faolin felt a surprising stirring of excitement within him. "Why must there be fighting?" he asked. "Can't you conclude a peace with these people from the North? If they're starving, perhaps they should be helped."

"My friend Eric, one can't share when he barely has enough for himself. That's the history of all the native tribes. The northern tribes are many. When they have been without food, either they have died or another tribe has died."

"But why don't they join the UWG? That would give them security."

Forest Path shrugged. "I don't know. The Nauryan tribes are very proud of their way of life, especially those of the North. They will struggle to retain it at all costs."

Faolin rubbed his cheek thoughtfully. "Will your old tribe be successful?"

"They've always driven the raiders away before. But

other tribes haven't been so fortunate. And the old village isn't as strong as it was."

"Well, please watch the situation as closely as you can, and let me know when anything happens. I'll inform the New Hope village board. This is very important to us. I'm glad you got the news to me as promptly as you did."

The next four days passed without further news. Faolin told the settlement board members about the struggle going on in the native territory; but, although they were interested and concerned, they didn't share Faolin's growing fascination with the problem. They were still in the midst of self-congratulation over how they were going to control the blight and of speculation as to what the grain prices would be in New Markwell this winter.

On the evening of the fifth day after his conversation with Forest Path, Faolin had just finished washing up after working in the fields and was dressing for dinner at the New Hope Common Hall. There was a knock at the door of his apartment. He went to it and saw, on the other side of the screen, the haggard, red face of Dr. Newberry. Faolin hadn't seen Newberry in the four years since his first journey to native territory. In those four years Newberry's face had aged ten.

"Doctor Newberry! Come in. Come in. How I've wanted to see you again." Faolin opened the door and Newberry, panting heavily and soaked with sweat, staggered in. "What in the world has happened to you? Why are you here?" Faolin well knew the reason he hadn't seen Newberry: the village elders had undoubtedly forbade the doctor from making any contact with the settlers. It must, then, have taken something momentous to bring him here now.

"I've come from the village," Newberry said, still gasping for breath. "Left late this morning. Never thought I'd get here."

"You came the whole way by foot?"

"Ran as much of it as I could. May I sit down?" Faolin held out a chair and Newberry collapsed into it.

"Sorry to barge in on you like this," Newberry went on. "We've got a lot of things to talk about, I know, but there's no time now. We've got a desperate situation over there. Need help bad."

"The raiders from the North?"

Newberry looked surprised. "How did you know?"

"Some of the exiles saw the men marching out five or six days ago. They guessed that's what it was."

"Well, our men marched back--maybe I should say crawled back--last night. It was horrible. Only about half of them returned, and they were a bloody mess. I spent the night treating their wounds. They were routed. A lot of them aren't fit to fight again. The village is in extreme danger. These Northerners are stronger than ever before. They could attack the village now at any time."

"What do you want of us?" Faolin felt again an unexpected thrill of excitement in response to Newberry's news.

"I want you to get those exiles back to the village to help fight off the raiders. We don't have a chance otherwise. The village elders are too proud to ask the exiles themselves."

"But we need every man here to ward off the crop blight and help get the harvest in."

Newberry stood up and faced Faolin. "Eric, you will have no more Nauryans to work on this project ever if the raiders are not defeated. Once the village is taken, the exiles will be indefensible, unless they want to move in with you. And from all I know about these raiders, I suspect they aren't going to let a few border markers stop them. They may not even let your brown skin stop them. Please believe me. Your harvest is nothing compared to what's at stake here."

Faolin backed away. "You're asking a lot. We've suffered to get to this harvest."

"I tell you, Eric, if the exiles don't help us, this harvest may be your last."

Faolin stepped to the door and stared out into the night, thinking. Oddly, he found that his thoughts were not centered on the harvest, but on the fighting . To a man born in a land that had not seen war for over a hundred years, and who had been taught since birth to resolve disagreements without force, the prospect of men battling with other men for survival was disgusting, frightening, and senseless. Yet at the same time it held the same challenge Faolin found in exploring new territories, in struggling against nature.

Abruptly Faolin turned back to Newberry. "Of course you're right, Doctor Newberry. The raiders must be defeated, even if we lose the harvest. It won't be easy to persuade the village board, but we can act despite what they say." He paused, taking in Newberry's expression of relief. "What's more, Doctor, I want to go along. I want to see the fighting myself."

Newberry looked up at these last words, his eyes measuring the sincerity of Faolin's expression. "Are you sure about that?" he asked slowly. "It'll be dangerous and unpleasant--barbaric. And you know you can't help the natives. That would be directly contrary to the non-intervention laws. You could be shipped back to New Markwell for counseling if you did--and if it's found out."

Faolin smiled. "Are you asking me not to do it?"

Newberry returned the smile, but said nothing. He lowered himself slowly back into his chair, his head nodding. "There's no time to lose, but I must rest."

"I'll get started right away. You can stay here as long as you like."

Faolin got the village board to meet in an emergency session that night. As he predicted, the board balked at interrupting the work in the fields, but Faolin's emotional pleas finally prevailed. A number of the territorials, apparently sensing the same challenge, curiosity, and excitement that Faolin felt, asked to join him in accompanying the natives.

What Faolin had not anticipated, however, was the opposition he faced from the native exiles themselves. Forest Path put the problem to Faolin bluntly during an interruption in the discussion with the leaders of the exile camp the next morning.

"There will be constant disagreement. The village elders will insist on commanding any action by us, since they have always done so. But we'll die at the hands of the raiders before submitting to the rule of the villagers again. There are strong feelings here, my friend Eric."

"Can't you accept their command in order to save your families?" Faolin asked. "Once the raiders are defeated you can return to your separate ways."

"You forget," Forest Path replied, "that we can always escape the raiders by emigrating to the UWG. The raiders won't follow us to your cities. This we would do rather than submit to the villagers."

Faolin envisioned a collapse of the whole settlement of New Hope. The territorials now knew they couldn't realize their dreams alone. "There must be a way to join your groups together," he said.

"The village elders won't let us lead the fighting. But they may let you. We would certainly follow you."

"Me? Why would they accept me if they won't accept you? Besides, I know nothing of warfare."

"We'll tell you what we know. It's not much. You can do it, I'm sure, for we have faith in you. It's the only way. And the villagers have no choice but to accept you. They need our help, and you are not of a lower clan."

Faolin declined again, but only half-heartedly. He found himself more and more caught up in the new experience of man fighting man. Where events would lead he didn't know, but he was not afraid to find out.

12

On the 11th of September, the combined Nauryan force set out from near the Komisaw village, heading northeastward up the mountain, in search of the enemy. Two hundred bowmen dressed in brown- and green-dyed sheepskins led the way, followed by a hundred hatchet men. Faolin, Jones and seven other territorials, together with representatives of the ruling bodies of both tribal groups, brought up the rear. With misgivings by all, but little reluctance on his part, Faolin had assumed the role of arbitrator. The villagers had balked at his leadership, but they had agreed with the exiles to allow him to resolve their differences in command decisions.

On the morning of the third day out one of the advance bowmen spotted the raider encampment strung out in a north-to-south direction along a ridge that protruded from the side of a steep mountain. The observers who climbed the mountain to inspect the enemy camp returned to report that the raiders were starting to strike their hide tents. They would he ready to move on, doubtless against the village, within twenty-four hours.

The elders of both factions shook their heads in dismay at the raiders' choice of a camp. To the north the mountain totally blocked any approach. To the south the treeless ridge on which the raiders were camped stretched on for miles, making any attacker from that direction visible long before his arrows came within range. To the east, on the other side of the encampment, the ground dropped away steeply into a valley, except for a few narrow ridges, perpendicular to the main one, that could scarcely hold two men abreast. Only to the west, from whence Faolin and his men came, was there a broad, tree-covered approach to the ridge. But it was in this direction that the constantly-manned defense positions of the raiders faced.

By the time all this information was gathered, the warm September sun had set. If there were to be an attack, it would have to come the next day. Faolin and the territorials sat with the native leaders in a small clearing about two miles from the raider camp, swatting insects and debating their course of action.

"I think," said Tall Branch, one of the elders of the village, after the findings of the observers had been discussed, "that it would be foolish to attack such a well-defended position. It would be best to wait until they move. We may be able to trap them in a valley or a canyon."

"That's wishful thinking," said Thundercloud, whom Faolin remembered from his meetings with the exile camp leaders. We've marched the trail from the village. Where are the valleys and canyons we are going to trap them in? We passed through none. If we don 't strike the raiders in their camp we can't hope to destroy them. Cutting off part of a worm will not kill it."

"But," said Tall Branch vehemently, "it's better to take a small victory than a defeat. Our last attack, which you know little of, was against their camp. They're invincible on their own ground."

"If we can't take them on their own ground, we may as well lay down our bows and hatchets and run away," said Thundercloud.

Tall Branch and Thundercloud glared at each other. The remaining natives looked to Faolin, who sat in the circle the men had made, the light of their small fire flickering on his face. As he listened to the others he stared at the ground where he stirred the loose pine needles with a stick. He looked up at the silence, and saw the others' eyes returning his gaze. He stood, realizing that the initiative had passed to him. Could he handle the responsibility? He found himself eager to try.

"When the raiders move, how do they move?" Faolin asked. "I mean, do they move in a column? Who goes first?"

Clear Spring, one of the village elders and the leader of the last attack on the raiders, cleared his throat. "In the past they have always moved in columns of four or five where they can," he said. "The bowmen march in the front and rear. The hatchetmen are mixed among the others. When they're attacked, they disperse in all directions."

"So," said Faolin, "they may be vulnerable in the middle, but we can't take their bowmen if we attack at the center." He started walking slowly around the circle of men, his arms behind his back and his head down. When he was halfway around he stopped.

"We must attack them in their camp," he stated decisively, "but we can't risk a direct frontal assault." He turned to

Jones, who had accompanied the observers. "Hiram, how many men can we get behind the ridge by dawn?"

Jones swallowed. "All of them, Eric, if we hurry. But it won't do any good. The entrances to the ridge from the other side are so narrow we can't attack with more than twenty-five men at a time."

"Of course, of course," Faolin muttered, resuming his pacing. He completed his tour around the circle and started another when he stopped again and turned suddenly to Thundercloud. "Do you have twenty-five men who can fight like three hundred?"

Thundercloud hesitated. "We have many men who can fight well, but twenty-five can never win against such a foe."

"Very good," said Faolin. "But can twenty-five *look* like three hundred in the early dawn?"

Thundercloud smiled, perceiving Faolin's plan. "With another ten bowmen behind, they can, if they approach from a place which will hold only twenty-five." His smile suddenly disappeared. "But such a plan would place the lives of those twenty-five in great peril."

"Surely," said Faolin, "it is worth imperiling a few Nauryan lives to save hundreds."

Thundercloud stared. "Your reasoning is sound, but it's not the reasoning of a citizen of the UWG."

"We're not in the UWG," Faolin replied. "There are no battles there." He looked at the other men. All wore silent, implacable expressions. "Besides," Faolin continued, "we can give our hatchet men an advantage they've never had before." He nodded toward Jones, who rose and went away from the fire into the blackness. He returned a moment later, carrying a rolled blanket. After a quick glance at Faolin, Jones stepped into the circle, lay the blanket on the ground, and unrolled it. The Nauryans, villagers and exiles alike, gasped.

"Guns!" exclaimed Thundercloud. "You're willing to give us guns?" he asked Faolin incredulously.

Faolin smiled. "Not give. Loan. There are nine of us territorials and twelve guns. We'll use our guns in the main attack. That will leave three to be carried by the men on the other side. It will make them much stronger. Now what do you think about the plan?"

"You can be in much trouble for bringing guns into native territory," Thundercloud said.

Faolin's smile disappeared. "We're already in much trouble for being here." He glanced sharply at the natives. "I assume our pledge of secrecy extends to the guns." The Nauryans nodded. "And if we win, we need not worry about the raiders reporting us."

"They have little contact with the UWG," Thundercloud acknowledged.

"Very well," said Faolin. "There are only twelve guns, and they are for small game hunting. But perhaps they will make our enemy a little less confident. That can decide the battle." He looked again at Thundercloud. "We have no time to lose. Which of your men would be able to undertake this mission?"

Thundercloud shook his head slowly. "I can't make that choice. All of our men will fight courageously."

"As will ours," added one of the men from the village.

"We'll need ten bowmen and twenty-five hatchetmen. That's one squad of bowmen and two and a half squads of hatchetmen, isn't it?"

Thundercloud nodded.

"Very well. Name me the squad leaders. I'll choose the squads."

Thundercloud looked at another of the exile leaders. "Shining Fish knows the names of both our men and those from the village."

At Faolin's request Shining Fish recited the names, and Jones wrote them down. To Faolin's surprise, the bowmen squad leaders included Forest Path, and the hatchetmen squad leaders included Swift Stream. How, Faolin wondered to himself, could these inexperienced youths be placed in leadership positions? The answer, on reflection, was obvious. It was because they were his messengers. After all, he was only slightly older than they and had no more experience in these matters. What to do about them? Faolin's initial inclination was to choose others for the dangerous mission on the other side of the ridge. But that would reveal an obvious favoritism, would it not?

Faolin reviewed the list as Jones had written it down. Finally he said, "I choose Long Bow and Darting Rabbit from the village, and Strong Back and Swift Stream from the exile camp. Please summon them here immediately. I'll inform them myself." No one questioned Faolin's choices. "I'm going to my campsite until they are here. After I've talked with them we'll discuss the rest of the attack." He walked away from the Nauryans, motioning for his fellow territorials to join him.

13

As the first light appeared the next morning, Faolin searched the eastern sky. He could see no sign of clouds. The clear, starlit night would give way to an equally clear dawn. Faolin sighed with relief. Nature was cooperating. He nodded to Jones to give the sign that the attack was on. As the word passed along the line of men who stood or lay concealed in the thicket barely a hundred yards from the raider camp, hearts beat faster and muscles tensed.

Moments after blazing sun first appeared above the mountains to the east, Faolin could hear shouts from the raider camp. Shortly afterward came the popping of the hunting rifles from the other side of the ridge. Faolin stretched out his arm to signal his men to remain in place. Let them take the bait, he thought. Let them take the bait.

Faolin could see men running in the raider camp. Should he give the signal now? The popping of the rifles continued, and the yelling. Faolin waited. Two minutes went by. The rifle fire and the yelling continued. A wrench of feeling swept through Faolin for those brave men on the other side of the ridge. Tears started to form in his eyes. The rifle fire became more sporadic. Had he waited too long? He dropped his hand, and the hatchet men rushed forward from the underbrush in front of him, under a rain of arrows from the bowmen, who then moved forward behind the hatchetmen.

Faolin and the other territorials didn't rush in with the Nauryans. They concealed themselves behind trees and used their rifles to snipe at the exposed raiders. But the distance and the general melee in the raider camp prevented them from having many clear shots. Faolin wasn't sure they had hit a single raider. He grew fearful that his plan wasn't working.

Long minutes passed. The gunshots from the other side of the ridge had stopped entirely shortly after the main attack. The shouts and screams of battle could still be heard, but they had diminished. Faolin could no longer see any fighting on this side of the camp. Had the Komisaw carried the battle to the raiders' center? Or had the attack been stopped? There was no way to tell.

As he waited, Faolin became more and more uncertain, more and more worried. If the battle was going well, he should have had word by now. He looked apprehensively at the other territorials. They were looking back at him, their eyes asking him what they should do. Should they rush into the camp to help the Komisaw? Faolin asked himself. That would be foolish. They couldn't make any difference. No, they should flee, before they too were captured. At least they should retreat to a point further away from the raider camp.

Faolin was about to order the territorials to fall back when he spotted one of the young Komisaw tribesmen running full speed toward him, away from the scene of the battle. Faolin checked carefully to see if the man was being followed. He wasn't. Faolin decided to wait for him.

"Mister Faolin," the young man shouted excitedly as he approached. "Mister Faolin, we've won. We've won." Faolin and the others stepped hesitantly out into the clearing to receive the runner. He gave his report: The plan had worked perfectly. The initial attack from the east had drawn the raider defenders from the western side of the camp. With the early morning sun in their eyes, they had been unable to measure the size of the attacking force on the east. The main body of Komisaw troops had swept into the camp virtually unopposed. They had captured the raider chief and his lieutenants, and the fighting ended soon afterward. The victors were now herding all the people in the raider camp--men, women, and children--into a large circle at the center of the camp. As Faolin had been told, the raiders had no UWG adviser with them. Casualties in the raider camp were high, but the attacking force suffered little.

Faolin was jubilant. He hopped around excitedly and hugged the bewildered runner. Then he gave the young man instructions to carry back with him. The herding operation was to continue. There were to be no executions or tortures until Faolin had met with the Komisaw leaders. And, as Faolin had planned from the beginning, none of the territorials would themselves appear before the raiders or their presence otherwise be made known.

The runner left. Faolin, Jones, and the other territorials returned to the concealment of the trees and undergrowth. As they laughed and jabbered wildly in a release from the deadly tension, another Nauryan burst in on them. Faolin turned just in time to see Forest Path coming at him, his face and eyes shining.

The laughter stopped. "Leave us for a few minutes," Faolin said to the other territorials.

"It's a good victory, friend Eric," said Forest Path after the others left. He was fighting off tears.

"It is, but you didn't come here to tell me that."

Forest Path stepped forward and grasped Faolin's arm. He lowered his head and cried openly. "They've killed our friend Swift Stream. I saw his body. Cut almost in half. I feel as if my own heart was cut out. It's more than I can bear."

Faolin took Forest Path's shoulders and raised his head

gently. "How did he fight?" Faolin asked.

"Like a madman, they say. With the strength of ten men. He killed a dozen himself, before he was slain." The tears still ran down Forest Path's cheeks.

"Then think of his bravery. Immortalize Swift Stream in your mind. He has saved your tribe. He was at the lead of the attack from the east. Without him, we would have failed."

Forest Path rubbed his eyes. He backed away from Faolin and tried to stand straight.

"Swift Stream wanted to be there," Faolin continued. "I asked him if he would take his squad to the east side, and he thanked me for asking him. It was his choice and his destiny, to die to save us."

"What will I tell Dawn Breeze? She'll be heartbroken."

"Tell her to be proud. If you like, I'll come with you."

"Oh, please do. Thank you, Eric." His tears gone, Forest Path looked around him. "I must return to my duties."

"Yes. We'll talk again later."

Forest Path left. Faolin returned to his friends, but could no longer participate in their merriment.

At mid-morning the native leaders met with Faolin in a wooded area out of view from the raider camp.

"It is our custom," said Tall Branch, "to slay their leaders and take an arm of each of their warriors. I see no reason why the custom should not be followed today."

"I believe," said Thundercloud, "that we should ask our advisor Faolin for his advice. He has brought us victory. Perhaps he can bring us peace."

Tall Branch grunted but made no objection. All eyes again turned to Faolin.

"This time," began Faolin, "I'm ready for your question. The raiders have been defeated before, but they have returned. I suggest that you do something that will insure against future raids. You are now in the best position to set advantageous terms for a permanent understanding." He paused and looked around. "What I have to suggest necessarily goes beyond the question of what to do with the raiders. But the raiders cannot properly be dealt with until other measures are taken.

"We are on the brink of an era when food supply need never be a reason for tribe to fight against tribe here. We can buy peace by guaranteeing the raiders a food supply--but on our terms. I suggest we impose no punishment on the raiders, but rather that we exact from their leaders a pledge that they will live peacefully in their own area if we promise to see them through times of famine."

Tall Branch opened his mouth to speak, but Faolin didn't give him a chance to interrupt. "Such an understanding will also require a common front against the raiders. I therefore suggest that the government of your tribe be reunited--that the exiles return to the village but be permitted to continue their agricultural work. Further, that their elders be represented on the village Council in proportion to the number of adult males in their camp." He looked squarely at Tall Branch. "That is merely providing them equality. It is the least you can do after they have saved your village from destruction."

Tall Branch stood up. He looked at the other village elders. "We can't do that. We have lost too many men. The exiles will control our Council."

Faolin had of course already made that determination. "Without the exiles your village would have been lost," he said.

Tall Branch turned to his fellow villagers. "Tell him we can never accept his suggestion."

"Sit down, Tall Branch," said Clear Spring. "We are in no position to disagree. Besides, I believe we have greatly underestimated this young man. We have lost much because we didn't join him earlier. Let us not lose more."

Tall Branch remained standing. "This is all a conspiracy between the territorials and the exiles," he said.

Thundercloud scrambled to his feet and faced Tall Branch. "I swear to you, Tall Branch, that this is the first we've ever heard of such a plan." He smiled. "I'm not even sure we wish to be reunited with such as you."

Tall Branch turned back to the village elders. "I demand a vote of our Council on this outrageous plan."

Before the others could respond, Faolin spoke. "I had hoped, Tall Branch, that you would see the wisdom of my suggestion. I would remind you that if you do not, the exiles will be forced to conclude a separate peace with the raiders. Unless you are willing to join them, they will have no reason to pledge their food supplies in exchange for protection for your village. And of course they will not let your men inflict any punishment on the raiders, for that would interfere with their peace treaty."

"Tall Branch," said Clear Spring, "I'm sure our Council will vote to approve Faolin's plan. We have no alternative." He looked around at the other village elders, most of whom nodded their assent. Tall Branch, seeing this, sat down wordlessly, hostility still flashing in his eyes.

The proposed treaty with the raiders was concluded easily. Their chief did not at first believe the offer made to him, but when he finally understood that it was in earnest he wept openly. Faolin and the territorials, hidden behind the rocks on the mountain above the camp, watched as the raiders packed and left, marching back to the north around the mountain. A dozen of the raiders remained to transport a temporary supply of grain back to their home after the rest had gone.

As the reunited Komisaw men trudged back to their village with their happy news, Forest Path and Faolin walked together for a time.

"Why didn't you ask me to take my squad to the east side?" Forest Path asked.

Faolin walked on for a time, thinking, before he answered. "Because Swift Stream's name was mentioned by your leaders first among the courageous warriors," he finally said. "And he was so eager to do it."

"Was my name mentioned?"

"Yes, but we also needed courageous fighters for the

main attack."

"I wish that I could now trade places with Swift Stream."

"We can't change the past. Swift Stream will be remembered as a savior of his people."

"I know. That's good."

"I have something else for you to think about. I intend to propose that you be named to the village Council of Elders. Would that be appropriate?"

Forest Path stopped walking. "Me? Oh, I'm much too young. It is against all tradition."

Faolin took his friend's arm and pulled him along. "Many things are happening here that are against tradition. I have a feeling that our work has just begun. It's necessary to have people on the Council who won't oppose progress. Could you accept the responsibility if I ask you?"

Forest Path hesitated. "I suppose I could, but . . ." His voice trailed off.

"What of your people? I'm not concerned about those few such as Tall Branch, but what would your fellow exiles think of me if I were to suggest such a thing?"

"They think so much of you, friend Faolin, especially now, that they would never question your decision."

"Then I intend to do it." He put his hand on Forest Path's shoulder. "Consider yourself an elder," Faolin said with a laugh.

14

Faolin and Forest Path left the main house of the Muskrat clan. They had just brought the news of Swift Stream's death to his family.

"I was surprised how calmly they accepted it," Faolin said.

"This is a hard life, my friend Eric. Most families have lost at least one of their children. It has to be accepted."

"Soon, Forest Path, so much tragedy will not have to be a part of your lives. I promise you that."

When they reached the cluster of buildings that belonged to the Blackbird clan, they briefly told their news to the older members of the family, then sought out Dawn Breeze. She was in the shrine room. Faolin paused at the door.

"Perhaps I should wait outside," he said.

"Why?" Forest Path asked.

"That is your sacred room. Some of your clan might object if I enter it at a time like this."

"Oh, no. You've been in here before. You're always welcomed. Your presence at our shrine honors us."

Faolin shrugged and followed Forest Path into the small room. Despite its relocation, it looked just the same as Faolin remembered it--the same blankets and low benches. Dawn Breeze sat on one of the blankets, facing away from the door. Her hands were on her lap, and several of the relics from one of the many containers were laid out on a bench in front of her.

"Dawn Breeze. Why are you here?" Forest Path asked softly.

The girl turned to face the two men. The dim light from the doorway gave her face a softness that Faolin thought made her even lovelier than he had remembered.

"I felt a need to come here to meditate," she said. "I've been so fearful since you left. But my fear must have been wrong. You are here with our friend Faolin. You have won?"

"We have won," said Forest Path, "thanks to Faolin. The raiders have returned to their homeland."

Dawn Breeze looked at Faolin. "You change our lives

more and more every day," she said, a smile flickering on her face. "We cannot resist you." She looked back at her brother. "My fearfulness stays with me. I sense that you have other news."

"Yes," Forest Path said solemnly. "Swift Stream has been killed."

"Oh!" Dawn Breeze exclaimed sharply but softly. She put her small hand to her mouth. "How . . . When?" Her eyes began to moisten.

Forest Path looked to Faolin. Faolin swallowed to clear the lump in his throat. "He helped lead the attack that took the raiders away from our main force," Faolin said. "They say he fought like ten men. It was his bravery that won the battle. Without him we would all have been lost." Faolin searched Dawn Breeze's face for some sign of understanding, but her expression remained unchanged. A tear started down her cheek. Faolin wanted to say more, to cover up this painful silence, but he couldn't find the words.

"He wanted to do it, Dawn Breeze," Forest Path added, his words rushing. "It was his wish to go. He was so happy to be chosen for the task. He wanted to fight them, and he saved us all."

Without any warning, Dawn Breeze lunged at Faolin. "Why did you come here?" she screamed. "Why do you do this to us?" She pounded on his chest, then began to claw at him, crying and sobbing the whole time. Faolin made no move to step back or defend himself. He was immobilized. For a brief moment he found himself strangely welcoming the attack. It was as if he had, without thinking, adopted her screaming accusations as his own. When he regained his senses and thought to protect himself, Forest Path was already pulling Dawn Breeze away from him. It took all of Forest Path's strength to contain the struggling, kicking girl, but Faolin couldn't move to help him. Instead, he backed away across the room.

Then, as quickly as she had begun, Dawn Breeze stopped and collapsed onto her knees, her head bent forward and her hair touching the floor.

"I'm sorry," she sobbed. "Sorry. Sorry. Sorry. It's too

much to fight. It's too late."

Forest Path leaned over and touched her shoulder. "Dawn, it is we who are sorry to bring such dreadful news. I understand how you feel. Even I cried when I learned. I felt I couldn't live with myself. But it will pass. You've faced death before."

"I know. I know," said Dawn Breeze. "Please leave me alone with my grief. I wish to suffer this alone."

Forest Path looked up at Faolin. They nodded to each other and quietly left the room.

"Perhaps it was wrong of me to be here," Faolin said when they were outside.

"No. Not at all. It's good she can suffer this way. She'll get over it sooner. We're glad you came."

As soon as he could excuse himself, Faolin left Forest Path and the exile camp and started back toward New Hope. Jones and the other territorials had gone there directly, and the settlers in New Hope would be waiting to see Faolin. He looked forward to their greeting and to the comfort of being with his own people again.

While the natives were off fighting, the irrigation ditches had become clogged, and the settlers who stayed behind had been too few to prepare the fields for flooding. As the fields had dried, the blight crept in, and now it was too late to recover the grain it had touched. By a monumental effort, the territorials and the natives managed to flood the fields closest to the lake in time. They saved a third of the crop-- enough, at least, together with the earlier harvest, to carry them through the winter and to make good the pledge to the raiders, but still not enough to ship to the market in New Markwell.

The New Hope village board reluctantly approved Faolin's commitment to the raiders, on his assurance that it secured the future. More than one board member remarked, however, that he was getting tired of being told that he would have to wait until the next harvest before he could buy the things he needed. For Faolin, the failure of the late crop and the settlers' approval of his achievements gave neither the disappointment nor the pleasure he might have expected.

Faolin found himself, for the first time he could remember, unable to give more than a portion of his attention to the affairs of New Hope. The battle with the raiders, and the events following it, had changed him. He craved excitement and challenge, and what the settlement offered was no longer enough. At the same time, no matter where he was, or what he was doing, his thoughts insisted on returning to one subject: Dawn Breeze.

Clearly, Faolin told himself, Dawn Breeze had attacked him only because she needed to vent her feelings. There had been no personal animosity toward him. How could there have been? He had not killed Swift Stream. He had certainly never done anything directly to her.

But had he somehow transgressed an unknown Nauryan custom that Dawn Breeze or Forest Path had not mentioned for fear of embarrassing him? Most of the time the Nauryan natives seemed as open and comprehensible as any UWG citizen; but in some matters there was no way to explain their behavior. What had Dawn Breeze been doing with the relics in the family shrine when they intruded on her? Had he interrupted some private religious rite? Despite the fact that he, unlike other territorials, was welcomed to the Blackbird Clan shrine, he knew virtually nothing of that clan's--or the tribe's--religious rites.

After several weeks Faolin's preoccupation had not lessened. He missed a village board meeting--something he had never done before--and he let the others begin the planning for the winter work and the next spring's planting without him. The problem, Faolin finally told himself, was that he had to know the reasons for that strange outburst in the Blackbird shrine. Cooperation of Nauryans and territorials was essential to this enterprise, and if some unknown factor threatened that cooperation, he should be aware of it. To find out the reasons for what happened, he would have to see Dawn Breeze.

On a cold, gray day in late October Faolin went to the house of the Blackbird clan. As he rode into the exile camp he noted that many of the houses were gone--no doubt already moved back to the old village. He saw as he dismounted in front of the main Blackbird clan dwelling that parts of the clan's outbuildings were being taken down. It would be more difficult, he thought, for these people to get to the fields once they moved back to the old village. He made a mental note to suggest that they establish a summer camp near the border.

Forest Path greeted Faolin and took him to a side room of the house where Dawn Breeze waited. All but the impending confrontation evaporated from Faolin's thoughts as he neared Dawn Breeze's presence. He felt himself beginning to sweat and wondered, strangely, if he would be able to speak to her the questions he had framed so many times in anticipation of this meeting.

Dawn Breeze smiled warmly when she saw Faolin. She rushed forward to greet him and offered him her hand, which he grasped for a moment. It was warm and dry, and Faolin was embarrassed at his own cold, moist palm. Dawn Breeze looked directly into Faolin's eyes. His eyes met hers briefly but could not hold them and glanced away uneasily toward Forest Path. Faolin began to feel foolish, as well as nervous. How could he have imagined that there existed some underlying animosity that must be disclosed? Yet he was also relieved and inwardly pleased to find Dawn Breeze so friendly.

The three of them sat down on low stools, in the Nauryan fashion.

"We're very pleased to have you here," said Forest Path. "But your message perplexed us. Why do you wish to see my sister and me? I suspect it is something more than a social call."

"Something more, yes," began Faolin. "But not so much more. I felt I left very abruptly when I was last here, and I missed the chance to enjoy your hospitality, especially of such a beautiful hostess." He glanced at Dawn Breeze, and she smiled. He had not really meant to say those last words, but her reaction made him glad he did.

"Oh, that was my fault ," said Dawn Breeze. "I behaved like a crazy person. I was very upset, but I'm better now. I can see things more clearly." She looked at her brother, then back to Faolin. "I had a feeling you would return soon."

"Dawn Breeze often has feelings about things that may happen," said Forest Path, slightly scornfully.

"Do they happen?" Faolin asked.

"Sometimes. Not always," said Dawn Breeze with a shrug. "But my feeling that you would return was very strong." She smiled again.

Faolin felt more relaxed. "I must confess," he said, "that I've been troubled about what happened here ever since I left. I thought that perhaps I'd violated some sacred custom and that you were too courteous to tell me. That's why I wanted to return."

"You violated no sacred custom of mine," said Dawn Breeze. "Did he violate any of yours, Forest Path?"

"No--at least not any that I remember," Forest Path said with a grin.

Faolin smiled too. "You're right to make fun of me. I can see that my worry was silly. But please understand my concern that we--territorials and Nauryans--remain on open and friendly terms. We need each other and should avoid any kind of behavior that will put us at odds. If we know when feelings are hurt, we can do something about it."

"Don't worry, friend Eric," said Forest Path. "We're very happy with our lot, especially now that you've made it possible for us to return to the village."

The three sat silently for a moment. Faolin had resolved the problem he came to resolve. There seemed nothing else to say. But he didn't want to leave these good friends. They apparently were waiting for him to decide what to do next.

"I noticed many houses gone as I rode into your camp," Faolin finally said.

"Yes, they've already returned to the village. We will he going soon."

"Forest Path was helping to take down some of our buildings when you came," said Dawn Breeze.

"Well, I hope I didn't interfere with your work."

Forest Path shook his head. "Oh, no. We can finish at any time."

"When do you plan to go?"

"We'll go to the village tomorrow if the work can be finished," said Dawn Breeze.

Faolin stood up. "In that case, I must be delaying your job. Please don't feel you should stay here because of me. Please return to what you were doing."

Forest Path also stood. "Very well, if that is your wish." He turned to Dawn Breeze. "You'll see that Eric is comfortable until he's ready to leave?"

"Yes, brother."

"I must be going very soon anyway," Faolin said. "It's just as well."

Forest Path stepped up to Faolin and shook his hand. "You may stay as long as you like. It was good to see you again, friend Eric. Please come see us in the village." He nodded to his sister and left the room and the house.

Faolin looked at Dawn Breeze, who still sat on her low stool. He felt uncomfortable again. Dawn Breeze seemed more beautiful every time he looked at her.

"Yes, you will have to come to see us in the village," she said, breaking the silence. "We will not be in the same place. We've taken the houses of one of the clans that had many of its men killed by the raiders. It's a larger area than we had before, and nearer the center of the village. Grandmother said it was only right that we live there, now that Forest Path is on the Council of Elders. The women who traded the place to us were happy, because now we've taken the obligation of providing for them. Many others from here have also taken places near the center of the village." She shook her head. "It's very strange. When we left the village we were the outcasts. Now we're returning as the equals to the shepherd clans. The villagers seem to accept it, but--"

"Just a minute," interrupted Faolin. "I'm having trouble

keeping up with all you are saying.. Do you always run on so when Forest Path leaves?"

Dawn Breeze blushed and looked down. "I'm sorry. I talk too much when I'm uneasy."

"There's no reason to be uneasy now."

Dawn Breeze looked up. "I can't help it. A person naturally feels awe in the presence of the Protector."

"The Protector?"

"Yes. Of our legends. We're not afraid to call you by that name, now that we're certain. The victory over the raiders has proved it."

"I don't understand."

Dawn Breeze smiled in a way that said she would go along with Faolin's little pretext. "I am the keeper of the legends for the Blackbird Clan. Shall I tell you the legend of the Protector?"

"Please do." Faolin sat down again.

Dawn Breeze drew up her knees and wrapped her arms around them. She stared into space beyond Faolin, as if she were looking at something far away. "The legend has been passed down in the Komisaw tribe longer than anyone can remember. Many years ago-- many, many lifetimes ago--the mountains opened and the spirit of the mountains spoke with a wise man of our tribe. The spirit told him about how to live one's life in harmony with nature so that one will not suffer from nature's cruelties. And among the things he said was that when we strayed from the Right Way, there would be suffering until a brown man--the Protector--came to put us back on that path."

"And you think I am the brown man?"

"Forest Path and Swift Stream thought that from the beginning, because it was also told by the spirit of the mountain that the Protector would come unannounced, and that we would be tempted to kill him and must resist that temptation."

"They did almost kill me."

"That made them certain. And by their faith, they managed to convince others of the truth of their belief. That is why we came here. The others, who stayed in the village, did not believe that you were the Protector, or that your way was the Right Way, so they didn't come. But they believe now." She stopped. "Did no one tell you this after the battle with the tribe from the north?"

"No. But I must tell you that I'm not a god. I'm not your Protector."

"But you are. The spirit of the mountain said: the Protector will deny himself ten thousand times, to test your faith, but you must believe." She smiled. "We all learn that when we're very young. It's what we say when the rains go on too long, or when the sheep become barren, or when a plague comes to us. We have faith that nature will approve of us again if we only have patience."

Suddenly Faolin understood the meaning of the spring ceremony that had been performed around him each year. He held up his hand. "Please believe me. I'm not this Protector. Surely the legend must say more that doesn't fit my appearance here."

"Oh, it does. The Protector of the legend wears clothes of gold and comes from over the mountains. But Forest Path has explained that. If you did all those things, you could not test our faith. When the time comes, you will reveal all these things to us."

"Look, Dawn Breeze, that's a very fine story, and I hope your Protector does come some day. But I am not he. I'm only a man."

Dawn Breeze smiled again. "Oh, the Protector is a man. The legend says: he will laugh like a man and cry like a man, and he will feel the needs and the desires of a man." At this she looked into Faolin's eyes and blushed. So did he.

Dawn Breeze stood up suddenly. "There are other parts of the legend that I can't tell you now. Maybe someday, but not now. Perhaps someone else will tell you." She put a hand to her eye as if wiping away a tear and turned her head momentarily away from Faolin. When she looked at him again the smile was back on her face. "It is right that you are here. I knew you would come. We'll do what must be done." She approached Faolin, reached out and took his hand gently. He stood slowly, unsure of the feelings that coursed through him. He could think of nothing to say.

"Protector . . ." she began.

"Please. You shouldn't call me that."

"Friend Eric, will you take me on your horse? I've always wanted to ride on one."

"Yes, of course. I'd like that. Where shall we go?"

"To the rock. It's not far. I want to stand on it one more time before we return to the village."

Forest Path, when they told him, seemed to accept their desire to go riding as perfectly natural, and he went back to his work. Faolin's horse, rested from the ride to the exile camp, carried them swiftly out into the clearing that led to the pine forest at the edge of the large rock that jutted into UWG territory. Dawn Breeze sat behind Faolin on the horse, exclaiming her delight as the wind whipped her face and hair. Faolin liked the feeling of her arms around him.

When they neared the edge of the rock, they slowed. Dawn Breeze pointed out a narrow path that she said led through the pines and out along the rock's crest. Despite Faolin's many journeys around the rock, he had never been on top of it. He urged the horse forward along the path. Soon they were immersed in the dense trees, and Faolin had to look hard to find his way.

"Can you tell if we're still on the path?" he asked.

"Yes, I think so. But gods don't get lost."

"I thought you said the Protector is a man."

"Well, he's part man and part god. A man, but descended from the gods."

"A bastard, then?"

Faolin felt a small hand strike him on the upper back, not hard. "Don't talk that way. It's improper, even for you." Faolin turned around and thought he saw, in the dimness, a trace of a smile that Dawn Breeze was trying to hide.

Faolin turned to the front and leaned low over the horse's head to follow the trail. He stopped the horse.

"I'm going to have to get down," he said. "I can't find

the path." He dismounted and took the reins and led the horse as he walked slowly ahead.

"I think we're still on the path," he said after a minute, "but I'm not sure."

"Let me help you. I've been here before." Dawn Breeze also dismounted and joined Faolin.

"Yes, this is the path," she said. She pointed. "See how it turns to the right up there, just at that large tree." Faolin looked in the direction indicated and shook his head. "I'm afraid I don't see it. Perhaps you should lead the horse."

"I don't know much of horses. Come, I'll lead you and you lead the horse. It's not too much further until we're out of the trees." She reached out and took Faolin's hand. The touch of that small, warm hand ignited a surge of desire inside Faolin. It was as if a river of feeling had lain just under the surface of Faolin's thoughts, ready to erupt at the slightest stimulation. Faolin drew Dawn Breeze to him and held her close for a few seconds. She didn't resist. Then, embarrassed, he slowly released her. Their eyes met for a long silent moment. Finally, Faolin stepped back.

"I couldn't help myself. You're very attractive."

"You've been without a woman for a long time?"

"Yes."

Dawn Breeze moved back next to Faolin. "You may take me if you like." She put her hand gently on Faolin's chest.

"Take you?"

"Yes. Lie with me here. It will be good." Again Faolin stepped back, this time more out of shock than embarrassment.

"I would like to, Dawn Breeze, but it would be wrong."

Dawn Breeze looked hurt. "You don't want me?"

"Oh, yes. Yes. Of course I do. More than anything. But it wouldn't be right."

"I don't understand."

"You're a child, not even of age among your own people. We are of different races, different customs. Strangers.

Uncommitted to each other."

"What of these things?"

"In my land, it isn't the custom for a man to . . . lie with a woman he has not married."

"Even when neither are married?"

"Yes."

"But why? Is it against your laws?"

"No, it isn't illegal. And some do it. But they're held in disgrace."

"That seems to me strange."

"It isn't. There are sound reasons for the custom. A society that wishes to progress can't permit itself to become overly preoccupied with sexual matters, or burdened with unwanted children."

Dawn Breeze turned away. "Those reasons do not make any sense to me. We have no such strange customs."

"You don't mean to say that you have . . . "

Dawn Breeze turned to face Faolin. "Of course. Since I have been old enough to enjoy it. It is one of the ways a girl prepares herself for marriage."

Faolin stared at Dawn Breeze in amazement. Her revelation did not decrease his desire for her, but he couldn't help but think of her as he had thought of the girls he had seen in the new towns along the Westland coast. No, not that, he told himself. She was simply uncivilized. A barbarian with primitive customs. But it wasn't her fault. Unlike the prostitutes of the UWG frontier towns, she knew no better. Faolin felt insanely jealous of the other men who had held this young girl.

"What . . . what if there are children?" Faolin asked, desperate for something to say.

"They belong to the girl's clan, of course, and stay with her after she marries. Many men will choose a girl who has already borne sons." She looked to the ground, as if embarrassed. "I have not borne any children."

Faolin   was   intrigued,   as   well   as   shocked   and disappointed. "Does a girl of your tribe go with other men after she marries?"

Dawn Breeze shrugged. "Not so much. Only if her husband asks it, or if she wants to shame her husband so that he will leave her clan."

"In the UWG it is against our customs for a married man or woman to have relations with another in any circumstances. Your ways are very different from ours. But your life is much different, too."

"I would like to know more of your life. Doctor Newberry never told us of these things. Tell me, have you never been with a woman at all?"

Faolin looked down and shuddered, trying to repress the memories of youthful acts at the Pinedale Home. "Not for a very long time. I don't have very pleasant memories of it. I was publicly scolded."

Dawn Breeze stepped back to Faolin's side and took his hand again. "I can erase those memories for you, if you wish."

Faolin put his arm around the girl and pulled her next to him. "I do wish it, but I can't change the feeling of wrongness."

"Is it wrong in the UWG to be with the girl one will marry?" Dawn Breeze said, softly and hesitantly.

"Not so wrong, but . . ." Could it be, Faolin thought, that this girl wants to marry me? The prospect stunned him. His desire for her swept aside feeble doubts about their deep cultural differences and Faolin's own life plan.

Faolin grasped Dawn Breeze by her shoulders and looked deep into her eyes. "Do you mean," he asked, "that you would like to be my wife?"

"Oh, yes. As soon as I reach the proper age."

"Then it will be," Faolin declared. He picked her up and twirled her around several times, then put her down and placed his arm around her gently. "I love you, Dawn Breeze."

She smiled a knowing smile, but there was a glint of moisture in her eye that did not escape Faolin's notice.

"What's this?" he said, kissing her eyelid. "You aren't sad?"

"Oh, no," she said, putting her arms around Faolin's neck and clinging to him. "I am just so happy. Our marriage will bring great joy to us and to our people. I know. I know."

They silently moved, arm in arm, to a shaded carpet of soft pine needles.

"You have much to learn," said Dawn Breeze afterward, "but I will teach you."

"We will have a lifetime for it."

They led Faolin's horse further along the path until the forest gave way to the rocky hill. They rode out onto it. From there they could see for miles. The lofty perch gave Faolin a feeling of omnipotence. He wondered if just perhaps he could be the Protector of the Nauryan legend. They stayed for a few minutes, then rode back to bring their news to Dawn Breeze's people.

15

Barbara Strongarm and her husband rode a bus to the meeting. He worked intently all the way there on the notes for his speech, scribbling quickly, crossing out, scribbling again. Barbara watched him for a while, hoping he would look up and maybe chat with her for a minute. But he didn't. She gave up and gazed out the window. The woods and fields that covered the fifteen miles between Wendell and Painterville slid slowly by.

The 1928 Congressional election campaign was underway, and Robert Strongarm was a candidate for Congressman from Eastern Agronica's 4th District. He had passed the candidates' examination on his first try (without taking advantage of the Nauryan equalization factor). He had high hopes, too, since the incumbent had just withdrawn from the race. From now, early April, until the end of May Strongarm would be giving his speech at least three nights a week. Barbara wondered to herself how her husband could work so long on a speech when the campaign regulations so closely controlled its content. Yet, knowing Bob, she fully expected that he would revise the speech for each meeting. She knew that she was not going to be able to sit through every meeting Bob went to, but she had resolved to come to as many of the early ones as she could, to provide Bob moral support--as if he needed it.

The bus slowed as it entered Painterville. The road became bumpier. Barbara watched Bob struggle to keep writing despite the bouncing of the bus. They soon reached the central area of the town and stopped in front of the small depot, where they got out. A gray-haired man in his fifties met them and took them to a black, squarish car that had the words "Eastern Packing Co." stenciled on the doors. They drove to the factory complex on the far side of town. Painterville, like so many Agronican towns of its size, was organized around its few large industries. Bob would be visiting its chemical plant and its tool and die works next week.

The car crunched up a gravel driveway and stopped by the factory assembly hall. The employees and their families who were gathered inside stood and applauded politely as Barbara and her husband entered and walked down the center aisle to the front of the room. Bob's opponents had already arrived. Barbara noted that the auditorium was less than half full. She sighed to herself. When she was a child, the assembly halls were always bursting for the campaign speeches. These days, people seemed to have other things they preferred to do. The gray-haired man showed Barbara to her seat in the front row. Bob joined the other candidates on the stage, and the program began.

The first speaker, determined by lot, was a man from the south end of the District named Brackett. He droned on, giving his views on the questions set out in the official campaign format. Barbara found it very difficult to listen. She hoped she wouldn't have the same trouble when Bob took the podium. Unfortunately, he had been cast in the last position.

As the first speaker gave way to the second, Barbara's thoughts drifted. She remembered the first time she met Bob, just after he came to Wendell to work in the city administrator's office. He had caught her in the midst of a late-blooming rebellion against conventionality, and his angry, intense manner had attracted her very much. She had admired him for rejecting the equalization bonus and leaving the law school at Brockton to take up a new career. Within a year they were married. The government's policy of encouraging marriages between Nauryans and Browns was at its height then and helped to overcome any misgivings she had.

In the years since, Barbara's rebelliousness had dissipated, but Bob's intensity had only increased. She now dreamed of the most conventional sort of cozy family life, raising their son and keeping house, receiving her housewife's subsidy. But Bob couldn't live that life. He worked too long and too hard, whether he was at his office or at home. He didn't have any time, and perhaps didn't have any capacity, to relax and share good feelings. It was as if he had continually to prove that his Nauryan ancestry was no handicap, long after he had succeeded in doing so. It was the natural thing for him to enter this campaign. He had talked about running for Congress for years.

Finally Bob's turn to speak came. Barbara concentrated on him. She didn't find it as difficult as she feared. He had a directness and a flexible style that made him easy to listen to. He moved through the format: tax rates, production incentives, medical care, the transportation system, housing, and so on. The audience seemed to Barbara to pay close attention to Bob, and when he finished they applauded heartily. She felt that he had made a much better presentation than any of the others.

Then came the questions from the floor. There weren't many. Fifteen minutes into the question period the Chairman recognized a heavy-set, middle-aged man sitting near the front of the room who had been trying vainly to be recognized since the candidates finished their prepared speeches.

"I would like to ask about something," the man said, "that wasn't on the format. I don't know if other people have noticed this, and I haven't seen any statistics on it, but it seems to me that there's been a lot more stealing going on than there used to be. My apartment was robbed last year, and I know other people--not just in Painterville--who have had the same thing happen to them. I wonder if the candidates would tell us what they think ought to be done about this."

The man sat down. The privilege of giving the first answer had returned to Brackett, and the Chairman repeated the question.

Brackett stood up and responded eagerly. "I'm glad to hear that question," he said, "because I've noticed this problem too, and I've given it some thought. Quite frankly, I think the matter ought to be included in the format."

Brackett looked around the room, took a sip of water, and went on. "I've talked to some people in the District Police and Counselling Administration, and they agree with you." He nodded at the questioner. "They say there is definitely an increase in theft here. They've never kept statistics on it before, because there's been so little in the past, but they're going to start next year.

"Now, these people in the District PCA office tell me something that's very interesting. While there are more thefts being reported, they aren't catching as many offenders as they used to. And of the ones they do catch, very often they're turning out to be prior offenders.

"From these facts--and they're going to be documented—I think we can see why we're having more thefts. It's because, number one, people think maybe they can get away with it without being caught, and, number two, we're not curing the offenders we do catch."

Brackett's gaze returned again to the man who had asked the question. "With all that in mind, I think I can answer your question--namely, what do we do about this situation? To me, the answer is clear. We've got to make the police more of a deterrent, and we've got to try something a little stronger than counseling on offenders." He paused for effect. "I know some people aren't going to like this suggestion, but I say we should give our policemen guns, we should allow them to search for stolen goods, and when we catch a thief--certainly if he's a second offender--we ought to do more than talk to him. We ought to give him a good, sound punishment."

A murmur ran through the audience. Barbara was surprised. She looked at Bob. She could tell he was upset. He clenched and unclenched his fists, crossed and recrossed his legs. But Brackett wasn't finished.

"Now let me say one more thing, " Brackett continued. "In more than half the cases where offenders are caught, the police find them to be under the influence of alcohol. I know that most of us here would never dream of touching alcohol, and for good reason. But there's a growing number of people--especially among certain groups and types--who do. In my opinion, ladies and gentlemen, it's this alcohol that's got a lot to do with increasing crime. It makes people lazy and unproductive, and undermines their morals. I think that the Congress ought to pass laws making alcoholic beverages illegal, and I'll propose such laws if I'm elected. Laws prohibiting alcohol would only support what the vast majority of us believe, and I think they would put an end to what is fast becoming a serious problem." With these words Brackett sat down.

The candidate whose turn followed Brackett's rose and, still obviously thinking about the question, started to move to the microphone. But before he could get there, Barbara saw with a shock, Bob had bolted out of his seat and grasped the microphone first.

"Mr. Chairman," Bob said, "I know this is irregular, but if the other candidates don't mind I'd like to speak next. I ask this privilege in order to respond directly to Mr. Brackett's statements."

The Chairman appeared displeased, but Strongarm was already at the microphone. He looked at the other candidates. They shrugged their assent--probably preferring the additional time to formulate their own answers, Barbara thought. "Very well," the Chairman said.

Barbara watched as Bob looked out silently over the audience. His look clearly said that this was a very important matter, well justifying his interruption of the normal order. Barbara felt less embarrassed about her husband's conduct.

"Ladies and gentlemen," Strongarm began, speaking slowly, "our government is founded on the twin pillars of freedom and equality. We've never before worried about crimes of theft, despite our great freedom, because our policy of equality has made it impossible for one man to have more than his neighbors. Now, we are told that, for some reason, such crimes are being committed, and often. Why this should be mystifies me. We all have more today than we ever did in the past, and if we continue to work as hard as we do, we shall all certainly have much more in the future. Our government is dedicated to expanding production so that everyone can have more of everything.

"To begin with, then, I'm very skeptical of these rumors about increases in thefts. There aren't any hard figures to substantiate them. Before we attempt to do anything about this supposed problem, we should at least make sure it really exists.

"But even if there has been an increase in crime such as the question assumes, I can't agree with Mr. Brackett's solution, for that solution, in my opinion, strikes against that pillar of freedom on which the government is based. If we start chipping away at that pillar, it's going to crack and break. If police carry guns, if they can search someone's home for stolen property, if they can punish offenders, then, believe me, we're all going to be affected.

"If in fact there's an increase in crime, we must fight it in a manner that's consistent with our basic principles--by the tried and tested ways that have brought the world peace and harmony for the last 125 years. If, as Mr. Brackett suggests, counseling isn't curing offenders, then let's improve the counseling process. Better yet, let's prevent crime from ever arising by instilling proper values in our youth, by education and example." He smiled briefly. "I'm sure most of you who are my age will agree that the lower school behavior courses aren't as important in our children's lives as they were in ours. That would be a good place to start. Because I firmly believe, my friends, that no amount of restriction or punishment is going to enforce behavior patterns that even a small minority of our society doesn't believe in.

"Now, there's one more thing Mr. Brackett stated that I must comment on. He spoke of a supposed alcohol problem and mentioned that 'certain groups' of our citizens seem to be prone to it. I think I can afford to be explicit where Mr. Brackett was too polite. I assume when he talks about 'certain groups' he means Nauryans. We all know that there is an unwritten and unspoken belief that Nauryans who have come to be citizens of the UWG tend to drink alcohol and tend to be lazy and unproductive. The belief may even be correct, though I assure you there are many, many Nauryans who don't fit it.

"But even if many do, there is certainly no statistical or other basis for assuming Nauryans are committing crimes, as Mr. Brackett implies." Barbara could see that Bob was seething now. She guessed that the others in the audience could sense it, too. They were very quiet and their attention was riveted on Bob. "I personally resent his suggestion. And as to any alcohol problem, in any part of our society, I reject the suggestion that prohibition of alcohol will solve it. As I said before, we can't change people's behavior by making it illegal. When people are happy in their lives, and when they know the counterproductive effects alcohol produces, they won't turn to it as a release. If there is an alcohol problem, the solution lies in education and proper treatment of all citizens so as to make their lives fulfilling." He paused. "And if the problem is a Nauryan one, the solution lies in ridding our society of the kind of unspoken assumption of Nauryan inadequacy that was revealed by Mr. Brackett's comments."

Strongarm nodded toward the questioner and sat down. The rules of the meeting prohibited applause until after all candidates had answered the question, but those rules didn't stop this audience. They stood and cheered Strongarm for half a minute before the Chairman could end it. Barbara took it all in. For some reason the Nauryan issue often brought forth this kind of a response, especially when Nauryan rights were defended by Bob's fervor. Whether Brackett meant his comments to apply to Nauryans or not, he had made a slip that cost him dearly with this audience. Barbara was sure he would not do it again.

They managed to catch the last bus back to Wendell. Bob had put his notes away. He leaned back in his seat with his eyes closed and his hands folded across his stomach, but Barbara could tell from the way his jaw muscles were working that he wasn't relaxing.

"I thought it went extremely well, Bob," she said.

He opened his eyes. "You do? You know me. I can't keep from worrying."

"Your presentation was much better than any of the others. The audience listened to you."

Bob smiled. "That's good." He closed his eyes again and seemed to unwind a little.

After a few minutes Barbara said, "They sure went for that Nauryan stuff."

Bob opened his eyes again and sat up. "I'm not sure what you mean by that."

Barbara shrugged. "I mean, your response to Brackett was very convincing. I think the audience really believed in what you said."

He searched her face for a moment after she spoke. "I hope so," he finally said. "Brackett's ideas are very destructive."

"Yes."

Bob again sank back into his seat and closed his eyes, this time with his back turned toward Barbara. She could sense that his mind was starting to work on his next speech. The rest of the trip back to Wendell passed in silence.

16

The steel-tipped arrow hummed through the air, then glanced off the moving clay target, breaking off a small piece, and, its energy spent, dropped headfirst into the ground. Han watched the flight of the arrow without expression. As soon as it fell, he fitted another to his heavy, curved bow and drew it back. Another target leaped into the air. The arrow struck this one squarely in the center, and the target burst into a thousand fragments. Han, his turn over, slid the bow over his shoulder, turned around sharply, and strode away from the shooting line. The small group of court families and their attendants watching the contest smiled their approval. Han touched his forehead in acknowledgment.

At the age of 17, in the summer of 1928, Han already showed the poise and bearing of a veteran Warrior. Inwardly at this moment he was highly pleased with himself. He had made his best score ever in the archery contests of the mid-summer festival. More important, he had decisively beaten his brother, Changa. Han eagerly searched the group of spectators for his father, the Emperor. Oddly, he was not in his place at the center of the group. Then Han spied him, off to the side, engaged in an animated conversation with several of his ministers and with two brown-skinned men from the UWG mission. The Emperor had not even watched the contest! Han moved toward the group as the next contestant took his place at the shooting line. As Han approached them, he was aware of the conspicuous absence of Yim Jinsa, who had been the First Minister of the Empire since Han was a small child. The old man's death just a week before the festival had greatly saddened Han, and Han fretted excessively about who the

Emperor would choose as a replacement.

Han reached the group and stood at the edge of it without speaking. The two foreigners nodded at him. His father and the others went on talking without noting his presence. They were discussing dams and hydroelectric power. After a minute of listening to them Han, boiling inside, squared his shoulders, turned, and marched off in the direction of the New Palace. As he turned to go, he observed one of the foreigners, the one they called Halburton, watching him. Han fancied that he could read in the man's eyes a curious mixture of suspicion, awe and pity. The suspicion and awe Han liked, for he had cultivated it in his few conversations with members of the UWG mission, but the possibility that one of the foreigners would feel pity for him made Han cringe.

Han walked alone across the field and through the gardens to the walls of the New Palace. Someday, he thought, his father would have to recognize his military prowess and give him the honor he deserved. Han found himself daydreaming of how it would be if he allied himself with one of the vassal lords and fought his father and brother for the Empire. But the vassal lords were a relic of the past. Today it was the owners of the great new factories who held the power, at least in Northern Chansu. And, in any event, how could any rival for the Empire hope to overcome the superior weapons from the UWG that had enabled Han's grandfather to win and hold the Empire? Only by obtaining equal or better weapons, and this meant obtaining the friendship of the UWG. That was a most unpleasant prospect. Han disliked the foreigners for many things, but above all for their lack of respect for nobility--or, more precisely, for their treatment of lesser persons with equal respect. They seemed, indeed, not only to miss the subtleties of social hierarchy, but to consciously ignore them. This Han felt demeaned them. The foreigners were worse than Worker class; they were classless. And, despite their outward display of cooperation, Han believed that they wished to export their classless ways to Chansu. Chansu must not let down its guard against them.

Inside the walls, in the New Palace courtyard, Han

paused for a moment, trying to decide what to do next. His mind made up, he went directly to his apartment and sent one of the servants to fetch Tama.

Han knew that he had not given Tama leave to attend the contests, and normally only the priests of the palace temple would go, leaving the rest of the huge temple assemblage, including the concubines, behind. But occasionally his father or mother would release them for the day, on account of the festival. Han had not seen anyone other than the priests about this afternoon and prayed that no such release had been given. He desperately needed refuge from his father's indifference.

The gods answered his prayers. Tama appeared at the door of his apartment, her large eyes calm and expectant. She was a big girl, almost as tall as Han, yet with very delicate features. She was two years older than he and looked even more mature than her years. But what attracted Han to her was neither her appearance nor her age, but the sense of inward tranquility that surrounded her. Many of the young girls from the temple had a calm, quiet manner--undoubtedly a result of their similar training, for virtually all were given to or adopted by the temple priests while still infants--but Tama had the power to transmit it to others by her soft voice, her supple hands, and even by her mere presence. Han often needed her talent.

But this time the quiet could come later. As soon as the girl was inside the door he attacked her voraciously, directing all his pent-up feelings against her body. Tama didn't resist, but accomodated as best she could, understanding Han's needs.

Afterward, Tama stayed with Han in his apartment. He sat sullenly in a soft chair in the large living room while she sat on the floor across the room, strumming quietly on a Chansu guitar. They had scarcely spoken to each other since she came. A huge tray of shrimp and rice cakes they had ordered lay untouched on a table.

Tama stopped playing and put her instrument aside. "Why are you so unhappy, Prince?" she asked. "You don't eat. You don't talk. I don't know why you ask me to stay."

Han looked at her. The muscles tensed in his neck. Finally he spoke. "I asked you because I need someone to make me happy. You aren't doing so."

"I'm sorry, Prince, but I can do nothing to help you when you are like this. You must look within yourself. I would be glad to listen to you if you want to talk. Sometimes that makes you feel better."

"Yes, I suppose I can talk to you," sighed Han. "You at least will carry my words no further than the temple." He glared at her.

"I have so vowed to you and to the Gods." Tama moved across the room and sat on the floor in front of Han. She took his hand in hers and held it gently. "Has your father again insulted you, my Prince?"

"No!" Han answered emphatically. "I'm troubled about the fate of Chansu, not about myself."

"To my uninformed person, the future of Chansu appears bright."

"Yes, Tama, it is bright if it continues in the path my father and his father have set it. That future can be a glorious one. More glorious, I'm sure, than you have ever imagined. But what troubles me is the fact that there are those who would divert us from our great destiny, and I feel powerless to stop them."

"That is certainly cause for concern. What, may I ask, is the threat that you fear?"

"The immediate threat results from the death of Yim Jinsa, and the possibility that he will be succeeded by someone who doesn't share Jinsa's views."

"Yim Jinsa was a great man, devoted to the Emperor and to the Emperor before him."

"You knew him?"

"No. I've seen him many times at the temple, but I know of him only through the words of others in the temple."

"Well, there's a danger that he may be followed by one of the Warriors of the South. My mother is pressing strongly for the appointment of her nephew, Bin Shona."

"I can't believe that the Emperor would appoint someone who wouldn't continue Jinsa's policies."

"He won't if he perceives the truth. My mother and her relatives, including Bin, want to reverse all the progress that has been made in the last thirty years and return Chansu to the ignorant state it occupied before the coming of the Easterners."

"They wish to expel the Easterners?"

"Yes. But that's not what troubles me. I would expel the Easterners too if we had other means of obtaining their knowledge. I can't stand their classless ways. But we'll never free ourselves from their power, nor achieve our destiny, if we again hide ourselves from the rest of the world."

"My Prince, I think perhaps you worry more than necessary. I can't believe your father would ever permit this to happen. He has repeated so many times his dedication to the enlightenment of Chansu begun by your grandfather."

"Of course he won't permit it if he sees it. But he may be deceived. My mother is a very clever person."

"That may be. But your father is also. You underestimate him, perhaps."

Han jerked his hand away from Tama's and stood up suddenly. He raised his arm as if to strike her, then, catching her eyes in his, dropped it slowly. "Don't contradict me, Tama. You have no knowledge of these things. You have never even spoken with my father."

Tama remained on the floor and bowed her head slightly. "You are correct, my Prince. My knowledge comes only from rumor and supposition in the temple. I beg your forgiveness."

Han sat down again and lightly caressed Tama's hair and neck with his hand. "There's more to my concern than the replacement of Jinsa. For many years now my brother Changa has joined in the meetings my mother has held with her relatives to plot the reversal of the Emperor's policies. Changa claims that he doesn't subscribe to their extreme views, but he admits that he feels their position has merit. If Changa succeeds my father on the throne, there 's no question in my mind but that all is lost. And this," he said, looking directly into Tama's eyes, "I am certain my father does not realize."

"You must inform your father of these things."

"He won't see me. And if he sees me, he doesn't listen. Once I tried to tell him that Changa was coming under mother's influence. He just laughed and said Changa will grow out of it."

"Perhaps he is right."

"He's not!"

"Then you must devise a means of showing him the truth."

"I've spent my life trying to get my father's attention. You know this. We've talked about it many times."

"Perhaps you try too hard. Perhaps you can reach your father through one of his other ministers. There are many ways, my Prince. It may take years, but be patient. And ask the gods for guidance. They will see that Chansu's proper destiny is fulfilled."

"I think sometimes, Tama, that the gods have made me their instrument, so strongly do I feel this need to keep our homeland on the proper course."

"Then they will see that you succeed." Tama smiled at Han. After a moment his sullen expression lifted and he too smiled. She had worked her magic again.

"You've helped me again, Tama. Thank you. I have confidence now." He paused. "Yes, the gods will help me, because the course I follow is the one that will bring honor and glory to Chansu."

PART THREE

March 1948-July 1948

1

Report to the Information Ministry
Re: Chansu Political Situation
From: David Halburton
Date: March 19, 1948

    Our sources in the palace temple
report developments that should be given your
immediate attention.

    As you know, for a number of years
there has been considerable in-fighting regarding
the successor to the Emperor. Changa, the
Emperor's older son and presumptive heir, has
been strongly supported by the Empress and by the
conservative elements. Han, the other son, has
obtained the reluctant support of many of the

Emperor's present administrators and of the new
industrial interests.

You also are familiar with our
evaluations of these two men. Changa, though he
seeks to diminish UWG influence, is reasonable
and easy to work with. Han has often been
aggressive and hostile in his dealings with us;
we don't have a clear idea of his ultimate goals
as far as the UWG is concerned, but we doubt they
are in our long-run interests.

Two weeks ago we reported to you that
there were rumors that the Emperor was seriously
ill. We speculated then that, if the rumor was
true, we could expect the dispute over the
succession to come to a head. We also guessed at
that time that the Emperor would not take the
affirmative act necessary to alter the normal
succession to Changa.

We now have had it confirmed from our
temple informant that the Emperor is indeed ill.
He has suffered a stroke that, we understand, has
totally impaired his ability to communicate.
Although the Emperor is now obviously unable to
make any designation as to a successor, we are
informed that there is in existence a document,
purportedly signed by the Emperor several months
ago, which names Han as his heir. Changa and his
supporters will undoubtedly contest the document,
but they will have a difficult time of it, since
most people in the present administration tend to
favor Han.

If the Emperor doesn't recover
quickly, we expect that Han will move to take
over the government, and we expect that he will

be successful. We are unsure whether, if this
happens, there will he any immediate effect on
the UWG Mission in Shinso, but we strongly
suggest that all shipments of personnel and
equipment to Chansu be delayed until the outcome
of the present situation is clearer.

2

The early April rain that had already lasted two days pounded on the metal roof of the radio building that sat in the center of the UWG Compound at Shinso. The yellowish light from the building's windows weakly penetrated the blackness outside and revealed activity within that was unusual for the early hours of the morning. Inside, a young man, headphones over his ears, worked feverishly at the transmitter. An older man, thin, bespectacled and white-haired, paced nervously back and forth across the linoleum floor of the control room.

Outside, some hundred yards away at the main gate to the compound, there was also a flurry of activity. Eight men in dark red rain gear that glistened with wetness swarmed in front of the entrance. They showed some papers to the Chansu guard on duty. He abruptly stiffened, saluted, and opened the gate. The eight men rushed through. Four of them remained just inside the gate. The other four made directly for the radio building, where two of them banged loudly on the door while the other two watched at the windows.

The young man at the transmitter looked questioningly at the older man. The latter shrugged. "Turn it off," he said tiredly. "We've done all we can." He moved to the door. "I'll let them in."

3

Tom Short, the Assistant Director of the New Markwell Communications Center, yawned and stretched, then went about his usual morning chores of turning on office lights and starting the coffee brewing. As he passed by the radio room he noticed Rogers, the night operator, bent over the short wave equipment. It was seldom that there was any long-distance radio communication going on at this hour of the morning. It was still night in the islands of the Western Ocean, and messages from the east now usually came in over the cables. Short opened the door to the soundproofed room. Rogers looked up briefly, then motioned Short to be quiet. Short sat down, curious.

After a few more minutes of manipulating the equipment, Rogers finally sat back and pulled off his earphones.

"They must've stopped," Rogers said. He looked at Short. "You won't believe it."

"Won't believe what?"

"Here, read this." He tore off a page of handwriting from a tablet and handed it to Short. "It came in from the Chansu mission about twenty minutes ago and then cut off." He stood up. "I've got to set up an emergency phone call to Preston. They're going to want to know right away. Bring it on in as soon as you finish."

Short took the paper. As he quickly read the brief message, his eyes and mouth opened wide in astonishment.

4

 The day had not started out badly, Strongarm reflected, as he sat in his office, digesting the disagreeable lunch he had just eaten in the government cafeteria. He had awakened early, after a good night's sleep. As usual, he jogged for a mile along the path that wound through his apartment building complex on the outskirts of Preston, the UWG's capital city. He took a cold shower and dressed, then woke Barbara. They ate their usual silent breakfast together, he scanning the morning newspapers. He was mildly disappointed at not finding anything in them about his proposal, but there was no real reason the morning papers should mention it.

 After breakfast, the motor pool car picked him up promptly at seven and took him to his office. He had been there almost an hour, working on his statement, when the unpleasantness began with the first, and worst, of the phone calls.

 "Mr. Strongarm," the unfamiliar voice on the other end said. "I'm Lieutenant Wilson at the 18th District Police Headquarters. I'm sorry to bother you, sir."

 "What can I do for you, Lieutenant?" Strongarm prided himself on being accessible to people, but why had his secretary put this call through, especially on this day, of all days?

 "I'm afraid we've got your son here, Mr. Strongarm. Your son, Paul."

 I have only one, thankfully, thought Strongarm. "Why is he there?" he asked cautiously, expecting the worst.

 "He was apprehended along with two other young men several hours ago, Mr. Strongarm. The arresting officer claims they were stealing radios from an appliance store stock room, and the owner of the store confirms it. We haven't talked to any of the young men, of course, except to get their names. You know the regulations."

Oh no! thought Strongarm. Not now! Not today!

"Has my son called a lawyer?" he managed to ask.

"No, Mr. Strongarm, he refuses to call anyone. That's why I telephoned you. It's probably not exactly proper for me to do this, but I thought someone ought to know who could help your son. I assume you won't try to use my calling as a technicality to get him off. I don't think you would be successful."

"Of course not. And I appreciate your calling. Tell me," he asked casually, "has the arrest been recorded on the public records yet?"

"No. We're required to wait eight hours."

It would be out in time to make the evening papers, Strongarm thought. He cursed silently. "What's the treatment if he's convicted?"

"The charge is theft of personal property without violence. The treatment for that is one to three years of therapy, depending upon response. There probably won't be any restraint imposed if it's a first offense—we're checking on that--and if he behaves himself. He will have to be put on limited surveillance."

"It is a first offense, Lieutenant." Though hardly unexpected, Strongarm thought to himself.

"Yes, Mr. Strongarm." He would, of course, look it up anyway, and Strongarm expected him to.

"I appreciate your calling, Lieutenant. I'll get a lawyer for Paul right away."

"Will you be coming down to see him yourself?"

"I will if I can get away. Today is a pretty busy day for me. If I can't, I'll see if I can get his mother over there. Thanks again for letting me know." He hung up.

Why, Strongarm asked himself again, did the boy have to do this today, the day Strongarm had been working toward for most of his life, the day of his first major proposal as a member of the Prime Council? It was almost as if the boy was doing it on purpose. But why? They should have asked Paul to submit himself for voluntary therapy two years ago, after the alcohol episode. Well, Strongarm sighed, they couldn't claim to be surprised. He called his lawyer and sent him to see Paul. Then he called Barbara at work and asked her to go too. He promised to send a motor pool car around for her, if one was available. Then he tried to blot the matter out of his mind and turned to the important business of the day.

That had been the first thing in the morning. Afterward, until about ten, Strongarm had been able to do some more work on his press statement. But then the other calls started.

The first came from Tom Hillflower. Then it was Warren Earlyspring, Strongarm's doctor. Then came half a dozen more, until Strongarm was forced to have all of his further calls held. He hated to admit it to himself, but he didn't stand up very well under repeated criticism, especially when it was from his fellow Nauryans.

The conversation with Hillflower had set the pattern for the rest. It had started off with the normal pleasantries, but Hillflower had quickly turned to the subject of his concern.

"Bob," Hillflower said, "word has it that you're going to introduce some proposal today about the equalization policy."

"You know very well I am, Tom. The initial hearing is scheduled for this afternoon."

"Bob, I wish you and I had had time to sit down and talk about this thing. It's got a lot of our friends very concerned."

"I realize that. But I don't think you could have changed my mind. This is something I've been in favor of for most of my life."

"Bob, if they eliminate the equalization policy, a lot of people are going to have to readjust their whole lives. It's going to produce a lot of disillusionment and anger."

"I know that, Tom. But I'm convinced it's the right thing. We don't need a crutch anymore. Our whole problem is that we think we do. Believe me, this thing makes us second-class citizens. Only by getting rid of the equalization policy are we ever really going to make ourselves equal."

"That's all very idealistic, Bob, but it's not very practical."

"I'm doing what I think is right. Why don't you give it a chance."

"What am I going to tell my son? He's got his heart set on medical school."

"All I can say, Tom, is that if he can't make the medical school without the equalization bonus, he ought to be setting his heart on something else."

That essentially ended the conversation. After a few brusque final words, Hillflower hung up. But the ones that followed carried on the attack, with similar results.

The calls made Strongarm feel very much alone, as if every other member of his race had turned against him. He had tried to reason patiently, but they wouldn't understand. Non-Nauryans understood, many of them, but very few of his fellow Nauryans. Sometimes their thick-headedness enraged him. It was infuriating to dedicate all one's energies to helping his brother, only to have that help maliciously spurned.

Strongarm didn't really know that it was the lunch that had brought the leaden weight and irritation to his stomach. He liked to complain about the food at the government cafeteria, as did everyone else, but even he suspected that it was as much the anger and the criticism that caused his discomfort. He pulled out his silver-cased watch, worn from so many years of use but still functioning. It reminded him of his long-dead parents who had given it to him and the law school at Brockton, where he had first used it, and of his own experience with the Nauryan equalization policy; but he quickly put these thoughts aside. It was now past one-thirty. The Prime Council meeting was less than half an hour away.

A freshly-typed draft of Strongarm's proposed press

statement lay in front of him on his desk. He picked it up and read it again:

Today, April 4, 1948, the Prime Council voted, ___ to ___, to consider the repeal of all Nauryan Equalization laws. Formal hearings will be scheduled later this week. The Council's vote was made over the determined opposition of a number of Nauryan leaders. The proposal was, however, brought before the Council by Robert Strongarm of Agronica, a Nauryan himself. Strongarm is the newest Council member, having been elected to the post by Congress in mid-1947. Shortly after the Council vote, Strongarm issued the following statement regarding the Council's action:

"The Council's recommendation today marks a great step forward in the history of the UWG and in the history of the Nauryan race. I sincerely hope that Nauryans and non-Nauryans alike will support it and urge the Council to formally recommend its approval to the Congress.

"I realize that many of my Nauryan brothers have opposed this step, and their opposition is understandable. It is not easy to give up advantages and subsidies that we have had for many years. But those advantages were never intended to be permanent. The founders of our government adopted the Equalization Policy only to compensate Nauryans for the educational and cultural deprivations of life outside the mainstream of civilization. That justification no longer exists. In the last 150 years we Nauryans, with the help of the UWG, have overcome the handicaps of our distant past. Continuance of the

```
Equalization Policy now can be justified, except
with respect to new arrivals from the native
territories, only on the theory of a permanent
disability. If the policy continues, it becomes an
official declaration of Nauryan inferiority. Such a
declaration is untrue and obnoxious and must be
rejected by us all, Nauryans and non-Nauryans
alike."
```

Not nearly persuasive enough, Strongarm said to himself. Too statesmanlike. He wished he had more time to work on it, but if he made any more changes his secretary could never get it retyped before the Council meeting. He started to think about how this press statement would look in the newspaper underneath (he was sure it would be underneath, if not relegated to a later page) the story of Paul's arrest. But he forcibly put the matter out of his mind. He could do nothing about it now.

     Strongarm again reviewed the prospects that the Council would vote consideration of the proposal. Henry Smith, of Agronica, would undoubtedly support the measure. His indecisiveness wouldn't let him do it until he had listened to interminable evidence offered against the proposal, but he would go along.

     With Smith and Strongarm himself supporting consideration, only one other Council vote was necessary to obtain a majority. Rolf Cornettia, the Council Minister from Doltony, appeared to be leaning in favor of the recommendation, though for the wrong reasons. That rough, irascible, and uneducated man undoubtedly had in mind the effect of the measure on the non-Nauryans, who would clearly be benefited in job competition by the measure. The number of Nauryans in Doltony these days had shrunk far below that of the other Regions of the UWG. Cornettia was not without appreciation for the original merit of the Equalization Policy, but he would be eager to accept the argument that the policy was no longer justified.

     Mildred Carter, the senior member and Chairman of

the Prime Council, from Agronica, would likely oppose consideration. She had been on the Council much longer than any of the other members, and she tended to assume that past policies and programs of the government possessed merit in direct proportion to their age. She would be a difficult person to budge.

The remaining Council member was an enigma. This was Mindra Parthupta of Brahmastan. Although a woman of brilliance and insight, Parthupta often seemed indifferent to Council action on many issues. She had not yet expressed any interest in the Equalization question. Strongarm tentatively classified her as favoring consideration, but only because he believed that she, more than any other Council member, had the incisive mind to appreciate the rightness of the measure which he felt so deeply.

On the whole, Strongarm reflected, prospects were quite favorable. When he added the influence he had with respect to this measure as a Nauryan himself, success appeared extremely likely. His stomach began to feel a little better.

Strongarm checked his watch again. Ten minutes to two. He got up slowly and put on his suit coat. He placed the press statement in his briefcase, and closed it, then left his office, turning off the lights as he went out the door. He nodded to his secretary as he passed her desk and went down the stairs and outside. It was quite cold for April and he walked briskly across the courtyard and through another door, then down a corridor to the large public Council Room. Strongarm no longer noticed the ornate carving and wood paneling that made this room look so different from most government meeting halls, and from Council members' own offices. He did notice that five or six reporters had already assembled in the press booth at the back of the room. This pleased him, and he smiled at them. Recent Council meetings had seldom drawn more than three reporters. He took his seat at the Council table, the first member to arrive.

Henry Smith came in a minute later and took his place across from Strongarm. They nodded at each other but didn't speak. The other Council members arrived soon afterward, except for Mildred

Carter. She still had not arrived at ten minutes after two. Strongarm grew very impatient.

"Where is Mildred?" he asked, with a trace of annoyance in his voice.

"She was on the telephone when I stopped by to get her," said Mindra Parthupta.

They waited, Strongarm sitting silently, the others talking quietly among themselves.

At two-twenty Carter hurried into the Council Room. She glanced uneasily at the Reporters in the press booth. Strongarm could tell from her expression that she was upset.

"I'm sorry to be late," she said, "but a matter of some urgency has arisen. Our scheduled meeting must be canceled. I'd like to invite all the Council members for an informal chat in my office."

The Council members looked questioningly at each other. A reporter burst out of the press booth. "You can't do this, Madame Chairman," he said. "You've scheduled a meeting on the Equalization Policy. If you have business to discuss, you must do it here. The Information Act requires it."

Carter looked contemptuously at the reporter. "The matter I'm referring to isn't on the agenda. When we're ready to deliberate policy, we'll call a meeting on it. You'll be informed of the matter as soon as the Council members know about it. That much I'm certain we're entitled to do."

The members collected their papers and filed out of the Council Room and down the hall toward Carter's office. Strongarm felt greatly relieved at having the equalization policy discussion postponed. Any other day would have to be better than this one, though he dreaded the prospect of facing further entreaties from his Nauryan brothers before the next meeting. He also wondered what could be important enough to postpone the best-covered Council meeting in months.

When they had at last all crowded into Mildred Carter's office, she closed the door and spoke quietly. "I've got some serious news from the Information Ministry. Just before noon, our time, the Communications Center in New Markwell received an urgent message from the Chansu mission. The Mission Director, a fellow named Halburton, suspected something was afoot and requested immediate evacuation. I was about to call you in when another message came. I'm afraid it's too late for evacuation now."

"What do you mean?" Smith asked.

"The second message isn't from the mission at all. It's from the Emperor of Chansu." She paused. "I'm afraid that the entire Chansu mission has been captured by the Chansu army and is being held for ransom."

The other Council members sat in shocked silence for a moment after hearing Chairman Carter's news.

"Were there . . . were there any casualties?" finally asked Henry Smith.

"Not that we have been told of," Carter answered.

"What are the demands?" asked Rolf Cornettia, the Council member from Doltony.

"Basically they are asking that we agree to supply them with certain raw materials that are in limited supply in Chansu. Rubber and copper, for example. They give a long list of reasons why we should do it, but mainly they claim that it's only fair that all people in the world share its wealth. I'm having copies of the communication made for us."

Strongarm spoke for the first time. "Let's not be too hasty to judge these people until we've reviewed the communication, Mildred. Their statement, as you relate it, doesn't sound so unreasonable."

"To me, their actions speak more clearly than their words," interjected Cornettia.

Just then Carter's secretary came into the room, carrying some papers.

"Oh, good," Carter said. "Here are your copies. I think the best thing to do is for us to read these over before we discuss the matter further."

"Shouldn't we say something to the press?" Henry Smith asked.

"We'll have an announcement for them later in the day. But I think we should have some consensus as to how we're going to deal with this before we give it to the press, don't you?"

The others agreed, then began studying their copies of the Chansu message. The message wasn't long--less than two pages of double spaced typing--and it wasn't, thought Strongarm, a very clear proposal. In a few minutes the Council members were ready to resume. None wanted to delay the discussion any longer than necessary.

"This will be a preliminary discussion of policy alternatives," said Carter. "We will not of course debate the selection of policy until our public meeting." The other Council members ignored this ritual, and inaccurate, statement which Carter used to open all their private meetings.

"Let me begin," continued Carter, "by suggesting the alternatives I see. First of all, we can meet the demand, or at least part of it, sign the agreements, and hope that the Chansu release the hostages. Whether we continue to observe the agreements after their release is another question, but of course by then we will already have delivered a considerable amount of material.

"Second, we can simply ignore the request and hope that the Chansu will have the decency to let the hostages live.

"Third, we can attempt some sort of military action in order to obtain the release of the hostages.

"I'd be pleased if the Council would suggest some further possibilities."

Henry Smith spoke first. He was a relatively short, slender man in his late fifties, with graying temples and a round, friendly face. "I suppose we could try to talk them out of it." He paused a moment, reflecting. "I don't suppose that's much use, though, considering the difficulties in communicating with them. I guess we shouldn't take a chance on sending negotiators over there who can't deliver anything."

Mindra Parthupta spoke next, in her typical brusque manner that many others found irritating. Though only in her forties, Parthupta had the face and behavior of a shrewish old woman. That her Brahmastan colleagues were so devoted to her continually amazed the other members of the Council, though they readily granted the acuity of intellect. "There are only two alternatives," she said. "Either we capitulate or we fight. Very simple problem. Hard choice. To me the decision is clear. To you, I don't know."

"May I ask something, Mildred?" interrupted Cornettia, ignoring the question invited by Parthupta, who now sat back in her chair with an expression that demonstrated she had overcome the problem and would now watch the others struggle with it. "You say military action," continued Cornettia, a hulk of a man with a large, slack mouth and a jowly face. "We're not in much of a position for that. We haven't fielded an army in over a hundred years."

"We've got a police force," ventured Smith. "I suppose that's no answer, though. They aren't trained in weapons. But why can't we raise an army"'

"Just who is going to fight?" asked Strongarm, showing a little impatience at listening to Smith's half-formed thoughts. "Would you go? Would your sons?" he demanded of Smith.

"Well, there's the possibility of conscription," said Smith. "But I suppose--"

"I will never support conscription," Strongarm declared. "That's a solution that's worse than the problem."

"Gentlemen. Gentlemen," interrupted Carter, raising. one of her thin, bony hands and casting a disapproving, schoolmistress glance at the men. "There are military means that don't involve armies. We have aircraft. We have ships. We can build bombs and cannon. The question now is whether we use military means at all. Let's look at the situation from a broad perspective before we get into the details."

"Well," said Strongarm, "let me just say this. Although

I can't agree with their methods, the Chansu do not make an altogether unreasonable request. Why shouldn't we share our wealth with them? It's the only answer consistent with our basic principles. It's the UWG way. As for the Chansu tactics, we must remember that they haven't had the benefit of our enlightened civilization for very long. Perhaps a sincere effort by us to share with them will help to teach them our ways."

"I'll go along with that," said Smith. "That makes sense."

"I have some serious reservations," said Cornettia. "The history of the Chansu shows they are a people without respect for the most basic human rights. We can't treat them as if they were like us. They're trying to blackmail us into giving up our hard-earned property. I think we ought to consider first what we might accomplish in the way of military action."

"Will you let their supposed lack of humanity deprive you of yours?" Strongarm asked. "They are people. They live and breathe and bear children, just as we do. They deserve the same treatment we accord to our own. I'm not agreeing with their methods, but we should ignore their methods if their requests are reasonable. I say they are."

"Let's think of the hostages," added Smith. "Military action is sure to endanger them."

"Not necessarily," said Cornettia. "They'll want to keep the hostages to bargain with."

"I think the question is, will meeting their demands really solve anything?" Carter said. "They may not release the hostages. And even if they do, we don't want to encourage them to pull the same trick again."

"Mildred, if there's any chance that meeting the demands will get us through this, we've got to try it," Strongarm said. "What they ask isn't unreasonable. Using force isn't the way we solve things. How do we ever expect to convert the Chansu to our principles if we don't keep them ourselves?"

Carter shrugged. "What you say is very logical, Bob, but my instincts say it's wrong. Still, I suppose we can try to do it their way, as long as we're prepared for something else if it doesn't work. What do you think, Rolf?"

"It won't work. But I suppose we've got to try it, as long as Bob is so insistent. How will it look in our public session if we vote against him?" He looked at Strongarm distastefully. "You've got us over a barrel."

"Yes, we've got to think of appearances," Carter sighed. "Shall we announce a unanimous recommendation to attempt to meet the demands?" She looked around at the other Council members. No one dissented. "All right. But I'm going to initiate an evaluation of our military options, too."

"You're not going to announce that, are you, Mildred?" Cornettia asked.

"Of course not." She smiled. "That's just for advisory purposes, not policy making. I certainly hope we are unanimous on that, too."

The Council members mumbled their assent as they began to gather their papers together, getting ready for the walk down to the Council room and their confrontation with the waiting press.

5

Some five hundred miles east of the UWG capital city of Preston, where the Prime Council and the Congress sit to chart the government's course, lies the city of Stevensburg. Unlike most cities its size in Eastern Agronica, Stevensburg has no old District surviving from pre-revolutionary times. Stevensburg existed before the revolution, but only as a small logging village, none of which has survived. Its growth came as a direct result of the revolution, for it was in Stevensburg that the Third Representative Congress of the new United World Government decided, in 1810, to locate the fledgling housing industry that would eventually provide the shelter for the entire population of the UWG.

The Third Congress built the first factory in Stevensburg because of the extensive timberland nearby, and because Stevensburg was not too remote from the population centers of eastern Agronica. In 1948, of course, timber was no longer as significant in the construction of housing, and the population centers were dispersed throughout the entire Region. Nevertheless, the housing industry was still centered in Stevensburg, in the presence of the giant Consolidated Housing Company.

Dorothy Harper was among the thousand or so architectural engineers employed by Consolidated Housing in Stevensburg. Her husband, Fred, worked as a project engineer at the new Research and Development Lab of the Agronica Electric Company just outside the city. They both performed their jobs well, but they cared little about their companies or company administration. They never bothered to vote their company stock. They would have liked to earn a little more money, but the scheduled 5% pay increase was not sufficient motivation for them to apply for advancement from their present positions. After five years of marriage they still enjoyed spending their time alone with each other and had thus far decided against having children.

On this particular early April day Dorothy waited in their apartment for Fred to return from doing the laundry, so they could have dinner together. They alternated weeks in doing the household chores; this week Dorothy was doing the meals and Fred was doing the cleaning and the laundry. While she waited, Dorothy surveyed the living-dining room that she had been trying for five years now, without success, to make look a little bit nicer than the thousands of identical rooms in the hundreds of other buildings in their apartment complex.

Somehow, they had never been able to save enough to buy the kind of curtains she liked. Not that the curtains would have been enough, anyway. Professionally, of course, she understood the impossibility of providing adequate and equal and reasonably-priced housing for 450 million people without standardization. But if only she could do something to make *her* apartment express a bit of individuality.

The door opened and Fred walked into the room, a large basket of clean laundry under his arm. He set it on the floor. "I'm glad that's done," he said. "When do we eat?"

"Half an hour," said Dorothy, as she stepped into the kitchen and slipped the frozen meals into the oven.

"You mean you're just starting dinner? Why didn't you put it in before I got back?"

"Because I didn't know how long you'd be," Dorothy answered, coming back into the living area. The laundry can be crowded this time of day."

"True, " Fred replied absently, avoiding a confrontation. "True." He sat down on the sofa and picked up the newspaper.

Dorothy stated at him for a moment. "Fred," she finally said, "we've got to do something about this apartment. It's beginning to depress me."

"What do you have in mind?" Fred asked, his nose still in the newspaper.

"For one thing, I'd love to get those curtains I've told you about. It wouldn't take long to save enough if we really tried."

Fred put the paper down. "You can save for them out of your income. I'm already saving for something."

"For what?"

"I've told you. A set of tools."

"Tools? You've never said anything about that. What do you want tools for?"

"I want to do some woodworking. I need something new to occupy my time away from the job. Especially when you go on weekend shift this summer."

"Why didn't you tell me?"

"I'm sure I did," Fred said, his voice raised a notch. "Remember a month or so ago when we were making plans for the summer?"

"But we were talking about things we were going to do together."

"I've been hoping you would take it up, too. "

"I've got to check the dinner," Dorothy said, stalking away into the kitchen. They both knew it wouldn't be ready for another twenty minutes.

Fred followed her. "Look," he said, "maybe what's bothering you about the apartment is the same thing that's bothering me. We just can't afford to do the things we want to do."

"Our incomes are the same as those of 450 million other people. What makes us so different?" Dorothy answered icily.

"Well, maybe it's the way we spend it. We thought we had to have that radio we bought last year. Now we hardly ever listen to it. We could just as easily still use the one in the common room. Besides," he went on, "our incomes aren't at the maximum."

"Do you think we ought to take the exams for a higher position?"

Fred shrugged. "It might be easier to make it. The newspaper says the Prime Council might reconsider the Equalization Policy."

"How many Nauryans do you expect to be competing in the next Supervisor Exam? And anyway, do you really want to go back to the Institute to prepare for it?"

"What have we got to lose? If we don't pass, we haven't given up anything."

"But Fred," Dorothy replied, this time in exasperation, "what have we got to gain? Even if both of us made Department Supervisor, we'd only have fifty dollars more a month, and a good part of that would go to taxes. Do you know how much those curtains cost? To say nothing of your tools." She paused. "Anyway, I don't want to be a supervisor. The job's bad enough as it is. That would just give me more to worry about."

"It's a good thing everyone doesn't feel that way. Who would run things?"

"But everyone does feel that way. At least at Consolidated. Maybe the dedicated scientists at your place are different."

"Now, Dorothy, *everyone* couldn't feel the way you do about your work, or no one would apply to move up."

"Well, I'm talking about people our age. Anyway, if you're so interested in your work, you go ahead and take the Supervisor exam."

Fred didn't say anything for a moment. Then he smiled sheepishly. "You're right, of course. What's the matter with us? My parents lived for their work. Yours, too. But work just seems to get in the way of our lives."

"We could go on subsistence grants."

"Then we would have even less money than we do now."

Dorothy watched Fred. He was a reasonable, sincere man. She moved next to him. Fred put his arm around her.

"Fred, I'm sorry I got angry with you before."

"It was my fault."

"No. It was nobody's fault. I mean, we both need something, but it's not curtains or tools. Or more money. Those are just distractions."

"You think we need a change in our lives? Children?"

"No!"

"Moving?"

"Maybe. Though I hate the idea of looking for another job."

"Well, let's think about it for a while. I'm ready to go somewhere else." He paused. "But I still want those tools."

Dorothy smiled. "And I want my curtains."

They talked about where they would like to move until dinner was ready. Dorothy served the plates, and they sat close to each other at the small dining table as they ate the tasteless fare. Halfway through the meals Fred got up and turned on the radio. They listened to music until they were almost finished eating, when the programming was interrupted for a special announcement about the day's Prime Council meeting. Fred snapped the radio off when the music stopped.

6

It was early spring in the 48th year of the Torgoona Empire. Lyn Wonan squatted on the ground in front of his wooden house, near the village of Betsu, some four hundred miles southwest of Shinso. He poked at the cooking fire with a stick, trying to extinguish it. His legs and back ached from his day in the fields, but he didn't mind. In another week his muscles would have re-accustomed themselves to the work, and he would enjoy it, as he always had. It pleased him to throw all his energies into a task that was for the good of Chansu.

Lyn's father and older brothers had left immediately after the evening meal for the village directive meeting. All males over the age of 20 in each of the villages of the Danksat Land Company were required to attend such a meeting each month, to be informed of the work schedule for the following thirty days. Next year Lyn would be old enough to accompany them. Lyn's mother and aunts, his brothers' wives, their children, and his younger unmarried sister were just now eating their evening meal in the kitchen, having finished their work of serving the men.

As Lyn completed his task he heard agitated voices in

the distance, coming from the village road. He listened carefully, his heart beating rapidly in the still night. With the others gone, he alone was charged with the defense of his home. He imagined an attack by wandering bandits, such as he had been told roamed this country many years ago. How to repulse them, he thought quickly. By deception or by bold attack? Then he recognized in the loudest and angriest voice the tones of his next-eldest brother, Janyan. The directive meeting must have finished early. Lyn walked around the house to the road to greet his father and brothers. He stood in the shaft of light cast by the bare electric bulb inside.

When his father and brothers saw Lyn, they grew silent. They walked on slowly toward him and came to a halt in front of Lyn and the house. They were looking at him, Lyn knew, but he could not clearly see the expressions on their faces. He was puzzled by their odd behavior. Then Lyn's father, Longlun, motioned them inside the house but beckoned Lyn to stay. Janyan hesitated for a moment, then joined his brothers. Lyn and his father stood alone.

"You have something to say to me, father?" Lyn asked.

"I do, but it's difficult."

Lyn's mouth felt suddenly dry. What had he done? "Is it something you learned at the directive meeting?"

"Yes, it is."

"But I've been fulfilling my quota."

"This has nothing to do with your work, Lyn." Longlun looked at the ground.

"Then what?"

Longlun put his arm around his son's shoulders. "You have heard, Lyn, that the people from across the ocean have threatened to bring Chansu under their rule."

"I've heard that in the broadcasts in the village."

"We learned tonight that the danger has increased. The Emperor fears that the people from the east may attempt to invade Chansu. It's important that we be ready to beat them back."

"But what does this have to do with us, father? We're

Workers, not Warriors."

"We were told that the eastern people have great forces. All men are required to serve in their armies. Because their numbers are so great, the Emperor has decided that we must borrow their method and that the Worker classes will supply men to aid the Warriors."

Both men were quiet for a minute. Lyn waited expectantly.

"Each village has been asked to supply so many men, and accordingly each family," Longlun continued. He paused. "We have decided that you and Janyan must go from our family."

Lyn felt a surge inside him. To leave his home, his village, his family--the place where his ancestors had lived for generations--this was a frightening, wrenching thought. Yet at the same time he could not help remembering the daydreams that filled his mind when he was younger during a long day in the fields. Dreams of the glory of being born a Warrior, of living by the Warriors' code, of fighting for the glory of the Emperor--a world he had thought forever denied to a young man of the Worker class.

"I hope," Lyn's father was saying, "that you will take this better than your brother. He thinks only his own selfish thoughts. He doesn't see that this is a much greater destiny for which he has been chosen."

"I understand, father."

"I know you do, son. And I know also that you see why you and Janyan were chosen. Your older brothers have children to care for."

"It is for the good of Chansu."

"Yes, for the good of Chansu. Come, let's go inside."

7

Shortly after dawn two days later a truck, painted the dark red color of the Chansu Defense Force, pulled into the village of Betsu, slipping and sliding along the muddy wagon trail. A small crowd, mostly women and children, gathered to watch as the first contingent of young men selected by the village was lined up and briefly interrogated by the two officers who had come with the truck. The children were excited. Trucks were still rare in this remote village, and so were members of the Warrior class, except during the occasional inspection visits. The women, however, wrung their hands and dabbed at their eyes with homespun kerchiefs as they watched their sons and husbands prepare to leave the village, perhaps never to return. For many, like Lyn Wonan's mother, this was only the first farewell. The truck would return in a few days to carry off still other sons and husbands.

Lyn Wonan stood in the line next to the truck as straight and as still as he could. He hoped to impress the officers with a soldierly bearing. In his hand he held the hardcakes, wrapped in a piece of cloth, that his mother had insisted he take with him lest there be no food on the trip. He watched out of the corner of his eye as one of the officers moved along the line questioning the men. Finally the officer came to him.

"Name?" the officer asked curtly.

"Lyn Wonan, sir."

The officer glanced up from his clipboard at the "sir."

"Your age?"

"Nineteen."

"You are a field worker?"

"Yes, sir."

"Do you read and write?"

"No, sir."

The officer made some notes on a paper he had with him. Then he looked at Lyn Wonan's package. "What do you have there?"

"Hardcakes, sir. My mother--"

"The Chansu Defense Army feeds its soldiers precisely what they require," interrupted the officer. He took the package from Lyn and placed it on the ground. Lyn wished he could return the cloth and the cakes to his family, since they could use them, but he said nothing.

When all the men had been questioned, the officers marched them to the back of the truck, and they climbed in. It was crowded inside and hot under the canvas top. After a minute the truck lurched and pulled away. Lyn Wonan felt a pang of sorrow as he glimpsed his mother standing in the crowd, waving at the truck as it left. But he also looked forward to the adventure that lay ahead. For so many years, since long before the Empire, the people who had been born in this village had almost without exception lived and died here. Now all was changing. For the past five years the young women of the village had been assigned to work for half of each year in the mills and factories at Nongoto, and some had decided to stay on at Nongoto permanently. Now many of the young men of the village, mere Workers, were being asked to leave the village to become soldiers and to fight along with the Warriors to defend Chansu, and Lyn somehow knew that many of them, including himself, would not be returning to the village, at least not to resume the ways of their fathers. It was an exciting time, thought Lyn, and he wondered to himself how life in this land would be once all these changes had produced their full effect.

The truck carrying the men from Lyn Wonan's village moved slowly eastward along the wagon roads. Several times the men were called out of the truck by the officers as it negotiated light wooden bridges. On other occasions they had to push the truck where it became stuck in the mud. Late in the afternoon they reached a medium-sized city, filled with many metal-roofed houses as well as with houses like those in Wonan's village. And in the center of the city, Lyn saw larger buildings than he had never encountered before. Not long afterward the truck stopped at a railroad line. The officers passed out a ration of bread to the men to eat while they waited for the train. Shortly before sunset it arrived, making what seemed to Lyn a terrific noise and puffing out large clouds of white smoke. Lyn had never seen a railroad before, and he was fascinated. The men climbed into large, bare boxcars, where they slept as best they could as the train rumbled northward through the night. Sometime around dawn it stopped, but the men stayed in the cramped cars until the sun was well up in the sky.

Lyn's second day away from home was taken up by more interrogation, a superficial physical examination, a pledge of loyalty to the Emperor, calisthenics, two meals of bread and a thin soup, and interminable waiting. That evening, well after sunset, Lyn found himself standing in front of a small dark red tent that had been assigned to him. The tent was one of thousands just like it stretching across a huge muddy field. The field was surrounded by a high fence that separated it from the Warrior class barracks and other camp buildings. Spaced regularly throughout the field of tents were small unpainted wooden buildings containing the latrines and washing facilities which the Worker class soldiers who occupied the tents stood in long lines to use.

Lyn, like the thousand-odd other recruits arriving that day, had been given a newsprint pamphlet and been told to spend the evening in his tent studying it. He had not had a chance to look at it yet but hoped that there would be pictures from which he could decipher its meaning. Now, standing finally in front of the tent, Lyn welcomed the sanctuary it offered. He bent over, lifted the flap, and moved inside. In the dim light Lyn half-felt, half-saw his way to a thin mat lying atop the damp canvas floor. He collapsed onto the mat and uttered a sigh.

"Rough day, Worker?"' came a voice close beside him. Lyn, startled, sat up. "Don't tell me you expected to have this enormous tent all to yourself."

Lyn looked at the source of the voice. All he could make out was the shape of another man lying on a mat next to the one Lyn occupied. Lyn was shocked at the tone of disrespect implicit in the man's words.

"Let's take a look at each other," the man said, moving to the end of the tent opposite the flap. A spark flickered, and then a lamp glowed, casting its light on a thin, weary face that looked to Lyn to be only a few years older than his own.

"Take a good look now," the other said. "We've got a pint of oil for this lamp to last a month. I figure that's about fifteen minutes a day. What's your name, Worker?"

"I'm Lyn Wonan."

"My name is Ryl Kolu. I've been here about two weeks. Did you just arrive?"

"Yes," said Lyn.

"They must have assigned you to our Group to replace the fellow who used to live here."

"I am in Group Crocodile-D. Is that your group?"

"Yes, it is. Amphibious training, but you don't know that yet. It's not going to be much fun."

"I don't think I've been brought here for fun."

"Well, remember this, Lyn Wonan, you do as the officers say, no matter how wrong or difficult it seems to you. Walti--he's the one who lived here with me before you--thought he knew better. They knocked him senseless. He may even be dead now."

"The officers are of the Warrior class," responded Lyn. "We Workers can't be soldiers unless they instruct us."

"You may just make it, Lyn Wonan," said Kolu, smiling. He had the kind of taut face that a smile couldn't change much, but his small mouth opened slightly and showed clenched, crooked teeth. "Now that we've seen each other, let's turn out this lamp."

"Wait, how am I to study this paper?" Lyn asked.

"They don't actually expect you to understand that. I think they pass it out to make recruits worry. They'll show it all to you eventually. Do you read, by the way?"

"No," Lyn answered. "Do you?" he asked hopefully.

"Some. But I'm not going to bother reading that for you." Kolu reached over and put out the lamp.

The two men lay back on their mats, silent for a few minutes.

"Where are you from, Lyn Wonan?" Kolu finally asked.

"A small village. Betsu. It's somewhere south. I don't know exactly where we are now."

"This camp is perhaps fifty miles from Shinso."

"Oh," said Lyn. He wasn't even too sure of the location of Chansu's capital city, except that it was many miles to the north and east of his village. After another wait; he asked, "Where do you come from, Ryl Kolu?"

"My home is also a small village, but not so far away. It's a three days' walk to the southeast. I know that, for I walked here."

"Were you also chosen by your village to meet the requirement?"

"No. I'm fortunate to have many brothers. Two of them were sent when the Emperor made his levy on our village. But that was during the winter."

"Then why are you here?"

"This spring they brought the machines into our village. They do the field work of many men. Because of them, there was no work for my family, and the inspectors arranged for us all to go to work in the factories at the city of Yenchi. But one of my sisters had been there and she told me how the unmarried men live. They aren't permitted to stay with their families. It's much worse than this tent, believe me. So I asked to join the Defense Force and they sent me here."

"I would have made the same choice. This is a great adventure and a great opportunity for us."

Kolu laughed. "I hope you're joking."

"I don't understand."

Kolu was silent for a moment in the dark tent. "You're not joking. Well, you'll understand soon enough. Believe me, I didn't come here because I wanted this. But the alternative was worse."

"Oh." Again Lyn felt ignorant. This other fellow couldn't be as disrespectful and impertinent as he seemed. Lyn must have missed something. They didn't speak for a long while. At last Lyn heard the sound of his tentmate turning over and yawning.

"Well, Lyn Wonan," Kolu said, "you'd best get to sleep. You may think you're accustomed to rising early for work in the fields, but Workers' hours would be a luxury here. We don't wait for sunrise to get started."

"All right. Thank you." Lyn too turned on his side, but the strangeness of his surroundings, so far from his familiar village; kept him awake for a long time.

8

The next morning, after pre-dawn lectures, exercises and breakfast, the training groups assembled just inside the gates of the campground. The Crocodile-D unit, composed of about fifty Workers, all of roughly the same age as Wonan and Kolu, was led by a training officer named Lieutenant Hun Lunan. He marched his men to a truck that took them several miles away to a large empty field, covered mostly by damp earth and occasional patches of weeds.

"Workers," Lieutenant Lunan addressed them after they

climbed out of the truck and assembled in lines before him. "Today we concentrate on personal combat. This will be very important in our ultimate plans. It's not just a conditioning exercise, so please pay close attention."

The eyes of the Workers fixed on the Lieutenant. They were pleased to be seeing some actual combat tactics, thought Kolu. Two weeks of conditioning exercises was not the sort of thing they had expected. He wondered how Lyn Wonan would be able to handle the combat tactics without the conditioning.

"The art of hand-to-hand fighting is an ancient one among the Warriors of Chansu," said the Lieutenant. "Perhaps you have seen exhibitions in the large villages and cities. Do not expect to learn the art as practiced by Warriors. It takes a training and mental conditioning for which you are not fit. But you shall learn some of the fundamental moves and positions. They will be ample against the uninitiated."

Lunan paused and looked over the group. "I require an assistant to help me with the demonstration. There is among you a new member, whose name is Lyn Wonan. This will be an excellent way to introduce him to the unit. Would he please step forward?"

Lyn, who had taken a place at the end of the back line, stepped briskly around to the front of the group. He bowed before Lieutenant Lunan.

"We will first demonstrate the importance of proper balance," said the Lieutenant. "Please stand at ease," he told Lyn. "Now try to resist me. That is a command." He then moved toward Lyn, feinted as if to push him over backwards, and pulled him quickly forward. Lyn tumbled, face downward, onto the soft ground. He quickly scrambled to his feet.

"You see," said the Lieutenant, turning to the group, "Wonan here was prepared for a backward thrust and was totally off balance for the opposite motion. We shall demonstrate again. Worker Wonan," he said to Lyn, "I again order you to resist me." This time the Lieutenant faked both a backward and a forward thrust and then neatly flipped Lyn to the side. Lyn landed harder than before and rose more slowly.

"Please observe also," Lunan said to the group, "the way in which the thrusts are made. The motions are very precise and specific and require much practice. You will be shown the basic moves as soon as we conclude the work on the matter of balance."

The Lieutenant turned again to Lyn. "Now, Worker Wonan, you know what to look for. I order you to resist me again. Don't allow me to disturb your balance." He advanced again on Lyn, took Lyn's arm and made quick movements, right and left. Lyn dropped into a crouch, carefully watching every motion the Lieutenant made. Lyn moved his feet swiftly and grasped the Lieutenant to counter the thrusts. The men locked for a moment, then the Lieutenant called "Stop" and stepped back.

"Very good, Worker Wonan," the Lieutenant said, panting slightly. "You're a rapid learner. We'll try again." He jumped at Lyn this time, but Lyn quickly stepped aside, denying the Lieutenant's momentum. The men locked again, and beads of sweat popped out on their foreheads. Lunan released his hold slightly, moved backward, then quickly reversed his motion. But at the same moment Lyn himself reversed direction, stepped back, and tugged lightly on the Lieutenant's arm. Lunan, unable to stop himself, sprawled on the ground. He leaped up quickly, his face scowling, his eyes darting.

The Workers stood silently, surprise registering on their faces. How he wanted to laugh and cheer Lyn on, thought Kolu, but he well knew how dangerous that would be. He wondered if the others in the unit felt the same way he did. Lunan again moved toward Lyn. This time he placed his arms as if to grasp Lyn for another throw, but when Lyn made a motion to defend himself, the Lieutenant quickly struck him a chopping blow under the chin. He spun the dazed Lyn around and caught him again with chops to the kidneys and the back of the neck as Lyn collapsed, unconscious, onto the ground.

Lieutenant Lunan, now breathing very hard, straightened up and turned toward the Workers. "This man shows some promise," he said, "though he of course lacks the Warrior's ability to anticipate all possible moves."

How could Lyn anticipate those blows he had never seen before? thought Kolu. He certainly had anticipated everything he had been shown, and then some.

Lunan looked toward Lyn. "Would you two men on the end in the front please revive Worker Wonan so we can continue our lessons?" They did so, but Lyn was much too groggy to continue . He had to be replaced by another assistant for the remainder of the morning's exercise.

Later, Lyn and Ryl sat together under a tree eating some hardtack that constituted their lunch for the day.

"Lyn, you did very well this morning in the fighting. You were better than Lieutenant Lunan."

"Oh, no. He knocked me out." Lyn rubbed his chin.

"Yes, but you matched him on everything he taught you."

"It was luck. No Worker can outfight a Warrior."

Ryl chewed his food slowly, thinking about what Lyn said. "Lyn," he finally stated, "I don't believe that any more. I think you could beat Lunan in a fair fight."

Wonan put the last bit of hardtack in his mouth, wiped his hands on his shirt, and stood up. "You have crazy ideas, Ryl Kolu. I don't want to listen to them. You are wrong." He turned and walked back down the grassy slope to where the unit was beginning to fall in for the afternoon's session.

9

 Dawn Breeze watched Silver Leaf, the young Nauryan girl who had been helping her, return to the kitchen to prepare another tray of mutton. For a moment she envied the girl, whose life, with all its possibilities, still lay ahead. Yet the very breadth of those possibilities disturbed Dawn Breeze. No longer was a girl from the Komisaw tribe bound to marry within it, for the Protector had "united" all the tribes within hundreds of miles up and down the foothills. Silver Leaf's clan could now arrange, if they wished, for a man of wholly different appearance, language and custom to come live with her as her life's mate. Or Silver Leaf could, as so many young girls seemed to do these days, abandon her clan entirely and go to live with one of the new territorials, whose numbers increased every year.

 In Dawn Breeze's youth things had been much simpler. A girl knew all the eligible males by the age of 10, and the one who would live with her was usually chosen by her clan within a few years afterward. Dawn Breeze felt a sudden longing for the old days, and for Swift Stream, dead these many years, then quickly put the thought out of her mind and returned to her work, arranging the baskets and bowls of food for the mid-day meal on the long table before her. It was close to heresy for her to question, even in thought, the great changes the Protector had brought to her people. Especially for her, whom the Protector had chosen for his wife, and who herself had initiated the changes she now caught herself disliking. The Protector had come, just as the legend had predicted, and had shown them the Right Way. The Nauryan tribes of Westland now lived in permanent peace, under the leadership of her tribe, and they enjoyed an abundance never before dreamed possible. How could anyone question such a result?

The drone of a small airplane sounded in the distance. Jones was returning, just at the time he had said in his radio message. Faolin and his guests would hear the plane also and would be rushing down to the lake, where the plane would land. Then they would come to the house for their meal. Dawn Breeze hurried to make sure the table was ready for them.

As she worked, she thought about Faolin, the Protector, and their twenty years together. Twenty childless years, though for some strange reason Dawn Breeze did not regret their lack of offspring nearly as much as did her husband. Twenty lonely years, too, for her. She had never fully realized until they were married that Faolin expected her to give up her birthright to her clan's buildings and property, and come to live with him, permanently. Once they were married, of course, she had no choice but to follow the word of the Protector. It might not have been so bad if he had been with her, but, except during short periods in the winter, Faolin always seemed to be riding around leading his troops, or supervising the planting or the harvest, or building roads to the river. For a native girl, used to the continual presence of grandmothers, aunts, and cousins, the shift to the life of a territorial pioneer woman was extremely difficult.

As the years had passed, Dawn Breeze's knowledge of the man she had married--she couldn't help but think of him as a man, despite the legends and the worship of the other natives--came slowly, and each new thing she learned about him had seemed, if not always expected, at least reasonable. Yet when she compared the Faolin she knew now with the Faolin she thought she had married, the differences seemed vast. She had thought she was marrying a god in the form of a man, who would one day, in a burst of revelation, shed his disguise and reveal his true identity to her. For a long time she had cherished a hope that this would happen, but she did no longer. She didn't doubt that Faolin was divinely inspired, but he was a man nonetheless--a man with as many weaknesses and imperfections as other men. Though she hardly dared admit it to herself, she simply did not believe everything that the legends said. Once, many years ago, when she first began to have her doubts, she tried to discuss her observations with Painted Mask, the shaman on the Council of Elders. He belittled her opinions and chided her for expressing them; since then, she had kept them to herself.

Oddly, though, at the very time she started questioning Faolin's divinity, Faolin himself, who had always before laughed at the idea that he was a god, began to act as if he believed it. Where in earlier days he had been passive during the spring rites, or had at most talked about the crops and the planting, he had now begun to acknowledge his worshipers' devotion. More disturbing was his increasing tendency to attack those who disagreed with him--or who he supposed disagreed with him--as if they had no right to criticize his divine will. This was not the revelation Dawn Breeze had once hoped for. Such behavior did nothing to persuade Dawn Breeze that her husband was anything more than a man.

Silver Leaf returned with another tray of mutton.

"Where shall I put this, Ma'am?" she asked.

Dawn Breeze took the tray. "I'll arrange it," she said. "Did you hear the airplane? They'll be here very soon."

"Yes, Ma'am."

Dawn Breeze looked over the table. "This is everything, isn't it?"

"Yes, Ma'am."

"All right. You can go on back to the kitchen. I'll join you there later." The girl left. Dawn Breeze put out the last of the food. She stepped back and looked at the plates of cold chicken and mutton, the stacks of bread, the bowls of sliced vegetables and fruit, and the pitchers of water and milk. That ought to be enough, she thought. She sat down and waited. Her legs and feet were tired.

The buzz of the airplane sounded again as it took off for its return trip to New Markwell, having deposited Jones and his companions. Not long afterward Dawn Breeze heard boisterous voices outside. She got up and went to the door. Faolin was striding along, as usual, about five steps ahead of the party of ten men who puffed doggedly along behind him, all gestures and loud voices. Dawn Breeze had to admire the figure of her husband, tall and straight, hair graying around the temples, his frame filled out in the last twenty years but as solid as ever. The men came up on the porch.

"Dawn Breeze!" Faolin called. Then he saw her in the doorway. "Dawn Breeze, Hiram has returned from civilization." He put his hand on Jones' shoulder and pushed him forward through the door. "I hope you've got enough good country food for him."

Dawn Breeze didn't answer. She held the door open as the men came through. Bringing up the rear, a little apart from the others, was Forest Path. He was the only Nauryan in the group and had been invited, Dawn Breeze assumed, only so that Jones' report could be carried back to the Council Of Elders in the village. Dawn Breeze exchanged knowing glances with her brother. They had talked on many occasions about the territorials and their rough manners.

The men attacked the meat and bread, eating mostly with their hands. Only a few actually sat at the table. The others, including Faolin, stood around it, moving from one plate or bowl to another, talking and eating at the same time.

Dawn Breeze started for the kitchen. "Wait," Faolin called to her, "you don't have to leave us, Dawn Breeze. Join us." He walked up and put his arm around her.

"I've already eaten," she said, removing the arm. The other men, who had been watching, looked away and resumed their own conversation.

"Well, stay anyway," Faolin commanded. "You'll want to hear Jones' news."

Dawn Breeze shrugged and sat down in a straight backed wooden chair in the corner of the dining room. Faolin returned to the men, and they all continued to eat. Slowly, as they filled themselves, they became quieter. Soon they were all sitting, on chairs or on the floor, waiting expectantly for Jones to start talking.

Faolin pounded on the table for silence. "Well, let's

hear about what's happening in the world." He looked at Jones, who sat next to him. "First of all, what about our contracts for this year's crops?"

Jones leaned back in his chair and smiled. He, unlike Faolin, still retained the boyish features he had possessed when he signed on as Faolin's assistant so many years ago. He was still tall and thin, and he had grown a droopy moustache. He seemed to have a twinkle in his eye most times he spoke, though the impression was misleading. Jones could be a very critical, demanding person at times. Dawn Breeze guessed he was a good bargainer.

"Well," Jones said, "I've got good news for you there. We're up an average of five cents a bushel for this fall. I've got the contracts all signed up in my bag."

The men around the table voiced their approval. Dawn Breeze, too, was pleased. Some portion of the increase--not a lot, perhaps, but some--would trickle down to the Nauryan natives who worked in the fields and returned each night to their villages. And they, unlike the territorials, were still exempt from the income tax.

"There's talk, though," Jones continued, "that the government is going to increase incentives for opening up new farms. I guess they don't like the fact that demand keeps pushing up the grain prices."

"Well, we can open up new farms, too," said Faolin. "We'll get our share of the tax breaks." He grinned. "We can't lose."

"What's the latest news about Chansu?" asked one of the men at the table. The people of New Hope received occasional short wave radio messages and they of course knew about the capture of the UWG mission in Shinso. But they were too far away to receive the regular radio newscasts, and mail was delivered only sporadically. Thus even in 1948 their information on current events was often a week behind the rest of the UWG.

"Nothing new. Apparently the government is going ahead with the plan of meeting the ransom. A fleet of cargo ships stopped at New Markwell just yesterday, on their way to Chansu."

"Lunatics!" exclaimed Faolin. "That's no way to deal with those bandits. You pay their ransom, and they'll just ask for more."

Jones shrugged. "People say we've got to save the lives of the mission. A lot of them also seem to think that maybe the Chansu deserve what they're asking for."

"Crap," said Faolin. "They don't deserve anything if this is the way they ask for it. And as for the mission, well, sometimes sacrifices have to be made. We know that." The others nodded their approval.

Dawn Breeze watched her husband. Sometimes he could be very opinionated. She wished for this discussion to pass.

"What else is new in the city?" someone asked. Dawn Breeze felt relieved.

"Well," said Jones, "every time I visit New Markwell I can't believe the change. It's only been a year, and it seems like the place is twice as big. New roads. New buildings. You've got to see it to believe it. I'll tell you, I'm awful glad to get back here. It's just too crowded for me. I can't see how all those people can stand it."

"What about our roads?" asked Faolin. "Any news?"

"Not really. I talked to the Deputy Minister of Development and he says they've got the plans ready, but he doesn't know when they'll start. They want to finish the roads up the coast first. I told him we could wait, since we've got good roads as far as the river."

Faolin belched. "That's right. After all, roads run both ways. Who knows what sort we'll get in here when we've got a road all the way to New Markwell. But it would be a help in getting in our supplies."

Dawn Breeze hated the thought of the roads coming in. Her people were even now barely able to cling to their heritage. Only the tax laws, and their devotion to the Protector, kept them in the native lands. An open door to the west would probably overcome that restraint. She had asked Faolin to stop the roads. He could do it, at least for a time. But he vacillated. He saw only his own needs and conveniences, not those of the natives.

"You know," Jones was saying, "things are changing in the city in other ways, too. The people, I mean. Would you believe you can buy a drink of alcohol right out in the open on Main Street in New Markwell? And some of the girls are wearing their dresses up to here." He put the edge of his hand just above his knee. "There doesn't seem to he any sense of what's right and proper any more." He shrugged. "People don't seem to work as hard, either. You know, not a single grain buyer is open on Saturday." He shook his head. "I don't know what the UWG is coming to."

Faolin pushed his chair noisily away from the table and stood up. "It's something you can sense whenever you get a newspaper. It's disgusting. Sensationalism. Writing about things that just aren't proper in a newspaper. No respect for government officials, either. You should read the things they write about the government ."

Jones nodded vigorously. "I've just seen it. Not once in a while, either. Every newspaper, morning and night. But not just the newspapers. The books, too. You wouldn't believe some of the books in the stores."

"There's a sickness there, gentlemen, a sickness," said Faolin. "It's in everything we get from the UWG if you look for it. They seem to have lost their way, and they're getting further and further off the path."

Dawn Breeze had heard these thoughts of Faolin before, though seldom with such intensity. But what struck her more than her husband's seriousness was the words he used. The people in the city had "lost their way," he said, and they were "getting further off the path." To a Nauryan of the Komisaw tribe these words had special meaning, by now well known to Faolin, and his use of them Dawn Breeze found disturbing.

"This Chansu thing is just another example of the sickness. The Prime Council should have the guts to stand up to those Chansu bandits. But you watch. They'll give in to everything, and we'll be in a bigger mess than before. I know. I understand these things."

"But Eric," said one of the men at the table, "isn't the whole philosophy of the UWG the fair and equal treatment of other people?" Dawn Breeze recognized the speaker as one of the territorials who had arrived in recent years, a stout, balding man named Weber. He was on the New Hope town board. "I mean, I couldn't agree with you more about the sickness in their lives, but this Chansu thing seems different. Equal rights is as important a part of the UWG as hard work and proper behavior."

Faolin glared at Weber through narrowed eyes. "Why are you against me, Weber?" Faolin asked.

"I . . . I'm not against you, Eric," the man said, surprised. "I just thought there might be some justification for fair treatment of the Chansu."

"I've often suspected that you latecomers are infected with the disease of the cities. This proves it. We can't permit your unsound ideas to spread and undermine our work here. You're attacking me now. Next time you'll be saying that *we* have departed from the basic principles of the UWG."

"Oh no," Weber protested. "I've never thought that."

Faolin examined Weber for a moment. "Very well. I don't want to be too harsh. For your attack on me, I must ask you to leave my house. Please do not return. But you may stay in New Hope as long as there are no further attacks on our beliefs."

Weber looked around at the others. They sat in silence and avoided his eyes. He rose slowly, went to the door and left. Dawn Breeze watched him go, saddened by the incident. She had seen her husband this way before, but never in front of all his most trusted advisers. She noted in their faces the same shock and sadness that she felt. Perhaps even more for, she guessed, they loved Faolin more than did she. She exchanged glances with her brother, who had been sitting in a corner of the room, a little apart from the others. She had told him about Faolin's behavior, and his eyes acknowledged her warnings.

"I'm sorry, gentlemen, for the incident," said Faolin. "I must confess, though, that I've been suspicious of Weber for some time." He looked over at Jones. "Now, where were we?"

"Oh, I was just going on about the changes in New Markwell," Jones said, almost apologetically.

"Yes, of course," said Faolin. He cleared his throat. "It's my opinion that the situation gives cause for concern. Personal indulgence seems to have become more important than hard work. People are looking for the easy way out. Let's consider ourselves fortunate to have avoided the decay. We must be vigilant to prevent it from happening here."

The others mumbled their assent.

"Well, Hiram, what other news do you bring us?" Faolin asked.

Jones was watching the other men. He turned to Faolin. "Nothing of importance, really." He paused. "Eric, I've not seen my family for two weeks, and I'm sure there's a lot of work to do at my house. I thank you for your hospitality"--he nodded towards Dawn Breeze–"but I think perhaps I should leave now. We can go over the contracts tomorrow."

"Leave? It's still the middle of the afternoon," Faolin protested.

"I've still got a lot to do today, too, Eric," said one of the men sitting near them. "And we start the inspection of the irrigation system first thing tomorrow morning." Several others added similar comments.

"Oh, very well," Faolin said reluctantly. "It's good to see that work still comes before pleasure here." He grinned. The others departed, one by one, mumbling their thanks to Faolin and Dawn Breeze at the door.

Forest Path was the last of the men to leave. Dawn Breeze looked at him as he approached. He appeared old to her—old and tired. His hair was mostly white now, though he was still in his forties, and the wrinkles stood out on his scarred gray face.

"I hope your children are well," Dawn Breeze said.

"They're all fine," he replied. "Black Earth is bigger and stronger than I am now. He'll be seventeen next month. We miss you. Please come to see us soon."

"I will when I can." Dawn Breeze glanced uneasily toward Faolin. "Tell me, how is Soft Rain?" Soft Rain was their cousin, who had taken Dawn Breeze's place as heir to the Blackbird clan.

"She's well also, but she doesn't care for the house as you would."

"I'd like to help her, but Eric insists I stay here." Dawn Breeze looked again at her husband, who had gone to the other side of the room.

"That is your duty," Forest Path said. He patted his sister's shoulder.

"The old ways keep changing more and more," Dawn Breeze sighed.

"Yes, they do. Well, I must be going. Do come soon. We can have a nice talk."

"I will. Goodbye, Forest Path."

"Goodbye, Dawn Breeze." Forest Path looked toward Faolin. "Goodbye, Eric," he called. "I'll make my report to the Council of Elders this evening." Faolin nodded. Forest Path left.

Dawn Breeze went to the table and started stacking trays and bowls.

"You don't need to do that. That's Silver Leaf's job," said Faolin.

"Yes, Eric." Dawn Breeze put the dishes down. "I'll call her." She started toward the kitchen.

"Wait. What were you and your brother whispering about at the door?"

Dawn Breeze turned and faced Faolin. "We weren't whispering. Forest Path asked me to visit him soon."

"Why?"

"He's my brother. We like to see each other."

"Well, I'm not sure you'll have time." Faolin paced back and forth across the room. "Dawn Breeze," he said, "I'm very worried about our settlement. I can't help but feel there are evil influences at work here."

"Why is that?"

"You saw what happened here today. I'm particularly worried about these newcomers. Weber is not the only one I've had doubts about. I didn't say anything before, because I had no evidence. Now I do."

"What do you propose to do?"

Faolin shook his head slowly. "I don't know. I don't know." Then he caught Dawn Breeze firmly in his gaze. "But I must do something. It's my task, as your legends say. And I will perform it."

"Yes, Eric, and I have faith that you will." Dawn Breeze waited. Faolin went to a chair near the window and sat, staring out into the afternoon sunshine. When it was apparent that he was lost in his thoughts, she quietly slipped out of the room into the kitchen. She would instruct Silver Leaf to wait to clear the table until after Faolin had left the dining room.

10

Han Torgoona, the Prince Regent, stood on the balcony at the top of the Old Citadel in Shinso. What more appropriate place, he thought, to celebrate his triumph? He watched with pleasure as the fleet of UWG cargo ships came into view in the distant mist of the fjord and slowly made their way to the harbor below him. If only, he mused, his grandfather, who had stood in this same tower barely fifty years before to supplicate himself before another expedition from the UWG, were alive to share this scene. But Han's grandfather was long since dead, and Han's own father, the present Emperor, was unable to comprehend what was happening. The Emperor spent his days in a chair in his room, staring at the wall, a silly smile on his face, his mind destroyed by his paralyzing stroke. Han's brother, Changa, and the Empress were under a more or less permanent house arrest in their apartments at the New Palace. Thus of the royal family, only Han was here to view the triumph. But that was only fitting, for the triumph was his.

The deep-water docks had been emptied for this occasion, and the six UWG vessels maneuvered up to them, where groups of laborers waited. The crews of the UWG ships were too busy bringing in their boats to notice that, far behind them in the fjord, a dozen small iron-clad warships had slipped into the channel and were beginning to lay thick cable across it. Nor did the crews of the UWG ships see the rows of red-clad troops waiting in and behind the low buildings that dotted the dock area. By the time their ships were secured and they had prepared themselves to negotiate the exchange of cargo for hostages, their position was hopeless. The Chansu forces swarmed unopposed aboard the UWG ships, took the crews captive, and marched them off along the docks toward the terminal building, where red-painted trucks waited to carry them to an unknown destination.

Rubbing his hands together and chuckling to himself, Han took in the whole series of events from his high vantage point. Only after the last of the ships' crews had disappeared into the terminal building did he leave his post. Inside, several of his officers and advisers waited for him. They had been watching through the windows.

"Everything has gone precisely as you planned," said Han's first minister. "I apologize for my doubts." He bowed his head.

"Lift your head. Your doubts were reasonable ones," said Han, magnanimous in the flush of victory. "After all, we would never have so highly valued a few lives. Now we know that we have correctly measured their will. They are incapable of resisting us. With these ships and their crews we have greatly improved our advantage. Let us continue to press it."

11

At 3:30 on the morning of April 29, 1948, Strongarm received an emergency call from Chairman Carter's secretary. He dressed and shaved quickly and was on his way to the Council chambers by shortly after four. All five of the Council members had arrived by 4:30, and the informal meeting in Chairman Carter's office began, with her usual remarks. She then proceeded immediately to the subject of her concern.

"At exactly 2:45 a.m. this morning, Preston time," she said, "our Communications Center in New Markwell received this message from Chansu." She held a thin sheet of paper in her hand. "I've made copies for you." She passed to each Council member a white-on-black reversal photocopy of the message. Strongarm read:

```
To: Rulers of the UWG
From: Han Torgoona, Prince Regent
     For Emperor Laka Torgoona


Receipt of shipments acknowledged. Ships
and crew remain to assist in improving
economy of Chansu. Their well being, and
that of UWG Mission in Shinso, depends
upon ability of the UWG to supply
```

```
additional aid to equalize Chansu.
Requests to follow from economic advisers.
```

"That isn't what we agreed to," Smith blurted.

"Of course not," replied Carter. " The question is, what do we do now?"

"Military action is the only answer," Cornettia declared. "If we had moved on the military front in the beginning, we wouldn't have to worry about 300 more hostages." He stared at Strongarm, whose mind was working hard to analyze this new development.

"We agreed to look into military alternatives while we were meeting the original demands," said Smith. "What have we found out?"

"I have all the preliminary reports," answered Carter. "Most are not very promising. As far as raising a volunteer army is concerned, it seems almost impossible. People just won't do it."

"Conscription is the only answer," put in Cornettia.

"Never," said Strongarm through clenched teeth.

"Look, don't get so jumpy," Cornettia said to Strongarm. "I just said it's the only way to raise an army."

"Let me finish, please," insisted Carter. "On the naval side, things are slightly better, but not much. We've got plenty of fishing boats and freighters that could carry troops if we had them, but none of them has guns, of course. We could probably pull some old cannon out of the museums and put them on the bigger ships, but it's questionable how well they'll work."

Carter placed the two reports she had summarized on the table and picked up a third. "The best alternative at the moment, at least according to these reports, appears to be aerial bombardment. We have aircraft with a 6000 mile range. If we could construct an airbase in the western Ellenberry Islands, we could get the planes within striking distance, allowing for a round trip flight. The experts say it wouldn't be too difficult to alter the aircraft to carry and drop high explosives, such as TNT, but they have some doubts as to how accurate any such bombing would be. The Chansu may have cannon that could knock down planes at low altitudes, though that is very questionable. The engineers would have to design and build the bombs, but they don't expect that to take too long."

"Let's get them started immediately," said Cornettia.

"They already have," Carter replied.

"Just a minute. We never approved the use of explosives to kill innocent people," Strongarm interjected.

"No one has been authorized to drop any bombs. That we must decide. But there was no harm in getting them started on the project in case we do decide to use them." Carter glanced at Mindra Parthupta, who sat listening to the discussion in her typical stony silence.

Carter cleared her throat. "There is one further possibility that has been raised along these lines that we should consider. As all of you probably know, scientists from Agronica National University have been working with the people at Agronica Electric to develop a means of releasing energy by atomic reaction. Some of them think it's the only long-range solution to the problem of producing enough electrical power. What you probably don't know--I didn't--is that a separate group at A.E. has been experimenting with the same power source to produce extremely strong explosives for large-scale earth excavation. In fact they've had several devices ready for testing for almost a year, but they haven't found a suitable place to do it. There's apparently a problem about a potential release of radiation that is harmful to life, so the test has to be in a very remote spot. In any event, our experts say in this report that such a device could possibly be adapted into a bomb that could be dropped from one of our aircraft. This would be an extremely destructive weapon."

"How destructive?" asked Parthupta quietly.

"Well," Carter said, glancing uneasily at Strongarm, "they say the blast itself could destroy maybe half a square mile. They're not sure about the radiation, but it might be destructive to life over a much wider area."

"That certainly sounds promising," said Smith, half smiling. Strongarm was shocked at Smith's statement. "How long will it take to get such bombs ready?" Smith added.

"The report isn't definite, but possibly within a month. It's a question of redesigning what we have to fit into an airplane and figuring out how to drop it. Apparently we have enough chemicals or whatever they use already in the power project to make a number of bombs. That's the only time-consuming aspect, and that's all finished."

"Where do these experts propose using this bomb, Mildred?" Strongarm asked sarcastically. "On cities full of women and children? This whole idea is crazy. I suggest we start talking about something reasonable."

"Look," said Cornettia, "we didn't start this thing. They did. And they've got to take the consequences."

"Innocent women and children didn't start it. And those who did start it thought it was the right thing for their people. As far as we know, they haven't harmed a single person. You're all talking as though you've already decided not to meet their demands. But we don't yet even know what the further demands are." Strongarm held up the message and waved it. "This says requests are to follow from their economic advisers. For all we know, the requests will be perfectly reasonable."

"I don't care what the requests are," said Cornettia. "It's the way they're making them. If we meet the requests, they'll think it's because they threatened us, not because the requests were reasonable. That's the way their minds work. They aren't UWG citizens; they're barbarians. And if we show weakness to them, they'll continue to prey on us. We've got to show them we won't give in. And if that requires the taking of lives, then so be it."

"That's absurd," Strongarm retorted angrily. "If we kill their people, they'll just kill ours. Look, Rolf, even if you're right-- which I refuse to concede--it makes no sense to bomb Chansu and kill thousands of their people. The least costly solution is simply not to send what they ask. They may still release the hostages. But even if they kill the hostages, we will have made our stand at the cost of the fewest lives." Strongarm turned to Carter, "Surely you can see, Mildred, that what Cornettia is proposing goes against every principle that the UWG stands for. We would be denying people of Chansu their very right to live, solely because we disagree with the policies adopted by their leaders."

Carter, who was still standing, looked down at Strongarm with the expression of a schoolmistress trying to calm an angry and misguided student. "Bob, we appreciate the point you're making. You may be right. There may well be some inconsistency between what Rolf is proposing and some of the principles which we learn in the primary schools. But Bob, you're relatively new to this Council. You haven't seen much of the kinds of decisions we have to make. And I believe all of us have seen instances where the so-called fundamental principles just have to be compromised. Those principles are wonderful ideals, and it's right that people should be taught that they should govern everything. But when you sit here, Bob, in the Prime Council, where the really important decisions must be made, where we have the responsibility for the well being of 450 million people, we've got to be right. And the right decision isn't always the one that maximizes freedom, or equality, or productivity. The right decision has to take into account human nature, which isn't always governed by the fundamental principles. In this instance, we're confronted with an enemy--with an opponent--who knows nothing of and cares less about our fundamental principles. We can't permit those principles to cause us to lose everything we have. We must meet the foe on his own terms."

There was silence for a moment. Strongarm sat, openmouthed, scarcely able to believe what he'd just heard.

Just then Parthupta spoke, breaking the silence. Her quiet voice was barely audible. "I will agree with our Chairman that this Council has occasionally departed from the course our basic principles might indicate. Whether that has been right or wrong, I am not nearly as certain as she. But in any case, in this instance Mr.

Strongarm has a valid point. Is it correct to take several thousand Chansu lives--maybe more--in an effort to save a few hundred UWG lives? An affirmative answer clearly places a higher value on a UWG life than a Chansu life, does it not? Of course," she smiled enigmatically, "the report you mentioned about the impossibility of a volunteer army suggests that we UWG citizens place a very high value on our lives indeed."

"You see my point," Strongarm said excitedly. "Certainly a Chansu life is not worth less than a UWG life."

"Just a minute," said Cornettia, "we're not just weighing lives here. We're talking about aggressive acts. We have to consider where the guilt lies."

"Gentlemen. Gentlemen," said Smith to Strongarm and Cornettia, who appeared almost ready to come to blows. "Let's see if there's some alternative solution. We don't necessarily have to actually *use* this atomic explosive. I mean, maybe all we need to do is show that we have it. If the Chansu know, surely they'll give up the hostages. Why don't we proceed to build it as soon as we can and then demonstrate it?"

"That seems a reasonable position," said Carter. "Can you accept that, Rolf?"

"Sure. As long as we don't waste any time. And as long as we've got some more bombs ready to use if one demonstration isn't enough."

"Bob?"

Strongarm thought for a moment. "No," he finally said. "The mere threat of using such a weapon is false to the humanity I thought the UWG stood for. Absolutely not." He looked at Parthupta.

"The Chansu are an inscrutable people," she said, still smiling. "It is difficult to know if they will react as Mr. Smith predicts." She said no more.

The discussion continued at length. Finally, Carter called for an informal vote on Smith's suggestion. It carried, 3 to 2, with Strongarm and Parthupta dissenting.

When the voting was over, Carter turned to Strongarm with an apprehensive expression. "Are you going to request a public debate on this, Bob?"

"Don't we have to have a public discussion anyway, under the Information Act?" Smith asked.

"I don't think so," said the Chairman. "Unless Bob or Mindra request it. We haven't recommended any 'government action.' We've just authorized a bomb test. Surely we wouldn't have to have public debate if the test was to be in the uninhabited swamps of the South Continent, where they originally planned it. A test in the Western Ocean isn't any different." She grinned. "If the test has any desirable side effects, they're purely fortuitous." She looked back at Strongarm.

Strongarm disliked the tortured logic they used to evade public discussion, but he admitted to himself that there were times when public discussion of Council decisions was not useful. Was he, he suddenly wondered, himself already guilty of the compromise of principles Carter had mentioned earlier? He put the thought aside. The question was, should he demand pubic debate on this matter? He envisioned them sitting around the Council table, before a bevy of reporters, discussing whether to observe the fundamental principles of the UWG, with some Council members arguing--and, indeed, possibly prevailing--that those principles should be ignored here. Such a debate, he foresaw, would have a shattering impact far beyond the matter at hand. Of course, perhaps the debate would skirt this basic question. But then, what was the point in having it? Strongarm looked around the table, and his eyes fell on Smith. From a tactical standpoint, Strongarm concluded, he was more likely to persuade the changeable and inconsistent Mr. Smith in private conversations than in public debate. The other two--Carter and Cornettia--were beyond convincing.

Strongarm returned Carter's stare. "I'll waive public debate--for now," he said.

"Mindra?"

"I will concur with Mr. Strongarm."

"Good," Carter said. "Now all we need to do is decide what action we're going to announce." She laughed. "I don't quite think we can avoid disclosing the message from the Emperor."

"It's going to take time to get our other plans ready," said Cornettia. "Why not just say that, although we have doubts, we're going to continue to assume Chansu's good faith. We'll continue to meet their reasonable demands, but will devise a means of delivering what they ask that doesn't create a risk of their taking more hostages." He looked toward Strongarm and Parthupta. "I'm sure even our two pacifists can agree on that."

The Council voted unanimously to adopt Cornettia's suggestion. Then they went home to get a few hours rest before the public session which they scheduled for ten that morning.

12

Fred Harper burst into his apartment, winded but bubbling over with excitement. He had run all the way from the bus stop. "Dorothy. Dorothy," he called.

Dorothy was sitting in the kitchen, sipping a cup of tea and looking out the back window. "What is it?"

Fred came into the kitchen and sat down next to her. He leaned over and kissed her on the forehead with a loud smack. "It's happened," he said. "The answer to all our complaints. I just heard about it today."

"What complaints?" Dorothy wrinkled her forehead.

"You know. Being bored. Wanting a change. Wanting to move. Well, the opportunity has come. We didn't even have to go looking for it."

"What do you mean?"

"Billings--you know, the plant supervisor--spoke to my unit today. The company has finally decided to run the tests, out in the Ellenberry Islands. They need three men from my unit, and he asked for volunteers. Just think, a paid vacation in the south seas."

"Great. What am I supposed to do for a job?"

"That's the best part of it. They also have to build housing out there, and they need someone with exactly your qualifications. Billings told me afterward that he thought we were the perfect candidates, because of your job. He promised to give me first crack at it."

Dorothy sipped her tea thoughtfully. "Is the pay the same?" she asked.

"Just the same. The company will move our things, too."

"How long would we be there?"

"Oh, I don't know. Not permanently, of course. Maybe six months. Maybe a year." Fred's high spirits were slowly waning. Why wasn't Dorothy more enthusiastic? He felt a bit angry at her.

"Would you like some tea?" Dorothy asked, holding up her cup.

"No, thanks. Look, Dorothy, this is exactly what we've been talking about for the last month. Can't you get a little more excited about it?"

Dorothy looked down at her cup. "I'm sorry, Fred. It's just so sudden. Somehow it's too easy. I keep thinking there must be something wrong with it."

"Well, there isn't. What could be?"

"Oh, what about the Chansu situation, for example? That still isn't resolved."

"Honey, the Ellenberries are thousands of miles from Chansu. Besides, they'll work that problem out soon. You just wait and see."

"What about those things you're working on? I don't

want to get blown up either."

"Perfectly safe. That's my job. I know those circuits. I help build them. There's no danger, believe me."

"But what if we don't like it there?"

"If we don't, we just look for another job. We're not giving up our freedom, Honey."

"Can we come back here?"

"Well, I guess so. We'd have to re-qualify for the jobs. But I thought the whole point was to get away from Stevensburg."

Dorothy looked up at Fred. After a moment she gave him a slight smile. "You really want this, don't you?"

"Yes."

"Okay," she said in a small voice.

"We'll love it there, Honey. We really will. This is the smartest thing we've ever done. We're going to live our lives." He put his hand gently over hers, then bent over and kissed her again. "Thank you, Dorothy. You won't regret it."

13

Lyn Wonan bowed low before the officer as he entered the classroom and sat on one of the hard wooden benches. An unusual mid-May heat spell had made the room stuffy and uncomfortable. A few days ago, when their classroom series started, Lyn had welcomed the relief from the physical abuse of the training program. Now, with the birds chirping and the scent of blossoms in the warm, moist air, Lyn longed to be outdoors again, for whatever purpose. With the physical training over, it was as if all this other business was meant only to mark time and keep them occupied. Lyn chided himself for this thought as soon as it came to him, Of course the classroom training was important, or the Warrior officers would not have ordered it. If he failed to appreciate it or benefit from it, the fault was his, not theirs.

The rest of Lyn's unit, all Workers like Lyn and his friend Ryl Kolu, followed Lyn into the room, bowed, and took their places. The officer stood and moved to the front of the room, his sword swaying at his side. He faced the class.

"Good morning, Workers," he said. "I am Won Palata, Captain, Instruction Corps. Please give me your attention, and I will try to put some military knowledge in those hard Workers' heads of yours." Captain Palata smiled broadly, showing a gold tooth. Then he opened a notebook and laid it on the high lectern in front of him. He perused it for a moment and then looked up. "The oldest saying in military teaching is, 'First of all things, know your enemy.' This day we learn the history and behavior of the eastern peoples." He reached behind him and pulled down a map of the UWG.

"The homeland of the UWG is these two continents more than 5000 miles to the east. The population is centered even further away, in the eastern half of the North Continent and the northeastern section of the South Continent." He pointed to the Region of Agronica and portions of the Regions of Brahmastan and Doltony. "But the people of the UWG are scattered in smaller numbers throughout the land. There are perhaps 500 million of them--ten times the population of our island. But don't let their numbers frighten you. Even if they were ten times ten greater in numbers than Chansu, we would have nothing to fear from them."

Captain Palata turned away from the map and took two steps toward the class. "Why is this, you ask? Why are 500 million people no match for the 50 million of Chansu? The answer is simple. In the 500 millions of the UWG, there is not one Warrior. Not one! There is not even a Worker class! The people of the UWG are classless, below all the classes of Chansu."

Captain Palata returned to his lectern. "It was not always so in the UWG. Once there were, as here, classes divided according to the natural laws. But the classes forgot the lessons of vigilance, or were corrupted, and were overthrown in a bloody struggle many years ago. The classless ones have taken the weapons and works of those they defeated and have sought to use them to carry their unnatural, unspeakable classlessness to the rest of the world. But no amount of weapons or works inherited from the dead can accomplish their goal. When the classless vermin killed their Warriors, they killed their spirit. They cannot regain it, for it was lost forever in the blood of their dead Warriors. Indeed, in all of this world, only here in Chansu does Warrior blood still run.

"So the UWG can never succeed in Chansu. Our spirit will prevail. The laws of nature are with us. But the Emperor has decreed that we cannot rest until the threat of the UWG is eliminated. The Emperor says it is not enough merely to stop the UWG from imposing their classless system here. The gods will not be satisfied until an ordered society such as ours is restored to all areas of the earth. It is that, and not merely driving the foreigners from our island, that is our task."

Captain Palata went again to his map and continued the lecture, discoursing upon the ridiculous institutions and customs of the UWG that evidenced its weakness. Lyn forgot about his longing to be outdoors and drank it all in eagerly. He felt honored that his lowly person could be a part of such a noble enterprise.

14

The Ellenberry Islands stretch southwestwards in a three thousand mile arc from a point in the Western Ocean about 750 miles from New Markwell. The larger islands in the group are at the eastern end of the chain. They are inhabited by a few administrators and sugar-cane farmers from the UWG and by a small "civilized" native population, physically and linguistically related to the Chansu, whose principal occupation is fishing. A large canning factory was built in the 1920's on the easternmost island, where the local catches are packed for shipment to the continent.

The eastern Ellenberries, with their moderate climate and dramatic scenery, are renowned as an ideal vacation spot. Unfortunately, very few UWG citizens are willing or able to set aside from their incomes the amount of money necessary to finance such an excursion. The relatively few, modest hotels on the eastern islands attest to the fact that visits are much more dreamed about than made.

The western two-thirds of the Ellenberry chain, where the arc swings back sharply to the northwest, is composed of fewer and smaller islands. None have been inhabited in modern times but there are occasional traces of past occupation on some of them. Archaeologists theorize that the western Ellenberries served as stepping stones for the ancestors of the Chansu to migrate to their descendants' present home, or for the ancestors of the people of the eastern Ellenberries to migrate from Chansu, depending upon which theory one adopts.

Of the extreme western islands in the chain, the largest is Hawk Island, so named because of the appearance of the birds, actually gulls, which at certain times of the year flock there in large numbers. About four miles long and a mile wide, Hawk Island, unlike most other nearby islands, also possesses a long, flat expanse of beach on its southern and eastern sides. The beach, the island's size, and its location some 2200 miles from the southeastern tip of Chansu made it the logical choice for an advance airbase from which UWG planes could strike at targets in Chansu.

Dorothy and Fred Harper looked upon Hawk Island for the first time on the morning of May 16, 1948. Their ship had reached the island during the night and now sat at anchor off the island's southern beaches. They stood on the rear deck, holding onto the railing as the ship rolled slightly in the choppy seas. It was a clear morning, with a brisk breeze from the northwest. But their spirits did not reflect the brightness of the day.

"It's cold here," Dorothy said, pulling her cloth coat tighter around her. "I thought the south seas were supposed to be warm."

"We're not in the south seas. This end of the chain is a lot further north than the islands you hear about. I didn't know we were coming way out here when I signed up; that's why I called it the south seas. But anyway, it still doesn't get as cold as Stevensburg."

"Well, it is now."

They stared silently at the island that was to be their new home. The high, barren ridge running down its center seemed ugly and forbidding. No trees could be seen anywhere. On the beach they spotted the small white dot that was the boat of the scouting party, but they were too far away to see its members.

"Oh, Fred, it looks like such an awful place. I'm scared. We shouldn't have come."

Fred put his arm around Dorothy's shoulders. "It'll be different when you get some buildings put up, and a window with curtains in it." He paused, thinking. "And there's no reason to be frightened. Nothing can happen to us here."

"But Fred, you said this might be a military base, not just a testing station." Fred had suspected the true purpose of the Hawk Island expedition even before the boat left Taradesh twelve days ago. Now he was convinced, though he still voiced doubts to Dorothy. Why else would the government have sent men and supplies to construct an elaborate airbase on Hawk Island? Why else would there be such a sudden urgency to test devices that had been sitting ready for a year? "Honey, we don't know that. Besides, they would surely have told us if there was any danger. Full disclosure, that's the way the government operates. It's the law. How many times have you heard them say that?" This point did bother Fred. Heretofore he would never have thought that the UWG would intentionally mislead anyone. Had he just been naive? He felt angry.

"Is that what you really think?"

"I don't really know, but yes, that's what I think." The qualification didn't keep the statement from being a lie, and Fred realized it. "Look, for all we know, the airstrip is just for refueling planes bringing supplies to Chansu. That doesn't present any danger." Now the lie was deeper. For several weeks Fred had been working on wiring diagrams that would permit testing the nuclear explosives by dropping them from a plane. Yet perhaps the project chairman had merely concluded that that was the safest way to run the test. It was inconceivable that anyone could be planning to drop these devices on Chansu.

"Oh, I hope you're right."

"What danger could there be, even if this is a military base? We're still two thousand miles from Chansu. The Chansu don't have any big airplanes or warships. For all the technology we've given them, they're still a very primitive people. They haven't changed in two thousand years. They've never--not ever--come this far away from their island, and I hardly think they're about to do it now. Believe me, there's nothing to worry about." Fred patted Dorothy's shoulder. What he said was perfectly reasonable and logical. He hoped Dorothy believed it. He wished that he could.

15

Ryl Kolu and Lyn Wonan, their minds dulled by a day of lectures, lay in their tent waiting for sleep.

"Lyn," said Kolu, "what do you think of the Easterners?"

"What do you mean? They're our enemies. They intend to conquer Chansu and impose their ways on us."

"Have you ever spoken with an Easterner?"

"Of course not. I've never even seen one."

"I have," said Kolu, matter-of-factly.

"How could you? It's not permitted."

"Except in performance of duty. When they brought the machines to my village, two Easterners came to explain their workings. I served as a messenger for them. They spoke to me of many things."

"It must have been very unpleasant for you."

"At first I found it difficult to accept their manner. They speak to everyone in the same words. They know nothing of the positions of respect. For example, they'll look directly at whomever they speak to, whether he's a Warrior or a Worker." Kolu paused, then went on. "But after a time I forgot these peculiarities. They were kind men, not cruel. Their manner comes from a difference of custom, or ignorance, not from disrespect."

"How can you know that?"

"I could sense it. That's the only way to explain it."

"They still want to overcome us, as they did with their own rulers many years ago. That's not kindness," Wonan pointed out.

"This point troubles me," Kolu admitted. "I asked them about it once, and they freely admitted that they overthrew their own rulers many years ago and killed large numbers of them. But they didn't kill them all. They've made complicated rules to prevent the heirs of the rulers from returning to power, as would be the natural thing to occur. Strangely, they seem very proud of what they've done. I'm sure they would like to see the same thing happen here."

"We must be prepared to prevent it from happening."

"Yet much of what they say about their land is very interesting," Ryl continued, ignoring Lyn's statement. "As they describe it, people there no longer remember or care about their class position. It's not so much like all persons becoming classless, they say, as it is like all persons becoming of the topmost class. But to me it seems like neither. In their land a man can pursue whichever occupation he wishes. He can speak to whomever he wishes and associate with whomever he wishes. He can even say whatever he wishes. And everyone is entitled to an equal share of the product of the land. It seems more like, to me, that every man can choose his own class. They have many very strong rules to preserve this situation."

"That's all most unnatural. How can they prevent the classes from separating themselves if they allow all the classes to live? Those who are strongest--the Warriors--will naturally rise to the top, as they have in Chansu, by their excellence in combat. I don't believe they've told you the truth. I believe, as the Emperor says, the classless have eliminated all the others and rule the land themselves. We must use the weapons they took from their rulers to prevent them from doing the same to us."

"They also told me that their machines were created after they overthrew their rulers, not before."

"Impossible. How can you believe them when they have stated their purpose is to overcome us? Ryl, my friend, I don't want to hear any more of this. Let's go to sleep."

Lyn turned on his side and within minutes was snoring lightly. Ryl lay on his back for a long while, trying to imagine life in the UWG, until his overworked mind also succumbed to a restless sleep.

16

The Prime Council's staff of advisers had planned well, and they had selected competent personnel. The Hawk Island airstrip and radio tower were built with only the most minor delays. Construction of the buildings took a little longer, but once the airstrip was finished, forgotten and unanticipated supplies could be brought in on one or two days' notice. By the end of June all the essential buildings were completed. The remaining ones could proceed at a more leisurely pace.

Twice before the end of June supply ships bound to and from Chansu stopped briefly off Hawk Island. These were the only occasions when the work stopped. Everyone was especially elated when the first ship returned from Chansu. At least the government had devised a plan of transferring materials without further UWG citizens being taken hostage.

The laboratory and machine shop where Fred Harper labored was the first building finished, and even before the middle of June he was hard at work on his specialty. He and his co-workers assembled, tested, checked and re-checked with excruciating care the devices of destruction they were commissioned to build. How much easier it would have been to do this work back in the well-outfitted lab at Stevensburg. Yet they had gone as far as they could there. It would have been much too risky to ship the bombs to this remote island fully assembled.

When the work in the laboratory building was completed, Fred turned his attention to the mechanical devices and controls in the aircraft that would fly the first test. This work was not so painstaking, and by July 12 Fred and the others celebrated its completion. It took two more days for the right weather conditions to materialize, and in the late morning of July 14, 1948, Fred found himself high above the ocean, two thousand miles northwest of Hawk Island, aboard the noisy, throbbing plane. Fred had never flown before, and in other circumstances the mere thought of being aboard any plane--let alone a huge four-engined transport over remote stretches of unfamiliar ocean--would have petrified him. But on this occasion Fred had other things that concerned him much more.

The pilot called back to the engineers and crew. Chansu

was now visible on the western horizon. Fred craned his neck to look out the narrow window. His heart leapt. There indeed was Chansu, a gray and brown smudge on the distant sea. That he could see it made it seem much closer than he knew it was. And if they could see Chansu, could Chansu see them? Did the Chansu have guns or planes to intercept them? Of course not. Yet who really knew what the Chansu were capable of?

But Fred had no time to speculate on that danger. He had another task, with even greater dangers. He and the others now had less than half an hour to make their final check of the circuits that would arm and free the bomb. They had gone over the circuits in minute detail before the bomb was placed in the aircraft, and again before takeoff. But with something like this, with all their lives at stake, they couldn't be too careful. The acceleration of takeoff, the frontal zone they passed through halfway here, either of these things might have disturbed the delicate wiring.

The circuits still tested out. Fred looked at the navigator, who had come back for a moment from the cockpit to review their progress, and shrugged. "We've checked everything we can," Fred shouted over the drone of the engines. "It tests okay." He made a sign of approval with his fingers.

The navigator smiled and patted Fred on the shoulder. Fred disliked his brave manner. "Well, let's see what happens," the navigator said. He walked back to the cockpit, motioning the others to follow him.

A few minutes later the navigator, now in his seat behind the pilot, pointed excitedly out the front window. The pilot nodded and moved his controls slightly. Fred, crowded together with the others around the cockpit door, didn't have a very good view out the window and at first couldn't see what the navigator was pointing at. Then he spotted it. A small gray patch on the blue ocean, dead ahead. An acre of uninhabited, barren rock protruding from the sea some twenty-five miles off the eastern coast of Chansu. The target.

On seeing it, Fred appreciated even more the wisdom

of the selection of this site for the test. It was far enough away from Chansu that the blast itself should do no serious damage, and the prevailing winds would carry any radioactive waste particles out to sea, away from the island. Yet it was close enough to afford an impressive demonstration of the bomb's power. Assuming, of course, that this was the purpose of the test--a matter as to which neither Fred nor the rest of his companions had been officially informed but which none any longer doubted. What other possible reason could there be for testing the explosive here?

But at the moment Fred's concern centered on himself. His palms were cold and moist, and a lump grew in his throat. He and the others in this small metal tube five miles above the ocean would be the closest humans to the blast, and by far the most vulnerable. The bomb's parachute would slow the drop enough to allow them to get twelve miles away from the center of the explosion. By their calculations, the aircraft should be able to withstand shock waves at ten and a half miles. But no one had ever touched off one of these before. A pencil and paper safety margin of one and a half miles gave Fred little comfort.

The plane banked slightly to the left, then straightened. "That's the best I can do," shouted the pilot. "We're dead on course." The navigator nodded. The responsibility for releasing the bomb fell to him. He had made a number of practice runs over Hawk Island with a dummy bomb and had devised some rough calculations for the timing of the drop, taking into account the height, the plane speed, the wind. They weren't perfect, but a direct hit was not essential; the bomb gave them a considerable margin for error, particularly since it was timed to detonate at about 1000 feet above sea level. And, of course, the navigator well knew that for the unspoken purpose of this test, he did not have to come anywhere near the supposed target.

Fred watched as the navigator nonchalantly flipped the first fateful switch. His heart pounded. No accident had occurred yet. The lamp Fred had wired so carefully showed that the bomb fuse was now armed. Fred glanced again at the light over the fuse lock switch. It still glowed reassuringly, indicating that the timer would not begin to run until the bomb was released. Now they waited, and the moments crept by. The navigator watched his instruments. After several long minutes, he pushed a gray metal lever and the bomb bay door opened with a mechanical growl, vibrating the skeleton of the aircraft. Fred felt the air pressure drop in his ears. The navigator's hand moved slowly over the remaining switch, hesitated, then quickly flipped it. The lock light went out and a third light went on, indicating that the bomb was released. The plane rose suddenly as the pilot struggled to retain control of the lightened plane. One of the men next to Fred ran back to check. He knelt and peered through the slits above the bomb rack, then looked back toward the cockpit, smiling and holding up his fist. The bomb was on its way!

Fred and the others watched the pilot anxiously as the plane leveled off. Up here, in the cloudless sky, it suddenly felt as though they were not moving at all. Couldn't the pilot give the engines more power? But of course he had given as much as he could. He had no more reason to hover over this site than they.

Seemingly endless moments passed and nothing happened. Had the mechanism failed? The co-pilot turned around toward Fred and the others, who were still gathered around the cockpit door. "Say," he said, "shouldn't you fellows get strapped in?"

Used to moving about the inside of the plane to prepare for the test, they had forgotten the most elemental precaution. Before Fred could reach his seat a blinding, unearthly light came from under and behind them, so strong it seemed to penetrate the plane's aluminum skin. Moments later the plane jolted and shuddered. Fred fell to the floor, his head glancing off the side of a metal cabinet. Then nothing.

The next thing Fred knew someone was slapping his face. He opened his eyes and saw the navigator kneeling over him. "Wake up," the man was shouting, as if from far away. When Fred's partly-opened eyes met his, the navigator smiled. "Hey," he said, "It worked. Nice job." Fred returned the smile and then sat up slowly. Someone from behind helped him into one of the cabin seats. He felt the lump on the side of his head. Had they really survived?

"Just take it easy now, Fred," the navigator said. "We're on our way home."

17

Virtually everyone in Larna, a medium-sized town on Chansu's eastern coast, experienced the explosion in one way or another. If they didn't see the flash that lit up the eastern sky and the towering mushroom cloud, they heard the thunderous roar and felt the still potent shock waves several minutes later. The more worldly residents of Larna attributed these happenings to some sort of earthquake, an event not unknown along Chansu's eastern coast. The more spiritual residents flocked to the temples for an explanation.

Thus it was that the local priests were the first to venture out into the sea to determine what had happened. And, while the local administrators were still trying to decide whether the blast was important enough to report to their regional supervisors, the priests had already communicated their findings to the High Priest at the New Palace Temple in Shinso.

Han Torgoona, the Prince Regent, sat at his morning meeting with his advisers at the long table in the Emperor's Meeting Room at the New Palace when a servant from the Temple brought the High Priest's request for an audience. Han dismissed the others until after lunch and sent word that he would receive the High Priest alone in the Emperor's private chambers. As he walked there through the Great Hall, Han thought about the man who had asked to see him.

Ever since he could remember, Han had disliked Pim Goodna. Before Goodna's election as High Priest, he had served as Priest of the Palace Shrine, and Han had known him since he assumed that position, when Han was in his teens. A fat, bald man with a perpetual scowl and unfriendly, piercing black eyes, Goodna had been a close advisor of the Emperor, Han's father, and had often in the past deigned to assume toward Han the same superiority and authority that the Emperor himself assumed. Now that he was Prince Regent and heir to the Empire, Han vowed he would no longer tolerate such behavior. This would be the first confrontation between them since the Emperor's disability, and Han looked forward, though not without some misgivings, to the opportunity to set things right with Goodna.

Han's thoughts turned from the High Priest individually toward the institution of the Priesthood generally. Han had felt for some time that the role of the Priests in relation to the Warrior class required revision. Persons who were naturally superior demeaned themselves by seeking advice from their inferiors, and such a practice, if carried to excess, could only lead to their ruin. Han did not question the need for the functions the Priesthood performed, even the giving of advice. The problem, as he perceived it, was that not all the functions of the Priesthood could properly be performed by the Priest class. The maintaining of the shrines, the raising of unwanted children, even the performance of the rituals--these were lesser tasks which inferior people could and should handle for their superiors. But when the members of the Priest class presumed to divine the will of the gods and advise their superiors as to how to act accordingly, they were overstepping all bounds of propriety. The answer to this problem, Han had recently concluded, was quite simple. The advisory functions of the Priesthood should be performed by members of the Warrior class. The Warriors undertook the important tasks in other lines of endeavor, leaving the mundane jobs to their inferiors. Why not also with regard to the Priesthood? Han resolved to take this matter up with his First Minister as soon as possible.

But for now Han had to accept the existing situation

as well as he could. The High Priest was coming to see him, and he must acknowledge the man as the preeminent interpreter of the mysterious forces which governed their lives. At least Han would have the satisfaction of knowing that Pim Goodna and his progeny would not long maintain their undeserved position of influence.

Han arrived in the Emperor's chambers, most of the rooms of which he had already appropriated. He sat down behind the large, ornately carved desk at which his father had so often received honored guests. His fingers drummed on the top of the desk as he waited impatiently for the High Priest to arrive. At last the door opened and a servant showed the visitor, followed by several young women from the temple as attendants, into the room.

Han remained seated. "Good morning, Pim," Han said, as familiarly as he could. Goodna looked even more disgustingly corpulent than the last time Han had seen him. The man bulged out of his white embroidered robes, and his jeweled necklace and bracelets pinched his soft flesh. Han resented the expressions of adoration on the faces of the attendants. How could they possibly desire to serve, much less admire, this revolting creature? He was about to ask Goodna to dismiss them when the High Priest himself, possibly anticipating Han's request, sent them out of the room with a snap of the fingers.

Without being asked, Goodna sat in the chair on the other side of the desk. "It's good to see you, Han," he said. "It's been too long since we last talked. How is your father?"

"No change," Han said curtly. "Quite frankly, we believe it's very unlikely that he will ever be able to resume his duties." Han watched carefully for a reaction from the High Priest. There was none. Damn him! Didn't he realize the precarious position he was in?

"That's very sad. Such a tragedy." Goodna crossed his heavy legs with evident effort.

"Why did you ask to see me?" Han asked.

Goodna puffed himself up with a deep breath. "There has been a sign, Your Excellency. A sign from the gods." He spoke these words in deep, rich tones that were not present in his ordinary conversation.

Your Excellency. Han liked hearing that from the High Priest. Perhaps Goodna was beginning to appreciate his new standing with Han. "What sort of sign?"

"We have received a direct and completely trustworthy report from the main temple at Larna. Yesterday, at about noon, the god of the sea and sky spoke to the people of Larna. There was a great flash of light, and a sudden wind from heaven. A small island in the ocean near Larna which held a sea shrine has disappeared.

"An island has disappeared?"

"All but a small bit at one end. The sea has covered it over."

"Perhaps it was an earthquake."

Goodna smiled condescendingly. "No earthquake comes in a blinding flash of light and a great roar of thunder and wind from a cloudless sky. Those are the works of the gods."

Han was puzzled. Could it really have been the doing of the gods? Or was this whole thing made up? Han doubted that Goodna would come to him with a pure fabrication. Yet he was also skeptical of a divine influence; Goodna was not above stretching the facts to suit his own purposes.

"You think it is some sort of message, then?" Han might as well hear Goodna out.

"Unquestionably, Your Excellency. More than a message, I would say. A warning."

"About what?"

"A warning to the people of Chansu to remain in their homeland. To disavow adventures to the east."

Han felt suddenly angry. The man had not changed his ways. Here he was, trying again to tell Han what to do, as always. But did Goodna know of the training camps, of the elaborate military strategies being drawn up this very minute in the War School? The High Priest had not been privy to any of the planning sessions. But of course no secret could be kept for long from the Priesthood.

Han momentarily repressed his feelings. "How do you know that is the meaning of the gods?"

"What else could be the meaning of a wall of fire and destruction in the eastern ocean? The gods know what mortals plan, and they show their disapproval, just as a parent will threaten a child who tries to leave the parent's protection. Be careful, Han Torgoona. Our gods will forsake us if we stray from our homeland."

Han could take it no longer. He stood up, his jaw set, the muscles tightening in his neck. "I've heard enough, Pim Goodna. You can't tell me what to do any longer. I'm not deceived by your robes and your talk of messages from the gods, and my father can't protect you now. Neither you nor any other faint-hearted worm is going to stop me. The Warriors of Chansu are going to fulfill their destiny. Our gods will be restored to the entire world."

Goodna stood also and glowered at Han. "You can't restore our ways by following the ways of the east. You will defeat yourself. Remember that, young man. The gods have spoken."

Young man! What happened to "Your Excellency?" "Get out, Pim Goodna. I don't want to hear any more. Your days as High Priest are few enough as it is. Don't make me shorten them more. Stay alive at least long enough to see the natural order brought back to the world. I want you to see that."

"All I can do now," said Goodna, reverting to his sonorous tones, "is pray for Chansu." He turned regally and marched, head held high, out of the room.

18

Han trembled with anger for long minutes after the High Priest left. Would he forever have to prove himself to men such as Pim Goodna, even after he was Emperor in title as well as fact? Would even his successes against the UWG be enough? Surely the ascendancy of the Warriors of Chansu to world domination would be sufficient to still the disapproval and the criticism. Therefore his plans must be carried out. He sat down again behind the huge desk to compose his thoughts.

Han was still sitting there fifteen minutes later when a servant, apologizing profusely for interrupting His Excellency, brought an urgent message of utmost importance that had just been received in the radio room. Han dismissed the young Worker impatiently, then looked at the typewritten sheet. He read:

```
To:   The Emperor and the Prince Regent of Chansu

         By now you have probably received
reports of an immense explosion 25 miles off
Chansu's eastern coast. Please be advised that
this explosion was no act of nature. It was
caused by the detonation of an atomic device
dropped from one of our aircraft. Other such
aircraft based within easy striking distance of
Chansu are at this moment being armed with
similar devices.
         The UWG abhors the use of such force. We
```

believe all people can live together in peace
and mutual respect for each others' rights. The
government of Chansu has, however, by making
hostages of UWG citizens, exhibited a disregard
for fundamental humanitarian principles. The UWG
has no alternative but to respond in kind, if
necessary.

We insist that you release our citizens as
soon as possible. If you do so, the UWG will
continue to consider your requests for
needed supplies. If you do not, we may be
required to use our atomic devices against
appropriate targets in Chansu itself.

Mildred Carter
Chairman, Prime
Council
United World
Government
July 15, 1948

Han dropped the message to the desk and laughed aloud. A message from the gods, Goodna had said. The High Priest was exposed as a fraud. No spirits of sea or sky had told Chansu to stop its ventures to the east. Only puny, classless men, who feared the restoration of the natural order to the world.

Tempted for a moment to call Goodna back and show him the message, Han gradually changed his mind. He picked up the message and reread it. Misgivings seized him. He hadn't known that the UWG possessed such weapons. And if he had he would never have thought the UWG capable of using them. Had he miscalculated? Was he leading Chansu to its destruction? Should he stop, alter his plans, before it was too late?

The answer to the last question came as soon as it was

posed. He couldn't turn back. His honor was at stake. To abandon his plans was to admit defeat, to admit that he would never prove himself, to negate the natural superiority of his entire class. This venture was his life. He would not, he could not, nullify his very existence.

Han read the message for a third time. The UWG would use force "if necessary." It "may" be required to use its atomic weapons against Chansu. Han's self-assurance began to return. These were spineless words. Reluctant threats. He grinned. He had not misread their will. The UWG had no Warrior class to match the Warriors of Chansu, who had achieved their ascendancy through their inborn ability, courage, and spirit. Those attributes would carry them to victory, whatever weapons the classless people of the UWG had inherited from their own now extinct Warriors. And as Han sat behind the great desk, thinking, ever so deliberately, a new plan--an exciting, bold, devastating plan--slowly took shape in his mind.

19

The fishing boat, its engines idling, bobbed slowly up and down as it drifted in the ocean dusk. On the deck a crew of five or six men appeared to be working on their nets. But inside, in the hold, there were no fish. Fifty uniformed men sat shoulder to shoulder around the sides, sweating and breathing the foul odor that permeated the place.

Several hundred yards away a similar fishing boat also drifted, and another the same distance beyond it. Ten miles to the northeast were three more such vessels. Eight miles to the southeast, three others. And so on across 1500 square miles of ocean. Forty ships in all, carrying a total of 2000 men, scarcely noticeable and not noticed by anyone in the vicinity.

Lyn Wonan was among those sitting in the hold of that first boat. He leaned his head back against the metal bulkhead and tried to sleep, without success. The rolling of the ship still, after over a week, made Lyn's stomach vaguely uneasy. When the ocean was rough, he had been able to survive only by lying flat on his back and staring at a point on the bulkhead above him. But he accepted his seasickness without comment or complaint, knowing that it was a necessary part of the great adventure in which he was participating.

Ten days ago, on July 18, the orders for this voyage had been announced to Lyn's training group by Lieutenant Lunan, his unit's commanding officer. All the Crocodile units which had completed at least two months' training, he said, were to participate. They had boarded trucks that very afternoon which took them to the docks at Shinso. The boats had sailed that evening. All the Workers in Lyn's training group were in the hold of the ship with him, confined to their dismal hole except for a thrice-daily stroll around the deck, one Worker at a time. Lyn's friend Ryl Kolu was at this moment dozing next to Lyn. Lieutenant Lunan and the five other Warriors who had joined him for this mission stayed above deck in the crew's quarters. Each day, however, one of them would descend into the hold to lecture the soldiers on the plans for the battle that was to come, which changed a bit each day as a reconnaissance team completed its work.

Their final lecture had just ended. In another hour, as soon as it was completely dark, the forty fishing boats would engage their engines and begin converging on the small dot of land known as Hawk Island. If all went according to plan, the boats would swing around to the north of the island and touch the shore within seconds of each other beginning at approximately 1:00 a.m.. Their common objective was a long stretch of narrow beach lying beneath the bluffs at the northeast end of the island, where its rocky spine met the sea. With climbing equipment half the soldiers would scale the bluff, march down the ridge, and position themselves behind the UWG base. Meanwhile the rest of the troops would march as far as they could go without danger of detection around the eastern perimeter of the island toward the base. When all the troops were in position, those on the beach would begin moving on the base. If opposition was encountered, they hoped to draw it toward them, so that the troops on the ridge could then enter the base unopposed and proceed directly to the primary objective: the four large buildings that lay along the runway between it and the ridge. The troops moving from the ridge would attack those buildings first.

Lyn reviewed the attack plan over and over in his mind as he sat leaning against the cold metal bulkhead. Several of the other Workers had resumed their week-long dice game in the center of the floor, but the pitch of their voices betrayed their rising anxiety. They, Lyn could tell, worried about whether they would live through the night. Lyn worried also, but not about death. His fear was that he would not comport himself bravely--that, at the decisive moment, the Worker he was would betray the Warrior he tried to be.

20

That same evening, July 28, 1948, on Hawk Island, Fred Harper worked past his normal quitting time making the final wiring adjustments on the third and last of the remaining bombs. When he finally left the brightly-lit hangar it was almost dark outside. It wasn't Fred's habit to work late unnecessarily, but he didn't mind this evening. It felt good to get a job completed. Also, things were not all they should be in the prefabricated duplex where Fred lived, and he welcomed a chance to put off another confrontation with Dorothy.

Basically, Dorothy was bored, and Fred could understand why. After rushing around the clock to get the base built and the bombs assembled and tested, now there was nothing to do but wait until the government told them the job was over and they could go home. There was the island to explore, but that had taken Fred and Dorothy all of half a day. The rest of their time together since the test, until the day before yesterday, they seemed to have spent complaining--about their lives, the island, and each other. Fred had received temporary relief when his superintendent decided two days ago to move the three bombs from the assembly building into the aircraft which had been adapted to carry them. The move was designed to make it possible to get the bombs into the air on short notice, though Fred wondered why, if that was an important requirement, the construction team had built the hangars at the western, upwind end of the runway. But the hangars weren't Fred's concern, and he had welcomed the new job. Now, however, it was all finished.

Fred breathed deeply as he strolled along the edge of the runway toward the administration building and the rows of prefabricated houses beyond. He walked slowly, savoring the warm, moist breeze and the approach of night. The sound of the waves tumbling onto the beach beyond the runway soothed him. How ironic, he thought, that a place of such peace and calm harbored the most destructive devices men had ever built.

Fred resisted the temptation to stay and instead quickened his pace. Somehow the thought of the bombs made the spot seem lonely. Besides, Fred was several hours late and the more he delayed, the angrier Dorothy would be when he arrived home.

The duplex Fred and Dorothy occupied stood in a row of others just like it to the north of the east end of the runway. Two additional rows of identical buildings ran along behind theirs, on the uphill side. Dorothy and her colleagues had designed the houses by altering plans their company had made for a small village in one of the reclaimed areas of the South Continent, where the standard apartment dwellings were not necessary and could not be easily constructed. The dwellings were prefabricated from metal, plastic, and prestressed concrete at the Consolidated Housing factory in Stevensburg and thence shipped by rail and boat to Hawk Island, where they were assembled under Dorothy's direction at the same time Fred was assembling the bombs. Each living unit, occupying half a building, contained a bedroom, a living-dining area, a small kitchen, and a toilet. Each row of houses shared bathing facilities provided in a separate building in the center of each row. There were few married couples among the men and women working on the island, and no children, so in most cases two men, or two women, occupied a living unit.

The Harpers' house was next to the last one in their row. Fred stopped momentarily in front of it. Then he went in. Dorothy was sitting in a canvas chair reading a magagine, which she put down as Fred entered.

"Hello," Fred said, as cheerfully as he could.

"Hello yourself. Where have you been?"

"I had to finish wiring in the last bomb."

"You could have done it tomorrow."

"I wanted to get it done." Fred walked to a chair across the room from Dorothy and sat down. "Have you eaten?"

"No, I was waiting for you."

"I told you at lunch I might be late."

'Not three hours late."

"Okay. I'm sorry." Fred stood up. "I'm also hungry. I'll put some dinner on. How about meatballs?"

"Sounds terrible."

"What would you like?"

"I don't know. I don't feel much like eating."

"How about some chicken? You've always—"

"No! I'm sick of all that stuff. Every can tastes the same. You go ahead and get yours. I'll heat something up later."

"Okay." Fred went into the kitchen and emptied the contents of a can into the saucepan on the stove. He came back to the living room. Dorothy was staring at the wall, her arms crossed and her mouth set.

"Another boring day, Honey?" Fred asked. He pulled

up a chair next to her and reached over and took her hand.

"How long do we have to sit here, anyway, not knowing what's happening? We don't even know whether anybody on Chansu saw your bomb go off, or what the government is doing about it. Are we going to have to explode another one?"

"I don't know. We're ready if we have to." Fred no longer even tried to pretend their mission wasn't a military one. It was an accepted fact by everyone on the island. "I'm sure they're just negotiating; one explosion ought to be enough to convince anybody. They couldn't have missed it. Anyway, we're perfectly safe and comfortable here. Let's go swimming tomorrow."

"People think there are sharks out there. Anyway, I don't want to go swimming. I want something meaningful to do."

"Should we apply for a transfer back to Stevensburg? I'm sure we can be replaced now."

"That's not fair to the government. We told them we'd stay until the job was finished."

"But we are finished. For the most part, anyway."

Dorothy looked at Fred. Then her eyes drifted away. "Oh, Fred, I don't want to go back to Stevensburg, either. What's bothering me isn't just this place, and being misled, and all that. It started before we even got here. It's just that it's so awfully isolated here that there's nothing to keep me from thinking about it."

"Thinking about what?"

"Oh . . . emptiness, I guess. Lack of fulfillment. I don't know."

"Think about your work, Honey. You've accomplished a lot. Surely that's worthwhile."

"Is it? What's so fulfilling about designing twenty-four identical little cubes? Same size, same shape, interchangeable pieces. Or even twenty-four apartment developments? Or twenty-four hundred? They're all the same, Fred. None of it is original. They ought to have machines doing it."

"That's unfair, Dorothy. You're working on improving

things, not making them all the same."

"You really think so? If anyone tries to design something really new, you know what happens? The superintendent smiles and says isn't that clever, but we can put up three standard buildings in the time it takes to do that, so how can anyone afford it?" She paused. "You know, something about this island makes me see it more clearly. We don't think about the sameness at home, because that's the way everything is. But out in a place like this there's no existing pattern to conform to. So when we build twenty-four little boxes, identical down to the last screw, the drabness of it stands out. It's just depressing."

Dorothy turned away from Fred, closed her eyes and leaned back. Neither of them said anything for a minute. Finally Dorothy opened her eyes and looked at her husband. "Fred, I guess I am hungry. Could you put something on for me, too."

"Sure. What would you like?"

"Anything. I don't care."

Fred went back to the kitchen and opened another can, which he poured into a second saucepan. He turned the fire down under the first pan, then returned to the living room and stood just inside the door.

"Fred, would you sit down a minute?" Dorothy said. "I want to ask you about something."

"Sure." Fred sat down again in the chair next to Dorothy's.

"Do you think," Dorothy began slowly, "that maybe I should give up my job and take a housewife's grant. Wouldn't you like to have children?"

"Well . . . I don't know." The question came as a surprise. "You've always been so sure you didn't want any."

"You've suggested it every now and then. What do you think now?"

"I know I've mentioned it in passing. But if you have children and take a housewife's grant, you can't change your mind and go back to work until the kids are old enough for a day home, and you've always said you disapproved of sending children to a day home."

"Fred, I know what I've said before. I'm asking what do you think. If you think at all."

"Look, I'm just saying what's going through my mind. If you want a report on my final conclusion you'll have to wait a bit. It isn't the sort of question one can answer right off."

They glared at each ether. Fred got up and began pacing back and forth across the small room. "I just don't know what to say to you," he said, feeling oddly guilty. "Of course it would be nice to have children. And if you're sure you want to do it by taking a housewife's grant, let's do it. But if you do, it means abandoning your work for a while--there's no way around that. I'm not sure you would be happy sitting around the apartment every day, not being productive." He was tempted to mention the loss of freedom children would impose, but he thought better of it.

"You think we shouldn't."

"I can't decide for you. You're the one who has to weigh these things. I do know that I'm not ready to share taking care of children, if that's what your hinting at. But as for the housewife's grant, that's up to you, and I don't know how you feel."

"You sure don't. Oh, the hell with you. You're no help at all." Dorothy got up and walked to the window. She pushed aside the curtain and looked out. "I just can't stand this place," she said evenly. Then, glancing briefly at her husband, she went back to her chair, picked up her magazine, and buried herself in it.

A short while later Fred and Dorothy ate their dinner in silence. Afterward Dorothy resumed her reading and Fred tried to write a letter to his family in Preston, whom he hadn't seen in four years. About midnight they both gave up on the evening and went to bed.

Dorothy went right to sleep, but Fred couldn't. Dorothy's soft, slow unconscious breathing brought back the loneliness that had touched Fred out on the runway on the way back from the hangar. Fred sought escape from the feeling by reconstructing in his mind the circuits he had been wiring the last two days. He felt satisfaction at having installed the three bombs in just two days. He had taken almost a week wiring in the test bomb. As he thought, however, an uncertainty formed in the back of his mind. Something was nagging at him about the safety circuit that prevented the arming of the bomb below 10,000 feet. Suddenly, he realized he had made a mistake. He had wired the safety circuit through the wrong box. Or had he? He couldn't have made an error like that, could he? Oh well, he could check it out in the morning. He turned over on his side. But wait, were they going to take the planes out in the morning? He had left a message that the wiring was completed, so they might be tempted to. If they did, and if he had made the mistake he thought, there would be some pretty confusing readings on the instrument panel. No danger, really, but he had better change his message. Oh well, he couldn't get to sleep anyway. A walk might do him good. He threw off the light blanket and got out of bed.

21

Fred heard the strange popping noise, coming from the direction of the administration building, just as he reached the hangar. He peered into the moonlit darkness but saw nothing and heard no more. It must have been the waves on the beach, he thought.

The lights still glared inside the hangar as Fred entered it through the small door on the east side. No one was there. The three planes sat side by side in the cavernous building, their upward pointing noses giving them a regal appearance, like huge animals resting proudly in their lair. Fred marveled again at the ingenuity that had created this huge structure on such short notice in this remote place. He remembered that when the hangar was first built, the occupants of the base had taken turns standing watch over it at night. Although the watch assignments were still posted on the bulletin board, no one bothered to follow them any more. After all, what was there to watch for?

Fred glanced at the bulletin board and saw his message that the wiring of the bombs was completed. He started to take it down when the popping noise repeated itself. It was followed by a loud bang. Looking back toward the base through the still-opened door, Fred thought he saw flames, but the bright lights inside the hangar made it difficult to make out anything outside. Alarmed, Fred went to the metal switch box on the wall and turned the lights off.

The sudden darkness seemed to carry with it a muffling silence. Fred stepped back to the door. He did see flames rising from near the administration building. In the moonlight he could also make out shadows of people running about. Whatever it was, he'd better get back and help. But first he would turn on the runway lights. He returned to the switch box, put on the runway lights, and raced back to the door. What he saw at the far end of the runway stopped him in his tracks. His heart pounded, and an electric shock surged from his belly throughout his body. He was suddenly drenched in sweat.

As the first shock wave passed, the sight took on meaning. He could see hundreds, maybe even thousands, of men spilling from somewhere in the darkness out onto the lighted runway and around the lighted portions of the administration building. Where did they come from? His mind next registered the fact that they all appeared to be dressed identically, in dark-colored clothes. Uniforms? Uniforms. Oh no, he thought, and he uttered a short, involuntary cry as the conclusion hit him. They are invading the island! They're after the bombs. But who? It could only be the Chansu. Another wave of panic swept over him. His life was in grave danger.

As he watched, still standing in the doorway, he

realized that in a matter of minutes they would be coming for the hangar. In fact, it appeared that a small group was heading this way now. With great effort he forced himself to move out of the doorway, back into the hangar. He slammed and locked the door. Where to go? There was another door at the far end of the hangar. It served no purpose, since the base was all located in the other direction, but it had been part of the prefabricated sections and had not been removed. Fred began groping his way through the dark interior of the hangar toward that back door. He started to break into a trot once he estimated where he was, but then he slowed. How could he survive out on the island without food or weapons? The Chansu would probably know he was there, since he had turned on the runway lights.

Suddenly he remembered. Inside each plane was a survival kit, to be used in case of a forced landing in a remote place. There would be food, warm clothing, and a gun. Also a radio. He chose the last aircraft in the hangar, searched out the switch for its interior lights and turned them on, and scrambled up and into the cockpit. As he looked for the kit, he dimly recalled that just a few short hours ago he had been working in this very plane, wiring in the bomb.

The bomb. The Chansu were after the bomb. The bomb and the craft to deliver it, they were right here. And he, Fred Harper, was the last man in the entire UWG who stood in their way.

But he couldn't stop them. What could he do? He was one man against hundreds. A small bore rifle in a survival kit that he hadn't even found yet was his only weapon. It was hopeless.

Then the realization that he strove to avoid crashed in on him. He did indeed have a weapon, an invincible one. He had the bomb, and he knew how to unleash it. In two minutes, three at the most, his trained fingers could make the adjustments that would blast the plane, the hangar, the Chansu troops--indeed, the whole island-- into vapor and dust.

And himself. And his wife, and his friends, and all his countrymen on the island. But mainly himself. He had found the subject of death creeping into his thoughts often in his life, but he had shunted it aside. He couldn't shunt it aside now. Death. An end to all his plans, all the things he wanted from life but had not yet received.

Fred found himself staring at the cable that ran from the cockpit to the bomb rack. At its end lay the mechanism that he could make destroy his world. He followed it with his eyes but stopped when they met the back wall. There, neatly strapped into place behind a small locker, was the survival kit.

He shook, and sweat broke out again all over him. He had an overpowering urge to urinate. He had to do something. By ending his world, he could perhaps save the world of thousands or millions in the UWG. But that was only a probability, a possibility; there was no certainty that the Chansu would use the bombs. What was a certainty was that if he exploded the bomb, he, and he alone, would be the killer of hundreds of people on this island, including his wife and his good friends. And if he destroyed the island, the UWG would likely be back with more bombs, to be captured or used against the Chansu. So other lives would be lost whichever way he turned.

Relieved, Fred jerked the survival kit out of its bracket and held it tightly as he left the cockpit and jumped through the door of the plane to the hangar floor. He ran to the back hangar door, slipped through it, and found himself, panting and lungs burning, climbing slowly through the darkness up the rocky ridge away from the base.

In the urgency of the moment, Fred had forgotten all about the wiring problem that had brought him to the hangar and the message that was still pinned to the bulletin board. Nor had he even noticed that his set of plans for the installation of the bomb in the aircraft still sat, rolled up, tucked into a metal bracket just outside the bomb rack of the plane he left so hastily.

Fred had been climbing for only a few minutes when, looking back, he saw in the moonlight dark forms converging on the hangar. They swarmed into it. He climbed on. When he next looked back he could see a group of men emerging from the back door, which he had stupidly left open. They would be searching for him! Fred climbed harder, clawing furiously at the sharp, scaly rock until his hands bled. He could hear urgent voices drifting up from below, but it didn't sound as if they had seen him. He was almost at the top of the ridge.

Suddenly a blinding light exploded over his head. A flare. Fred froze in shock. Should he stop moving? No, they would surely see him against the black rocks. He scrambled on upward. If only he could make it to the top, he would be out of sight from below. He reached and pulled himself slowly upward. It was the top. He rolled over it and onto the flat crest of the ridge. As he did a gunshot cracked from below, and a bullet twanged off the rock not five feet under him.

Fred crawled to the center of the ridge, where he could stand without being seen from below. He spun around, confused. He couldn't go back toward the base, because the Chansu were there. He could only go westward, toward the end of the island. Perhaps he could find a hiding place there.

He ran, as well as he could over the uneven rock. Twice he fell, scraping his arm and knees badly. He couldn't hear anyone behind him, but he knew they were there. The flare had died, but there would be another. As he ran, Fred became conscious of a roaring below him. The sea! He slowed down, and just in time. Not ten feet ahead, the crest of the ridge ended abruptly. Fred approached the edge cautiously, on hands and knees. He remembered now, from his brief exploration of the island. There was a straight drop of several hundred feet. The same to the north and the south. The slope he had climbed back by the hangar gave way here, at the westernmost end of the island, to perpendicular walls. Fred panicked. He was trapped!

22

Lyn Wonan and Ryl Kolu were in the first Crocodile Unit to reach the hangar. Lyn didn't know why the decision had suddenly been made to send his squad to secure the hangar as rapidly as possible, but he didn't question the decision or even wonder about it. For him, it was enough that Lieutenant Lunan had given the order. He would obey it with every resource he possessed.

The first man in the squad to enter the hangar, Lyn sensed that someone was there, or had just left. He saw the lights glowing through the windows of the plane on the far side of the hangar. Ignoring the huge planes, the likes of which Wonan had never seen before and which under other circumstances would have awed him, Lyn quickly searched the inside of the huge building with his electric torch. He found no one, but he noted the open door at the other end of the building.

By this time Lieutenant Lunan, the Unit Commander, had arrived. Lyn reported briefly.

"Why didn't you search the planes?" Lunan barked.

Lyn hung his head. The Lieutenant ordered several of the other men to search and guard the planes until the inspection team arrived. Then he, along with the rest of the squad, including Wonan and Kolu, went out the back door.

They stopped to allow their eyes to readjust to the darkness. Lyn could see that the hangar was the last building at this end of the camp. Beyond it the beach stretched on for several hundred yards, narrowing to a small sliver. To the left was the sea and the sound of the surf. To the right, only a short distance from the hangar, the sand abruptly gave way to the sloping sides of the rocky ridge that ran down the center of the island. It would be difficult, Lyn thought, to find anyone out here now. The moon was bright, but there were too many shadows in which a man could hide.

"Send up a flare," ordered Lunan. "Then step back next to the hangar. We don't want to make ourselves targets."

The bright glow of the flare hurt Lyn's eyes at first, but as soon as he could he searched out the places where the shadows had been. There was nothing along the beach or at the base of the ridge. He shifted his gaze upward. At the edge of his vision something white moved against the black rocks, high up on the cliff. It was a man.

"There. Up there," Lyn shouted, pointing.

The Lieutenant and the others looked. "Well, shoot, you fool," Lunan yelled when he saw the man. He stepped beside Lyn, jerked Lyn's rifle from his shoulder and aimed at the moving figure. Just as he fired the figure disappeared over the crest of the ridge.

"After him, all of you," the Lieutenant shouted, leading the others over to and up the side of the ridge. As Lyn started to rush forward after his commander, he felt a hand on his arm restraining him. It was Kolu.

"This is craziness," Kolu said. "There is only one man. What can he do now?"

Lyn jerked his arm free. "It's our order. We don't question it." He went after the others and soon caught up to them. Kolu followed reluctantly.

It took them longer than Lyn estimated it would to reach the top of the ridge. When they did, there was no trace of the enemy. The Lieutenant sent up another flare. Visibility along the top of the ridge and down the slope on the other side was excellent, but still they saw no one.

"The enemy has gone along the top of the ridge," Lunan announced. He sent four men back toward the base. He ordered Wonan and Kolu to come with him in the other direction, toward the western end of the island. The rest he sent back down to the hangar.

The three men spread out and walked slowly westward, searching for a sign of their quarry. Lyn was on the northern flank, and he looked for a place where a man could hide, or where he could have gone down the other side of the ridge without being visible in the light of the flare, which had by now spent itself. But the slope of the ridge on the north side soon turned into sheer walls, and Lyn knew that no man could climb down those.

The ridge's crest, some thirty yards wide where Lyn and the others had come onto it, gradually narrowed to less than fifteen. Then, suddenly, it ended in a straight drop to the sea. Lyn wouldn't have detected the edge if he hadn't been walking slowly and hadn't heard the noise of the surf far below. He motioned the others to stop.

"It's the end," Lyn said to the others.

Lieutenant Lunan approached the edge and looked cautiously over. "The enemy couldn't have escaped this way. Come, let's join the others."

"Perhaps the man fell over the edge. It's difficult to see," Kolu said.

"That's possible. Send up another flare."

When the light was up all three of them leaned over the side and looked down. They couldn't see the side of the cliff all the way to the bottom, for the top of the ridge protruded out over the side, and the wall just beneath the overhang was out of their line of sight. But they could see the rocks below, and there was no sign of any broken body.

"He's not there. He--or they--must have gone the other way," said Lunan. They stepped back from the edge and started in the other direction.

Lyn stayed on the north side of the ridge. Perhaps this time, from this angle, he thought, he could see a hiding place. His thoroughness reaped its reward almost immediately. Not ten yards away from the end of the ridge, along the north edge, showing through the small rocks and dirt which had obviously been placed to cover it, a brown strand of rope caught Lyn's eye. He had missed it earlier in the shadows, but the light of his torch from this side was just barely enough to reveal its presence. He rushed to it. The rope was looped tightly around a heavy boulder several yards from the side of the ridge and then ran to and over the edge. Lyn called the others, then peered cautiously over the edge where the rope went. It was tight against the side of the cliff, which explained why Lyn hadn't caught sight of it earlier, and which also suggested that something was putting tension on it below. Here, however, as on the end of the ridge, the top overhung the sides of the cliff, so that Lyn couldn't follow the rope all the way down. He could see where it disappeared under the overhang, but he couldn't pick it up again further down the cliff.

"What is it, Wonan?" the Lieutenant demanded. Lyn pointed out the rope and reported his observations. "You should have seen it when you first went by. We've wasted a lot of time." Lunan bent down and looked over the edge, then turned to Wonan and Kolu. "Another flare," he said. "Then pull that rope. We'll see what it's attached to below."

Lyn and Ryl did as they were told. The rope was fastened to something below, but on their second pull they managed to free it. They looked over the side quickly, half expecting to see a body falling to the rocks below. Instead, all they saw was the rope, dangling in the air, its end about fifty feet below them.

"Well, they didn't make it to the bottom with that rope," Lunan laughed. "They must be just under the overhang. Perhaps there's a cave." His face went serious. "Worker Wonan, I want you to go down the rope and get them."

Lyn's heart skipped, and he felt ashamed at the reaction. "Yes, sir," he said, and he picked up the rope.

"Sir," protested Kolu, "he'll be an open target. Shouldn't we just leave the enemy there? Perhaps we can shoot at him from below."

Lunan glared at Kolu. "I give the orders here, Worker. You know nothing of these matters."

"It's craziness. He'll be killed, for no purpose. The enemy presents no danger there."

The Lieutenant started to move toward Kolu, his arm raised in anger. Lyn feared that Kolu might strike back. He resented Kolu's intrusion into his affair, but he didn't want Ryl to suffer the consequences of harming a Warrior. He turned on Kolu himself and pushed Kolu to the ground.

"I obey my order," Lyn said. "It's not your place to interfere."

Ryl stared up at Lyn from his sitting position on the ground, his face registering a mild shock. The Lieutenant slowly lowered his arm.

"Very well, Wonan, then get on with it," Lunan said.

Lyn checked the rope. It was strong and securely fastened to the large boulder. Then he made sure of his weapons. A knife in its scabbard at his waist, where he could reach it quickly. His rifle slung over his shoulder, not so immediately accessible, but available. He stepped to the edge and picked up the rope in one hand. Then he turned and saluted the Lieutenant.

Lunan returned the salute lazily. "We will be ready with a flare," he said. "Call us when you want it."

"Yes, sir." Lyn gripped the rope firmly with both hands and began lowering himself over the cliff, bracing his weight with his feet against the rock wall. As he went over, he glanced at Kolu, who still sat on the ground where Lyn had pushed him, still wearing an expression of shock, mixed with worry. Lyn felt a sudden, brief surge of compassion for his friend. Then all he could see was the black side of the cliff, and his thoughts turned to the difficulty at hand.

Lyn was exhilarated as he moved slowly down the rock face. It felt good to use his muscles and skill. He was oblivious to the rocks that lay a hundred yards below, just a slip of the hand away. He was serving his Emperor. He was doing the job of a Warrior!

Almost before he knew it he was at the end of the overhang. He looked up briefly and saw the shape of the Lieutenant's head and shoulders, staring down at him. Kolu was not watching. Then he focused his attention on the problem before him. If he were to continue to lower himself below the overhang, the lower part of his body would he exposed to any enemy that was under it long before Lyn could ever see them. He wasn't afraid to do that if it was necessary. He would obey his orders. But maybe there was another way.

Slowly, gradually shifting all his weight to his arms, Lyn walked his feet to the side and up to the level of his head. The strain on his arms and back was terrific. Then, inch by inch, he lowered his head until he was almost upside down, just above the bottom of the overhang. The blood throbbed in his head. He was about to lower himself a little further when he realized that all would be shadow under the overhang. His throat tight from his awkward position, he called up to the Lieutenant for a flare. Lunan didn't waste a moment. Within seconds the flare burst in the air, somewhat above Lyn but far enough out from the cliff to give light underneath. As quickly as he could, Lyn moved his head downward.

There the man was! Crouched on a narrow ledge, not ten feet away, staring back at Lyn, his eyes full of fear. There was no cave, as the Lieutenant had speculated. Just a narrow ledge no more than a foot wide, no more than ten feet long.

The man had a rifle which he held across his body, as if it were a shield. He also had a flashlight, pointed toward Lyn, its glow overcome by the flare. At once Lyn realized how exposed his own position was. Only his eyes and the top of his head protruded below the overhang. But he couldn't move back up the rope in this position! His muscles ached just holding himself where he was. He had to do something. Slowly, he moved his feet to the side, staring at the man as he did. The man remained frozen. Why didn't he shoot? Lyn wondered. As Lyn's feet reached the bottom of the overhang, he swung himself around to an upright position. As he did, his rifle slipped on his shoulder, the catch on the strap opened, and the weapon fell down into the sea. Whatever sound it made was covered by the roar of the surf. Now Lyn was fully exposed, but still the man did nothing. Lyn swiftly scrambled back up the rope until he was protected again by the rock.

Now what should he do? His feet found a crevice in the rock and he cautiously transferred most of his weight to them, resting his strained arms. The man was, as Kolu had said, completely harmless there. Now that his rope was pulled away, he couldn't leave his ledge. He would eventually starve, if he didn't first fall into the sea. There was no logical reason for Lyn to go after him.

But the Lieutenant had already rejected the idea of leaving the enemy there. Lyn's orders were to take the man, and that was what he would do. The question was how to do it. Lyn still had has knife, but he must get close to use it. It was just as well, for it would be next to impossible to use a rifle while hanging on the rope. Lyn had never used a weapon of any kind on a human before, but the thought of doing so now didn't trouble him. This man was an enemy, a classless person who planned to destroy Chansu. Killing him would be no different from killing a wolf that threatened Lyn's village.

How, Lyn wondered, had the man himself reached that ledge? He must have swung over to it on the rope and found something to grab onto. Well, Lyn could do the same. He shifted his weight back to his arms. They felt strong again. He began to slide down the rope. No flare this time. Lyn knew where the man was, and Lyn would be enough of a target silhouetted against the night sky, without a flare to make an even brighter background.

As Lyn reached the bottom of the overhang he kicked off with his feet and loosened his grip on the rope ever so slightly. His stomach lurched as he began to fall away from the side of the cliff. Then he tightened his grip, his hands burning and his shoulders straining.

Slowly, ever so slowly it seemed, the rope pulled him back toward the cliff, under the overhang and toward the ledge. As he began his pendulum swing he saw the enemy's flashlight snap on. As its beam searched for him, it glinted on the man's rifle barrel. Surely he will shoot, Lyn thought. But no shot was fired.

Now Lyn moved faster, at the bottom of the arc. The man, slightly above Lyn, was shouting something at him, wholly unintelligible. With steadily decreasing speed, Lyn moved upward, upward toward the little light. The light moved, and Lyn caught sight of the man's face again. A face full of fear. Not, Lyn thought, the face of an enemy.

Then Lyn was almost abreast of the man. The rifle barrel was thrust out at him, not to shoot him, not even to knock him off the rope, just to push him away.

Lyn's upward swing was ending. He would not reach the cliff behind the man to take a handhold. Quickly, Lyn reached for the outthrust rifle. He missed. He grabbed again and caught it. But in doing so Lyn's grip with his other hand on the rope gave way.

Lyn was holding onto the rifle barrel. There was weight for a moment at the other end, then suddenly there was none. Lyn fell. The man had let go of the rifle. No. Incredibly, the man was above him, falling too. He had held on, trying to save Lyn! A scream. Not me, thought Lyn. Warriors die bravely. He held his mouth shut tight as the rocks came up to meet him.

PART FOUR

July 1948-August 1948

1

The news that the Chansu had taken Hawk Island arrived in Preston at about three o'clock on the afternoon of July 29, 1948, while the Prime Council was in public session. A messenger brought two messages from the Communications Room directly to Chairman Carter at her seat at the Council table. The first was a garbled, incomplete transmission from the UWG radio officer on Hawk Island. The second slightly later one came from the "Chansu Defense Force--Supreme Marine Commander." It said simply: "Hawk Island now a territory of the Chansu Empire and will he defended as such."

Carter paled visibly as she read the messages. Her discomfort was obvious to the other Council members and to the three reporters in the Council Room.

Henry Smith had been reading a prepared statement on new tax legislation when the messages arrived. As attention shifted to Carter he slowed and stopped. He looked at her expectantly. "Is there some problem, Mildred?" he asked.

Carter still appeared shocked. "No, I'm quite all right, Henry. Please go on with your statement."

"Wait a moment, Madame Chairman," said one of the reporters, a thin, wiry man with bushy eyebrows. "If this is official business, we're entitled to know about it."

Carter glanced questioningly at the faces of the other Council members. Silently, she passed the messages to them. Cornettia and Smith, who read them first, reacted much the same as Carter. Parthupta remained as impassive as ever. Strongarm, the last to read them, responded with an unmistakable look of contempt directed toward Carter.

"Well, do we have the information or not?" asked the reporter.

Seeing no negative response from the other Council members, Carter held the messages before her, her hands trembling slightly, and spoke. "We have just received word that the Chansu have landed a force on Hawk Island in the Ellenberry Islands and have claimed it for their own."

Strongarm felt relieved that Carter had not decided to delay the disclosure. Perhaps she had concluded that the secrecy business had gone too far. Or maybe she just thought that the bare fact of the capture of Hawk Island wouldn't seem too important. If the latter were true, though, she had made a grave error; her mannerisms alone betrayed the terrible significance of the messages.

The reporter looked puzzled. "Where is Hawk Island, if I may ask?" he said.

"At the very western end of the Ellenberries," answered Cornettia, trying to help his Chairman. "Now, shall we return to Mr. Smith's statement?"

"Mr. Cornettia. Mme. Chairman," said the reporter, obviously fishing for something that would explain the concern he had seen when the message arrived. "This appears to me to be a matter of urgent public interest. I think under the Information Act we ought to be entitled to some more information."

Cornettia started to speak, but Carter, somewhat rejuvenated, interrupted him. "We have no more information than this. The radio messages are public documents. You may examine them. We will have public deliberations on the matter as soon as sufficient information is available. In the meantime, perhaps it would be best for the Council to adjourn to make further inquiries." She smiled at Smith. "I can see, Henry, that this matter seems to have taken attention away from your statement. I would imagine you would rather continue it at some other time, anyway."

Smith nodded. The bushy-eyebrowed reporter sat down. But before the Council could act on Carter's suggestion another reporter, a young and energetic woman, leaped to her feet. "Madam Chairman," she said, "I would like to ask you one question before you adjourn. Do you think that this action by the Chansu could have anything to do with the atomic explosives test reported in the Ellenberries about a week and a half ago?"

The blood drained from Carter's face again. She looked helplessly at the other Council members. They all averted her eyes, except Strongarm, who stared at her stonily. "Yes, I believe it might," Carter said, her voice not much louder than a whisper.

"There couldn't possibly have been any atomic explosives on Hawk Island, could there?" asked the young reporter, excitedly and fearfully.

There was a long pause. Finally, Carter spoke, in a louder and firmer voice. There was no way to avoid the issue now. "I believe there were," she said.

"Oh no!" exclaimed the reporter, clapping her palm to her forehead. "Oh, no!"

2

The next morning, July 30, 1948, the Prime Council members found themselves sitting uncomfortably on the dais of the Grand Chamber of the Capitol Building, looking at the 350 members of Congress gathered below. The hot lights for the television cameras glared down on them. Strongarm sweat heavily. What a misfortune for the Council, he thought, that the first live telecast of a session of Congress was going to involve this debacle. Why couldn't it have been his own proposal for elimination of the equalization laws, finally approved for consideration by the Council a month ago but still not acted upon? Why, indeed, couldn't it have been anything other than this?

The members of the Congress Information Committee, who had been waiting just below, now walked single file up the stairs and onto the dais and took their place at a table opposite the one at which the Prime Council members sat. The great hall quieted. The Chairman of the Information Committee, Representative Childone from West Doltony, adjusted the microphone in front of him and spoke, in the high-pitched twang of a Swampland farmer.

"Members of the Prime Council, fellow Representatives, and citizens of the United World Government," he began. "This extraordinary meeting has been convened by a unanimous vote of the Congress, taken late yesterday, as a result of certain facts of extreme importance to all of us, which became known only yesterday. The Congress apologizes for the short notice afforded of this meeting, but I think everyone will agree that the matters at stake are of such urgency and such moment that any further delay would have been highly dangerous.

"The Prime Council and the Information Committee of the Congress met a short while ago to agree on the procedures for this unprecedented session. We will proceed immediately with questioning from the Committee, and the Council members may make as long or short a statement as they like in response. The senior member of our Committee, Representative Briggs, will begin."

Briggs, a thin gray-haired man in his seventies, peered at the Council members over the tops of his rimless glasses. "Mrs. Carter," he finally said, in his soft polite voice, "could you please begin by telling us about the messages you received yesterday afternoon and the events leading up to them?"

Carter did so, first reading the messages and then briskly ticking off the events that preceded them: the initial capture of the UWG mission in Chansu, the holding of the supply ships, the Prime Council's informal decision to proceed with the development of the atomic device, the testing of the device, and the warning to the Chansu.

When she finished Briggs smiled at her politely. "Well," he said, "of course we were all aware of the Chansu mission and the ships, and of the tests. But how did knowledge of the Prime Council decision to threaten Chansu elude us?"

"Because the Council did not consider that any government action decision had been made," Carter answered. "We didn't hold any public hearings on the matter."

"Yet you built an air base and sent three aircraft and four atomic bombs to Hawk Island. You exploded a bomb next to Chansu and threatened them that you might explode another one right on top of them."

"That's correct."

"May I interject something here, Mr. Briggs?" asked Cornettia. Receiving a nod from Briggs, he continued. "Speed and secrecy were very important on this, you must understand. Public debate would have cost valuable time and perhaps forewarned our enemy!"

"You mean you actually believe that there are Chansu agents around here reading our newspapers?" Briggs asked. There was a small ripple of laughter from the floor of the hall.

"No, I don't. But we don't really know what the Chansu are capable of. Take Hawk Island, for example. The Chansu had never gone that far from their island before. For all we know, they're able to monitor our news broadcasts."

"All right," said Briggs, serious again. "Are you saying that a violation of the Public Information Act was excusable, or that there was no violation?"

"Both," Cornettia snapped.

"Tell me," continued Briggs," was the decision unanimous?"

"No." Cornettia had taken over from Carter in fielding the questions.

"What was the vote? If you bothered to hold one."

"Three to two."

"Three to two! That close, and yet you failed to call a public hearing. Who voted against it?"

"I did," spoke up Strongarm. "Mrs. Parthupta and I."

"Why didn't you ask for a public debate? You could have forced it," Briggs said.

Strongarm spoke directly and forcefully. "I can't speak for Mrs. Parthupta, but I didn't believe a public hearing would change the result of the vote, and I felt that a public airing of the Council's disagreement would have been detrimental." Strongarm still hesitated to expose the policy decisions that lay behind the actions of the majority of the Council. He hoped that the Information Committee would not ask him to elaborate on why he thought a public airing would be detrimental.

"What about the Information Act, Mr. Strongarm? What did you think about that?"

"I felt at the time that the Council's action was probably not covered by the Act. I realize now that there may be some doubt about that conclusion, but we were hardly in a position to submit the question to a court."

"May I say something else?" asked Cornettia.

"Certainly," said Briggs.

"Public hearings would not have changed anything. We would have taken the same action. I think that is the gist of what Mr. Strongarm is saying."

"Well, this is not the proper time for a debate, Mr. Cornettia, but I would suggest to you that the violation of the Information Act can't be excused even if you are correct. And let me pose one question for your thoughts." Briggs' voice rose. "Isn't it just possible that if the same action was adopted after public debate someone might have suggested we take adequate steps to protect Hawk Island from an invasion?"

Briggs stared at Cornettia for a long moment. Then he looked down at his notes. Finally he spoke again, in his normal courteous tones. "Council members, there are a great many more questions I would like to ask about how and why these secret decisions were made, but we are facing a problem that demands a solution, not recrimination. I will therefore only state that these matters of improper secrecy will be fully investigated at the proper time, and I remind the Council, as far as its future conduct is concerned, that its tenure in office is at the discretion of a majority of the Congress. Your position is already precarious. I think I speak for the Congress in stating that both we and the public feel we are entitled to know about *all* decisions of any significance made by the Prime Council from here on out."

Briggs sat back in his chair as a murmur of approval filled the hall. Chairman Childone banged his gavel and leaned forward to his microphone. "The most important matter at hand is what we do about the Chansu occupation of Hawk Island. The Committee has asked me to pursue that subject. First of all, Mrs. Carter, what threat is there at present to the UWG, now that the Chansu have our aircraft and our atomic bombs?"

Carter rubbed her narrow chin thoughtfully before she spoke. "Mr. Chairman, we haven't had much time to analyze the situation. The Prime Council hasn't really discussed it--not even informally." She smiled weakly. "In my own view the present danger isn't great. Those aircraft have a maximum range of 6,000 miles. Hawk Island is too far away from the UWG to permit any strikes against us, though I suppose the eastern Ellenberry Islands are within their range. But they do have the bombs and the planes. They can move closer. Or perhaps they can increase the range of the aircraft."

"I suppose, by the same token, Hawk Island is outside the range of our aircraft, too," said Childone.

"That's correct--at least as far as any present airstrips are concerned. We could expand one of our airports in the eastern Ellenberries, or build a new one."

"How long would that take?"

"The Hawk Island base was built in a little over a month, once the materials were there."

Childone scratched his head. "It looks like a standoff, at least for the moment," he said.

"Excuse me," interrupted Parthupta, "but I think we make a serious error of judgment if we assume the Chansu are subject to the same limitations as we. We say Hawk Island is not within range because our planes cannot fly there and return. Who is to say the Chansu require their planes to return?"

"That's ridiculous," said Cornettia. "No one would intentionally sacrifice his life that way--to say nothing of their few planes."

Parthupta smiled politely at Cornettia. "You know little of the Chansu. They don't necessarily share our regard for life--or our logic. And they may know more about our behavior than we do of theirs."

Childone whispered briefly with one of the Committee members seated next to him. He then turned to Parthupta and said gravely, "I take it that what you have in mind, Mrs. Parthupta, is that it is less than 6,000 miles from Hawk Island to our cities in Westland. What about that, Mrs. Carter?"

"I suppose it's possible for them to attack us, if they're willing to give up their lives and their planes. I agree with Mr. Cornettia that this is very unlikely."

The discussion had caused an increasing volume of noise from the floor of the hall. Childone banged his gavel. "Well, regardless of whether there is a present threat or not," he said, "what does the Council propose to do about the capture of Hawk Island?"

Carter answered. "As I told you earlier, Mr. Chairman, the Council hasn't yet had a chance to consider any action. We've been too busy preparing for this." She swept her hand in the direction of the television cameras. "We do have a starting place, however. When this whole affair with Chansu began we had extensive reports prepared on possible means of responding to the situation. Those reports were written with the objective of freeing the hostages held in Chansu, but they could as well be applied to the object of freeing Hawk Island. Let's not forget, incidentally, that the Chansu may be holding hostages there, too."

Childone consulted briefly with several other Committee members. "Do we have these reports?" he asked.

"No. They were requested by the Prime Council. Surely you don't consider those to involve government action."

"No, but of course they would have been disclosed if there had been public debate on the subject," Childone replied. "What do the reports say?"

"Well, in brief, they consider the possibility of air, naval and land action against Chansu. The air attack seemed the most promising, providing we could build a base close enough."

"It permitted us to mount a significant attack without much danger to our own people, you see," interjected Cornettia.

"Yes," Carter continued. "Naval action seemed less promising because of the time to build proper warships, and of course the Chansu do have military vessels. Land action was rejected because of the impossibility of recruiting troops--unless, of course, we resort to conscription."

"And several Council members have been and always will be opposed to conscription, for whatever reason," put in Strongarm, feeling a need to demonstrate the depth of his feeling on the subject. "No end can justify such a means."

"I'm sure many members of the Congress share that attitude, Mr. Strongarm," said Childone. "But how do we know that troops can't be raised voluntarily?"

"Would you go?" asked the unusually talkative Parthupta, in her usual quiet voice. "Would your sons?" Childone sat for a moment, staring at the Council members. He didn't respond to Parthupta's question. He didn't need to. "Well," he finally said, "obviously the reports must be reconsidered in light of the present situation. We can't drop explosives on the island if UWG citizens are being held there."

"Mr. Chairman, the Prime Council plans to hold a formal session to deal with that very matter just as soon as your Committee is finished asking us questions," said Carter.

Childone bristled and leaned toward his microphone, then apparently thought better of it and drew back. "The Committee will take a five minute recess for consultation," he finally announced.

The consultation required less than two minutes. The Committee members returned to their chairs on the dais and then waited for the representatives to scurry back to their seats on the floor. When a reasonable order was attained, Childone said, "It is now a little before eleven o'clock. When can the Prime Council meet if we adjourn now?" Carter looked at the other Council members, then back at Childone. "We must consult certain advisers in the executive department. We can then hold our meeting directly after lunch--say two o'clock."

"Very well. The Committee recognizes that the immediate danger must be taken care of. We can wait to resume these hearings until after that is done, perhaps even later this afternoon." Childone turned toward the television cameras. "The Committee apologizes for starting something that must be interrupted, but I think we can all agree that the interruption is necessary." He looked back at the Council members, with an expression on his face as if he had just thought of something. "Of course, the Prime Council won't mind holding its meeting here, in front of the cameras, will it?" he asked innocently. "I'm sure the public will be interested, and there could hardly be a more appropriate occasion for the first television coverage of a Prime Council policy session, could there?"

Childone's request was not, Strongarm knew, as impromptu as he tried to make it seem. Strongarm dreaded the thought of holding the Council meeting here, but the Council could hardly refuse. Strongarm suddenly realized what he was thinking. He wished that all the Council's deliberations could be private. How could he have ever come to such an untenable conclusion? Of course the debates must be open to the public, and what better way to do it than by television.

Chairman Carter did not bother even to consult with her fellow Council members. "Of course," she said. "The Council would be pleased to conduct its meeting here."

"Very well," Childone said, with a look of triumph. He pounded his gavel. "This session of the Information Committee is adjourned until further notice. Unless there are objections from the Congress," he looked over the silent faces in the hall, "we will reconvene here at two o'clock for the Prime Council's policy session." He banged the gavel again, and the Committee rose and began to file down off their platform, while the Prime Council members waited their turn to leave.

3

Strongarm assumed the two o'clock hour was set so that the Council could meet informally at one. Carter confirmed the assumption shortly after the adjournment, then suggested the Council members go their separate ways for an early lunch. Strongarm went instead to his office, where he sat for a long time staring out the window and thinking about impossible alternatives.

Shortly before noon Strongarm's phone rang. His secretary was out, so he answered it himself. It was Carter. "Can you come to my office right away?" she asked. "It's urgent."

It took Strongarm only a few minutes to make his way across the courtyard, hot in the late July sun, and into Carter's office. He was surprised to find all the rest of the Council present, including even Parthupta, who seldom ever spoke to her fellow Council members except at scheduled meetings.

"Robert, thank you for coming so quickly," Carter said. Strongarm grew apprehensive. Carter seldom called him 'Robert.' Carter reminded him very strongly of his mother when she had wanted him to do some especially unpleasant task. "Since we left the Congress there has been a crucial development," Carter continued. "This message was received not more than twenty minutes ago." Carter handed him a sheet of the red-bordered lightweight paper he recognized as coming from the Council's Communication Room. It read:

```
To:    Prime Council of the UWG
```

```
We now possess your planes and your atomic
explosives. As recompense for your contemptible
threat to use them against the Empire of Chansu,
and to further equalize the disparity in wealth
that divides our nations, we demand that you
cede all Ellenberry Islands to us forthwith.
Refusal to do so will result in mass destruction
of your land and your people.

                          Han Torgoona
                          Prince Regent of Chansu
                          In   the   Name   of   the
                          Emperor            .
```

Strongarm looked up from the message. "So soon," he said.

"Yes, so soon," said Carter.

"The equation takes on a new balance," said Cornettia. "It's no longer only hundreds of UWG lives at stake."

Strongarm slapped the message down on the table. "The equation wouldn't have changed if we had taken the humanitarian approach. They're only doing to us what we did to them."

Carter picked up the message and looked at it, then at Strongarm. "You may be right, Robert, although I have my doubts as to whether the Chansu needed our example to make this threat." She waved the paper. "But be that as it may, we have made a mistake. We should have listened to you. But we can't change the past. We must deal with this threat. Surely you concede that."

"I agree that we should do something. What that is, I don't know. I hope it's not too late to avoid military action." He looked at the other Council members present. "What has been suggested?"

Henry Smith answered. "We thought of course we would press on with what was mentioned this morning--building a new air base, or increasing the size of an old one, within range of Hawk Island. We've also asked the engineers to see if they can't somehow extend the range of the existing aircraft. But Mildred and Rolf don't think that we have enough time for either. Besides, there's the problem of the UWG citizens who may still be on the island."

"We're going to send a message to Chansu asking for time to decide," said Carter. "But I would guess that we won't get enough--not if they really mean what they say."

"Surely we'll have further negotiations with them," said Strongarm.

"You mean give them the Ellenberry Islands? Never," said Cornettia.

"You don't mean to suggest that, do you, Robert?" said Carter.

Strongarm collected his thoughts. Would the Ellenberries be enough? Or did the Chansu just want them as stepping stones, as Cornettia and Carter believed.

"I wouldn't rule anything out. After all, they have much less land than we. It would make sense for them to expand to the Ellenberries. It's the nearest land to Chansu. Of course, we couldn't do it unless they give us back our bombs."

"Strongarm, you're--" exploded Cornettia.

Carter held up her hand to stop Cornettia. "Just a minute, Rolf," she interrupted. "Of course we're open to negotiation, Robert, and we're going to do what we can. If the Chansu really want to coexist peacefully with us, we will agree. But you must admit that we have to be prepared for a military contingency."

"If they strike first."

"Yes, of course. If they strike first."

The others were silent for a moment, looking at Strongarm. He had a feeling that there was more to be said. "So where is all this leading?" he asked. "You aren't sure of the value of a new air base. What else is there?"

Smith cleared his throat. Carter and Cornettia looked at him expectantly. "We believe that we have to be prepared to make a direct invasion of Hawk Island," Smith said. "That's the only way to get our bombs back without unduly endangering any hostages." He stopped for a moment. "Short of negotiation," he added belatedly.

"Wouldn't that take too long to get ready? And who's going to do it?"

Smith smiled. "That's what I asked when I first heard the idea. But the fact is, we're almost ready for an invasion right now. You remember that when we decided to pursue the air power strategy, Mildred also mentioned that her staff had explored the possibility of naval action. Well, the report was pessimistic, but nevertheless the staff went ahead to put together the best equipment they could. It was designed for a possible invasion of Chansu, but it can certainly be used against Hawk Island."

"What kind of equipment?"

Smith looked to Carter. She nodded and took over the explanation. "We have three ships, armed with cannon. The guns are more than a hundred years old, but we've made them work. The ships also have small mortars that will fire explosive shells."

Strongarm shook his head. "I guess we all have our secrets these days, don't we? What else don't I know about?"

"It was no secret. Actually, it was the staff's idea, not mine. I just told them to go ahead and make any preparations they thought were necessary. Thank goodness they did."

"Where are these ships?"

"We had them stationed in New Markwell. When we got the message from Chansu yesterday we immediately dispatched them for the Ellenberries."

"We have everything we need for an attack on Hawk Island, Bob, except for one thing," said Smith. "And that is the men to make it. If we can find them, they can be flown to the eastern Ellenbernies to meet the ships, and they can be at Hawk Island in about ten days--if it becomes necessary, of course."

Strongarm was beginning to understand the odd circumstances of this meeting. They had all agreed on a plan of action, but for appearances sake they wanted it to be unanimous, and they had some doubts as to whether he would go along with it. He looked at Smith. "If this meeting is designed to get me to go along with conscription, we can stop right now. You four can vote it, but I won't go along, and I'll tell the people this time why it's a mistake. Conscription isn't any better than domination by Chansu. Can't you see that? It's against every principle the UWG was founded on."

"It may well be, Robert," said Carter, "that we will have to have a showdown on the conscription issue. Quite frankly, I'm not at all sure how that question will be decided." She glanced at Parthupta and Smith. "But there is perhaps another solution. There may be another source of volunteers."

"I thought we had a study saying there wasn't any way to raise volunteers," said Strongarm.

"That's true," Carter said. "But that study only considered UWG citizens. There is another possible source." Strongarm felt confused. What was Carter talking about?

"I don't get what you're driving at," he said. "Everyone who lives in the UWG is a citizen--by definition."

"Well, I don't mean to get hung up on a legal point. But the fact is that there is a large group of people in the UWG who share neither the burdens nor the benefits of our society. That is the group I'm talking about."

Strongarm suddenly grasped the direction of Carter's remarks. He felt a little weak in the knees and, realizing he was the only one standing at the meeting, moved to a nearby chair. "You're talking about the unadapted Nauryans," he said. It was quite clear now why he had been summoned last for this conference, and why he had been treated with such peculiar deference.

"Yes. Tribal warfare is hardly unknown among them."

Strongarm didn't know where to begin. The whole idea was inconceivable, outrageous. "But their primitive fights are far different from what we face."

"In most cases, perhaps so. But they are limited by their weapons. With the weapons we can supply them, they will be much more effective."

Strongarm studied Carter's eager, sincere face. "You've got quite a few secrets, don't you? I suppose you've already been training the Nauryans for this job."

Carter shook her head. "No, you're wrong there, Robert. Oh, I'll admit that the possibility of recruiting the natives was mentioned in one of the early reports, but no one ever thought seriously about the idea until yesterday."

"The suggestion is absolutely contrary to our non-intervention policy."

"Robert, extraordinary difficulties sometimes require extraordinary measures. No policy, no matter how old it is--short of our basic principles, anyway," she hurriedly added, "is inviolable when it comes to preserving the UWG's very existence. Besides, we're not considering forcing the natives to do anything; we're just trying to find some volunteers."

Strongarm stood up. "It's perfectly clear why I was the last one to be brought in on this--why this whole meeting has been directed at me. You want me to be the message boy to the Nauryans. You assume they'll listen to me, because I'm one of them." He cast his eyes downward and shook his head slowly. "You have a lot to learn about Nauryans." Then he looked up, fire in his eyes. "But that's only a small part of your misjudgment. You want me to ask native Nauryans to risk their lives to save you, because your lives are too precious to be risked. Surely you can see how degrading that is." He turned toward the door. "The answer is no. I'm leaving."

"Bob, wait," Henry Smith stood and stepped to Strongarm's side. Strongarm resented even Smith's familiarity. "Bob," said Smith, "there is one thing you should at least consider. As a friend, if for no other reason."

Strongarm turned back to Smith. "All right, Henry, I'll listen to you--as a friend."

"It's true--we can't deny it," said Smith, "that we're asking the Nauryans to risk their lives where we're afraid to risk our own. But there's more involved here than the relative expendability of lives, which you mention." He paused to catch his breath. "There's also a judgment that here is a task of the most crucial importance that the Nauryans are more fit to perform than any other persons in the UWG. If they're willing to volunteer for this operation--and remember, no attack may actually ever be necessary, if we can negotiate something--if they volunteer for this dangerous job, they will have the admiration and the gratitude of 450 million people."

"As you know," Carter added, "some of us don't feel as strongly as you that the Nauryans are treated as second-class people. But if you're right--if they are--surely there could be no better way to change the situation."

"One more thing, Strongarm," said Cornettia. "I'm going to be blunt about this. While what Henry and Mildred have said is true, and ought to be reason enough, we're willing to make practical concessions. You do this, and you have a unanimous vote of the Council to repeal the equalization laws. You might win without it, but it's bound to help you in the Congress."

Strongarm, now confused, sat down again. He found himself looking at Mindra Parthupta. For lack of anything else to say, he spoke to her. "What do you think?"

Parthupta drew a deep, silent breath. "I think," she said, "that there is much merit both to your position and to that of the others. The Council's request is of course, at least in part, premised upon a lesser worthiness of the lives of the Nauryans. Yet if they volunteer for this mission, it would possibly change that judgment. I think, however, that the most important effect has not been mentioned--and that is the effect this task may have on what the Nauryans think of themselves."

She smiled her knowing smile. "I can foresee that this effect could possibly be more far-reaching than any of you dream."

Strongarm felt himself being persuaded, though he disliked showing that Parthupta or anyone else on the Council could change his mind. "Do you join in this request?" he asked her.

"Reluctantly, but yes," she said. "Domination by the Chansu is not the worst fate that could befall us, but I suppose we're not fit to accept it. If there are weaknesses in our system, my judgment is to let others exploit them."

As usual, Strongarm found himself not fully understanding what Parthupta meant. But it was clear that the other four members of the panel were unanimous in their request to him. Perhaps he had been too quick to reject it. Recruitment of the Nauryans would not further decrease their status; it only reflected their status. And, as Smith and the others had said, volunteering for the task could improve the situation. Moreover, if negotiations with the Chansu, which Carter had promised to pursue, were fruitful, the Nauryans would not actually have to face any danger. Strongarm made up his mind. He would swallow his pride and go along with the request.

The other Council members responded happily and thanked him profusely. And, having made this decision, Strongarm had no difficulty in going along with the further Council decision to avoid mentioning the Nauryan request at their public meeting. After all, there was no point in talking about it until the natives had actually agreed to go along with the proposal.

4

Strongarm and his chief administrative assistant, Tom Greenbough, a Nauryan in his mid-twenties, departed by plane for New Markwell late on the afternoon of July 30, 1948, directly after the Prime Council policy session held in the Hall of Congress. They took with them two small suitcases and a thick briefcase full of hastily assembled reports, of varying currency and authenticity, on the Westland natives. Strongarm's absence from the next morning's resumed hearings of the Information Committee would be attributed to preparations for the new air base. Chairman Childone would be dubious, but Strongarm didn't care now. He wouldn't have to face any questions until he returned. And then he hoped to have something much more newsworthy to talk about. Despite his still mixed feelings about his mission to Westland, he was glad to be doing anything that excused him from the hearings.

Strongarm and Greenbough first flew to Taradesh on the last of the three daily flights from Preston. They arrived in Taradesh at nine in the evening, local time, and boarded a waiting plane which had been chartered in advance for them from Agronica Aviation for the remainder of their trip. The charter was necessary because the next regularly scheduled flight to New Markwell didn't leave for a day and a half.

As Strongarm and Greenbough entered the chartered plane, the pilot and co-pilot came back from the cockpit to greet them. They seemed unusually cheerful and helpful. Then Strongarm remembered that the UWG Investment Ministry had only recently decided to buy stock in Agronica Aviation in order to strengthen it as a competitor to General Air Machine. Actually, Strongarm would have preferred to charter a plane from GAM, but its only available craft was in New Markwell on its regularly-scheduled run. Strongarm resigned himself to the flight. Perhaps his presence would do AA some good.

The twelve hour flight through the night to New Markwell did nothing to impress the two passengers. The pilot flew the longer coastal route, but the weather made the air every bit as rough as that on the direct route over the high mountains. The food served on the plane was mediocre, the seats were uncomfortable, and the temperature of the cabin was almost unbearably cold. Strongarm tried to sleep but could manage no more than a few catnaps before being awakened by the cold and the bouncing plane.

When they finally arrived at the New Markwell airport on the morning of the 31st Strongarm felt irritable and out of sorts. His rumpled suit and unshaven face didn't help his disposition. He even resented the time it took to set his silver pocket watch back another four hours. He hoisted himself out of his seat and made his way down the aisle to the door, responding to the smiling faces of the crew with a frosty stare. As he climbed down from the plane, squinting against the early morning sunshine, he was struck by the incongruity of the long, wide runways and the tiny concrete-block building that housed the terminal facilities. They made him think of this airport as a refueling point, a stopping place, but not a destination or a beginning.

Strongarm had visited New Markwell once before, fifteen years ago, when he was on the Agriculture Committee. That time the Committee had traveled leisurely by sea and had followed an easy schedule while in Westland. Strongarm had then had an opportunity to travel around its capital. He remembered it as a small town with straight streets and many small brick or frame buildings with little ornamentation. As he and Greenbough now drove into the city for their meeting with the Regional Director, he saw the straight, wide streets he remembered and the spartan decor, but everything else had changed incredibly. The city seemed to have doubled in size, and the small buildings had given way to the same precast concrete and steel structures that predominated in Agronica. Whereas fifteen years ago automobiles had been rare in this frontier outpost, they now filled the roads, even at this hour in the morning. Strongarm was surprised at the changes and felt irrationally angry at the city for failing to conform to his expectations. It was the time change, the travel, and the lack of sleep, he told himself.

The driver asked Strongarm if he and Greenbough wished to go to their hotel room first. "Is the Regional Director at his office?" Strongarm asked. He pulled out his watch to check the time. Seven-thirty.

"Not yet, but he lives only half a mile away. He can he there in fifteen minutes if you wish. Otherwise he'll be in from nine until five."

"Just how often does a member of the Prime Council come here?" Strongarm demanded. "I thought Schaefer would be at the airport. Now you tell me he's not even at his office."

"Mr. Schaefer thought that after the flight you would want to rest. If he came to the airport, chances are the reporters would find out. We understood that you were going to be very busy and would just as soon avoid the reporters."

Strongarm had no answer to this. "Well, take us to Schaefer's office and get him there. I want to get on with it. We do have a lot to accomplish, and not much time."

The rest of the trip into the city passed in strained silence. At last the car stopped in front of the low-roofed, glass and concrete headquarters of the UWG Westland Region office. It stood across a wide green park from the larger and older buildings that housed the elected Westland and Territorial government.

Normally, the visit of a Council member to a regional or Territorial capital would be cause for numerous luncheons, banquets and other affairs arranged by the local officials. In this instance, however, Strongarm had not even notified the local officials that he was coming. His sole objectives in New Markwell were to make the transportation arrangements to reach the native tribal leaders, and to discuss his request with Donald Schaefer, the Regional Director for the UWG's Native Populations Administration, which operated directly under the Welfare Ministry in Preston, rather than under the Territorial officials. The sooner he did these things, Strongarm thought, the better. If there was time afterward, he would pay a courtesy call on the local authorities.

The driver unlocked the building and showed Strongarm and Greenbough to a small conference room just inside. Then the driver telephoned Schaefer's home and left in his car to pick Schaefer up. Strongarm meanwhile sat in the room, drumming his fingers on the clean, plastic-surfaced table. He asked Greenbough to see if there was anything available to eat or drink, but Greenbough returned a few minutes later empty handed. Just then Strongarm heard a car squeal to a stop in front of the building. A short, thin, white-haired man, like Strongarm still unshaven, rushed into the building, red-faced and panting.

"I'm sorry I wasn't at the airport to meet you, Mr. Strongarm," he said.

"It's all right. We didn't want to get the press involved. We've got a lot to do, and we don't want any delays."

"Yes. Well, I should have been here. I didn't realize this was such an emergency. But I'm ready to start now."

"Good. Can we get some coffee and breakfast first?"

"There's nothing in the building. I can send the driver out."

"We would appreciate that. Then come back here and let's get down to business." Strongarm still felt irritated. He had to force a softness into his voice.

Schaefer took their orders and relayed them to the driver, then returned to the conference room.

"Now," Strongarm said, "the reason we're here is to recruit native Nauryans to fight for the UWG against Chansu. This is a very crucial matter. We need all the information you can give us on how to approach them."

Schaefer's face showed surprise and shock. "We---we had no idea. . . ." His voice trailed off. He looked at Strongarm questioningly. "That's a very drastic proposal. What about the non-intervention policy? Do you have some kind of authorization from the Council for this?"

Strongarm nodded at Greenbough, and the assistant pulled out from the briefcase the letter, signed by all members of the Prime Council, which Strongarm was to present to the tribal leaders. Schaefer read it over carefully. "It seems to be in order," he finally said. "I didn't mean to question you, really, but this is certainly a departure from past policy. I had to be sure. I can understand why the Council has taken this step, of course."

"What do you mean by that?" Strongarm asked.

"Well, the natives in the northern areas have demonstrated quite a lot of military skill in recent years. Or, I suppose I should say, one tribe in particular has. Instead of several dozen more or less independent bands, we've got this one tribe--the Komisaw tribe--which has brought the other northern tribes under its control. The whole structure of the native societies has changed in their area. As a matter of fact, we've been wondering if this development doesn't call for a reordering of the whole approach of our administration up there." He paused, then lowered his voice slightly. "Confidentially, Mr. Strongarm, I haven't said anything in the reports," he nodded toward Greenbough's bulging briefcase, "but I'm concerned that we're losing ground with the northern natives. They aren't so dependent on us any more. As a matter of fact, more and more of the tribes are turning down our counselors. The Komisaw tribe hasn't had a counselor since Dr. Newberry died eight years ago."

"You mean they've even refused medical assistance?"

"From us, yes. But they do have another source. The natives, especially the Komisaw tribe, have developed a close relationship with the settlers up there."

"Well, perhaps the settlers are doing the job of your Administration for you."

"That could be. Unfortunately, they don't like to talk to us much about their relationship with the natives. We do know that many of the natives work on the farms up there, rather than on their own land."

"Doesn't that deprive them of their official status as unadapted natives?" Greenbough asked.

"Not as long as they continue to live in native territory," Schaefer answered. "And as far as we know they still do."

Strongarm reflected on this information from Schaefer. He had thought the Native Populations Administration kept closer contact with the natives than this. His job now appeared even harder than it had before. Yet at least it seemed clear where the point of contact with the natives should be.

"I take it from what you've said," Strongarm stated, "that our request should probably he directed to this Komisaw tribe."

"I would think so. Yes, definitely."

"Now, who should we be getting in touch with? Is there some tribal chief?"

"There is, I'm sure, a tribal Council. I'm sorry to say, though, that we don't even have a record now as to who is on that Council. Our last list is over eight years old."

"And you don't have a counselor with the tribe any more?"

"No, as I said."

Strongarm scratched his head. "Do you suppose we can just walk in on them cold, without any introduction? From what I know of Nauryans, I have my doubts about that."

"It would be best if we had someone they knew make the initial contact for us. I'm thinking about the settlers up there."

Strongarm suddenly saw some hope. "How well do you know them?" he asked.

"Well, at least we know their names. They're UWG citizens. They don't come down to New Markwell any more often than they have to, though, so I doubt if there's anyone around here who knows them very well."

"Do they have any sort of local government up there? A town board or the like?"

"Yes. The center of the settlement is the town of New Hope. I'm sure they have a board. I don't know who's on it, though."

"Well, I suppose they would be the best bet. Let's telephone them."

Schaefer shook his head. "No telephone. Just radio. They've got a little receiver and transmitter up there, I'm sure. That's the only way to reach them."

"Well, let's do that."

"Yes. Certainly." But Schaefer remained seated at the conference table, a thoughtful expression on his face.

"Is something wrong? Another problem?" Strongarm asked.

"No. No problem. I was just remembering something. When I last heard from Newberry, a year or two before he died, he mentioned that there's one settler in particular up there who has a lot of influence. This fellow was one of the original scouts for the settlement party, and he's married to a Nauryan woman--a native, I mean." Schaefer glanced out of the corner of his eye at Strongarm. "The man I'm thinking of may be on the town board anyway, but even if he isn't, he may well be the man to talk to."

"What's his name?"

"That's what I was trying to remember."

Greenbough pulled a report out of the briefcase and leafed through it. He stopped at one of the pages. "Was the name Faolin?" he asked. "Eric Faolin?"

"Yes, I think that's it," said Schaefer. "How did you find it?"

Greenhough smiled proudly. "What you said rang a bell--about a scout for the territorials who married a native. He's mentioned in several of the reports from the early nineteen-thirties.

Apparently there was an investigation of him for violating the non-intervention policy. The Administration wasn't able to find any substantial evidence, so of course whatever they did find was expunged from the records."

Strongarm frowned. "Do you really think that's the man we want?" As he spoke Strongarm realized what he was implying. "Of course, we shouldn't hold that investigation against him," he added hastily.

"Now that I'm thinking about it," Schaefer said, "I have this recollection that Newberry was never completely candid with us about this fellow. His reports were inconsistent--incidentally, you don't have Newberry's reports, I don't think. We only sent summaries of the counselors' reports to Preston. But some of us felt that Newberry was either exaggerating Faolin's influence, or understating it. The reports we got didn't ring true. Since Newberry died, I guess we really haven't pursued the matter. It's difficult, you know, when they won't accept a counselor. And those settlers up there don't tell us any more than the natives do."

Strongarm resented the inefficiency of this operation. How could they do their job with so little information? But he didn't want to incur Schaefer's animosity now. He still needed the man's help. "I understand," Strongarm said. "It's impossible to get information when no one will voluntarily supply it. Well, we'll just have to proceed on what we have. It seems the choice is between the town board and this Faolin, assuming he's still up there. What do you recommend?"

Schaefer thought for a moment. "Normally, I'd suggest we go through the regular channels--the town board. But I've got this feeling that Faolin is the man. I wish I could remember better exactly what Newberry said. It wasn't all in his written reports, either. I say we try to contact Faolin first."

Strongarm got the strong impression that the Native Populations Administration did not receive a full measure of cooperation from the local authorities. But if that was true, his presence wouldn't necessarily change the situation. "All right," he decided. "Let's see if we can get in touch with Faolin. If we can't, we'll try the town board as a second alternative."

Schaefer nodded and rose from the table. "I'll get right over to the Communications Center. It's just next door." The driver with a hot tray of eggs and bacon came into the room as Schaefer left. Strongarm and Greenbough attacked the food eagerly.

5

Strongarm and Greenbough, accompanied this time by Schaefer, were airborne again before ten o'clock. They rode inside a small seaplane that took off from a quiet backwater of the Strange River ten miles northwest of New Markwell. They were lucky to find a pilot, a grizzled, sunburned territorial operating his single craft under the pretentious title of the Westland Charter Aviation Service, who had made the trip to New Hope several times before.

Strongarm slept during most of the first leg of their journey up the coast, and when he awoke on their landing to refuel at Barton, some 400 miles north of New Markwell, he felt greatly refreshed. From Barton the plane headed inland through a clear, cloudless sky. Strongarm now watched with interest the terrain passing below them, where the heavily farmed coastal area gave way to the bush country, with only occasional small patches of cultivated land clustered around the rivers and streams. He asked Schaefer countless questions and wandered off into detailed discourses on farming gleaned from his days on the Agriculture Committee. Schaefer and Greenbough smiled and nodded politely but seemed to find it difficult to concentrate on Strongarm's words as they blended into the drone of the airplane's engines. The pilot, sitting next to Schaefer in the front seats of the plane, gave no indication he heard Strongarm at all.

Finally, shortly after five o'clock, the pilot pointed out a small lake ahead of them. They descended and circled it a few times. The sense of excitement and well-being that Strongarm had found for the last few hours began to fade as his thoughts returned to his task.

As the plane flew low over the lake Strongarm noted the fields of grain stretching off in every direction, laced by the network of irrigation channels. "That's certainly impressive," Strongarm said. "I had no idea they had so much land under cultivation. It must be a large settlement."

"Not so large," Schaefer replied. "Still well under a thousand territorials, including children. As you know, the incentive legislation encourages larger ownership up here."

"How do they manage to work it all?"

"Native labor, I suppose. It is surprising, though. Work like that is decidedly contrary to their natural inclinations."

"You don't think Nauryans are fit for the work?" asked Strongarm frostily.

"Oh no, no. You misunderstand. I was referring to their social structure. The natives have always held agriculture in very low regard. That's one thing that's made them reluctant to come into the UWG as full citizens."

Strongarm turned back to the window. "You know," he said to no one in particular, "I admire the people who created this. Sometimes I think they're the true achievers of our world."

"I'm taking it down now," announced the pilot, cutting Strongarm off. "You can see the docks on the south end of the lake." With that the plane banked sharply and then began its final descent. It landed in a spray of water and taxied up to the end of the largest dock. The pilot cut the engines and opened the door, and the occupants of the plane climbed out on the dock. It seemed to Strongarm very silent after the roar of the plane ceased. Thick, tall trees surrounding the lake cut off any noises from beyond, save the occasional call of a bird. No human was in sight.

The group stood on the dock for a minute, wondering what to do. Then Strongarm heard a sound from a path that led from the other end of the dock back into the trees. As he watched, a Nauryan boy emerged, moving toward them hesitantly. He carried a crust of bread in one hand; the other was empty. The boy stopped when he reached the dock.

"Do you come to see the Protector?" the boy asked, in a small voice.

"We come to see Mr. Eric Faolin," Strongarm answered.

"Yes," said the boy, bowing slightly. "The Protector Faolin dines now. If you will come with me, I will take you to his house." He turned and began walking back up the path. Strongarm and the others followed.

"I'm not sure I understand this," said Strongarm sternly. "Just what is the relationship between this Faolin and the natives?"

"I don't know. I really don't," Schaefer replied. "As I told you before, we haven't been able to get much information about the tribes up in these northern areas for years."

"Well, I'm going to find out," said Strongarm. He went ahead and caught up with the boy.

"Tell me, son," Strongarm said, "how is it you happen to be here instead of in native territory?"

"My family works here," the boy replied. Strongarm noticed that the boy's speech carried only a slight native accent.

"They work on Faolin's farm?"

The boy glanced at Strongarm as they continued along. The trees that circled the lake had thinned out now. "My family shares this farm with Protector Faolin and others. But we do not live here. The far away rulers do not let us. They would take away our other land if we did."

"What does this Faolin do for you?"

"He is our Protector. Without him we would be nothing. He shows us the way. He helps us to raise ourselves." The boy looked up at Strongarm curiously. "You look like one of us," he said. "You should know of Protector Faolin. Has he not helped you to rise also?"

"I've helped myself," said Strongarm bitterly. "And your people would do well to follow the same course. I'm very anxious to meet this Faolin."

Strongarm dropped back and let the boy lead the way. He spoke to Schaefer. "This Faolin appears to have some sort of unusual hold over these people. I'm suspicious. I hope you'll make a thorough investigation of this matter at the appropriate time."

They continued on for perhaps half a mile. The wooded area had given way to bushland. Then abruptly the bushland stopped and the party was walking between fields of grain that stretched away as far as they could see. Ahead of them was what looked like another clump of woods, but as they got closer they could see that beyond several rows of trees was a group of buildings. The buildings separated themselves into a large frame house, two or three work buildings, and a big rectangular structure that reminded Strongarm of provincial meeting halls in the agricultural communities of Agronica. The boy led them to the front door of the house. An old Nauryan stood on the porch watching them.

"Hello, Gold Feather," the old man said to the boy when he was close enough. "Are these the people from the aircraft?"

"Yes, they are," said the boy. "I have brought them from the lake."

"What is your business?" the old man asked, directing his question to Schaefer.

"I'm the Regional Director from New Markwell. I radioed earlier that we would be making a visit today. We wish to see Mr. Faolin."

The old man turned to Strongarm and his assistant. "And what is your business?" he asked. "Do you wish to see the

Protector for guidance? I would warn you that he is a busy man and must turn many away."

"We want to see Faolin about other matters," said Strongarm. He struggled to contain his feeling of outrage.

"They're with me," said Schaefer. "They're UWG citizens from the Region of Agronica. They have no connections with the Westland tribes."

"I will announce your arrival," said the old man, still cautious. He went inside. In a minute he returned. "The Protector is still dining, but he will see you when he finishes. He wishes you to know that you may eat with the workers in the assembly hall if you are hungry."

"No, thank you," replied Strongarm curtly. "We will wait. We would like to come inside."

The old man looked back and forth from Strongarm to Schaefer. "Very well," he said. "Please follow me." He led them inside the front door to an entrance hail with bare wood floors and several wooden chairs placed against the walls. "Please stay here," the old man said.

Greenbough and Schaefer sat in the chairs. Strongarm himself stood in the center of the hall. He shifted impatiently from one foot to the other.

Fifteen minutes passed. Twenty minutes. Strongarm was now pacing back and forth across the entrance hall. "Schaefer," he said. "I want this whole operation investigated as soon as possible."

"Yes, Mr. Strongarm," Schaefer replied. "I presume you want us to wait until this Chansu affair is concluded."

"I suppose. I suppose." Strongarm looked down the narrow empty hallway that led from the entrance hall back through the house. All the doors in it were closed. "Such rudeness I have seldom encountered."

"Faolin probably doesn't know you're here, Mr. Strongarm. I didn't tell him who you are."

"That makes no difference. He knows we've traveled all day just to see him. How am I to deal with such a man? We should have gone to the village board directly."

They waited another fifteen minutes. Just as Strongarm was about to propose they leave, a man, a territorial, appeared in the narrow hallways. "Mr. Schaefer," he said, "would you and your party please join me?" He led them back along the hallway and through one of the doors. They entered a large room. Strongarm was surprised at its size and the opulence of its furnishings. The light wood paneling and the half-dozen well-stuffed armchairs did not seem at all in keeping with a rugged frontier life. The man directed them to the chairs. As they followed him a door at the opposite end of the room opened and two more territorials entered.

"Good evening, I'm Eric Faolin," one of the men said to Schaefer. "You must be Director Schaefer. I'm pleased to see you." Faolin and Schaefer shook hands. "Let me introduce my companions. This is Paul Farnham," he indicated the man who had led the group into the room. "And this is Hiram Jones, my chief assistant." He indicated the other. "We've been discussing the fall's harvest."

"Mr. Faolin," said Schaefer, "I'd like you and your friends to meet Mr. Robert Strongarm, Member of the Prime Council of the United World Government. And this is his assistant, Tom Greenbough."

Faolin's companions stared at Strongarm in disbelief. Faolin himself showed no surprise. "I thought I recognized you, Mr. Strongarm, from your pictures in the press. This is indeed an honor. Perhaps you would be so good as to speak to your brothers while you're here. It would be very inspiring." He turned to Schaefer. "You didn't say in your message that Mr. Strongarm would accompany you. Is there some reason for the secrecy?"

"Yes, there is," said Strongarm. "Secrecy and urgency. We've been traveling for a long time. Perhaps we can get right down to the reason for this visit."

"Certainly," said Faolin. "Let's all be seated." They all sat down except Strongarm. He moved over to the nearby window, then turned to face the group.

"First I would like to ask that your friends excuse themselves," Strongarm said. "There's no slight intended, but it is essential at this point that secrecy be kept to a maximum."

Faolin moved his hand and the others got up and left the room without a word.

"Thank you," said Strongarm. "Mr. Faolin," he went on, "you may be aware of the recent difficulties we've been having with the Chansu."

"I understand they're holding our mission as hostages and that we're meeting their demands to keep the hostages alive. An unwise response on our part, in my opinion, Mr. Strongarm."

Strongarm suppressed a desire to argue the point. "We've also taken steps to move weapons into position--some incredibly powerful bombs--to be able to force the Chansu to release the prisoners."

"I've heard about a bomb test. I wondered if it had anything to do with the Chansu matter. Does the UWG really intend to use these devices against Chansu? Or is it just a bluff?"

Strongarm stared for a long time at Faolin. He found himself disliking the man more and more. "That question isn't very important right now, Mr. Faolin, for we've lost control of the bombs. The Chansu invaded the island two days ago and captured them. The news apparently hasn't reached here yet."

Faolin's eyes narrowed. "That's an unbelievable catastrophe!" he said. He showed emotion for the first time in their meeting. "Those people are inhuman. They'll use those bombs against us without question." He paused. "How could we have let such a thing happen?"

"The more important question is, Mr. Faolin, what can we do about it? That's why I'm here. The UWG has no armed forces, yet if those bombs must be recaptured, it can only be done by force."

Strongarm hated this. It was bad enough having to make a request he didn't believe in. Now it appeared he must argue the responsibility for what had happened. At this point he wanted nothing but to get this affair over with as soon as possible, whether he was successful or not.

"And you would like the Nauryan tribes to do the job for the UWG, since they do have warfare experience," said Faolin.

"Yes. If our other plans to get the bombs by negotiation don't work. We've come to see you since Mr. Schaefer believes you may be able to help us persuade the tribal leaders to give their assistance."

"Where are the bombs located?"

"They were captured on Hawk Island, at the very western end of the Ellenberry chain. We assume they're still there."

"Why don't you just drop another bomb on the island?"

"We don't have an air base close enough for a plane to fly there and return, and we're afraid there may still be UWG citizens on the island."

"Even if the plane can't return, and even if hostages are killed, an air strike would probably cost fewer lives than an attempt at recapture."

"We can't look at it that way."

Faolin shook his head slowly. "I know. I know. And no pilot will make the flight." He paused. "How will you get an attack force to the island?"

"Don't forget that we're still hoping to settle this by negotiation. But if we have to send troops, we'll fly them to the middle Ellenberries, from where they will go by ship. The ships are already on their way."

"Your negotiations won't do any good," Faolin scoffed. "Do you have weapons?"

"Yes. Rifles, and cannon on the ships."

Faolin rose from his chair and walked to the window across the room from Strongarm. He looked outside at the late sunshine, then turned to Strongarm. "We'll do it," he said.

"I beg your pardon," said Strongarm.

"I said we'll do it," repeated Faolin. "We'll be ready to leave in thirty-six hours, if necessary. We can train en route."

"Well, we had better consult the tribal leaders, then," said Strongarm, confused.

"That's not necessary. They'll do as I say." Faolin, smiling, walked back to Strongarm. "We can discuss the plans later. You and your companions must be tired and hungry from your trip. I'll have some of the men take care of you before they return to their village for the night."

6

Strongarm sat alone in his apartment back in Preston. He pulled out his watch. One a.m. He still hadn't fully recovered from his journey to Westland and often found himself, as now, unable to sleep at his normal bedtime. It didn't help that Barbara was still working at the newspaper, and that his son, Paul, only recently off surveillance and still undergoing counseling, was out who knows where with his friends.

Strongarm put his watch away and leaned back on the sofa. The report he had been trying to read slid off his lap and onto the bare wooden floor of the small living-dining room in which he sat. He didn't bother to pick it up; he was preoccupied with other matters.

The aftereffects of Strongarm's trip to Westland were not entirely physical. He had, it was true, accomplished exactly what he set out to do. The Nauryans had readily volunteered for military service. The news that they had, reported on Strongarm's return, was gratefully accepted by a worried Congress. Congressman Childone had even decided to postpone his hearings until after resolution of the Hawk Island affair, and if things worked out it was a good bet that the hearings might be permanently forgotten. The press was full of praise for the Nauryan sacrifice. Yet Strongarm remained uneasy about the situation. He hadn't expected to deal through this man Faolin and, not having even talked to the native leaders personally, he felt little sense of accomplishment over the success of his trip. Cornettia could have done as well--perhaps better, for Cornettia and Faolin would have understood each other.

It wasn't only the absence of personal achievement that disturbed Strongarm. He strongly disliked the influence Faolin seemed to have over the native Nauryans. He distrusted Faolin's motives. Was the man helping the natives make a noble sacrifice, or was he exploiting them? If Nauryans were to die to save the UWG only because some sharp territorial conned them into it, Strongarm's efforts would have lessened, rather than furthered, the cause.

Strongarm was pleased that the Nauryans were being praised, whatever the reasons for their volunteering. But was even that praise constructive? Were the Nauryans being accepted as fully-accredited equals, or were they simply being applauded for an unusual talent that happened to be needed at the moment. This of course took Strongarm to deeper questions. What did he want for Nauryans? Was what he wanted possible? Perhaps excellence in one important line of endeavor was enough.

But Strongarm wasn't equipped at this moment to follow out his train of thought. Perhaps, he told himself, the negotiations with the Chansu will end the matter here, with Faolin and his troops still on their ships in the Western Ocean. He allowed himself to believe there was still a good chance that no attack would be necessary. After all, Carter had promised that she would negotiate in good faith. Any reasonable demand that would include the giving up of the bombs by the Chansu would be met. Why would the Chansu insist on keeping only three bombs, however powerful? And even if the negotiations didn't bear fruit, if they could only be extended for two more weeks, an airstrip within range of Hawk Island would he completed. But would the Prime Council actually approve bombing the island when some UWG citizens might still be there?

Still uneasy, with nothing resolved, but comforted by the thought that the negotiations could solve the problems, Strongarm picked up from the floor the report he was reading and searched for the page where he had stopped.

The telephone rang. Strongarm ignored it at first. He resented the interruption. He sighed. He had no more reason to be up at that hour, he supposed, than whoever it was on the phone had to be calling. Besides, he wouldn't mind talking to someone. He walked over to the phone and took the earpiece off the wall. "Hello," he said tiredly.

"Bob, this is Henry Smith. Did I wake you?"

"No. I was working. What do you want at this hour?" Strongarm sounded less worried than he felt.

"I'm just calling for . . . to give you a sort of a report ."

"About what?"

"Well, I don't know exactly where to begin. I'm calling at Mildred's suggestion. There have been some developments in the Chansu matter."

Strongarm's insides went cold. He didn't want to debate about Chansu. Not now. Whenever the topic turned to Chansu, he had to fight for something. He was too tired to fight tonight. "What developments?" he asked, almost involuntarily.

"One hour ago we received a radio message from the Prince Regent of Chansu. They will under no circumstances give up the bombs. We have only their word that they won't use them. They renew their demand that we cede them the Ellenberries within forty-eight hours, or else we must 'suffer the consequences,' whatever that means."

"Do you think they're bluffing?"

"I don't know. I'd hate to take the chance."

"Well, I suppose we're going to have a meeting about it. How soon?"

There was silence on the other end.

"Isn't there going to be a meeting? Surely Cornettia isn't going to rely on their word about the bombs," Strongarm said.

"Bob," Smith began slowly, "Mildred, Rolf and I already had a short discussion about it. They're with me here now. The three of us have agreed on a plan."

"I see." Strongarm's stomach was in a knot. "So you're calling for my opinion right now, over the phone." Arguing in a Council meeting was difficult enough. Trying to argue to the Council over the telephone through Smith was impossible. "Well, what's your plan?"

Another pause. "Bob," Smith said finally, "we're not proposing to debate over the phone. As I said, this is really more of an information call. The three of us are a quorum and a majority, so we've already adopted a resolution. We think the emergency justifies our action."

"What's the resolution?" Strongarm choked out the question.

"That the Nauryan troops be instructed to move on Hawk Island immediately and use whatever force is necessary to occupy and secure it."

The sinking sensation that struck Strongarm was followed closely by an unexpected sense of release. They had, legally or illegally, taken the responsibility away from him. "Can't I say anything to make you change your minds?" he asked, but the question was designed, he realized, more to confirm his release than to request that responsibility be returned to him.

"The instruction to the Nauryans has already been sent."

Strongarm didn't know what to say. "I hope you're right," he finally managed. He could hear the resignation in his own voice. He felt, more than anything, useless and worthless. Would a Nauryan voice never be heard when a crucial decision was to be made? At least Smith had the decency to avoid the words of polite deference that usually marked such occasions.

"Yes," said Smith. "We hope so too. We should know soon." He paused. "Well, good night, Bob."

"Good night, Henry." Strongarm hung up the phone, then leaned his forehead against the wall and closed his eyes. He stayed there for a long time.

7

Two weeks after their capture, the last of the UWG citizens on Hawk Island had already made the trip to join their countrymen in the mission compound at Shinso. Only the Chansu Defense Force remained on Hawk Island, ready to defend it to the death.

Lieutenant Lunan had returned to Chansu in command of a shipload of prisoners and with great hopes for a promotion. He had been replaced by Lieutenant Bin Warnow, a much younger Warrior.

"Workers," Lieutenant Warnow addressed the men under his command as they assembled for a late afternoon inspection, "I have some very good news that has just come to us from Shinso. A great honor has been bestowed upon all Workers who participated in the capture of this island. The Emperor has decreed that each village from which one of you came will be given a special festival day in your honor.

"There is also a special message to you from the Emperor. I will read it." He held a sheet of paper in front of him. "It says: 'To the Worker troops of the Chansu Defense Force on Hawk Island. Your homeland congratulates you on the noble assistance you have given to the Warriors of Chansu in achieving their great victory. With such assistance we will soon fulfill our destiny of bringing order and harmony to our world and eliminating those who would impose upon us the artificial, classless and cowardly ways that offend our Gods.'" Lieutenant Warnow smiled. "Such words from the Emperor are indeed--"

A brief scuffling in the midst of the ranks in front of the Lieutenant interrupted him. "What is this?" he asked.

"Please pardon us, sir," said a thick-necked, broad-shouldered Worker standing near the disturbance. "We were only quieting one of our number who has not been well."

"Who is it?" asked the Lieutenant. "I'd like to hear what he has to say."

The ranks parted and Ryl Kolu stepped slowly but steadily forward, a red bruise forming on his left cheek. His eyes darted about rapidly.

"I spoke, sir," Kolu said in a quiet, calm voice. "I said that kindness and peacefulness don't offend the gods. My gods don't love death."

"That is an insolent comment, Kolu," snapped the Lieutenant. "You could be executed for such impertinence." He looked for a moment into Kolu's face. "I'll spare you that this time, Kolu, because I know of your friend's death and how it's affected you. But that excuse is not going to save you from a proper punishment. And next time, I warn you, it won't save your life." The Lieutenant motioned to several other men. "Take him to the detention center. There will be twenty lashes for this."

Kolu shook off the arms of the men sent to him and strode off on his own toward the detention center, as calm and steady as before. The men hurried after him, surrounding him to prevent any attempt at escape.

When the UWG personnel occupied Hawk Island, they constructed a one-story assembly and recreation hall with an outdoor patio just to the north of the east end of the runway. The Chansu, seeing no need for such facilities, quickly converted it into a detention center for Workers who didn't measure up to the strict requirements of the Warrior officers. Ryl Kolu's fellow Workers ushered him to the entrance to this facility. They stopped smartly in front of the detention center captain and relayed Lieutenant Warnow's order. The captain nodded curtly and dismissed the men, who ran back to their unit. Two other Warriors, the prison guards, were summoned from inside the center.

"Come with me," the captain said to Kolu. Kolu, flanked by the two guards, followed him as he turned and walked into the building. They went down a dark corridor. A heavy wooden door stood closed at the other end. The captain rang a bell. Slowly the door opened, revealing two more guards and beyond them a gate, made of metal bars. On the other side of the gate Kolu could see what must be the prison yard, surrounded by a tall wooden fence with barbed wire at the top.

The captain looked at Kolu and smiled. "Your punishment will come tomorrow, Worker. You will have the rest of this day and tonight to think about it. I assure you it will be painful. You will not want to speak disrespectfully of the Emperor again." The guards took Kolu up to the gate and opened it for him. He walked inside and the gate clanked shut behind him. He could see about a dozen others--all Workers--lying about the prison yard.

The sight of his fellow Workers stirred in Kolu an uncontrollable anger. He whirled around and faced the two gate guards. The captain and the other guards had already left.

"You bastards!" Kolu screamed. "You cowardly bastards! You are parasites. Leeches. May the Gods favor the easterners. May they destroy you and your evil ways. May they let us all live free and equal." Before he finished, the guards were in the yard, going at him. He didn't give an inch of ground. He felt only the first blow, a hard chop to the side of his head. He realized but vaguely that his body was being twisted and pummeled as he lapsed into unconsciousness and collapsed onto the ground.

8

Eric Faolin sat at a round oak table in the common room of the lead ship carrying his attack force to Hawk Island. With him at the table were the half dozen officers, all territorials, whom Faolin had picked to lead the attack. A large map of Hawk Island lay spread out in front of them.

"Eric has asked me to prepare several alternative attack plans," said Hiram Jones, stretching his long, stringy neck as he looked at the faces around the table. He sat at Faolin's left. His short-cropped hair and sunburned skin made him look younger than the other middle-aged men to whom he spoke. "Basically, we must choose between an attempt to infiltrate the island secretly and a direct frontal assault." He pointed to the map. "If we try to take the island by stealth, we'll have to land in this wide area on the north side which is hidden from the base by this ridge running down the center of the island. If, on the other hand, we make a direct assault, we must go straight for the base. That will mean a landing somewhere along the southeastern edge of the island."

Jones looked at the others again. He tapped the top of a stack of papers next to him. "There are a great many details to discuss under either plan," he continued. "But it seems to me we ought to first decide the overall strategy. Both alternatives have their disadvantages. If we try to reach the base secretly from the north and are discovered before we can get over or around the ridge, it will be extremely difficult to penetrate to the base. On the other hand, if we make a direct assault, there will be a much greater loss of life, even if we are successful."

Jones stopped speaking. The eyes of the officers lingered for a moment on the map, then swung to Faolin. He sat stiff and straight in his chair. "Your thinking tracks my own, Hiram," Faolin said. He looked around at his comrades, all of whom had participated in the native tribal campaigns with him. "We've faced this sort of a decision before. The battle against the Pillican tribe, for example. I'm sure you all remember that. To my mind there is only one answer." No one else spoke. Faolin cleared his throat, and the merest shadow of sadness crossed his face. "We can't worry too much about sacrificing lives. The lives at stake here, though they are ours and our friends', are nothing compared to the lives that will be saved if we succeed. We must take the plan that best assures success."

The others nodded in agreement. Faolin rose from his chair and walked around the table behind his officers. "We believe that the Chansu themselves captured the island by landing secretly on the northeast side first. They will undoubtedly have patrols all along the northern coast watching for a similar attack. Our chance of landing secretly is not good." Faolin passed all the way around the table and returned to his chair, standing behind it. "Furthermore, it is essential that we prevent any aircraft from leaving the island, but without destroying them. We must capture all the planes and bombs intact. The surest way to accomplish that is to bombard the runway with the cannon and mortars which we have on our ships. Once the bombardment begins there can't be any secrecy. Therefore, we may as well adopt the approach that requires the least secrecy. If men must die, let's do our utmost to see that their deaths aren't in vain." He sat down again, while his officers visibly relaxed, glad that the first decision had been made, however dangerous it might be.

9

When Kolu awoke it was early evening. He lay on his side in the prison yard. The side of his head was swollen, and he could barely move his left arm and leg. He sat up painfully and looked around. The other prisoners sat around the yard in silence, eating something from small wooden bowls. He noticed a bowl on the ground next to him, with a flat wooden spoon next to it. He reached over and picked it up and smelled it. It appeared to be a grain meal paste with bits of fish, and it smelled rotten. He tasted some and spat it out. Then Kolu became aware of the gnawing in his stomach. He picked the bowl up, and, with small mouthfuls swallowed quickly, managed to put away about three-fourths of the contents. Then he tossed the bowl aside.

One of the other prisoners nearby raised his head and looked at Kolu. "You had better not do that," the prisoner said. "They will return for the bowls soon. If you don't have yours to hand them, they may beat you again."

"Thank you," said Kolu. He crawled over to his bowl and picked it up. Then he moved over toward the prisoner who had spoken to him. "I'm Ryl Kolu," he said.

The other man glanced at a nearby companion, then back at Kolu. "I am Don Karga."

"Why are you here?" Kolu asked.

The other dropped his eyes to the ground. "I was late reporting for guard duty. We both were." He looked again at his companion, "We know why you are here. Your life is in great danger."

Kolu fixed his eyes on Karga. "I don't care to live in a world where I'm treated as an animal," he said steadily. "You aren't men if you accept it."

Karga looked nervously at his friend. "This is treason. We don't want to discuss it. We wish to live." He started to rise, but Kolu grabbed his arm tightly.

"Don't leave. Hear me. I'll speak softly," Kolu said in a harsh whisper. Karga reluctantly lowered himself again, but backed away from Kolu. Karga's companion stayed where he was, a blank expression on his face.

"You're in a filthy prison yard because you were late for duty. The Warriors are late for duty, too. Are they thrown into a detention center and whipped?"

"They are Warriors," answered Karga.

"They are men. We are men. There's no difference." The others stared at him. "You don't see," continued Kolu. "I know, it's difficult. I myself have seen clearly only since we came to this island. A great and good man, a Worker, came here with me. We trained together and fought together. He honored me with his friendship, which I can never repay. The man died in an act of great bravery--he died for what he thought was the benefit of Chansu." He paused to catch his breath. "When he died it troubled me. Then suddenly I saw why. This man, a Worker, died doing a thing a Warrior wouldn't do. It all became so clear. The merit of a man doesn't come from the family into which he's born. It comes from within him. And every man should be measured by the merit within him."

The other two glanced nervously around them, to make sure no one was listening, or to find a place of retreat, away from this crazy man. But the intensity of Kolu's manner made it impossible for them to escape.

"What do you know of the ways of the UWG?" Kolu asked. No answer. "We have been taught to hate them. We've been taught that their way is unnatural and that it is our destiny to restore order to their society. Do you know that in the UWG all men are equals? All receive an equal share of the wealth. All have equal opportunities for every job. Why should we--you and I--fear the UWG? We should embrace their ways. The Warriors fear them, of course, since their way is a threat to the Warriors' privilege. But you and I--we all who are Workers--should have nothing to do with fighting for that."

"You don't know the UWG," the friend of Karga said accusingly.

Kolu pointed his finger at the man. "You are wrong. I worked with advisers from the UWG in the fields of my village. I knew them well. They were good men, and what they say is true."

A noise came from the gate. It was opening. Karga and his companion scurried away. The detention center captain entered the yard, flanked by two guards. He marched straight over to Kolu, who, through force of habit, stood and lowered his eyes as the captain approached. Suddenly, catching himself, he raised them and stared directly into the captain's face.

"Worker Kolu," said the captain, "I see that you're awake. Good. I'm here to inform you that the detention council has considered Lieutenant Warnow's report on your behavior of earlier today. We find your actions inexcusable and detrimental to our forces. You will remain in custody here indefinitely, after the lashing which will be administered tomorrow morning. That punishment has been doubled. I also warn you that the next disloyal statement will result in an immediate sentence of death." The captain looked up at the sky. "All in all, we have been extremely lenient. You can thank Lieutenant Warnow for that. He asked that you be given one more chance. But that is all you have. Good day, Worker Kolu." The captain nodded his head slightly, turned abruptly, and marched back out through the gate, followed by the two guards.

Kolu watched the captain go. Then he burst out laughing. He walked over to where the other prisoners had gathered to watch. "He is ludicrous," said Kolu in a low voice. "How can he hope to suppress the truth by threatening me? I don't care to live where I'm less than a man." The others started to move away.

"Hear me!" demanded Kolu, louder now. The laughter had disappeared. "We must not bow before such a wicked system any longer. We must fight it." He turned his face upwards, to a sky where the stars were just beginning to show themselves. "I pray to all the gods of Chansu, and especially to the patrons of the Workers. Weaken the arm of the Warriors. Give strength to the UWG. Let them defeat the Warriors of Chansu and bring to us their way of freedom and equality." He dropped to his knees. "Hear me, Gods. Deliver us!"

Kolu rose to his feet and staggered after the group of prisoners. They dispersed, watching him with fascination. Kolu was suddenly overcome with exhaustion. He stumbled over to the solid wooden fence. He leaned against it and looked around. His head ached fiercely. After a moment he nodded, then slowly slid down the fence to the ground, where he lay, occasionally twitching, in a deep sleep.

10

Ever since he was old enough to understand them, Black Earth had thrilled to the stories of that dramatic battle against the northern raiders, when the fate of the entire Komisaw tribe hung in the balance. Sitting on the floor in front of his father, Forest Path, Black Earth had exulted in the great victory and cried when told of the death of Swift Stream, his father's great friend and his aunt's betrothed.

But by the time Black Earth, only just turned seventeen, had grown to maturity, the battles were over. The Komisaw tribe had established its peaceful authority over every other tribe within hundreds of miles, and those farther away did not oppose the Komisaw's wishes. So, regretfully, with a feeling of loss at being born too late that his father never understood, Black Earth gave up his dreams of being a great fighter and resigned himself to a life of farming, of someday following his father into the Komisaw Council of Elders, and of furthering the interests of his mother's clan.

But then, only ten short days ago, the Protector had sent his request to the Council of Elders for men to fight against the Chansu. Black Earth heard about the request from his father during the evening meal that same day and became so excited he couldn't eat. For a moment it appeared that his mother would deny him permission to go on account of his age, but his father took his side and between them they persuaded her.

Black Earth didn't have to wait long for things to happen. The five hundred volunteers from the Komisaw tribe began training the very next day, while Faolin sought recruits from the other tribes. After only two days the painstaking task of ferrying the 2,500 men to their ships in the Ellenberries began. Black Earth had scarcely seen an airplane before, much less flown in one, but he found the long, island-hopping jaunt aboard the cramped little two-engined transport plane exciting. He felt no fear over the long empty stretches of open water, nor did he see such fear in any of the two dozen Nauryans who accompanied him.

But now the adventure was about to begin. Though Black Earth still looked forward to it with exhilaration, he couldn't deny the fear that now made him restless and tense inside. He stood with the others in his battalion on the deck of their rolling ship, following in the dimming light the stick held by the battalion commander, a territorial named Wilson, as it moved across the large map in front of them, the map's corners flapping in the wind. Black Earth had difficulty hearing everything Wilson said over the noise of the wind and sea, but fortunately the commander repeated everything enough times for Black Earth to understand. As described, the task was not difficult to understand. Black Earth and the rest of this battalion were to land on the beach at dawn under cover of artillery, advance as far as they could, and dig in on the beach if they were stopped. It was a dangerous task, Black Earth could plainly see, and a chill went through him as he thought of running, fully exposed, up the beach in the face of the Chansu guns.

Wilson finished his explanation and laid his stick on the deck. He faced the five hundred gray faces before him. "I hope you Nauryans all understand this," he said, "because not only your life but the life of the guy next to you depends on your following my instructions to the letter. If you aren't sure what you're supposed to do, talk to one of your fellow natives about it. If you still aren't sure you understand, then come see me and I'll explain it again. It's really not that hard."

Black Earth bristled at these words, his fear momentarily forgotten. He resented being talked down to. Increasingly since Black Earth reached his teens he had found himself, as now, suddenly inflamed at a territorial's choice of words or facial expression. He had asked his father about it several times, but Forest Path had chided him for imagining things. But he had not imagined. This man Wilson might as well have said, "I'm afraid you natives are too stupid to understand me." Who was he to speak that way, especially now? Black Earth would willingly fight and die to save a civilization of which he was not a part, but he wasn't going to be ordered to do it, like some sheep. It did not escape Black Earth's attention that the entire command of this mission was in the hands of territorials. No Nauryan had made the decision to engage in a frontal assault on Hawk Island. Yet it was Nauryans who would die in the assault, not the territorials who sat in the safety of their ships. If Nauryan skills were necessary to accomplish the invasion, shouldn't they be at least in a position of equal authority?

Black Earth's thoughts were interrupted by the opening of the door leading to the bridge. Wilson stopped his exhortation as Eric Faolin stepped through the door and walked to Wilson's side. Black Earth felt a flood of relief and his anger dissipated. He would do anything for the Protector. In his anger he had momentarily forgotten that Faolin, not Wilson and the other territorials, was the leader of this force.

"Members of the combined Nauryan tribes," Faolin said to the men after Wilson introduced him, "tomorrow morning our great task begins. Mr. Wilson has explained what must be done to win the battle. It is a dangerous and difficult task I ask of you, but you can do it. I have fought with some of you before, and with your fathers, and I know you have the courage and skill to prevail. Indeed, of all the peoples of the UWG lands, we alone have the ability to stop this dangerous enemy. Those at home will be watching us and waiting. Not just our own families and tribes, but hundreds of millions throughout the UWG, for their safety and security depends upon us. This may be the most important battle ever fought. So rise to the occasion. Follow my commands faithfully. Execute the tasks assigned you bravely. You can and will do these things, and we will achieve victory that will ensure the blessings of the Right Way to you and your children, and to millions of others." Faolin stopped and raised his outstretched arms, then bowed his head silently for a full minute.

Another thrill coursed through Black Earth's body, but this time it was neither fear nor anger. It was pure excitement at being part of such an important adventure--more important even, he secretly told himself, than the great battle against the northern raiders of which he had heard so much. That battle merely saved the Komisaw tribe. This battle was for the future of the entire UWG.

11

As darkness fell, Faolin ordered all exterior ship lights extinguished. His three vessels glided on over the water to their destination. The sky was fair but moonless, giving little illumination but permitting the navigators to determine their position with great accuracy.

Shortly after 1 a.m., on August 19, 1948, the lookout in the high tower on the lead ship called an urgent message to the bridge, awakening Faolin from a nap. The lights of a small boat, moving in a course perpendicular to theirs, were approaching from the north. Faolin ordered his ships to shift course away from the small boat and into a circle that would bring them back to their original position, but behind the other boat. The lookout announced no course changes by the other vessel, and the radio operators, scanning the broadcast bands for possible Chansu patrol boat communications, heard nothing. Faolin and his officers hoped they had avoided detection. There was no wavering in Faolin's decision to proceed.

At 4:00 a.m. the lookout first spotted the ridge of Hawk Island and the lights of the base against the horizon. At 5:00 a.m. the ships of the UWG force dropped anchor, after maneuvering into a line paralleling the southern shore of the island. The Nauryan troops had already begun preparations for the landing and now began lowering their motley collection of small boats into the water. The first wave of troops then climbed down into the boats and, at Faolin's signal, moved off to their staging point. Black Earth, in a little rowboat jammed with seven other men, was in the first wave. As they moved off, he watched with a sinking sensation as his ship slowly receded into the still black night. His face was taut and he gripped his rifle firmly, as did those standing next to him. He envied the rowers and resolved to offer them relief as soon as it seemed appropriate. The hard physical work would take the edge off his cold nervousness.

As soon as the first wave was away from the ship, the rest of the boats were lowered and the second wave took their places in them and shoved off. By short, coded radio signals Faolin coordinated the efforts of the men on all three ships. Faolin checked the chronometer on the bridge. 5:35. Dawn was creeping into the sky to the east. If they hadn't been seen yet, it would only be a matter of minutes.

Faolin peered out through the windows of the bridge and attempted to follow the landing boats with binoculars, but it was still too dark. He turned and left the bridge and walked down the metal stairs to the main deck. Jones was there with the chief gunner, supervising the securing and aiming of the artillery. Faolin looked over the cannon and mortars, cold and gray in the first morning light. The cannon were well over a hundred years old and had been maintained only as museum pieces. The mortars were fairly new but had not been designed for military purposes. Faolin longed for the kind of weapons the UWG could have built him, if there had been time. How strange, he thought, that the UWG's future depended so much on these few antique and improvised devices.

"It's 5:43," said Jones. If we stick to our schedule, we should begin firing in two minutes."

"I've done the best I can," the middle-aged Nauryan gunner said apologetically. "We can correct as the light gets better."

Faolin looked at Jones. "I think it's going to take a few minutes longer for the second wave to reach its station. The first wave is probably waiting for the guns, but let's hold off just a minute."

They all stared off into the gray-blackness. Faolin thought the island was becoming visible, but he wasn't sure. He looked away, then back. Nothing. The seconds dragged. The light increased so slowly it was barely perceptible.

"I think I can see the ridge," Jones finally said, matter-of-factly. Faolin looked where Jones was pointing. Yes, that was it. A jagged edge of black against a slightly grayer sky.

"Very well," Faolin said. "Let it begin."

Jones gave a signal, and the chief gunner did likewise. The Nauryans manning the guns turned to their weapons. The firing of the first cannon split the early morning stillness and lit up the deck.

Black Earth, resting at the oars of his overcrowded boat, heard the cannon boom. He listened for the impact and thought he heard a dull crash from high up on the ridge above the base. More cannon fired, the other ships joined in, and now a mortar shell exploded on the ridge. Thank the Protector they were long instead of short. Then a different sound came, three quick cracks of a rifle, close by. The signal to advance. Twelve hundred men in the first wave moved toward the beach. As Black Earth strained against the oars he looked back over his shoulder to the island. Lights came on around the base. He thought he could see figures scurrying around under them. He turned back to his work and poured everything he had into the rowing. "Trust the Protector," he heard one of the older men in his boat say solemnly. "He will show us the Way." Now Black Earth could hear for the first time the Chansu guns chattering on the beach. He looked around again and saw the deadly ripples the bullets were churning in the water less than a hundred feet ahead.

As the boats closed the final yards toward the beach Faolin stood on the bridge of the command ship with Jones, watching through his binoculars. There was enough light now to see the landing taking place, but Faolin's attention was focused on the runway and the hangars.

"Hiram, the shells are still hitting 200 yards beyond the runway. Get them in."

"They're afraid to overadjust. They don't want to hit our people."

"I don't care. We can't let those planes get up."

Jones dashed out the door and down the stairs to the guns. Faolin remained on the bridge, his glasses fixed on the island. Suddenly he tensed. Did he see movement at the hangar? Yes. One of the doors was opening slowly. He swung the glasses back to the runway. No hits yet. As he watched, three shells exploded well behind it, amongst the buildings. He glanced quickly at the attack force. The boats seemed to be at the beach now, but it was difficult to tell if they had stopped moving.

Jones returned. "They're correcting," he said, breathing hard.

"I hope it's in time."

Faolin looked again. The strikes were coming closer to the runway, no doubt about it. As he watched, a shell burst on the near side of the runway. Faolin's hopes rose. "They're zeroing in on it now. Just a little more time is all we need."

He turned the binoculars back to the hangar. The doors were open now. Slowly, as Faolin watched, one of the large four-engined bombers emerged. He felt helpless and frustrated at his inability to stop it. His glasses swept across the runway. Still intact, as near as he could tell, but the shells and cannonballs were dropping on both sides of it now. Yet the plane kept on moving. Surely, Faolin thought, the guns would find their mark before the plane got turned around at the other end for a takeoff. As if in answer to Faolin's hopes, an orange ball of fire erupted not 30 yards behind the plane. Faolin sighed in relief. He turned to Jones.

"We did it. A square hit on the west end of the runway."

"They're good men," Jones said jubilantly. "I knew they could do it."

"Let's keep it up."

Faolin again trained his glasses on the island. The light now was providing good visibility. He wondered to himself what the Chansu would do. He had always realized that, once defeat faced them, the Chansu might decide to detonate the bombs. This Faolin had taken as an acceptable alternative, since it would remove the threat the Chansu posed. But now that he faced it as a cold, imminent possibility, a shiver went through him.

Faolin looked for the plane where he had last seen it, but it was gone. He looked back at the hangar. Not there. He ran his field of vision along the runway. There it was. But instead of slowing down, it was speeding up. A tightness gripped Faolin's chest. He put down the binoculars and looked out the window behind him. The ship's flag was flapping lazily toward the southeast.

"What's the matter?" asked Jones, sensing Faolin's concern about something.

"The plane's still moving. Can they take off to the east with a slight wind behind them?"

"I don't know. The runway is supposed to be long enough for a no-wind takeoff."

Faolin looked once more. The plane was making good speed now. Shells burst around and behind it, but not in front. The helpless feeling returned as Faolin watched the craft lift slowly, pass only yards above the buildings at the east end of the base, then climb into the sky and bank sharply to the north.

12

Inside the prison yard on Hawk Island Ryl Kolu and the other prisoners were asleep when the first cannonballs from the UWG boats crashed high on the ridge above them. They didn't awaken immediately, but as explosions from the mortar shells followed they began to stir. The sirens which started a moment later jolted them awake.

At first Kolu couldn't remember where he was. He was confused. He felt drugged. His jaw hurt fiercely, and moving his head made him ill. He could hardly lift his left arm. Gradually the events of the preceding day came back to him, and with them came the anger and the hate that he had felt at the Warriors. Anger and hate that must have been bottled inside him for a long time.

He remembered also now the things he had said the previous night, and the prayer he had made. He felt gladness and relief as the memory returned. How right he had been. How stupid not to have seen so clearly before.

Only after the memory was complete did the clamor in the camp impinge on Kolu's consciousness. His first reaction was fear, then puzzlement. What could be causing this noise, this excitement? Slowly the realization came. It could only be an attack on the island. It could only be the UWG trying to recapture its base. Kolu was jubilant. His prayers had been answered.

He turned to the prisoner next to him, a young, sallow-faced Worker with bad teeth, and poked him in the side. The youth looked terrified.

"The prayer is answered. The UWG has come to liberate us."

The youth stared at Kolu. Then he got up and moved away. "They're trying to kill us," he said shakily. He stopped. "Do something about that with your prayers."

Kolu stood and stepped toward the young man and grabbed his arm. "Follow me. Help me tell the other prisoners. We must fight for our own liberation."

"What can we do?"

"Follow me and I'll show you."

"You're crazy." The youth backed away again.

"Follow me!" Ryl glared at the young man. As if transfixed by the intensity of Kolu's words and manner, the young man followed meekly behind Kolu as he started across the yard to the next prisoner. That man's reaction was the same. The magnetism of Kolu's sense of purpose and fearlessness, coupled with the other prisoners' desparate fright as the exploding shells came closer and closer, drew them to him. In a matter of minutes they had placed themselves in his hands and huddled on the ground next to the guard house gate, waiting anxiously for his instructions. Kolu himself, his pain now ignored, listened carefully to what was happening outside the yard. He could hear men running, in the direction of the beach. Between explosions he thought he heard gunfire coming from there. The attacking force must, he thought, be landing on the beach.

Kolu now moved to the door of the guard house. Without being observed, he noted that the two guards on duty were still there, talking excitedly to each other. He slipped back to the other prisoners, his mind working feverishly to devise a plan.

Then he heard the aircraft coming toward him. The noise of its engines drowned out the exploding shells as the plane drew nearer. Kolu ducked involuntarily and several prisoners screamed as it suddenly appeared in the air above them, narrowly missing the roof of the detention center. He watched it, his heart pounding, as it sailed beyond them into the sky. He wondered to himself whether the launching of the aircraft would stop the UWG attack. He prayed silently but fervently that it would not. As the noise of the plane's engines faded away, he could still hear the shooting from the beach. That reassured him.

13

The plane was gone, back to Chansu. There was nothing that could be done about that. But the artillery had succeeded in rendering the runaway unusable for the rest of the planes. We can still capture those and the remaining bombs, thought Faolin, and we must retake the island.

Faolin looked through his glasses again at the action on the beach. The Nauryans were there, in large numbers. But they were prone on the ground. Were they dead? No, of course not, they were firing their weapons. Faolin looked back at the water. The second wave was coming in. He watched the progress of one squad as it advanced up the beach. He winced as one, then two, then three were cut down. But the rest pressed forward until they, too, took a position on the ground with the others, just behind a low rise that separated the sandy beach from the sparse grassy area between the beach and the runway.

Faolin turned to Jones, who still sat disconsolately in the cabin. "Get the artillery away from the runway now. Our men are too close. Try to hit some of those buildings, but stay away from the hangars," Faolin said. Jones left to relay the orders. He didn't move quite as fast as he had before.

Black Earth had been one of the first men on the beach. Six of those who landed with him had fallen, one while still in the boat, two in the water, the other three dashing with him up the beach. But by some miracle he survived, for which he gave silent thanks to the Protector. He was also one of the first to reach the rise in the ground behind which he and hundreds of other Nauryans now crouched. The rise came where the beach ended and performed the function of a shallow trench. Sand and a ribbon of small stones ran under Black Earth's feet and along the base of the rise, giving way to a crumbly soil where the side of the trench rose against his bent body.

In a random pattern the Nauryan troops would rise briefly above the protective wall to fire their guns. But from Black Earth's observations he knew the bullets from the Nauryan rifles were not having much effect. The Chansu defenders were heavily fortified, and rifle fire would never silence them. Black Earth shuddered at the thought of a massed attack on the guns, but he feared that no other tactic would work. He looked toward the attack leader some seventy-five yards down the beach. Faolin was in radio contact with the leader and would know what they should do. Black Earth breathed deeply. He was prepared for anything the Protector asked of him. He looked at the sky. If only the artillery could reach the Chansu guns. But for them to attempt to do so would certainly endanger the Nauryans, who were so close.

Black Earth wondered what the Protector was planning. He had watched the aircraft rumble down the runway and slowly lift into the air while the attack force was still pouring onto the beach. From the focus of the early artillery attack, Black Earth guessed that the Protector had meant to stop that plane. What effect, he wondered, would that plane have on us now?

On the bridge of the command ship Faolin, Jones and the ship's radio operator huddled around the bulky transmitter-receiver that they were using to contact the attack leader. After much fiddling and cursing, the operator finally produced a signal from the beach.

"Command ship, come in please," came the voice from the small loudspeaker.

The operator flipped a switch and nodded to Faolin.

"This is the command ship," Faolin said into the large circular microphone. "What is your situation?"

"We're on the beach, but we're pinned down here behind a low ridge."

"How many enemy are there?"

"It's difficult to say. We've only seen a few hundred, but there may be many more."

"How many have you lost?"

"Almost twenty-five percent, dead and wounded."

"Good," said Faolin after a short delay. "Then you're strong enough to continue the assault."

There was a pause. "They've got a lot of guns there, sir." The coldness of the reply was apparent even over the buzz and crackle of the radio.

"Do you think you can do it?"

Another pause. "If it is your wish, we will," the attack leader answered. "Is it possible for the guns on the ships to stop the Chansu guns?"

"Just a minute. We'll discuss it." Faolin switched off the transmit switch and turned to Jones. "They're worried about continuing the attack."

"Perhaps if we waited until night?"

"Definitely not. It would be catastrophic to change our strategy now. We would lose the entire element of their unpreparedness.. We must press on now or retreat. I don't want to give up."

"All right," Jones replied. "Then we'll have to see if we can knock out those guns. I'll put the most accurate artillery on it." He stood.

"Can they do it without hitting our men?"

"There's a fair chance."

"Then do it. We'll go at it for twenty minutes, but no more. Then we must attack." Faolin picked up the microphone again, then looked at Jones. "Wait here until I find out what I can about the Chansu gun positions."

He nodded to the radio operator, who reestablished contact with the attack leader.

"Now listen carefully," said Faolin into the microphone. "We're going to put our best artillery on those guns for twenty minutes. You'll keep advising us as to how we're doing. But after twenty minutes, no matter what, we must attack. Can you manage it?"

"Yes, sir," came the firm answer.

"Very well. First we'll need all the information you have on the Chansu gun positions. We want to make sure we go after all of them."

Before Faolin received an answer he heard a high-pitched whistle from above the ship. A moment later the sound of an explosion came from somewhere off to starboard. The bell of the bridge telephone rang urgently. "Tell the attack leader to stand by," Faolin said to the radio operator. He picked up the telephone receiver.

"This is the lookout, sir," came the voice after Faolin acknowledged. "There are two boats approaching from the west, around the island. They're shooting at us, but they haven't hit any of our ships yet."

Faolin delayed his response for a moment, thinking furiously. The decision was not difficult, but a twinge of regret stayed his hand. Finally he spoke into the phone. "Thank you for the prompt report," he said. "I'm going to put Jones on. Give him the exact position of the enemy ships, and he'll relay them to the chief gunner." He looked toward Jones. "Forget the guns on the island. Enemy ships are approaching from the west, around the island. Get the coordinates and put your guns on them." He held out the telephone receiver.

"How can we?" Jones blurted. "We'll have to move the ship to re-aim the guns. We'll lose all our coordinates on the shore."

"You worry about those other boats, " Faolin said firmly. "You have full authority to order our ships to maneuver. I'm holding you accountable for our fleet and nothing else. I'll take care of the attack force." He shoved the phone into Jones' sweating hand and while Jones began speaking over it he returned to the radio. "Get me the attack leader again," he ordered the radio operator. "They're just going to have to move without any more help from the artillery, and the sooner the better."

14

High in the air due west of Hawk Island the UWG bomber and its Chansu Defense Force crew climbed slowly into the sky. Pol Natuma, the pilot, checked over the instrument panel carefully. He still smiled in satisfaction at getting the craft airborne. Natuma had arrived on Hawk Island less than a week ago, having been summoned along with the few other Chansu who had experience piloting aircraft. But neither Natuma nor any other Chansu had flown planes like this before. Their training had been confined to the smaller planes used for intra-island hops. Until he arrived on Hawk Island, Natuma had never even been inside one of these giants, which had been used by the UWG in Chansu only for transoceanic flights. This morning, in fact, when Natuma was aroused from his sleep and rushed to the hangar in the midst of the UWG bombardment, was the first time any Chansu had ever flown such a plane. Natuma had spent his time since he arrived on Hawk Island studying the flight manual which had been found at the Hawk Island base and familiarizing himself with the cockpit, but it was barely adequate preparation. He still was surprised that he had been able to get the plane through the shells and into the air traveling downwind. He wondered if he would get it and its deadly cargo down again as easily.

The thing that bothered Natuma most now was the bank of switches and lights installed directly to the left of the main flight control panel. These switches, mentioned nowhere in the flight manual, obviously controlled the enormous gray metal bomb that rested in the plane's belly. Ordinarily, Natuma wouldn't have given much thought to these controls. He was transporting the bomb, not dropping it. But Natuma had noticed soon after takeoff that several lights at the top of the panel were glowing brightly. What did that mean?

As Natuma looked over the switch bank, he saw something that made him start. Another light winked on, this one labeled "Bomb Fuse Activated." Natuma tensed. Bomb fuse activated? Had he inadvertently activated the bomb? Was this a built-in defense mechanism to prevent the Chansu from using the bomb? There was a switch under the light, He reached his hand toward it, then stopped. He swallowed hard, then snapped the switch down decisively.

Natuma could not, of course, have known that the atomic bomb in the plane had built into it a safety mechanism that made it impossible to arm the fuse below 10,000 feet. Nor could he have known of the wiring error Fred Harper had made that caused the arming light to come on improperly when the safety mechanism disengaged at that altitude. By flipping the switch, Natuma put the fuse in the armed position, rather than the disarmed position as he thought. Even this error would have been inconsequential, however, were it not for Natuma's lack of complete familiarity with the subtleties of the language of the UWG, though he read and spoke it fluently. For now, still anxiously puzzling over the bomb control panel, Natuma's eyes fastened on another burning light with a switch under it labeled "Fuse Activation Lock." In the language of Chansu the translation of the UWG word "lock" also meant something like "lever" or "switch." The Chansu would never have used their equivalent word to describe the safety mechanism that prevented accidental activation of the bomb fuse while the bomb was still secured inside the plane with the bay doors closed. Natuma did not realize that when, after agonizing indecision, he flipped this switch also as a further precaution against a possible built-in defense mechanism, he was in fact turning off the one remaining safety device that prevented fuse activation. Once having thrown this switch, there was nothing Natuma could have done to reverse the mechanism he had set in motion, even if he had realized what he had done.

15

The blast tore open the sky. A few miles away, in the detention center yard on Hawk Island, the first sign of the explosion was the sudden brightness, like another sun, that appeared in the western sky.

Ryl Kolu leaped to his feet. "The gods have answered again," he exclaimed, as the brightness grew. The other prisoners, trembling, looked at Kolu in awe. "They have answered again," Kolu repeated. "You must know now that I speak the truth."

As the light, after reaching the intensity of ten suns, gradually began to fade, the first shock wave reached the island. Kolu, feeling as if a huge hammer had struck him in the chest, dropped to the ground. The blast shook the guardhouse. Pieces of the roof fell to the ground just beyond the prisoners. Then, with a great cracking sound, the whole guardhouse tilted crazily. Kolu could hear the guards yelling on the other side of the gate. Braving the ferocious winds that followed the shock wave, he crawled to the edge of the gate. Looking beyond it, he could see the guards unlocking the door on the other side of their enclosure and scurrying through it and down the long corridor that led through the detention center building.

When the guards were out of sight, Kolu raised himself slowly and, shielding his eyes against the swirling dust, tried the door on his side of the guardhouse. It was still locked tight. He began to feel around the edge of the door with his hands. The lock side was flush with the metal frame. He moved his hands over the top and around to the hinge side. Elation spread through him. The top hinge was torn off. He felt the bottom hinge. It was still on, but twisted. Three or four men could easily pull it off. He lowered himself to the ground and crawled back to the other prisoners.

16

When the sudden brightness lit the western sky Faolin was scrutinizing a map of the Hawk Island beach, radio microphone in hand, ready to give his signal to attack. He looked up, out the front cabin windows, now pointed westward. He knew almost immediately what it was. He became oblivious to the sound of the cannon firing and the shells from the Chansu ship exploding only a hundred yards away. The brightness caught Faolin's eyes and held them. Then, as if emerging from a magnificent dream, Faolin cried out in pain. His eyes felt as if they had been pierced by knives. He closed them and turned his head to the side, then slowly opened them, his hand shading them from the glare. A mist seemed to cover everything, but it slowly disappeared. The pain left and Faolin could still see.

He jumped up from his chair, jubilant. "The bomb. It's gone off," he exclaimed. "How did that happen?"

"The attack leader is still standing by," the radio operator reminded Faolin.

"It's a sign, don't you see," Faolin said. He picked up the microphone. "Attack leader, how are your men taking it?'

"What was that in the sky?" the voice asked.

"That's the bomb the Chansu tried to get away with. They didn't make it." Faolin wondered to himself if one of the UWG engineers had managed to booby-trap the plane before being captured.

"The men were afraid it was some sort of Chansu weapon. Hold on - -," the voice on the radio said in alarm.. A clanking, then a burst of static issued from the loudspeaker. A moment later, the shock wave hit the boat, and it lurched wildly in the water. Faolin was knocked to the floor. The sharp, incredibly loud clap of sound from the bomb ripped through his head.

When the shock wave passed, Faolin got up, his ears ringing. He could see that a violent wind was still buffeting the ship.

"Have we lost contact with the attack force?" Faolin asked the white-faced radio operator who was now working the switches and dials with trembling hands.

"I don't know," the operator answered.

"Keep trying. We've got to attack now," Faolin said. He picked up the telephone. Several quick calls told him that the ship had suffered no serious damage and that the other UWG boats also appeared to be intact.

The door to the bridge burst open. It was Jones. "Was that the bomb?" he asked, panting.

"Couldn't be anything else," Faolin grinned back. "How are your guns?"

"The blast knocked them around. We're getting them back in firing order."

"What about the Chansu ships?"

"They've stopped firing too."

Faolin pursed his lips and ran his fingers through his hair. "How long to get your guns ready?"

"I haven't really looked at them. I'd guess ten or fifteen minutes."

Faolin struck his palm sharply with his fist. "Do it in five," he said speaking rapidly. "Get everyone you can on every gun on every ship. We'll start moving in on those Chansu ships right now. It's a gamble, but we have an edge if we move. Tell your gunners that if they don't get our guns ready first, they're dead, because they will be."

Jones gulped. "Yes, Eric," he said. He moved slowly toward the door.

"Come on, man, move. Don't you see this is our sign? Our moment is now. If we delay, the spirits may abandon us."

Jones hurried out of the cabin, but not without giving Faolin a quick questioning backward glance.

Faolin looked toward the radio operator. The operator nodded and pointed to the microphone. Faolin picked it up and began calling. The attack leader answered right away.

"How are your men?" Faolin asked.

"They seem to be all right, but very scared. What was that?"

"Shock wave from the bomb. Don't worry. The spirits are with us now. We must attack as soon as possible. How soon can you be ready to move again?"

"Ten minutes. Maybe less."

"Make it less. Hit the Chansu before they recover. It's our best chance. It's the opportunity the spirits have given us. We're going to take advantage of it."

"Yes, Protector. Shall we stay with the same plan?"

"Yes. I want every man in the attack. Now, move."

"Yes, sir," the attack leader replied. Then there was silence. Faolin nodded and the operator switched the radio onto standby. "Get me the other ships," Faolin said. He picked up the ship's telephone and called new orders to the engine room and the pilot's cabin, then he pulled out his charts. The boat started throbbing as the engines came to life and swung it around to the southwest. Faolin made some rapid calculations and called additional instructions to the pilot. The leaders of the other two UWG ships came onto the radio and Faolin gave orders to them. He watched through the window of the bridge as his ship began moving off to the southwest away from the island, the other UWG ships following along in its wake.

Now he had to wait. He paced impatiently around the cabin. The delay was intolerable. So much hung in the balance. But he was confident. He knew his people would prevail. The spirits had given him the sign.

Faolin reviewed his strategy. He intended to place the enemy ships between the UWG fleet and the island, limiting their freedom to maneuver. Once in position, if all worked out, his ships would turn again toward the Chansu boats, and would have optimum firing conditions while at the same time presenting the Chansu guns with less of a target. All this, of course, assumed that the Chansu would not take prompt evasive action. The total success of the plan required that the enemy ships stay on their present course for at least five more minutes. It also required that the Chansu guns remain disabled at least until the UWG ships completed their passage across that course. But even if neither of these developments occurred, Faolin's fleet would be no worse off than they were now--as long as Jones was successful in getting the guns in working order.

Faolin wondered how Jones and his men were doing. The shock wave had probably not harmed the guns themselves very much. After all, they were built to absorb the force of a violent recoil. But Faolin worried about the metal tracks on which the guns were mounted. Hastily assembled and installed and far lighter than the heavy guns sitting on them, the tracks were more susceptible to damage. Faolin thought momentarily of going down to check on Jones's progress but he decided against it. Jones could get the job done just as well without him.

The Chansu ships had now come into plain view on the horizon. Faolin watched them carefully through the starboard window of his cabin. They appeared motionless in the distance, but the waves thrown off by their bows cutting through the water told Faolin they were still closing. Then, almost imperceptibly at first, the wave patterns began to change. Faolin picked up his binoculars and looked through them. The lead Chansu vessel was changing course, to the southeast! Faolin looked down at his chart and made some mental calculations. The Chansu had recovered too soon. Their new course would give them an advantageous firing angle before the UWG ships had boxed them in. But if Faolin's ships turned back now, the Chansu might be able to pin them against the island. No, the plan had to continue despite the increased risk. The spirits had given their sign. The Protector's guns would be ready first.

Faolin decided that now he must go check Jones's progress. But he didn't have to. At that moment Jones appeared through the door to the gun deck.

"Eric," he said. "We may have to change our plan."

"No. I've seen them and thought it over. We have to go on."

"Seen what?"

"The Chansu ships. I saw them change course."

"What?" Jones rushed to the window and looked out. He picked up Faolin's binoculars for a better view, then put them down heavily. "Eric, we've got to change our plan now. That wasn't what I came to see you about. It's the gun tracks. I'd thought they'd just come unbolted, but that's not the whole problem. We've secured all the bolts, and the tracks still won't work. They must've got twisted in the blast. It's going to take forever to get them all straightened out."

"All the guns?" Faolin asked, dazed.

"All of them. And on the other ships, too. We can fire the guns all right, but we can't aim them."

"How long to fix them?"

Jones shook his head. "Days to do them all. It will take a couple of hours for each track."

Faolin's shoulders slumped under an oppressive feeling of helplessness. His logic told him that there was only one alternative--to run. To run and hide until the guns were fixed. But he couldn't abandon the men on the island. He wouldn't.

Faolin straightened and spoke forcefully. "Forget about the gun tracks. There's no time. Just get as many guns as you can pointed over the starboard side, level with the deck. Chop up the tracks and weld them in place if you have to. We're going to go in and give them a broadside. That's all we need as long as their guns don't work."

As if in answer to Faolin's order, a whistling sound came from above them, followed by a loud explosion very close to the stern of their ship.

Faolin's eyes met Jones's. "That changes nothing. It's all we can do. Get on with it." Jones dashed out of the cabin.

Faolin picked up his charts to plot the next course change, straight at the lead Chansu ship. Another shell whistled overhead, this one landing off the port side. How can this be happening? Faolin thought. The spirits have given their sign to me. They couldn't abandon the Protector now, after he had come so far. Had he done this to himself? Had he unknowingly exercised his powers in favor of the enemy? Another shell exploded, again to port but closer than the last. Could it be, Faolin thought, that the sign was not to him, but to someone else?

17

"The guards are gone," Kolu said excitedly to the other prisoners when he returned to where they sat. "We can escape."

They sat dumbly, staring at him.

"Come," Kolu insisted. "I need three men to get the door off."

"There's no place to go," said one of the prisoners stiffly.

"Do you want to stay here, trapped in a cage, while the shells fall on you?" Kolu demanded. "If you want to live, follow me."

Kolu walked back to the door. The winds had died down now, and he could hear an occasional short burst of gunfire from the beach. After a moment two of the prisoners got up and came after him. The rest followed. Kolu directed the efforts of the three strongest prisoners in loosening the top of the door and then pulling it down so they could get through. He led the group into the guard's enclosure. It was still empty, but he found two guard's jackets and two guns behind the wooden table. He quickly put on one jacket and took a gun. He asked another prisoner, a big, balding man named Jintu, to do the same.

"We'll check the rest of the building," Kolu told his companions. "You wait here until we tell you to follow."

Kolu and Jintu tried the heavy wooden door on the other side of the enclosure. It was unlocked. They opened it slowly part way and peered down the corridor on the other side. The electricity in the building was out, but there was enough daylight filtering in for them to see. Kolu and Jintu opened the door all the way, stepped through, and closed it behind them. They moved silently down the empty corridor, pressed tightly to one wall, Kolu in the lead.

When they were halfway to the other end, Kolu heard voices. He stopped. After a moment the two guards entered the corridor at the other end. They were grumbling about being ordered to return to their post. They obviously didn't see Kolu and Jintu. Jintu started to turn around. Kolu reached out and grabbed his arm tightly, holding him. He motioned Jintu to get back against the wall and wait. Jintu obeyed.

The guards approached slowly, talking loudly to each other. Kolu held his breath and waited what seemed like forever. When the guards were twenty feet away, he dared wait no longer. He stepped quickly into the center of the corridor and fired two quick shots. He caught the guards squarely in their bellies, and they both crumpled to the ground without a sound.

Jintu's mouth and eyes opened wide in fright. "You've killed them," he exclaimed. "Two Warriors. We're done for now." He dropped his gun, turned, and ran back to the other prisoners.

Kolu watched him go. Then he picked up the dropped gun and continued stealthily down the corridor. When he reached the guards he frisked them hastily. He removed their two sidearms and some ammunition and stuck it in his belt. Then he continued on to the end of the corridor and looked through the door to the outside. He observed with relief that no one was around. In the distance he could see men scurrying about, taking up positions and fortifying buildings, but they were too far away to have heard the shots. He noted that several of the buildings had been damaged by the shock wave.

Kolu watched carefully for several minutes. The entire base wore a look of disarray, as soldiers were called from their sleeping areas, only half-dressed, to perform tasks at distant stations. Kolu knew, however, that behind the seeming confusion lay a firm logic, emanating in unquestioned orders from the base central headquarters. At last he made up his mind. He knew what had to be done. He turned and dashed back to the other prisoners. He found them huddled together in the guard's enclosure, desperately afraid. When he entered he sensed immediately their hostility to him.

"You killed the guards!" the one named Karga shouted. "To kill a Warrior means death. Death to us all. Why didn't you return here?"

"Be quiet," Kolu ordered. "If you stayed here, you faced death. I'm offering you life. The gods are with us. You've seen it. Do what I say and you will live. Ignore me, and death is certain."

The prisoners listened meekly as Kolu described his plan.

"You make us traitors," Karga exclaimed when Kolu had finished.

"You're already traitors in the eyes of the Warriors. I offer you the chance to become patriots in the future of Chansu." He paused. "And I offer you the only path to life. If you stay here--or if you try to escape from the base--you have no chance."

One by one the others reluctantly agreed to follow Kolu's orders. He assembled them into two squads, taking command of one himself and putting Jintu in charge of the other. They marched down the corridor, out of the building, and into the roadway. The prisoners' lack of jackets and boots didn't arouse suspicion in the confusion of running, half-dressed men.

Not two minutes after they were out of the building an enormous clatter of gunfire erupted from the direction of the beach. Kolu and his men jumped when the sound began but quickly realized that the fire was nowhere near them. Shortly afterward the loudspeakers announced the beginning of the attack, exhorted all to give their utmost for the Emperor, and issued bursts of commands directing various units here and there across the base. Kolu smiled. He knew the added frenzy caused by the attack would help them.

Kolu noticed that most of the others they passed were running. He ordered the prisoners to do the same. They were not far from their objective. Fortunately, it lay between them and the beach, so that it didn't look as if they were marching away from the action. Kolu selected the roadway that ran behind the building. The major fortifications would be in front. As his group passed, running at a trot, he directed them at right angles toward the building. He saluted the sentry by the roadway. "Reinforcements," he said quickly. The sentry returned the salute.

The next obstacle was the four guards at the rear entrance. They held up their hands as Kolu and his men approached. Kolu halted his group directly in front of them. "What unit is this?" one of the guards asked. Kolu didn't answer. There was no hope of bluffing. He raised his gun and fired rapidly. Three of the guards fell. The other scrambled back to the door. Jintu caught him square in the chest. Swiftly Kolu moved his men inside as the bullets from the sentry's gun struck the side of the building behind them. The prisoners had managed to retrieve two more guns from the fallen guards. Kolu slammed the door shut and looked around. Unbelievably, the hallway inside was empty. Kolu silently thanked the gods.

"You stay here with your men and stop anyone who tries to come in," Kolu ordered Jintu. Then he turned to the sallow-faced young prisoner named Lingnan, who had once been assigned to janitorial duties in the building. Lingnan's unfocused eyes showed an odd detachment, and Kolu had to speak his name twice to get his attention.

"How do we get to the command post?" Kolu asked. The youth didn't answer. Kolu grabbed him by the shoulders and shook him. "The command post!" Kolu repeated.

"Second floor," Lingnan replied, shaking his head.

"How do we get there?"

"Stairs in front." Just then the sound of footsteps came from around the corner of the hall, toward the front.

"Is there a back way?"

"Yes." Lingnan pointed to a door across the hall.

"Are there guards?"

"I don't know. Probably only in front."

Kolu looked around. He now heard voices coming from the front, getting closer, but apparently unaware of what was happening. "All right," he directed the two prisoners who had the handguns taken from the prison guards. "You stay behind, just inside that door, and guard the bottom of the stairs, in case anyone tries to follow us up." He paused, looking at their uncertain faces. "Don't worry. In five minutes you'll be safe."

Kolu grabbed Lingnan's arm and shoved him ahead. He motioned the two others in his squad, one of whom had a rifle from the dead guards outside, to accompany him. They went across the hall to the door, opened it, and started up the stairs. The two prisoners with the handguns followed but stayed at the bottom step and closed the door. A window halfway up looked out on the rear of the building. Kolu could see a group of guards running up, about seventy-five yards away, following the sentry, who had obviously gone to get them. So far Jinta was holding his fire. That was good.

"Who's there?" came a voice from above them.

"Reinforcements for the guard," Kolu answered crisply. "There's been an attempt to break into the building." He reached the landing and turned around it, facing up the stairs. The two guards at the top looked at him warily, but their guns were down. Kolu fired. The two men slumped and fell partway down the stairs.

"Hurry," Kolu shouted, charging up the stairs, leaping over the bodies of the guards. He burst through the door at the top, followed closely by Lingnan and the other two prisoners. This was it, Kolu thought. They had made it. The base command center. He recognized several officers and the base commander, sitting at a desk under a picture of the Emperor, along the side of the large, white-walled room.

Kolu sent the man with the rifle to the door at the front of the room. If any guards had been stationed there, they were pulled downstairs by the attack. Kolu and the two others rushed straight at the commander's desk, and he stuck the barrel of his weapon in the commander's chest. The two prisoners flanking Kolu made it difficult for anyone in the room to get a clear shot at him, and the prisoner at the front of the room, who had now shut and locked the door, held his gun ready to stop anyone who tried.

"One shot and your commander is dead," Kolu yelled. The officers in the room, stunned at the suddenness of the intrusion, stood in open-mouthed silence. Those with sidearms made no effort to reach them.

"Stop the fighting," Ryl said to the commander. "Send out the surrender signal."

"You are a crazy man," the commander answered, calmly. "We are driving them back. We are winning. The Emperor's arm is with us."

"These aren't Warriors," called one of the officers. "These are Workers. Look at their trousers. Listen to their speech."

The commander looked up at Kolu, then at the others. "Workers," he said in a clear, self-assured voice, "you are out of your place. Put your weapons down. We must concentrate on the attack."

Kolu sensed a wavering in the two prisoners next to him. "We aren't Workers," he replied, in a voice equally clear and confident. "We are citizens of Chansu. We demand you surrender this island in the name of the people of Chansu."

"I will give my life to defend this island for the Emperor," said the commander, folding his arms across his chest.

"I'll kill you if you don't surrender for the people of Chansu," Kolu said tautly.

"I won't do it."

Kolu looked briefly around the room, carefully noting the position of each man in the room. He was amazed at the clearness of his head and the speed with which he could take everything in. He looked back at the commander. Without further hesitation, he pulled the trigger. The noise shattered the tense silence, and the commander slumped at his desk. In virtually the same instant Kolu swung his gun at the second-in-command, the senior officer standing closest to the commander's desk, whom Kolu had recognized and identified by the insignia on his uniform. He moved toward the man, the two prisoners going with him.

"You are in command now," said Kolu. "Give the order."

The officer looked at Kolu contemptuously, then like his dead commander folded his arms across his chest and turned away, toward the window. Kolu caught him with a blast in the lower back that almost cut the man in two. Then Kolu moved his gun to yet another officer, much younger than the first two, but with the neatly-pressed uniform and insignia that made him now the acting commander. Kolu recognized him for the first time as Wan Konder, the officer who had been in charge of the training camp. Kolu felt instinctively that this was the weak link.

He was right. Konder sweat and shook almost uncontrollably. He looked around at his fellow officers. Tears began to run down his cheeks. His eyes came to rest on Kolu. He moved his mouth, but no sound came. He cleared his throat with a harsh, coughing sound. His gaze fell to the floor. Slowly he turned and moved toward the communications equipment near the dead commander's desk. "I will give the command," he said almost inaudibly. "I will give the command."

18

"Mister Faolin!" The pilot's voice over the ship's telephone was almost hysterical. "The rudder controls are gone. We can't maneuver at all. You've got to cut the engines."

Faolin paused as the sound of a shell bursting just off the bow momentarily interrupted communication. "Thank you for the report," he said, "but we have no choice. We're going straight in. If we ram them, so much the better."

Through the drifting smoke Faolin could now see the men on the decks of the enemy ships, coming directly at them. The Chansu boats were smaller than he had originally thought--fishing boats, perhaps. Maybe that explained why his ship was still afloat, even after suffering a direct hit near the stern and two partial hits amidships. The Chansu guns were not designed for quarry so large. The blessing of the spirits hadn't left them entirely. There was still hope.

Faolin made his calculations by eye now, ignoring the charts. He measured the speed of the lead Chansu vessel against that of his own. His brief hope left him as another shell burst under the bow, sending a shock wave through the deck under his feet. His ship would clearly pass to the right of the lead Chansu ship, and further to the right of the other Chansu vessels. And all his guns were on the starboard side, useless. If there was any chance of inflicting damage, only the two UWG ships following his could do it. And they were outnumbered two to one. He ordered the radio operator to raise the ship behind, to tell its chief officer what his responsibility was.

Faolin hesitated. Something had happened. Something was different. What was it? Was it in his mind? His hearing? No. He could still hear the throb of the ship's engines and the sound of the wind outside. But there were no more explosions. No more whistling shells. No more distant guns booming. He focused his glasses one more time on the Chansu ships. Their crews stood idly around on the deck, watching the approach of the UWG ships, ignoring their guns. Was this some kind a deception? What were they doing? As Faolin watched, the lead Chansu boat hoisted an odd triangular black flag. He stared, motionless, as the dark piece of cloth climbed haltingly up to the top of the rigging.

"Mister Faolin. Mister Faolin." The radio operator was calling to him.

Faolin slowly put down the glasses. He felt as if he were caught up in a confusing dream. "What is it?"

"It's the attack leader on the island, sir. He came on before I could reach the ship behind us. He says he's been trying to raise you for five minutes. He says it's very important."

Faolin took the microphone. "Yes, this is Faolin. What is your report?"

The additional distance made the voice on the loudspeaker less clear, but Faolin could hear enough to understand. "The Chansu, sir. They've surrendered, I think. They're just standing around with their hands on their heads. We thought it was a trick at first, sir, but they're not firing back. Not at all. What should we do?"

Could it be that his power had finally prevailed, in the midst of all this misfortune? At the last possible minute. There was no other explanation. It had. He silently thanked the spirits who had given him the sign and the power. He felt giddy. "Do what we always do when we win a battle," he answered the attack leader, beginning almost to laugh. "Take their weapons. Make them your prisoners. But treat them with every courtesy. And get ready for me. I'll be ashore as soon as I can."

"Call the other ships. Tell them we've won," Faolin shouted to the radio operator. He handed the man the microphone and then rushed out onto the top deck. Jones was just coming up the stairs. They embraced, laughing, and went around to the other side of the ship. They were just in time to see the lead Chansu ship gliding silently by, not fifty yards away. Faolin and Jones returned the salutes of the downcast Chansu crewmen with great glee.

By the time the small rowboat carrying Faolin reached the beach the Nauryan troops had already herded several hundred Chansu into a tightly-packed circle and taken their weapons. Seeing them, Faolin had vivid memories of his first victory against the northern raiders. He felt secure in his destiny; it was clear now beyond doubt that the lot had fallen to him to save the world. He was indeed the Protector.

He walked slowly around the group of prisoners, looking over them, relishing his victory. As he did, the attack leader rushed up to his side. Faolin greeted the man jovially and congratulated him on a fine job.

"Thank you, sir," the attack leader said. "I hate to bother you with this, but we've still got a little problem. Some of them refuse to come. It's a very odd situation, sir. I think we'd better have an interpreter."

"What is it?" Faolin frowned.

"We've found their command post, but we can't get their officers out. The officers want to come, but there's a man there who apparently will kill them if they do."

Faolin's frown relaxed. It didn't sound so bad. "Well, let's go see what it's all about."

Faolin called to the young interpreter who had come ashore with him, and the man came running up. They had picked up the man at Westland University in New Markwell along with several others whose services were needed in running the ship and bringing the planes back home. Except when they were working, the group of them spent most of their time together, apart from both the Nauryan natives and Faolin's fellow frontiersmen. Faolin instinctively distrusted all of these outsiders, but at times their services were essential.

The interpreter and Faolin followed the attack leader to the Chansu command post, one of the UWG laboratory buildings located along the runway halfway between the hangars and the living quarters. It was encircled by the Nauryan troops. Faolin nodded to them as he passed through their ranks. He went into the building, where more Nauryans were waiting. The attack leader directed him up the stairs to the command room. Just inside the door stood yet more Nauryan troops, but in the middle of the room six Chansu in dark red uniforms sat close together around a table. At the far end of the room stood another Chansu, wild-eyed, and wearing a similar dark red jacket over gray pajama-like trousers. He held tight to an automatic rifle pointed at the six sitting men. Behind him ten or eleven more Chansu, one in a red jacket and the others in the gray shirts and trousers, leaned against the wall, looking frightened. Several of them had guns, all pointed toward the ground and obviously not intended to be used. On the floor Faolin saw two crumpled, red-clad bodies lying in drying pools of blood. Flies were buzzing around them.

"All Chansu are required to assemble on the beach," Faolin said through the interpreter. "That includes all officers."

None of the Chansu spoke for a moment. Several of the red-uniformed men at the table looked at the man behind them who was pointing his gun at them. The man with the gun slowly shifted his gaze in Faolin's direction. "I am Ryl Kolu," he said. "I wish to speak to the commander of the UWG forces." The young man at Faolin's side translated quickly.

"I am Eric Faolin, Protector of the Westland Nauryans, and leader of this expedition," Faolin said.

Kolu looked Faolin over closely. "Have you secured the island?" he asked. The interpreter continued to translate.

"We have, except for this building."

Kolu gradually lowered his weapon and smiled. He appeared exhausted. "We have done it," he said. "You may take them." He identified the six men for Faolin, and the two dead men on the floor as well.

"Who killed those men?" Faolin asked, looking first at his own soldiers, then at Kolu.

"I did," Kolu said. "To make them surrender."

Now Faolin began to understand why the resistance had stopped so suddenly. What sort of man was this Kolu? Why had he done it? Could Faolin himself, through a power given him by the spirits of which even he was unaware, have caused Kolu's act?

"You can take these Chansu down to the beach now," Faolin told the Nauryans at the door. "But leave him," he added, nodding at Kolu.

The Chansu officers stood and walked in single file slowly out the door. The Nauryan in charge ordered the men behind Kolu to follow.

"Wait, please," Kolu said. "Don't take them with the others. They should not be punished. They helped me."

The Nauryans looked at Faolin. "It's not our way to punish prisoners," he said. "They have nothing to worry about. They won't be harmed." He smiled at Kolu.

"But they are poor Workers," Kolu pleaded. "If you put them with the other Chansu, their lives will be in danger."

"We treat all prisoners equally," Faolin said. "And anyone who attempts to harm these men will be severely dealt with."

"You don't understand. Many of the Warriors would be glad to sacrifice their lives to kill me or these men. They will do it to avenge the Emperor."

"I find that very hard to believe."

"It's true. Our ways are very different from yours. It's my hope that we can change to be like the people of the UWG. That's why we helped you. I promised these men that if they helped they would not be punished. They came with me because I told them they would be making the future better for themselves and for all of Chansu. Please don't betray my words."

Faolin looked at the gray-clad Workers, who still stood, trembling, against the back wall. He thought it over. "Very well," he finally said. He turned to the Nauryan in charge. "Find a building where these men can be kept apart from the others, at least for now. We'll honor this man's request until we have a better understanding of the situation. Be sure to disarm them first."

As the Nauryans took the guns from Kolu's followers and led them out of the building, Kolu himself handed his gun to Faolin.

"Sit down, please," Faolin said to Kolu. The two men, with the interpreter, sat in the chairs vacated by the Chansu officers. The room was empty now except for them, the two Nauryan guards at the door, and the two dead Chansu officers on the floor.

"You said that you caused the Chansu surrender. How did you manage it," Faolin asked.

"We came in here and shot the commander."

Faolin scratched his head. "Who are you? Why are you dressed different from the others?"

"I am a Worker. I was with a Crocodile unit until I was placed in the detention center. The men who were with me were also prisoners. They are Workers, too. We escaped when the gods made the earth shake."

Faolin studied the man closely. He seemed so young. Yet there was an intensity about him that Faolin had seldom seen in any other man. "Why did you do it?" Faolin asked.

"As I told you. The way of the Chansu is wrong. The way of your people is right. I want my people to learn your way."

Incredible, Faolin thought. This could only be the intervention of the spirits. Or, he suddenly wondered, could this still be some sort of Chansu deception? Knowing defeat was imminent, could the Chansu have surrendered, leaving this Kolu to infiltrate Faolin's force? Faolin looked at the man again. If Kolu was what he appeared to be, he could be a valuable disciple of Faolin among the Chansu. Faolin likened him to Swift Stream and Forest Path in those early days in the Westland foothills. But he certainly could not place the man in his confidence now, before the Chansu were subdued. Despite appearances, no Chansu could be trusted at this point. Faolin lamented the difficulty of finding anyone who could be trusted outside his circle of Westland territorials and Nauryan natives.

"I admire your wisdom and courage," Faolin said. "I would like to ask your further help in spreading the word."

"Gladly," said Kolu.

"Unfortunately," Faolin continued, "we are not yet ready to do that. The fighting is not over."

Kolu looked puzzled. "I thought you said the island was secure."

"We've captured the island, yes. We must make sure it doesn't fall again."

"I see."

"I'm going to have to ask you to join your companions, for your own protection, as you yourself said. When the fighting is finished, we'll talk again. I hope you can return to Chansu to help complete the great task you've begun."

"Yes. That's what I want to do."

Faolin was impressed by this man. Impulsively, he extended his hand to Kolu. "You are a good man, Kolu. You've done much to help your people." Uncertainly, Kolu grasped the outstretched hand. The two men looked at each other for a moment. Then Kolu withdrew his hand, rose, and went with the two Nauryan guards to join his fellow Workers.

19

Two days later Faolin stood in the control room for the Hawk Island airstrip, searching the western sky, his hand shielding his eyes from the late afternoon sun. He looked at his watch and paced to the other end of the room, then returned to the window.

"It's after five," he said to Jones and a Nauryan aide, who sat at a table along the south windows. "They should have been back half an hour ago."

In the two days since the Chansu surrendered Hawk Island, much had happened. The Chansu prisoners, except for Kolu and his followers, who were still locked in one of the housing units, had been loaded aboard one of the UWG ships and were even now steaming for another island in the Ellenberry chain, 500 miles further east, where they would be held until it was safe to return them to their homeland. Faolin had radioed news of his success to the UWG, but he had feigned equipment damage and had not acknowledged any return messages. He was not going to let a soft, cowardly Prime Council interfere with his mission before complete success was at hand. The shelled airstrip had been quickly repaired, and at seven this morning one of the two remaining aircraft stationed on the island took off toward the west. Faolin now waited anxiously for its return.

Not until almost five-thirty did the speck that was the plane appear in the western sky. Slowly it came into full view. It flew past the island to the north, banked and turned, and swept in to land on the airstrip from the east. Faolin was waiting where the plane taxied to a stop.

The first crew member climbed out of the plane and threw Faolin a half-hearted salute. He turned and helped the other three crewmen through the small door. When they were all on the ground Faolin walked up to them.

"Well," he asked eagerly, "what happened?"

"It was really something," one of them answered, a youngish territorial named Carter. "It knocked us pretty good, and we must have been fifteen miles away by the time it went off, too! We only had three engines going most of the way back."

"The target. What about the target?"

Carter grinned. He had a toothpick between his teeth. "Caught it square on the nose. I don't think there's anything left."

Faolin rubbed his hands together and hopped from one foot to the other, unable to contain his pleasure. "Wonderful. Marvelous. Fantastic," he said. "And we've still got the other bomb left. It's working perfectly." As he moved closer to congratulate the men, two of them, who were standing a bit apart from Carter, stepped back away from Faolin's contact. They exchanged quick glances and started to walk away from the plane, without a further look at Faolin.

Faolin's first reaction was to stop the two. He recognized them as a pilot and navigator who had been assigned to the mission in New Markwell. Neither, unlike Carter, had ever been a member of the New Hope community. Faolin considered it impertinent of them to leave without being dismissed. Typical of outsiders. Faolin was not used to such insubordination, and he was about to call after them, but something about their manner made him reconsider. It almost seemed that, rather than being cocky and insolent, they were full of sadness. The way their heads were hanging and their shoulders moving, they might have been crying. He let them go on down the runway toward the residence buildings.

"What's the matter with them?" Faolin asked Carter.

Carter shrugged. "They were kind of upset the whole trip, especially coming back. I guess they didn't like what we were doing."

"That's just the kind of attitude that got us into this mess with the Chansu."

"It was like they felt sorry for the Chansu," Carter added.

"You can't do that, or you're beaten before you begin. I don't like to kill either, but how else are you going to deal with an enemy who wants to kill you?" Faolin stared after the two men. "I shudder to think what would have happened with people like them in charge. At least the Prime Council had the sense to bring us into this thing. We'll make sure the Chansu learn their lesson." Cheerful again, Faolin turned to Jones, who had joined him on the airstrip. "Well, Hiram, let's get that radio warmed up. As soon as possible. I've got a message for the Emperor."

20

The high wooden fence that surrounded the UWG mission compound in Shinso had been reinforced with steel braces, and barbed wire had been spread around the outside of it. Four guards were posted at the entrance gate and four others patrolled the fence, day and night. Except for deliveries of periodic meager food supplies and inspections, the gate remained sealed.

David Halburton, the Director of the UWG's Chansu Mission, along with all the other UWG citizens in Chansu, had been confined to the compound now for more than four months. It had been a particularly difficult ordeal for a man of Halburton's years, but everyone had suffered. A feeling of gloom pervaded the compound. During the first days of the confinement Halburton had held daily meetings of the entire community in an attempt to keep up morale, but those soon were abandoned as ineffective. Spirits had been bouyed temporarily by the addition of some three hundred seamen to their number around the first of May, but the ominous implications of their capture soon more than cancelled the brief boost the introduction of new faces had provided. The influx of prisoners from the Hawk Island base just two weeks ago had had only a depressing effect.

For the past several days, however, Halburton had noticed with curiosity a barely perceptible change in the manner of the guards who could occasionally be seen through the gate. They seemed to glance inside the compound more often, and often it appeared as if they might be discussing its occupants. Their conversation was certainly more abundant and more animated than it had been previously. Now something else had occurred that was odd. The inspection was two days overdue. Never before had the inspectors departed by more than a few hours from their schedule.

Halburton's reaction to these events alternated between fear and hope. From discussions with the captains of the impounded UWG vessels Halburton knew that efforts were being made by the UWG to free them. But he also knew the mind of Han Torgoona, the Prince Regent. Han would execute every man, woman and child in the mission without a second thought if he felt their deaths would be useful to him.

As Halburton sat alone in his room thinking of these things, one of the older children of a mission family brought him a message that he was wanted at the main gate. His heart pounded and he fought to control his nervousness and a touch of dizziness as he hurried there. He cursed the infirm old body that refused to move as it once had. When he finally reached the gate he saw just outside it an unfamiliar face. The man was dressed in the black and yellow robes of a Court official, rather than the red uniform of the Chansu Defense Force, which all the other recent visitors to the compound wore.

The man spoke, in the accents of the Warrior class. "You are David Halburton?" he asked.

"Yes, I am," Halburton replied, in Chansu.

"Would you please come with me?"

"Who are you?" Halburton struggled to place the man. Perhaps he had seen him at the Palace, but he wasn't sure.

"My name is Min Tago. We have never been introduced, but I am of the Palace staff. Now, shall we go?"

"Where? And for how long?"

"To the New Palace. It will not be for long. Please, we waste time. Let us go. It is in your interest to do so."

Halburton nodded reluctantly. Two guards, who regarded Tago with obvious curiosity, opened the gate for Halburton and closed it behind him. Tago led Halburton to a shiny black car bearing the Court insignia. They joined the driver and a palace guard inside and sped off through oddly deserted streets toward the New Palace. The occupants of the car were silent until they reached their destination.

Halburton, Tago, and the guard left the car in the palace courtyard and walked up the wide flight of stone steps that took them into the Emperor's administration building. Other palace guards saluted as they passed. Halburton was surprised to see none of the red Defense Force uniforms in evidence. There had been many of them on the palace grounds on his last visit, so many months ago.

Tago finally stopped in front of the thick wooden doors of one of the rooms the Emperor used for receiving visitors. "We are here," said Tago. "Please go in, Mr. Halburton."

"I assume the Prince Regent is inside," Halburton said, not moving. "I would like to know why he wishes to see me."

Tago smiled. "You'll find out. Please enter. I've been asked to wait here."

Tago pushed open one of the doors and Halburton went into the room. It was darker than the hallway, and Halburton didn't at first see anyone inside.

"Good to see you again, Mr. Halburton," came a voice, speaking Warrior class Chansu, from the other side of the room. The voice, Halburton knew at once, was not that of Han Torgoona. Han had never greeted him in such polite tones.

Halburton turned slightly and saw, standing stiffly behind a heavy table, the tall, thin and slightly stooped figure of Changa, Han's elder brother. Halburton felt considerable relief.

"My pleasure to see you, Changa," said Halburton. "I had expected to see your brother."

"Yes, I know," Changa said. "Unfortunately, Han has suffered some severe setbacks. In true and honorable fashion he has taken his life, leaving me to administer the Empire for our father."

Halburton was shocked. His trembling hands betrayed his suddenly rising hopes. Did this mean the confinement was over? He dared not ask the question directly. "Is that why you've summoned me?" he finally said.

"Yes, it is." Changa paused. "You and your people will be released today." He seemed disturbed and uncertain. "You will be free to return to your homeland. A representative of your government will arrive soon to make all the arrangements." He sighed.

"I don't understand," Halburton said. "What has happened?"

"You'll find out soon enough. I'd rather not talk about it. My brother made some very bad judgments, and the people of Chansu must pay for them. Now, go back to your people. Tell them it's over. They may do as they please. Go where they please." Changa seemed very weary.

"Thank you, Changa." Halburton moved toward the door. "I've always considered you to be fair and honest. I don't know yet what's happening, but I sense that you may need a friend. If you do, call on me."

Changa smiled weakly. "Thank you, Halburton. All of Chansu needs a friend now. Our fate is in your hands."

Halburton went out into the hall, where Tago waited. Tago led Halburton back to the car. Halburton's joints felt supple, his step springy, as if he were twenty years younger. He couldn't wait to return to the compound with the good news. Unanswered questions filled his mind, but he would have to be patient. He wondered who was responsible for this dramatic change of events. Whoever it was would have the undying support and gratitude of Halburton and every other person in the bleak mission compound.

21

Several times in the few days they had been together Ryl Kolu's fellow prisoners had begged him to lead them in breaking out of their quarters. It wouldn't have been difficult, Kolu knew. The building they were in was obviously built as a small residence, and its prefabricated panels could easily be breached. But where would they go if they escaped? They would probably be caught and lose whatever chance they did have to return home.

During this time Kolu continually fought down doubts about what he had done. The immensity of his act made it intolerable to entertain any second thoughts about it. Usually he would cast his mind back to his friend Lyn Wonan, and that would supply all the justification he needed. Still, why were these invaders from the UWG treating him so unlike what he expected? And who were all these gray-skinned soldiers? Was this invading force perhaps not from the UWG lands of which he had heard so much?

On the afternoon of the fourth day of confinement Kolu heard voices outside. He looked through the window to see the man named Faolin and several other brown-skinned men talking with the gray-skinned guards just outside. The guards saluted and left.

After a quick knock, the door burst open, and the brown-skinned men entered. Faolin, beaming jovially, was the last of them to come in.

"Kolu," Faolin called. Then, seeing him, Faolin stepped up to him and put his hand on his shoulder. "Kolu, we've done it. The Emperor has agreed to all our demands. The hostages have been released and as soon as it can be accomplished all of Chansu is to be incorporated into the UWG. The Emperor has asked all citizens of Chansu to cooperate with us." After his words had been translated by the young interpreter in Faolin's group, Faolin stepped back. "Well, what do you think of that?" Faolin said.

"Incredible," Kolu answered. He couldn't believe that the Emperor would ever have agreed to such a thing. Was this man mad? "It is wonderful," he added, deciding not to reveal his disbelief.

Faolin looked around at the others in the room. Then his eyes returned to Kolu. "I have reached a decision about you and your men," he said. "We have a strong need for native Chansu who can spread the teachings of the UWG among their own people. I would like to invite all of you to be missionaries in your own land."

Kolu glanced uneasily at the other Chansu. Were they thinking what he was thinking? "What would this involve?" he asked Faolin.

"Several months of training, maybe less. I would want you to work with me, and then you could teach the others. After that, you would return to your homes." Faolin waited for his words to be translated, then continued. "Of course, you'll no longer be confined. I apologize for that, but you understand that until the Emperor gave his order we couldn't afford to take any chances, even though you and your men appeared to have already proved your devotion to our cause."

"What is the alternative if we don't wish to become teachers of your doctrine?"

Faolin frowned. "Well, then," he said, "you will return to Chansu with the other prisoners. They will be taken back in a few days."

Kolu was baffled. This man couldn't be speaking the truth, yet he seemed so sincere. Kolu didn't wish to offend him. He stepped forward. "I accept your offer," he said. "I would like to know more about the ways of the UWG for myself, as well as for my people."

"What about the others?"

"They are uneducated Workers. They need help in making up their minds. Please let me discuss the matter with them privately."

"Very well, but I'd like an answer soon." Faolin took Kolu's arm. "I'm very glad you'll join us. You are obviously a man of ability. You can greatly aid our cause."

"Thank you," Kolu said, bowing slightly. He looked up at Faolin. "May I ask you, Faolin, how you managed to persuade the Emperor? He would not readily lose face in such a way, I know."

"That was why we had to use force."

"Force?"

"Yes. We had to demonstrate our power. There was no other way. We used one of our bombs. We didn't like to do it, but it was necessary."

Slowly the realization came to Kolu that perhaps Faolin had made no idle boast. Perhaps he had indeed subjugated the Emperor. And he, Kolu, had made it possible. What had he done?

Was this what he had wanted to happen? And what kind of destruction had he unleashed? "Was . . . was this bomb such a thing as lit the sky and shook the ground during your attack?" he asked, almost afraid to hear the answer.

"Yes."

Kolu hesitated. Should he go on? He must. "Where did you use it?"

Faolin looked around at his fellow territorials, then back at Kolu. "We destroyed a city in northeastern Chansu. It was the only way."

"What city?" Kolu almost choked getting the words out.

"Yenchi, I believe it's called. I suppose you know of it."

Kolu's chest tightened so that he could hardly breathe. He staggered backward a few steps until he found a chair and sat down heavily. He put his hands over his face.

"Are you all right, man?" Faolin's expression showed concern.

"My . . . my family is in Yenchi," Kolu managed to force out between sobs.

Faolin stepped back, obviously in great discomfort. "I'm very sorry," he said. "Of course I didn't know." He paused. "I'm sorry that it was necessary." He stood for a moment, watching Kolu, then motioned to his companions. "I'm very sorry," he repeated. "There 's no point in talking more now. We'll leave. I still hope you'll help us. Think of your loss as a sacrifice for the future of Chansu, and help us mold that future." He moved to the door. "I'm going to put the guards back at your door for a short time. Tell them whenever you wish to see me again." The other territorials went out. Faolin started to follow them but turned again to Kolu before closing the door. "You've done the right thing, Kolu. It's too bad that your family has been lost, but all the people of Chansu will gain from our efforts, believe me."

Faolin closed the door behind him. Kolu did not look up, but remained sitting, hands over his face, crying openly.

22

After they had finished noisily celebrating the Emperor's capitulation, the Nauryan troops on Hawk Island began preparing for their return to the UWG mainland. The UWG government, with which communications had magically been re-established, mobilized as much of its long range aircraft as possible, to spare the troops the need for another tiresome sea voyage. Faolin celebrated too, but mostly by drowning himself in self-congratulation and daydreams. He stayed on the island to supervise the return of his troops to New Markwell, where he ordered them to stay until he arrived to join them, and the return of the Chansu soldiers to their homeland. In a month or so Faolin would make a triumphant visit to Shinso. But first he had other things to take care of, such as a visit to Preston to receive the congratulations of the Congress and the Prime Council . They had already sent him the invitation, which he had fully expected, and he was carefully planning how he would accept it.

While he was waiting, supervising, and dreaming, Faolin repeatedly sought out the company of Ryl Kolu. At first Kolu resented Faolin's visits, but he soon found himself, to his own great surprise, willing to accept the man as if his family and the city of Yenchi, and indeed the Chansu Empire, had never existed. Thankfully, here, on this remote island, in these strange circumstances, it was easy to forget--or ignore--everything that had happened.

As soon as Kolu stopped inwardly resisting Faolin, he noticed that the man was exhibiting a warm, almost fatherly attitude toward him. Faolin would ask Kolu and an interpreter to accompany him on walks around the island, and he would patiently explain things about the buildings, or the aircraft, or the people. He introduced heavy doses of his version of UWG ideology into the discussions, and also went on at great length about his magnificent achievements, both in Westland and here. All this was done, to Kolu's amusement and annoyance, as if Faolin were talking to a child. But at least Kolu acquired from these monologues a smattering of knowledge of the language and customs of the UWG.

When it finally came time for Faolin himself to leave Hawk Island, he asked--or rather ordered--Kolu to come back to the UWG with him. Kolu was surprised by the invitation, and his feeling about it was mixed. He was curious about the UWG; he felt some distinction in being the first Chansu to visit it; he certainly had nothing to return to in Chansu; and he did not relish the thought of staying on this bleak island with his fellow prisoners, all of whom had decided against returning to Chansu without Faolin's protection. Yet he could not entirely forget what Faolin had done, and he resented Faolin telling him what to do and acting as Kolu's special benefactor. And, of course, he could not entirely suppress the lingering doubts about contact with the UWG that he had been taught since birth.

But Kolu did come with Faolin--he really had no choice--and as their plane touched down at New Markwell Kolu felt relief from the anticipation and the unsettling long hours in the air. What was to happen next was his fate, and he would ride with it, without resistance. He had already exerted his influence on his world, and he had changed it beyond his wildest imaginings; he was too tired and depressed to continue the effort. He would become an observer, not an actor.

A band and a small host of officials met the plane as it taxied up to the small terminal building. Faolin led the way out of the plane, followed by Jones and a group of other territorials, then Kolu and the interpreter. There were no Nauryans on this flight; most of them had returned earlier, and they were standing at attention in their ranks behind the officials.

As soon as Faolin and Jones touched the ground, they were surrounded by a group of men and women yammering questions. The press of people and their insistent questions seemed to Kolu a most inappropriate way to welcome home a hero. Even he, a lowly Worker from a poor farming village in Chansu, felt that the situation required more dignity, more restraint.

"Those are reporters," the interpreter shouted to Kolu. "They are getting information for the newspapers and magazines." Kolu nodded.

When Kolu and the interpreter had climbed down the steps from the plane, some of the reporters from the fringes of the group around Faolin detached themselves and converged on the new arrivals. Kolu found their shouting and their brashness even more obnoxious. He pretended not to understand either them or the interpreter who struggled to translate their questions.

After about fifteen minutes the band began to play and an unintelligible announcement came from a loudspeaker on top of the terminal building. The reporters, complaining, stepped back reluctantly, much to Kolu's relief. Now a group of men who had been standing off to the side came forward. They were dressed in dark suits that looked very warm under the hot August sun. As they stepped up to Faolin, smiling, he shook the hand of each. Then someone produced a microphone and a camera, and Faolin gave a short speech while the pictures were clicked off showing him standing amid the dignitaries. This was more in line with what Kolu had expected, and it seemed appropriate. The long minutes with the reporters were forgotten.

After Faolin stopped speaking, he looked around him. His eyes fell on Kolu, and he called to him. One of the territorial officers ushered Kolu and the interpreter over to the microphone.

"This," Faolin said, "is Ryl Kolu. He is our first convert. He helped us win the battle of Hawk Island. He is the first Chansu to visit the UWG. He will be our leading missionary among his people."

The other men smiled some more and came up one by one to shake Kolu's hand. For the first time he was acutely aware of his red skin in the midst of their brownish faces. Faolin introduced them. They were the governor of the Territory of Westland, the mayor of New Markwell, a man from the UWG Information Ministry (who conveyed the welcome of the UWG Prime Council), Representatives from the UWG Congress, members of the Westland Territorial Assembly, and countless others. Kolu was confused by the proliferation of titles and did not really understand what the functions of these men were, other than that they were governmental. How, he wondered, could the UWG manage to administer itself with such a variety and mixture of ruling officials, all of whom apparently considered themselves equal to each other? Surely they didn't plan to export this odd system to Chansu.

After the introductions they all moved to waiting automobiles, which took them from the airport into the city. Kolu was put in the car with the mayor of New Markwell, who described with great enthusiasm everything they passed. Along parts of the route people stood at the edge of the road, waving and smiling. This Kolu liked. He smiled and waved back, interrupting the mayor's continuous narrative.

Kolu was impressed with what he saw. He had never imagined that there could be so many vehicles--and this, he had been told, was only a small, undeveloped city compared with the rest of the UWG. The large buildings, too, impressed him. But he was also struck with their sameness. How did one ever find his way around in this huge, sprawling place? Each intersection they passed looked like the one before it. He shuddered at the thought of living one's life here, however much wealth one had.

When they arrived at the city center they went immediately into the large, plain dining room of the UWG Territorial Office Building, where they were seated at tables. As Kolu looked around at the gray-painted walls, the exposed metal beams, and the hard concrete floor he wondered whether the rumors he had heard so often of the wealth of the UWG were exaggerations. The meeting center of a village in Chansu was the equal of this room. Surely an event of this importance should be held in the most magnificent dining hall available.

Almost as soon as they were seated, large metal containers of food were brought to the table. Kolu wondered what it was. He sniffed. It seemed to have no odor. He turned to the interpreter next to him. "Why is food being brought so early? Is it the custom of the UWG to eat in the middle of the afternoon?"

The interpreter laughed. "It isn't the middle of the afternoon here," he explained. "It's early evening." He tried to describe how the time of day differed around the globe. Kolu thought he understood. He had noticed, he now remembered, that the shadows and the light seemed odd when he got off the plane. He had simply attributed it to being in a strange place. He had not experienced any similar change in travelling from Chansu to Hawk Island, but that trip had been slow, in a fishing boat, and any timekeeping had been done by others.

In addition to the interpreter, Kolu's table included the talkative mayor, a number of local government officials, and a teacher of modern history from Westland University. One of the local officials, a man named Benson, partly stood and pulled the food container to him.

"Let me serve, if you don't mind," Benson said. He proceeded to open narrow horizontal doors in the container and removed small trays of unrecognizable meat and vegetables, which he passed around. "Watch out, they're hot," he warned. Then he turned to Kolu and the interpreter. "We're really quite proud of this. It's brand new. They prepare the food in individual portions at Protein Industries, then pop it in here and freeze it and send us the container. When we're ready, we put the whole thing in a special oven, and in half an hour it's ready. Two men can serve several hundred people, if necessary. Very efficient, don't your agree?" He smiled. Kolu smiled back. The man obviously enjoyed showing off his device.

Kolu waited until the others began to eat, then followed their example. The square of dark meat on his tray cut easily. Kolu noticed that each square on each person's tray seemed to have precisely the same dimensions. But when Kolu put a small piece of it in his mouth, he couldn't taste anything. Puzzled, he tried a larger chunk. The texture was pleasant, but there was no taste! Kolu looked around at the others. They were eating away and talking as they did. Apparently they found nothing unusual. There were no condiments on the table, so Kolu ate the meal--or as much of it as he could--as it lay on his tray. He soon felt full, but unsatisfied.

Before everyone had finished eating, the round of speeches started. When it was over, more than an hour later, every person in the room, including Kolu, had been offered an opportunity to talk, and Kolu had a headache. He had not minded so much hearing again Faolin's boasting about his exploits on Hawk Island or the endless tributes to Faolin. But he resented being told about how the way was now clear to show the wonderful "people" of Chansu the enlightened ways of the UWG, and to secure for them their "human rights." And he was simply bored over endless statistics about increasing production, the relevance of which he could not comprehend.

When the meal was over, the speeches finished, and the trays and containers removed from the table, the reporters from the airport, who had been confined to one table during the dinner, were loosed on the celebrities. Kolu recoiled from their advances. In desperation he told the interpreter he didn't feel well and asked if there were a room where he could lie down and rest. The interpreter went off to inquire, leaving Kolu to stare uncomprehendingly at the reporters around his table.

Five long minutes later the interpreter returned, and he and Kolu excused themselves, shoving through the reporters to the door. The interpreter led Kolu out of the building and diagonally across a large open square to another building.

"What is this place?" Kolu asked.

"It's a hotel. The mayor has arranged for all of our party to stay here."

More gray walls and concrete floors met Kolu's eyes as the interpreter led him up two flights of stairs and down a corridor to a door. He opened it for Kolu.

"This is where you'll be staying. I hope you feel better soon. We'll be at the Territorial Office Building for another hour or so. Please come back if you feel up to it. Do you think you can find the way?"

"I'm sure I can." Kolu had no intention of returning to those reporters.

"All right. Apparently we're taking off on another trip first thing in the morning, so if I don't see you again tonight, I will then." The interpreter was obviously not fooled, Kolu thought.

Kolu thanked the interpreter, who then left. Kolu went into the room and closed the door behind him. It was very small and stuffy, but it was good to be alone. He stood in the center of the room for a few minutes, then stretched out on the bed. He had become accustomed to beds in the house on Hawk Island, and they no longer felt strange to him. In fact, in these cramped, austere quarters, away from all the odd foreigners, lying comfortably on his back, Kolu could almost imagine he was still in Chansu, that his family was nearby, and that there was work in the fields. He forced the thoughts out of his mind. They were too painful. He wondered, for the first time, if he could return home without his grief overcoming him. Was he doomed to stay a stranger here, forever?

Kolu thought about the people of the UWG that he had met. Why, he wondered, were people whose lives were governed by such humanitarian principles so cold and unfeeling? It was as though in the process of strictly observing each others' rights they had lost sight of human feelings. Even Faolin, in his way, exhibited more emotion than these others he had seen. Was it that, as Lyn Wonan had said, their laws changed the natural order, and thereby made them less than human?

Thinking of these things, Kolu became very sleepy. The strain of the trip and all the new surroundings had exhausted him. He let himself doze.

An authoritative knocking awakened him. He jumped off the bed, took a second to reorient himself, and then opened the door. Faolin, with the interpreter behind him, stepped into the room.

"Kolu, are you sick?" Faolin asked. "The interpreter said you weren't feeling well."

Kolu hesitated. He understood the question but waited for the translation. "No," he replied, "I'm fine now. I just needed a little rest."

"That's good." Faolin sat down in the room's single chair. "I was concerned when I heard about it, but of course I couldn't leave the reporters. Tell me, Kolu, what did you think of our little reception?

"I am very . . . impressed."

"Well, you should be. The entire government of Westland was there. I thought they seemed properly appreciative of what we did, didn't you?"

"Yes, I think so."

"They'll listen to us now, no doubt about that. And they certainly need to, the way things were going before we stepped in." Faolin lifted himself out of the chair and went back to the door. "Well, we all need some rest now. We leave for the airport at six. I'm glad you're all right, son. I want you along on this trip."

"Where are we going?" Kolu asked.

"Where? Why, we're going to Preston. That's the capital of the whole UWG. They have quite an affair planned for us day after tomorrow. If you think what happened today was impressive, wait until you see that. Believe me, some very important things are going to happen there." Chuckling to himself, Faolin left Kolu's room, the interpreter preceding him out the door.

Kolu returned to his bed, but the sleep he had found so easily a few minutes earlier now eluded him. He lay awake, thinking about his strange fate, until the early hours of the morning.

23

The dust-covered jeep bumped to a stop in front of the houses near the old Komisaw village center. Dawn Breeze noticed that yet another of the hide buildings had been replaced by a drab concrete block structure. She opened the door of the jeep and hopped out, still as agile as a young girl.

"You can go on if you want," Dawn Breeze said to the elderly Nauryan driver. "Come back and pick me up in an hour." The driver nodded and sped away. Dawn Breeze watched the jeep until it turned and disappeared behind another group of houses. Having a jeep at her disposal was a convenience few other Nauryan natives shared, but Dawn Breeze seldom took advantage of it. She didn't know exactly why.

A hand touched her shoulder. Startled, she turned and looked into the sad face of her brother, Forest Path. She hadn't heard his approaching footsteps in the thick dust. "Hello, brother," she said.

"Hello, Dawn Breeze." He took her hands briefly, then dropped them. "Why are your here?" He seemed worried.

Dawn Breeze smiled. "I have news. Good news."

Forest Path let out a breath and appeared to relax. "Our men?" he asked.

"They're back. Most of them. In New Markwell. They've won. Our spirits are very strong."

Forest Path looked into his sister's eyes. "And my son?"

"He is well. The message said Black Earth is with the honor guard, traveling with the Protector this very day to the capital city of the UWG, to receive the thanks of the people of the UWG."

Forest Path's frown disappeared. He took Dawn Breeze's hands again. "That's wonderful. My son alive. And with the honor guard."

"And our men victorious again."

"Yes, of course. Another great battle won. It's been a long time, but the Protector's magic is still as strong." He paused. "You must take great pride again in being the one chosen by him."

Dawn Breeze looked away. "Yes, I do," she said unconvincingly.

"I don't understand," Forest Path said, "why our men have not yet returned, if the battle is won. We need them for the early harvest."

Dawn Breeze shrugged. "The message said only that they are in New Markwell."

"Well, I'm sure the Protector will send them back when he no longer needs them. We can't question his decisions. He is always right. Tell me, did you speak with him yourself?"

"No. The message was from one of the other territorials. I didn't hear it at all. Red Axe, the driver, was at the radio when it came in."

"He will talk with you when he has time, I'm sure. The Protector has the welfare of millions on his shoulders now. Perhaps he has outgrown our little village."

"Yes, perhaps."

Dawn Breeze and Forest Path looked away from each other in silence for a few moments. Then Forest Path spoke. "Come, Dawn Breeze, it's hot out here. Let's go into my house where it's cool, and we can talk some more."

Forest Path took Dawn Breeze's arm and together they walked to the large nearby hide-covered building with the huge hawk symbol of the clan into which Forest Path had married painted above the door. Their steps kicked up little puffs of dust as they went.

24

August 28, 1948, was a beautiful day in the capital city of the United World Government. The clear midmorning sunshine on the cluster of government buildings in the city center made their soot-grayed facades look fresh and new. It was a day for visitors to see the capital at its best. A few minutes after ten-thirty in the morning the large doors at the east end of the Congress Building swung open. The first man to come out was Eric Faolin. He walked down the sloping concrete ramp and across the wide sidewalk, then paused at the bottom of the wooden steps that led up to the platform that had been hastily erected overlooking the broad Capitol Building grounds. He glanced upward, then began climbing the stairs. Halfway up he stumbled on one of the steps and almost fell. He kicked it angrily and continued on.

As Faolin climbed he could sense the murmuring of the crowd, which he had glimpsed as he exited from the building. But not until he reached the top of the platform and their voices rose to greet him did he realize its immense size. He blinked and looked out from the platform. Just before him, wearing new uniforms and standing in close ranks were the two score Nauryan troops of the honor guard who had accompanied Faolin on the flight to Preston the day before. Beyond them, as far as he could see, people filled the Capitol grounds. Their cheering and clapping grew even louder. Faolin stepped forward and turned to smile at the members of the Prime Council who were mounting the platform behind him. They returned his smile, all except Mrs. Parthupta, the Council Member from Brahmastan, whose stony expression was not altered by the noise of the crowd.

"I've never seen anything like this," Rolf Cornettia, the Council Member from Doltony, shouted to Faolin as he reached the top of the platform. He clasped Faolin's shoulder briefly as he passed him.

They all sat in wooden folding chairs that had been placed on the platform facing the crowd. The cheering continued. For the first time Faolin noticed the other platform, below and in front of the Nauryan honor guard, where technicians were busily moving two bulky television cameras about amid strands of cables. Faolin had never seen a television picture before. He had been told that receivers were set up in government buildings throughout Agronica and in those parts of Brahmastan that had television transmitters. He wondered how many more people would be watching him at those locations,

After a full minute Mildred Carter, the Prime Council Chairman, stood up and stepped to the microphone in front of them. She raised her hand for silence but the crowd refused to respond. After another unsuccessful attempt she turned to Faolin. "Can you make them stop?" she shouted. Faolin joined her and raised his hand as well. As he stood the cheering grew even louder, but when he raised his hand it magically died. Carter nodded her thanks to Faolin, and he sat down. She began her introduction, recounting the events of recent months.

Robert Strongarm, seated in the row of chairs behind Faolin, for once welcomed the beginning of one of Carter's long drawn out introductions. The other Council members, except of course the unemotional Parthupta, appeared to relish the sustained applause, but Strongarm took little comfort from it. The crowd was cheering Faolin, not the Council. To those people Faolin had come like a white knight to reverse the errors of the Council. Their adulation of Faolin only emphasized the magnitude of the Council's mistakes.

But the cheering bothered Strongarm for another reason as well. He had never before heard applause of such intensity and length. Strongarm felt that it was prompted by more than mere appreciation of Faolin. It was as if Faolin's appearance offered the excuse to release feelings that had been bottled up for a long, long time. The cheering had disturbed Strongarm, no doubt about it, and he was very glad when it finally ended. Yet he feared the cessation was only temporary.

The applause didn't surprise Ryl Kolu, who stood with Faolin's territorial officers just below the speaker's platform, behind the Nauryan honor guard. Indeed, the cheering for a national hero was one of the few things about the UWG that he did understand. People always revered their leaders and heroes, didn't they?

Kolu was still not sure why he was here. Faolin had scarcely spoken to him since they left New Markwell yesterday morning. Kolu was certain that Faolin didn't intend to mention Kolu's role in the victory at Hawk Island. Yet Faolin had said that he wanted Kolu to be present for this speech.

Kolu listened as Mrs. Carter began her introduction. He was startled to hear a woman's voice. How could a woman be a government official, he wondered. How humiliating for her husband. Surely the UWG didn't expect Chansu to choose women as leaders. Once again he fought off the second thoughts about what he had done.

Black Earth felt proud, proud as he had never felt before, standing in the honor guard before this great throng. He knew that he had been selected for the honor guard by the Hawk Island attack leader for his bravery in the campaign, but that wasn't the major source of his pride. Rather, it was that these thousands, and the millions they represented, were publicly acknowledging that Black Earth and his fellow Nauryan natives had accomplished something they could not--that Black Earth and his fellows possessed a skill and courage that surpassed that of five hundred million UWG citizens.

Carter droned on with her introduction, but Black Earth, basking in this glory, paid little attention. Of course, the

Nauryans owed their success to the Protector, who was not a Nauryan. But Faolin was no more a member of the UWG than he was of the Nauryan race. He was sent by the spirits to bring the Right Way. And Faolin had not won the battle of Hawk Island himself; he had merely showed the Nauryans how to do it, with their own abilities. For this, and for all his guidance in other matters, the Nauryans owed the Protector a great deal. Black Earth and the honor guard would, as the attack leader had made them pledge when he selected them, do everything in their power, even give their own lives, to ward off any possible threat to Faolin. For the present, however, in front of this adoring multitude, that pledge seemed wholly unnecessary.

In a special roped-off area next to the television platform, just to the right of where the members of Congress were seated, was gathered a group of important guests for this great occasion. All those UWG citizens who had been hostages of the Chansu (save the few who chose to remain at the Chansu mission) had been flown home in the past week, and all had been invited to come, at government expense, to attend this event. If anyone deserved to be present to show thanks to Faolin and his men, they did, the Prime Council and Congress had concluded.

At the very front of this group, David Halburton sat motionless in a wheelchair. The victim of a heart attack on the trip home from Chansu, Halburton's recovery had been slow, and he had not yet regained all his faculties. His fingers twitched in longing for the pencil and paper he couldn't yet use to record for his diaries and reports the events of this momentous day.

In the rear of the group, her arm brushing against the rope that separated the distinguished guests from the crowd, sat Dorothy Harper. She had almost not come, but a friend had convinced her that it was just what she needed to bring her out of the depression she had suffered since her return from Chansu. Seeing her former companions had indeed improved her spirits. She remembered the difficult journey from Hawk Island to Chansu in the foul-smelling fishing boat, not knowing the fate of her husband, and the hard times in the Shinso compound, with almost a fondness. Somehow the constant sense of crisis there had given a meaning to life that now escaped her.

Carter finally finished her recounting of recent events. With a small flourish she introduced to her fellow Prime Council members, the Congress, the distinguished guests, and at last presented to her fellow citizens the man who had stepped forward in their hour of need to preserve the ideals of the UWG for all mankind.

The applause was deafening, much louder than before, as Faolin stepped to the microphone. It thrilled him and convincingly confirmed his plans. He let the cheering go on a little longer than he felt he should, but he found it difficult to ask the crowd to stop. Finally he raised his arms for silence. He got it, but reluctantly. He began. "My fellow citizens, you honor me. But it is not I who saved our world from the Chansu menace. It is these fine young men in uniform you see before you. They and their companions, many of whom fell on the beach at Hawk Island, none of them even full citizens of the UWG, stepped forward when no one else could. I told the Prime Council I wouldn't appear here today unless I could bring a representative group of these men with me. So here they are." He held his arm out toward the Nauryans in the honor guard, who stood, stiff and expressionless, before the throng.

At this the crowd erupted again. The cheering was as loud as before, and Faolin let it go on for a long while again before he stopped it.

"The Westland Territory is a long way from here. And we're not as advanced as you. Out where I live in the remote part of the Territory, we hardly have any roads or automobiles. We've never even heard of television." Faolin nodded toward the cameras. "But we're a part of the UWG. We believe in it. And we're ready to defend it." More cheering.

"Now, I'm not going to tell you any more about what happened out there on Hawk Island. You've read about that in the newspapers. Mrs. Carter already covered it today. Hawk Island is something I'd rather forget. It was necessary, but it wasn't very pleasant. I'd rather talk to you about the future. And the first thing about the future that we must deal with is preventing another Hawk Island." Again there was applause. Faolin hadn't even expected it here.

"How do we prevent the Chansu from rising up again? The answer to that is simple: we must bring them into the UWG as partners with us."

Strongarm, sitting on the edge of his chair, felt uneasy. If Faolin wished to propose government policy, he should do so in the Congress or the Prime Council, not here.

"This will not be an easy task," Faolin continued. "The Chansu have a society with traditions that are directly contrary to ours. But it isn't impossible. As witness to that fact, there is present in my party here today the first Chansu to set foot on this continent in four hundred years, my friend Ryl Kolu." Faolin waved his hand in the general direction of Kolu, but Kolu made no move to acknowledge it. "Mr. Kolu has been converted to the sound principles of the UWG. Indeed, he knew something about our ways long before I met him. Mr. Kolu has agreed to serve as an official adviser in our task of reaching his brothers."

Faolin paused, and the crowd cheered again. Strongarm grew even more uneasy. This time Faolin let the cheering die down of its own accord before going on, in a more serious tone.

"But before we can ask others to adopt our ways, we must put our own house in order. Out there in Westland, we feel we have a better--a more detached--view of what is going on than you who are in the center of the UWG. For some time now we've been concerned about an erosion of the UWG's basic principles. The old moral code is breaking down. People aren't producing as hard as they used to, yet they want to consume more. People are abusing their freedom, to the detriment of themselves and others. Freedom for self-indulgence was not what the founders of our system intended. I'm sure you can recognize this deterioration in your lives if you look for it. Are you as happy as you ought to be? Is there sometimes a desperation to your lives that ought not to be there?" Faolin stopped and looked around. "The near-disaster at Hawk Island is only the most obvious of many examples of this breakdown." Faolin looked at the Congress and the Prime Council members, held up his hand, and quickly went on. "I must add that I don't blame your government. They are the victims of the breakdown, too." A murmur of assent came from the crowd.

"But when your government is also a victim, it is powerless to restore the way of life the UWG was meant to insure. For this reason, I am proposing today to organize a new authority, above the present government but not in place of it, to return us to the path from which we have strayed, at the same time we are persuading the Chansu to take that path."

Strongarm half rose from his chair, then sat back. He could feel what was coming, but he must be certain. The crowd was concerned, too. They stood silently now, waiting for Faolin to go on.

"Effective as of today, my advisers and I are assuming that authority. We will oversee all the acts of the Congress and the Prime Council, and we will propose a number of new laws, among which--." Strongarm had heard enough. While the other Prime Council members sat, dumbfounded, in their chairs, Strongarm jumped up and rushed toward Faolin. He pushed Faolin aside and grabbed the microphone. But before he could say a word, two huge Nauryan soldiers from the honor guard appeared before him. As they advanced toward him, Strongarm noticed how ludicrous they looked. Their fine new uniforms, so impressive from a distance, were flimsy rags, hastily thrown together. The arms of the nearest soldier stuck out six inches below his sleeves. Strongarm almost laughed. Then the soldiers were on either side of him and took his arms. He resisted, but they just strengthened their grip. They guided him easily back to his chair. As they did, his eyes fixed on the faces of the soldier on his right. Strongarm noted the man's pockmarked, sallow gray skin, his decaying teeth, and the fervor in his eyes.

"Why do you stop me, brother?" Strongarm asked in a hoarse whisper. "I'm on your side." The soldier made no response.

He and his companion forced Strongarm back into his seat. Strongarm clenched his fists in rage, then his muscles slackened and his chin fell to his chest. It's no use, he thought.

Faolin resumed. "I'm sorry for that." He turned toward Strongarm. "Mr. Strongarm, I understand your reaction. But you don't realize that your opposition is a symptom of the illness of the UWG. Please hear me out."

Faolin turned back to the crowd. "My advisers will propose and see that the Congress enacts laws to bring an immediate halt to the spread of practices that are inconsistent with the basic principles of the UWG. No longer will the press be free to encourage immorality or to tear down the reputations of fine men. A full behavior curriculum will be restored in the schools. And until people relearn their evils, we are going to make the use of stimulating drugs a crime.

"These are just a few of the things we intend to do. We will order a full statement to be published in tomorrow's newspapers throughout the UWG. I know that this announcement comes as a surprise. You may wonder whether we have the power to carry out our plan. I am certain that the vast majority of the UWG will approve it. If you look at your lives closely, you will see the sickness that needs to be cured. But if there are any who oppose us, let there be no mistake. We have the power to carry out our plan, and we will not hesitate to use it. I need only remind you that we have twenty five hundred armed troops, dozens of aircraft, and an atomic bomb at our immediate disposal at the New Markwell airport.

"How long will our supervision last? That I cannot say. My hope is that it will not be long. I believe the spirits are with me and will help me to show you the way. As soon as the basic principles are restored, and the Chansu are integrated into the UWG, we will return to Westland. The amount of time this will take depends, in the last analysis, on you, the citizens. I plead with you for your help and cooperation. We have helped you. We have brought you through a crisis that threatened the very existence of this government. Now let us put this government back on a sound footing. Let us right now resolve that our world will not be endangered again. Let us bring back the hard work, and with it the happiness and contentment, that we have lost. For your own benefit and for the security of the world, I beg your support."

Faolin stopped. The silence was overpowering. This, he knew, was a crucial moment. His task would be easy or hard, depending upon what happened now.

Dorothy Harper listened to Faolin's speech intently. It confused her. The man's approach was so simple and direct, yet wasn't what he was proposing itself inconsistent with the UWG's basic principles? But no, he was proposing only a corrective interlude, not a fundamental change in the government. He would assume authority only long enough to put the UWG back on the proper path. Dorothy well knew from her own experience that something had to be done to cure the deep unhappiness around her.

The speech stopped. Dorothy felt anxious. Why was everyone so quiet? Her anxiety increased as the silence continued. Then, as if she was an observer located somewhere outside of her own body, she heard herself yelling, "Yes. Yes. Yes. Yes." The others around her began to pick up the chant. Soon the entire crowd was repeating it, over and over, louder even than their cheering had been before.

www.ingramcontent.com/pod-product-compliance
Lightning Source LLC
Chambersburg PA
CBHW062008170626

46813CB00001B/70